SICK FUX

TILLIE COLE

DEDICATION

For the supporters of the Dark Romance Revolution.
I adore your black hearts!

"If all else perished, and he remained, I should still continue to be; and if all else remained, and he were annihilated, the universe would become a mighty stranger."

Emily Brontë, Wuthering Heights

PROLOGUE

THE FIRST TIME I met Heathan James he was picking the wings off a butterfly. When I asked him why, he turned his light gray eyes my way and said, "Because I want to watch it die."

I watched as his gaze rolled back to the squirming wingless insect in his hand. Watched his lips part as the sad creature withered and died in his palm. A long, soft breath escaped his parted lips, and a victorious smile tugged on his mouth.

I once heard of the theory that the simple flutter of a butterfly's wings, a tiny perturbation, that merest whisper of movement in the air, could start the process of building something much bigger; a tornado, devastating thousands. A tsunami crushing iron-heavy waves onto sandy shores, obliterating everything in its path.

As I looked back on the moment we met, this introduction to Heathan James, the man who became my entire world, the pulsing marrow in my bones, I wondered if his deadly act of ripping the wings from the bright blue-and-black butterfly started such a perturbation in *our* lives. Not a tsunami or a tornado caused by a simple flutter, but something much darker and more sinister, caused by stripping a beautiful creature of its ability to fly, to thrive. A path of destruction no one saw coming; the sweetest, most violent deaths carried out with the gentlest of smiles on our faces and the utmost hell in our hearts.

Heathan James was never the light in my life, but instead a heavy eclipse, blotting out the sun and anything bright, bringing with him endless, eternal night and murderous tar-black blood pumping through my veins.

Heathan James was the genesis of my soul's reawakening . . . a soul not meant for peace, but one handcrafted for death and murder and blood and bones . . .

Soulmates forged in fire, under the watchful gaze of Satan's mocking eyes.

Heathan.

Ellis.

Just a couple of sick fux . . .

CHAPTER 1

Ellis
Age seven

Earnshaw Estate
Dallas, Texas

"HE'S WEIRD."

I gripped my doll in my hand as I stared at Heathan James sitting on the grass. He was dressed all in black—black shirt, black pants . . . and strangely, a black vest with pockets. I'd never seen anyone but a grown-up wear one of those before. His hair was black—short at the sides but long on the top. It kept falling into his eyes. His eyes that looked silver in the path of the sun. They were actually light gray. I'd never seen that color in a person's eyes before.

"Ellis." Eddie pulled on my arm. I yanked it out of his grip.

"He's new. And he doesn't know anyone." I leaned in close to Eddie, my best friend and next-door neighbor. His Stetson shielded his eyes. He always wore a Stetson. Said he wanted to be a Texas Ranger one day like his uncle. I thought he'd make a good one. "I heard my papa talking to my uncles last night. I snuck out of my room and listened at Papa's office door. I heard him say Heathan's mummy didn't want him anymore. Said he scared her. So she gave him to his papa—Mr. James, the grounds keeper." I shook my head. "I heard he didn't want him either but had no choice. His mummy's nowhere to be found. She ran away and left him all alone."

Eddie's blue eyes widened. "His mama gave him away? What did he do to scare her?" I looked back across the grass at Heathan. He had a magnifying glass in his hands. He was burning ants. I shrugged in answer to Eddie's question. I didn't know what he'd done.

"He doesn't look much scary to me," I declared, studying him hard. "I think he's older than us. I heard one of my uncles say he's already nine." Eddie was eight. I was seven.

"When you met him yesterday, he was killing a butterfly." Eddie looked over his shoulder at Heathan. "He's killing ants right now. He's really weird, Ellis. Why does he keep killing things?" He paused. "I think he's too strange to be friends with." He took a deep breath. "My uncle says to stay away from kids like him. That they're the ones who will end up getting you in trouble one day. You know I can't get into trouble if I want to be a Texas Ranger."

"I wanna go talk to him." I pushed past Eddie and ran down

the slope of warm grass. I ran until I was out of breath and came to a stop beside Heathan. I made sure my headband was still in place and my hair was smooth.

Heathan didn't look up at me, so I peered over his shoulder at what he was doing. A pile of dead ants lay under the magnifying glass in his hands. Smoke rose from their little black broken bodies. "Watching them die too?" I asked, and his back bunched under his shirt.

A bird sang in the nearby tree as I waited for him to respond. "They died slower than the butterfly yesterday," he said eventually. "They tried to survive, tried to escape, run away . . . but they couldn't. I had them trapped. They fought hard . . . but I had to kill them."

I wanted a closer look. I crouched down opposite him and smiled when he moved the magnifying glass away from the dead ants. He was watching my face, I could feel it, so I lifted my eyes and smiled really big. "I'm Ellis Earnshaw. I never got to say that yesterday. I live here too." I pointed to the main house. My house. My papa's estate.

Heathan didn't smile back. He didn't move, didn't say anything. He just watched me. His eyes moved to the black headband in my hair, then down my blue dress, over my white apron and long white socks to my black shoes. Last of all, he looked at the china-faced doll in my hands. "This is Alice," I announced and held her out for him to see. She was dressed exactly the same as me. She even had long blond hair and blue eyes too.

"No." Heathan shook his head.

"No what?"

"*You're* Dolly."

5

I looked at my doll again. "I don't understand," I said, crinkling up my nose. I was so confused.

He pointed at me. "You're not called Ellis. Your name is Dolly. I decided on it yesterday. You look exactly like your doll. I named you Dolly. I don't like Ellis. It's a stupid name. It doesn't suit you."

I stared at him in shock, then looked down at my doll. I smiled again. "I like that." Heathan quickly looked away. "She's Alice. From Wonderland." I pointed down at my blue dress, white apron and white socks. "It is my favorite book *ever*. My mummy got me this doll last year. My papa got me the clothes so I would match." I hugged my doll close to my chest. "I wanna be just like Alice when I grow up. Go to new places, fall into a strange new world. I wanna meet the Cheshire Cat and the Mad Hatter." I shook my head. "But not the Queen of Hearts. She's a monster! She . . ." I leaned in closer. "She scares me."

"Why do you say 'Mummy'?" he asked.

My shoulders dropped. "My mummy was English. It's what they call their mamas in England." Heathan's eyes narrowed. I tipped my head to the side. "Well? Do you know that book? *Alice's Adventures in Wonderland?*"

Heathan shook his head. A piece of black hair fell forward and covered his left eye. I reached up to push it out of the way, but his hand snapped out and grabbed my wrist. I gasped and stared at his fingers on my skin. His hold didn't hurt me, but . . . but when I looked into his eyes, my heart started beating really fast. "No one touches me," he said through his teeth.

"Okay." I swallowed.

Heathan stared at me and stared at me, then he let go of my

6

arm. I pulled it back and rubbed at the spot he had held. Heathan picked up his magnifying glass and brought it back over the pile of dead ants. I never took my eyes off him as the rays of the sun hit the thick glass and began sizzling the black insects once again.

"Why do you wear a waistcoat?" I asked.

Heathan's hand froze. He looked at me out of the side of his eye. "A waistcoat?"

I pointed at his clothes.

"A vest?"

I laughed and shook my head. "A vest. Silly me. I get the two names confused sometimes."

"Why?"

My heart suddenly felt heavy, and I dropped my head. I played with my doll's hair so I wouldn't cry. "I told you. My mummy was from England. She was from a place called Oxford. I've never been there. But she would call things by different names sometimes." I pointed at his vest. "She called vests 'waistcoats.' Called the hood of a car a 'bonnet.' Silly things like that."

"Where is she?" Heathan asked, and I felt the tears in my eyes get bigger.

"She died last year." I hugged my doll tighter. "Before she did, she told me she would see me in Wonderland someday." I held up my doll. "She gave me this. She told me it would keep me safe."

"From what?"

"Bad people." I stared at Heathan. He didn't say anything. "She said there were bad people in the world. Some who were close by. She told me that Alice would keep me safe."

7

"Have you met any bad people yet?"

I shook my head. "No. I only see my papa and uncles around here. Oh, and my nanny, Mrs. Jenkins. There's your papa too . . . and now you!"

Heathan looked at my doll, then he looked away from me. He let go of the magnifying glass and ran his hand over the pocket in his vest.

"What's in there?" I leaned forward to get a better look. Heathan's hand slammed over the pocket to keep it closed. I looked up into his eyes. Whatever was in there, I didn't think he was gonna let me see. But he breathed out deeply and reached inside. I waited, holding my breath as he pulled out something shiny and gold. I leaned in closer and closer, until my head was hovering above his hand. My face was only an inch from his. Heathan met my eyes, then slowly opened his hand. Finger by finger.

"Heathan." My heart started racing. "It's a pocket watch?"

"It's getting late." He stared at the face. I frowned when I saw that the glass was smashed and the hands weren't moving. A long chain dangled from his pocket.

"Heathan," I gasped. I had to hold my hand back from touching the broken glass. "It's broken. It doesn't work," I said sadly.

Heathan looked confused. He held the watch up to his ear, tapped the side and said, "Tick tock." He held it out toward me. "Tick tock. Tick tock. Tick tock." His head tilted to the side. "It works just fine. Can't you hear it? *Tick tock. Tick tock. Tick tock.* Can't you see it?"

I stared at the watch. I studied it really hard. I couldn't see or hear anything. Then I realized Heathan was playing pretend. Just like I did with my tea parties. He wanted me to play along with his game.

"I can hear it!" I smiled. Heathan froze at my words, then his lip started to tug up at the corner and I thought I saw him smile too.

Kind of, anyway. It was sort of a smile.

I didn't think Heathan smiled all that much. He seemed sad. Different to Eddie. They were both serious. But with Heathan, it was different. I wanted to know why.

Then *I* froze. My hand flew to my mouth as I realized something. "Heathan," I whispered eagerly as I looked down at my doll. At my clothes. I looked at his waistcoat, then down at the pocket watch . . . "The White Rabbit." I scrambled forward and sat right in front of him. Heathan didn't move. "The watch . . . You're just like the White Rabbit from *Alice's Adventures in Wonderland.*"

I laughed and I laughed.

"Rabbit." I pointed at his chest. "Tick tock, tick tock, tick tock . . . you're Rabbit!"

"Dolly."

"Rabbit!" I agreed and smiled at our new names. "Dolly and Rabbit. Alice followed the rabbit down the rabbit hole. He took her to Wonderland. He took her from her dull world and into one of bright colors and magical creatures." I squeezed my doll. "And now *I* have met you. Have *you* come to show me a new world?"

I waited in excitement for his answer, then a shadow suddenly blocked out the sun.

"Ellis."

I peered up and saw Eddie standing tall above us. His arms were crossed over his chest. "Eddie!" I pointed at Heathan. "He's Rabbit and I'm Dolly! Can you believe it?"

"What?" Eddie asked, eyebrows pulled down real tight. "What do you mean?"

"From Wonderland!" I threw my head back in happiness. "Like that thing my mummy always said . . ." I tried to think. "Fate!" I shouted, remembering her words. "It's fate!"

Eddie's face screwed up. "Why have you never made me one of the characters from that book?"

I screwed my face up too. "Who would you be?" I hadn't ever seen Eddie as anyone from Wonderland.

He shrugged, then his face lit up and he tapped his hat. "I could be the Mad Hatter! I always wear my hat. So does he."

I studied his hat. I shook my head and laughed at his silliness. "You could never be the Mad Hatter."

"Why?" Eddie crossed his arms over his chest again.

"Because the Mad Hatter is *mad*, silly! You're not. You're 'sensible,'" I said with air quotes. "Mrs. Jenkins always tells me how you're a 'good boy' and very 'sensible in the head.'" I shook my head. "So you can't be the Mad Hatter, Eddie. It just doesn't suit. You don't belong in Wonderland." I looked back at Heathan to see him staring at me. "But Heathan and I . . ."

Heathan whipped his head around to look at Eddie. Then Heathan moved right beside me, almost in front of me, and glared at Eddie. Eddie swallowed. He went very pale as Heathan scowled at him.

"I'm going home now," Eddie said slowly, backing away.

"You wanna come with me? My mama said you can come for supper. Maybe take a ride on our newest colt." Eddie lived next door—well, on the next estate over. The Smith estate was a ranch. He snuck in through the hedges separating the properties to come see me. I didn't ever go to his house. My papa never ever let me. I'd never left our estate's grounds in my whole life.

"No," Heathan answered for me, and Eddie stepped back again. "She's staying here." Heathan held out his arm so I couldn't get past him. "Go home."

I slapped his hand and shook my head. "Silly Rabbit! You're being so naughty and rude!" I giggled, then looked up at Eddie. "I'm staying here, Eddie. You know Papa doesn't let me leave, yet you always ask."

"Fine." Eddie stormed away, arms crossed over his chest again. "Eddie!" I called out, seeing he was upset, but he didn't turn around. I sighed and sat back down. I didn't want Eddie to be sad or angry at me. It wasn't anyone's fault if he didn't belong in Wonderland.

Heathan turned to face me. "I don't like him."

"Rabbit. Stop that. He's my friend."

"Friends?" he asked. "I don't have friends."

My mouth dropped open in shock. "You do now." Heathan didn't reply, so I pointed at my chest. "Rabbit and Dolly, remember?" I laughed again when his forehead creased in confusion. I, for one, loved the sound of our new names. "You wanna see my favorite things?" I asked, changing the subject.

Heathan still looked confused, but he eventually shrugged. "Stay here," I said and leaped to my feet. I ran all the way back to my house and grabbed my sack of favorite things. I was out of breath by the time I got back to Heathan. He hadn't moved. Not a single muscle.

I placed the sack on the ground and opened the pink string keeping it closed right up. I began pulling everything out. I took the pink picnic blanket and placed it on the ground between us. My heart raced in excitement as I set out the tea set. When it was all arranged between us, I stood up and spread out my hands. "There we go! What do you think?"

Heathan looked at me, then down at the tea set on the ground. I dropped to my knees and steadied his cup and saucer in front of him. "It's Earl Grey," I said as I lifted the teapot and poured the tea. "Mummy's favorite. She always drank tea—six cups a day sometimes!" Once Rabbit's cup was full to the brim, I filled my own. I brought it to my nose and smelled it, laughing as the steam hit my nostrils. "It tickles!" I snorted and wiggled my nose. "The steam tickles my nose every time I smell the essence of bergamot. But I always do it anyway because it smells sooo good."

"You're talking funny," he said abruptly.

I rolled my eyes. "It's afternoon tea. Afternoon tea *must* be taken with an English accent. It's my favorite. When I talk like this I sound just like my mummy. My mummy always had afternoon tea. Every single day at four p.m. on the dot."

I was about to take a sip when, over the lip of my cup, I saw Heathan watching me weirdly again. His cup was still on the blanket between us. I wondered if he'd ever had afternoon tea before. If he hadn't, it was a travesty!

I leaned forward. "You need to drink it soon, Rabbit. While

it's hot. Just make sure you blow on it first. You don't want to get a burned tongue. That's the worst feeling in the world!"

Heathan leaned over his cup and then looked up at me through his hair. "There's nothing inside it."

My hand froze on my cup. I had to be sure to hold the handle and not touch the china. I didn't want to burn my finger. "What are you talking about, Rabbit? I just poured you a cup!" My head dropped to the side. "You have never had afternoon tea before, have you?"

Heathan slowly shook his head. I placed my cup on the blanket. "I normally have cakes and treats too. But silly me, I haven't brought them today. I wasn't expecting new company. New *acquaintances*, as Mummy would say."

Heathan frowned and stared down at his cup. The pink of the cup and blanket was bright against his black clothes. "Would you like me to teach you how to drink your tea properly?" I scooted around the edge of the blanket until I was sitting right by his side. Reaching down, I put my hand on his. I jumped when Heathan froze and snapped his head my way. I forgot he didn't want me touching him.

I couldn't help it. I always touched people. I was a touchy person.

I went to pull my hand back, sad, when he said, "No . . ." I could feel my heart beating faster in my chest. "You can leave it there," he said. But he sounded funny. His teeth were gritted together, like he was in pain or something.

I leaned in closer, until my arm pressed against his. "You smell good," I said. Heathan's eyes looked into mine. "And you have the prettiest eyes I've ever seen." His jaw clenched, and he

13

moved closer until his nose was near my neck. My eyes went wide as I wondered what he was doing.

He moved back, his nose near my nose, and said, "You smell good too." His eyes closed, and opened again a second later. "Like roses."

I smiled and nodded. "It is roses. It was my mummy's perfume." I made sure no one was around before saying, "I'm not supposed to wear it—Papa told me so—but I sneak a little bit on every day. Just a little drop behind each ear." I tapped behind my ear to show him. "Out of sight."

Tightening my grip on his hand, I looked back at the cup of tea before us. "To drink tea, you must take your fingers and put them through the handle." I nodded at Heathan and guided his hand down to the cup. I put his fingers where they were supposed to go. "Now you bring the cup to your lips." Heathan did as I said, never taking his eyes off mine. Just as the cup almost touched his lips, I sat up straighter and shouted, "Wait!" Heathan stopped. I slapped my forehead with the palm of my hand. "I forgot the most important thing!" I reached out and pulled his pinky finger out into the air. I clapped and smiled. "There. To drink tea properly, you have to stick out your pinky. It's the law when drinking tea. Mummy told me that in England, if you don't do it, the Queen can chop off your head." I slowly touched Heathan's black hair. "And your head is far too pretty to chop off, Rabbit."

I sat back, waiting for him to drink. "Go on then," I urged. "Take a sip." Heathan's eyebrows were still pulled down, but he took a sip of the tea, then lowered the cup and saucer back down to the blanket. "Well?" I held my breath.

"It was good," Heathan said, kind of awkwardly, but I still squealed in delight.

"It wasn't too hot?"

"Just right," he declared, and I moved back to my cup and took a sip too. I loved tea so much. But only Earl Grey. No other blend of tea was good enough. To drink Darjeeling, especially, was positively a crime.

"What else is in the sack?" Heathan asked as I placed my cup on the ground. I whipped around and pulled out my most prized possession. I shuffled on my knees toward Heathan and placed the boombox on the blanket.

Heathan raised his eyebrow. I pulled the bright pink boombox toward me and switched it on. "It was Mummy's. There's a tape inside. A cassette. It has all of her favorite songs on it. They are from the eighties. I don't really know what that means, but they are my most favorite songs in the entire world. I play them every single day."

I ran my hand over the loveheart stickers my mummy had stuck on when she was younger. I turned to Heathan. "You want to listen, Rabbit?"

He nodded. I rewound the tape until I found my most favorite song and pressed play. The music started. "This song is called 'Dear Jessie.' It's by a lady called Madonna. It was Mummy's favorite song in the whole wide world."

I swayed as the music started. Unable to sit down, I jumped to my feet and, holding my Alice doll in my hands, I began to dance and sing. I spun around, head tipped back as I sang the words out loud. When I could spin no more, I looked over at

Heathan. He was watching me with a strange expression on his face.

I dipped my shoulder and looked him right in the eyes. I danced and sang, moving toward him, putting on a show. I always put on shows for my papa and my uncles. Almost every night. They always asked me to dance for them in my Alice in Wonderland dress—it was their favorite dress of mine. I loved to dance for people. It always made them smile.

When the song ended, I dropped down beside him, out of breath. "Did you like that, Rabbit?" I pulled Alice to my chest.

His silver eyes ran down over my dress, then back to my face. "Yes," he said, his voice raspy. "I liked it a lot."

"Really?"

He nodded.

"I'm so happy!" I took another sip of my tea, and Heathan did the same. I poured us one more cup. When all the tea had been drunk, I reached into the sack for my final treasure.

I placed the book before Heathan. *"Alice's Adventures in Wonderland."*

Heathan picked up the book and ran his fingers over the old front cover. "Your favorite book." He opened the cover and started looking at the pages.

I gasped. "Can you read, Rabbit?"

Heathan's hands paused, and he looked at me. "Yeah. You can't?"

I shook my head. "I'm homeschooled. My papa is a very busy man and he doesn't get much time to teach me. I spend most of my days playing out here in the yard." I played with Alice's hair. When I flicked my eyes back to Heathan, he was still watching me. "Can . . . could you read the book to me, Rabbit?"

Heathan looked like he was going to say no, but then his shoulders dropped and he nodded. Smiling, I moved until my head rested on his leg. I heard Heathan breathing weird, but I didn't say anything. I looked up, and he was looking down at me.

He was very handsome.

"My mummy read this to me every night when she was alive. Since then, no one has read to me . . . until now."

Heathan swallowed, and then started at the first page. I smiled as he read. And he read well. *He must be really smart*, I thought. *Quiet and smart.*

I studied Heathan as he read. I listened to his voice, his strong Texan accent . . . just like mine when I wasn't using my English one. "Why didn't your mummy want you, Rabbit?"

Heathan stopped reading and looked down at me. His silver eyes seemed to darken. "No one ever wants me," was all he said.

"Your papa? Mr. James doesn't?"

Heathan shook his head once. "He doesn't want me either. But I've got nowhere else to go. He told me to stay away from him while I was here. So I do."

I felt my heart grow heavy with sadness. "Then I'll want you," I said quietly, and Heathan's eyes grew so wide they looked like two bright moons shining in the midnight sky. I put my hand in his and squeezed gently. "I'll be your friend, and you will be mine. Dolly and Rabbit. Friends of the Earnshaw estate . . . your first friend in the whole wide world."

I rolled to the boombox beside me and pressed the play button. As Mummy's tape played, I rested my head back on

Heathan's leg and gave him a huge smile. Heathan's hand left the book, then, really slowly, he lowered his fingers to my face and over to my hair. He straightened my headband. I thought he might smile at me, but he didn't. He looked back at the book. I closed my eyes as he read to me again. And all the time he did, I imagined I could hear the tick-tock of his pocket watch in his vest.

I knew I would like the sound very much.

Tick tock.

Heathan James.

My new friend.

Tick tock.

CHAPTER 2

Heathan

Two years later . . .

THEY ALL EXPECTED me to feel something. They all stared at me as we stood at the side of the grave. My papa was lowered into the ground, and I watched, detached, as his coffin was placed in the grave. The pastor said something, but I didn't bother listening. I was too busy wondering what was happening to his body as it wasted away in the wooden box. Wondering what his blood looked like after five days of being dead. Was it thick and red? Congealed, like Jell-O? Had it changed color? Had his skin turned dry, cracked, gray? Did he stink? Had he started to decay, lips losing flesh, pulling back from his yellowing teeth?

A hand slid into mine. I didn't need to look to know it was

Dolly. She was the only person who dared touch me. She was the only person who ever spoke to me. Just the way I liked it.

I lifted my eyes and saw Eddie Smith glaring at me from across the grave, that stupid hat on his head. He watched Dolly's head fall against my arm and hug it close. When he met my eyes, I smirked at him, eyes burning. She was *mine*. He had her once, but from the minute I came along, he no longer existed in her world. There was me, the only one in her life now. I'd told her that to be my friend, she'd have to cut Eddie loose. I didn't share. Especially not with straightlaced jerks like him. She chose me. In a heartbeat. The decision between me and Eddie had never *been* a choice. She belonged to me . . . and she knew it.

Eddie hated it, of course. I read it in his face every time he stared at her like she was a favorite toy he'd lost. Every time he looked at me with his ex-best friend on my arm, he radiated with hatred.

He *should* hate me.

I was never giving her back.

I was keeping her . . . forever.

Over the past couple of years, Eddie had come to the estate less and less. He was once a staple, but since I arrived, his presence was no longer needed. I saw him watching through the fence most days, but I'd made sure she'd told him he wasn't welcome.

He was now redundant in Dolly's life.

I was all she would ever need.

I would make sure of it.

"Rabbit?" Dolly's voice pulled me away from Eddie and his shit-scared face. When I looked down at her sad blue eyes, she pointed to her papa beside her. Mr. Earnshaw was holding out a bucket of dirt.

"Take a handful of the dirt, son. Throw it into the grave, on your papa's coffin." I did as asked. But I never broke away from Dolly's hand. She sniffed, and when I looked at her again, I saw her crying. I rubbed the tear from her cheek with my thumb, then brought the tear to my mouth.

It tasted of salt.

It tasted of her.

It tasted good.

The pastor said something else, and then everyone began walking back toward the main house. I saw Mr. Earnshaw and the "uncles," his business partners, walking at the front of the small crowd. It was just estate staff. Mr. Earnshaw and his business partners never really left the estate. We were alone all the way out here in the Dallas countryside. But I had Dolly. So I didn't care.

I was homeschooled, had been since I arrived. But, just like Dolly, I wasn't actually schooled by anyone. So I spent my days with her, drinking tea at her tea parties and trying to teach her how to read and write. She tried, but she wasn't too good. She knew the basics, but she struggled with most things.

It pissed me the hell off.

"You want to go to my bedroom, Rabbit?" Dolly held on tighter to my arm, her cheek against my jacket. I nodded, not saying a word, and let her lead me to the house and into her quiet room. I heard the sound of the adults in the main room on the floor below. But I didn't wanna be around them. I didn't like them. Being around them made me want to hurt them. Being around anyone but Dolly made me want to take a gun and pierce a bullet through their thick skulls. I didn't know why. Those were just the daily thoughts I'd had about people ever since I could remember. Most nights I fell asleep imagining what they would all look like dead.

Dolly sat on her bed, her china-faced doll, as always, pulled tightly to her chest. She was wearing black today. She looked weird not dressed in her blue dress, white socks and white apron.

I *hated* it.

I went to her closet and pulled out one of her many identical blue dresses. Her big shimmering blue eyes were fixed on me as I held out the dress. "Change into this."

Dolly looked down at her black dress and coat. "Papa said I had to wear black today. To honor your papa. Like I did at my mummy's funeral."

"I fucking hate you in black. You belong in color." I pushed the dress out again.

Dolly scowled. "*You're* always in black," she said and pouted her full lips. "Why can't I wear black too?"

I was getting annoyed. "I live in shade. You don't. You live in the light . . . now *change*."

I kept my eyes fixed on hers until she sighed dramatically and took the dress from my hand. The only bit of emotion I'd felt all day came flooding to my chest as she marched past me to her bathroom, stomping her feet. I felt my lip tug up at one corner. It was as close to a smile as I ever got.

And only ever for her.

She was always dramatic. Full of life. Pushed every one of my buttons.

Throwing the long black jacket Mr. Earnshaw had bought for me for today across a chair, I sat down on the bed. My hand dipped into my vest pocket and pulled out my pocket watch. I ran my fingers over the screen and watched the hands move around. Tick tock, tick tock, tick tock . . .

The bathroom door opened and Dolly walked out, once again dressed in her blue dress. Her Alice doll hung at her side. She smiled and held out her arms to the side, seeking approval for her outfit. She knew I loved her in these clothes.

Only in these clothes.

My living, breathing doll.

She walked to her vanity and sat down on the stool, flicking a glance to me in her mirror, giving me another coy smile. She hummed to herself, yet another song from her mama's mix tape. I recognized the song. She always sang and danced to this song. Over and over again, every single day. I didn't care. I loved watching her dance.

I sat back on the bed, my head resting against the brightly painted yellow wall. Dolly reached for the tube of lipstick that sat on her vanity—her mama's old lipstick.

Pink.

It was bright pink.

She applied the lipstick, squirted some perfume on her neck, then came to sit beside me. When she played, it was always dress-up. Dress-up and afternoon-tea parties. English accents and bright pink lipstick. She had a picture of her mama at the side of her bed. She wanted to look just like her; that was obvious. With her pink lipstick and long blond hair, she did.

"Rabbit?" Dolly lay down beside me.

"Yeah?"

"Do you feel sad?" Her eyes were so big. I could see tears in them.

"I ain't sad," I replied flatly and slumped down until I faced her. Dolly smelled of roses again—my favorite scent. *That perfume . . . her . . .*

Dolly laid her hand over mine on the mattress between us. "Your papa died. It's a sad day. You . . ." She looked nervous. "You can cry if you want. It's okay. I won't tell anyone."

I frowned. "I don't cry."

"Ever?"

"No." I tried to think of a time when I'd cried. There had *never* been one.

"You won't miss your papa?"

I thought about her question. Then I answered with the truth. "No."

Dolly gasped. "But you do miss your mummy though, yeah?"

I shook my head. "No." My eyes narrowed as I tried to read Dolly's shocked face. I thought of my mama. Thought of her as she dropped me off at the Earnshaw estate gates. Pictured her watching me in the kitchen before she gave me up. Thought of how she cried herself to sleep at night while whispering my name.

And I felt nothing at all.

"She means nothin' to me. No one does." As Dolly sucked in a quick breath, I felt something burn in my chest.

"I . . . I don't mean nothin' to you, Rabbit? Even *me*? Your Dolly?" A tear fell from the corner of her eye and rolled down her cheek. I watched the drop fall, and something ripped in my stomach. Her bottom lip was trembling.

My hand jerked out and I wiped the tear with my thumb. "Only you." Dolly held her breath, searching my face. I glanced down, not knowing what this feeling in my chest, and now my stomach, was.

"What?" Dolly asked, sniffing back her tears. She took my hand in hers and squeezed.

I looked at our hands and tried to imagine life if Dolly left me. If I never saw her again, like I wouldn't my mama and papa. This time I didn't feel nothing . . . I felt *everything*. I felt fire in my blood and anger so bright it burned my eyes.

"You mean something," I said through gritted teeth. "You ain't like everyone else. I couldn't give a fuck about anyone else. Not a single fucking soul . . . only you."

Dolly's wobbling lips moved into a slow smile. She threw her arms around me and hugged me. I couldn't stand anyone touching me but her. And *all* she did was touch me—hold my hand, hug me. Her hands were always on me.

No one else would ever come close.

"Good," she breathed. "Because you're my favorite person ever. Ever that has ever existed in all the world."

The rip in my stomach vanished.

Dolly lay back down, resting her head on her hand. "You're gonna live with us now, Rabbit."

I nodded. Mr. Earnshaw told me that after my papa had died. Told me he was my legal guardian, and that it had been arranged with my papa when I first came to live here. If anything ever happened to my papa, I'd belong to Mr. Earnshaw. Now I did. He said he was making a room up for me.

I wanted it to be the room next door to Dolly's.

Better still, I wanted to just share Dolly's room. I didn't really sleep anyway.

There was a knock at the door. We sat up just as Dolly's nanny, Mrs. Jenkins, came through. Her eyes narrowed on us lying on the bed, close. "Heathan," she said. "Mr. Earnshaw would like to see you in his office." She looked at Dolly and folded her arms across her chest. "Where are your mourning clothes, Ellis? It's disrespectful to dress in color on such a sad day as this."

"I told her to change," I said, sitting up. I didn't like Mrs. Jenkins. Didn't like how she spoke to Dolly, hovered around her. "I always want her in color." Mrs. Jenkins looked at me. I glared at her, my lip hooking into a sneer. "*Never* in black."

The blood fell from her face.

"Come, Mr. James," she said, flustered, and turned for the door. I looked at Dolly. Her head was bowed, her shoulders hunched. I got up from the bed and put my finger under Dolly's chin. Her head lifted slowly, and eventually so did her eyes.

"I'll be back soon," I promised. I tipped my head in the direction of her favorite book on the nightstand. "I'll read to you when I return."

She smiled, and everything was okay again.

"Mr. James!" I snapped my head to Mrs. Jenkins, who was tapping her foot impatiently as she waited by the door.

Putting my hand in my pocket, I ran my fingers over the face of my watch. I followed Mrs. Jenkins down the hallway. We were traveling the back route to Mr. Earnshaw's office.

Mrs. Jenkins looked back at me. When I met her eyes she quickly faced forward again. "There're no kids here today," I observed as we came to a halt at the private elevator that led to the hallway outside Mr. Earnshaw's office.

Mrs. Jenkins froze. She slowly turned to face me. "Wh-what do you mean?"

I studied her. Her cheeks flushed as the blood beneath her skin rushed to fill her bloated face. I wondered what that blood smelled like. Wondered how quickly it would spurt from her vein if I dragged a knife over her throat. "This hallway." I paused, my attention now on the throbbing pulse in her neck . . . *Tick tock, tick tock, tick tock* it sang out, drawing me in. It was getting faster and faster, like it would burst free from her neck at any moment. "I've seen kids walking these hallways at night, brought to the front door in a blacked-out van in the dead of night."

She swallowed.

"I watched them being brought into this home by you and Dolly's uncles, and then led up to this floor. To this back route to Mr. Earnshaw's office."

Mrs. Jenkins's mouth dropped open as she tried to speak, but just as she did, the elevator pinged and the door slid open. We stepped inside, and as the door shut, I said, "Both boys and girls. About my age, I would say."

Mrs. Jenkins's back bunched. She shook her head. "Really, Heathan, you have such strange delusions. You've seen no such thing." She laughed nervously, the sound grating on my bones.

"Children coming into this house in the middle of the night? Whatever would that be for?"

She was lying.

I didn't know why.

I'd seen them.

I knew it.

So did she.

The door opened, and I followed her toward the office. Mrs. Jenkins knocked, then she held the door open for me as I stepped inside. She shut the door behind me and left me alone.

I cast my gaze around the room. Mr. Earnshaw was sitting behind his desk, and Dolly's uncles were sitting before the fire. They were always here. I assumed some of them lived in this house—it was big enough—and I rarely saw them leave the estate. There were six uncles, and as I stood there, they all stared at me.

"Heathan!" Mr. Earnshaw got to his feet. He was dressed as he always was, in a dark pinstriped suit. His dark hair was slicked back, and he held a cigar in his hand.

He stopped before me and placed his hand on my shoulder. I froze. He wasn't Dolly. No one else was allowed to touch me. Just as I was about to rip his hand away, he pulled it back and sat on the edge of the desk. "How're you doing, son?" He shook his head. "Such a tragedy, what happened to your father. A freak accident. I'm so sorry. Life can be so unfair."

I didn't reply. Instead I glanced at Dolly's "uncles"—I knew they weren't really her uncles, just her papa's business partners, who she'd known all her life.

"How're you feeling about living here now? In this house, with us?" My attention went back to Mr. Earnshaw.

"Fine."

Mr. Earnshaw smiled, then he reached out and ran his finger down my cheek. Ice trickled down my spine at his touch. I didn't want him fucking touching me. Mr. Earnshaw dropped his hand and moved to the small bar at the back of the room. "We have your room all prepared. It will be on this floor, not far from my office—"

"I wanna be next to Dolly."

Mr. Earnshaw turned and made his way back to me, a drink of liquor in his hand. I frowned. "You've had a long day. You deserve it, son. Whiskey always makes things better." He pushed the drink into my hand.

"I wanna be near Dolly. I want the room next to hers."

"Now, son." He paused. "I see how y'all are with each other. It wouldn't be . . . *appropriate* to put you next to one another." He smiled, and I wanted to rip out every one of his lily-white teeth. "Ellis is still only nine years old. She turns ten very soon." The smile he gave made the hairs on the back of my neck stand up. "She'll be older before long, more of a young lady than a child and able to do . . . more with herself and others. You understand what I mean, yes? You're already eleven, almost twelve. You're already a young man, and as such, I want to keep you nearer me. To safeguard you."

I felt my eyebrows pull down, but just as I was about to argue, Mr. Earnshaw put his arm around me. "Come, have a drink with us." He led me to the circle of seats, and I sat in the

TILLIE COLE

spare one beside him. I met each of the uncles' eyes. They all were watching me.

I hated the way they were looking at me. It made my blood run cold . . . colder than it already did.

"To Derek James." Mr. Earnshaw raised his glass in a toast to my dead father. The uncles repeated his words and drank their whiskeys. Mr. Earnshaw's hand came underneath my glass and guided it to my mouth. I shook my head, not wanting the drink—I'd never tried alcohol before—but he kept going until the rim of the glass was at my lips. He tilted the glass higher, and the whiskey poured down my throat. He kept it there until I coughed at the burn. The glass dropped to the floor without smashing. I wiped at my mouth and faced Mr. Earnshaw in shock. He cupped my face. "It'll make you feel better, son. Believe me. It'll . . . loosen you up. You'll begin to like both the taste and the effect in no time." A pause. "We want you to be more relaxed around us. We're your family now."

Suddenly, I felt dizzy and the room started spinning. I hated it. I didn't like what the liquor was doing to me. I didn't like not being in control.

I must have fallen asleep soon after. When I opened my eyes, it was to find Mrs. Jenkins leading me clumsily to my new bedroom. It was only two doors from Mr. Earnshaw's office. She opened the door and I stepped inside.

The room spun as I dropped to the bed and fell asleep.

I never got to go back to Dolly and read to her.

* * *

I BLINKED my eyes open as there was a knock at the door. I lifted my head and rubbed my hand down my face. The knock sounded again, then the knob turned and Mrs. Jenkins entered my room.

"I wanna see Dolly," I growled the minute her eyes met mine.

"Mr. Earnshaw wants to see you in his office. Ellis is busy."

My jaw clenched, and I swiped my arm out along my nightstand. The glass of water beside me smashed to the floor, shattering on impact with the thin carpet. My arm ached at the movement. Mr. Earnshaw had invited me into his office every night this week with him and "the uncles." And every night, he'd made me drink his whiskey until I couldn't see straight anymore, telling me I needed to relax. Every day since, I had been barely able to open my eyes during the day. I felt weak. I couldn't remember much of what happened in the office after I'd drank, but parts of me always ached the next day. Parts I wasn't sure *should* ache . . . My head always felt fuzzy and I found it hard to focus.

"Heathan!" Mrs. Jenkins said. "Come along. They're waiting."

Wanting to fight it, but having no energy to do so, I got to my feet and followed her out of the door. I straightened my vest, skimming my fingers along the familiar pocket, feeling the watch inside. My stomach rolled as we stopped at Mr. Earnshaw's door.

Mrs. Jenkins knocked as usual. But when I walked through the door and she closed it behind me, things seemed different. Instead of being in front of the fire, the uncles were sitting in a circle in the center of the room. And instead of being behind his desk, Mr. Earnshaw was sitting in the circle too.

"Heathan." he said, turning in his seat to look at me. "Come here," he ordered. I walked toward him. "Move into the center."

I walked into the center of the circle and felt all of the uncles' eyes on me. My legs felt like they would give way at any moment. I was so tired . . .

"Now, Heathan," Mr. Earnshaw said. I looked at him sitting there, smoking his cigar. He acted like he was a king in this house. "We need to have a chat." I didn't say anything, just waited for him to continue. "About how you had no other family to take you in once your father died." He smiled. "So I agreed to be your legal guardian. This much you know." He shook his head sadly. "But what you won't know is just how much it costs to raise a child." I frowned in confusion. "Food and board. Your schooling—"

"We don't get any schooling. No one ever comes to teach us. Hasn't since I came here two years ago and I was told I'd get a tutor. None came."

Mr. Earnshaw waved his hand in the air dismissively. "Well, you see, Heathan, your papa owed me a lot of money." I looked around the fancy office. Nothing about the office made me think Mr. Earnshaw was in need of money. The whole Earnshaw estate was the biggest and most lavish thing I'd ever seen in my life. "I took the money he left you, in repayment . . . but it wasn't enough. And now I have you to care for. I have to clothe you, feed you." He shrugged. "It all costs money." He relaxed back in his chair. "You're a young man now, not a child. Question is, what are you gonna do to earn your keep? To pay back what is owed? It's a man's duty to never be in debt."

A chair creaked behind me. I turned around and saw Uncle

Clive had risen to his feet . . . and he was staring right at me. Uncle Clive was the biggest of the men. And by big, I meant fat. His hair was thin, and he wheezed when he breathed.

He disgusted me.

He reminded me of a roasting pig.

And worse, he always smiled. A huge, creepy smile.

Right now, that smile was on me.

Uncle Clive flicked his head toward the door. "Come with me, Heathan. I have an idea about how you can start these repayments," he said, and I felt my fingers twitch. "I want to help you . . . now that you're family." My skin prickled under his attention. He brushed past me, his arm against mine, and walked out of the door.

"Go with him," Mr. Earnshaw ordered sternly.

I made my feet move and stumbled out of the door after Uncle Clive. When I entered the hallway, he was waiting by my bedroom door. He walked into my room, and I slowly walked in behind him. I didn't see him at first, but when the door slammed shut behind me I realized he'd been waiting behind the door.

My breathing echoed in my ears. My palms grew wet with sweat. Then Uncle Clive moved. He took four steps in my direction, then he stopped. He started undoing his belt. His forehead was sweating like it always did, and his cheeks were mottled with red patches.

My nostrils flared when my eyes snapped to his. His pupils had dilated as he watched me. I stepped back and stepped back until the backs of my legs hit the edge of my bed. I tried to keep my balance, but my feet moved from under me and I fell to the mattress. The room spun from all the liquor I'd been given lately. I felt weak. I didn't like not being in control.

Then Uncle Clive was before me, his belt and pants undone.

I caught a glimpse of his heavily-layered stomach skin and I tried to get to my feet. But Uncle Clive pushed down on my shoulder. His free hand ran through my hair. "You really are a handsome boy, Heathan. And so big for your age—tall and broad. And those silver-gray eyes . . ."

"Get off me." I lurched to the side, trying to get away. But Uncle Clive was stronger than me. His hands did leave me, but only to reach into his pants. I closed my eyes, not wanting to see what he'd do next. His fingers gripped my shirt and he forced me back into the mattress. I struggled and struggled until his hand swiped across my face, making me dizzy. Uncle Clive's arm was braced over my throat, his legs kept my legs pinned down, and I felt him unbuttoning my slacks. He began to pull them down my legs. I tried to shout, to tell him to get away from me, but my voice was cut off by the arm on my throat.

He pulled my pants down until they were bunched at my ankles, then wrenched me to my feet by the collar of my shirt. He dragged me across the room and bent me over the desk, kicking my ankles apart with his foot. His hand pressed my head down to the desk until all I could smell was oak. I tried to struggle, to get free, but I couldn't . . .

I stopped trying.

I pulled out my pocket watch and stared at the face. I blinked, studying the hands, blocking out the pain that quickly came. Blocking out the grunts, the wheezing, the drops of sweat that showered the back of my neck . . . the feeling of him behind me . . .

"Tick tock," I whispered to myself as my cheek moved back and forth along the oak surface of the desk. "Tick tock, tick tock, tick tock . . ." I kept my eyes on my pocket watch, pushing everything else out of my mind until I heard the bedroom door close. The room was plunged into silence. But I couldn't move. My cheek stayed pressed against the wooden tabletop. Oak. I couldn't stop smelling oak.

My pocket watch caught the light and reflected a patch of gold onto the ceiling. It was flickering. I realized it was from the shaking of my hand.

I breathed.

I breathed.

I breathed again.

I clutched my pocket watch to my chest and rose from the desk. Pain shot through my spine, but I gritted my teeth and pulled up my pants, fastening them as tight as I could. My hands still shook. My breathing felt strange.

And I had only one place I wanted to go.

I darted across the room and quietly opened the door. I peered out into the hallway. It was empty. I ran across the carpet, jaw clenching when every step hurt more than the next. But I wouldn't cry.

I didn't think I knew how to.

I avoided the elevator and headed for the back staircase. I climbed each step as fast as I could until I was at Dolly's floor. Seeing her door was shut, I burst through and slammed it behind me. I ran to the corner of the room and slumped down the wall, keeping out of sight. I tried to catch my breath.

But I couldn't catch my breath.

Everything felt wrong.

"Rabbit?" Dolly's sleepy voice came from the direction of her bed. I didn't look over at where she would be. Instead I stared at my hand . . . stared at the blood coming from my palm. I slowly opened my fingers and saw that my pocket watch was still in my hand. The glass had cut my skin.

"Rabbit?" Dolly's voice was closer this time. But I felt myself rocking. Watched the hands on my watch as they traveled around the clock face.

"Tick tock," I whispered, swaying back and forth, back and forth. "Tick tock, tick tock, tick tock . . ." I tried to block it all out.

"Rabbit? Wh-what's wrong?" I felt Dolly drop down beside me. I smelled the roses from the perfume she always wore. She gasped. "You're bleeding." She ran for the bathroom. When she came back, she took the watch from my hand and covered my palm in a towel. "Are you hurt?" she asked. I finally let myself look up. She was dressed in a long white nightgown, but the black headband she always wore was still in place. And in her hand she held her doll.

She said there were bad people in the world. Some that were close by. She told me Alice would keep me safe . . .

Dolly's words from two years ago circled my head. It was what her mama had told her before she died.

Bad people.

She wanted Dolly protected from bad people.

Bad people close by.

Her papa . . . her uncles . . .

"Where have you been?" she asked. I looked into her blue eyes as she spoke. They were sad again. I had no words to say. "I've missed you so much. Mrs. Jenkins told me you have been busy with my papa and uncles." She stuck out her bottom lip. "Too busy to visit me. To play and to read to me." Her lip began to shake. "I've been so lonely without you. And now you look sad," she said, her shoulders slumping. "I don't want you to be sad." Her voice was now a whisper.

When I still didn't say anything, she drew back and tried to smile. "I think I know what will make you feel better." Dolly got to her feet and rushed to her mama's old pink boombox on her desk. She switched it on and began to dance.

And I watched her. I never took my eyes away from her as she swayed and mouthed the words to the song. She smiled as she danced . . . then another memory came into my head. Words she'd once told me as we lay out on her picnic blanket one summer's afternoon.

I always dance for my papa and my uncles. They love to watch me dance. I do it a lot . . . they love it . . . they always ask me . . .

"Stop," I said under my breath, but Dolly didn't hear me. She closed her eyes and raised her hands up in the air as she kept dancing. "Stop!" I said louder, but she still didn't hear. "Fucking stop!" I eventually screamed, loud enough that my voice cut through the music and my anger filled the air.

Dolly stopped dead and stared at me with huge blue eyes. "Rabbit?" she whispered, and her bottom lip trembled again.

37

"Turn off the fucking music!" I snapped. Dolly did as I commanded, with her head dropped and her face all sad. She turned, shy and nervous, and I eventually managed to hold out my hand. She clutched her doll to her chest like a shield, but she came forward anyway. When she was within reaching distance, I grabbed her hand and pulled her down to sit next to me. "No more dancing."

"Why?" She blinked her long lashes. "I love to dance."

"No more dancing for your papa and uncles," I said more firmly, and Dolly shook her head. "Promise me."

Dolly paused. "Can . . . can I still dance for you?"

I felt that strange feeling in my chest again. The one I had only ever felt around her. The one where my heart squeezed and my throat got really tight. "You can dance for me. But *only* for me."

"Okay." She played nervously with her hands in her lap.

I glanced down at my watch on the floor. "I want to protect you," I said, and Dolly looked up. I picked the watch up in my bloodied hand. "I want to keep you safe."

"From what?"

"Bad people," I replied. Dolly looked down at her doll, then nodded her head. Like she understood.

She always understood me.

But she had no idea of the danger she was in inside this house.

Dolly held her doll tighter. "Rabbit?" she whispered. I looked at her. She was so pretty. "Are you sad now? My heart is telling me you're very sad."

I went to shake my head. Went to say no, but when I opened my mouth, I nodded and automatically whispered back, "Yes."

Tears built in Dolly's eyes, and she lurched forward and threw her arms around my neck. We never hugged. At least I never hugged her back—she always hugged me. But today I let her hold me for longer than normal. I let her hold on. I didn't push her away as I normally would when I couldn't stand to be touched anymore.

I wanted *her* touch to replace *theirs*.

"You smell strange," she said against my neck. "You smell of smoke . . . like my uncles and papa smell." I closed my eyes and thought of my watch, thought of focusing on the hands moving around the face while it all happened. "I really wish we could escape to Wonderland right now, Rabbit. I . . . I think you need it." She sighed. I heard the smile on her face as she did. "Think of all the adventures we could have. All the colors we would see and all the people we would meet. If we could only find the rabbit hole in this house . . . There must be one somewhere. A way to escape."

I breathed in deep and smelled her mama's rose perfume again. Then I thought of her uncles and her papa. Thought of the kids I had seen being brought in at night in vans. I now knew what for. I didn't know where those kids came from or who they were. But now Mr. Earnshaw and the uncles had me too . . .

"Rabbit?" Dolly slowly reared back her head. She stared me in the eyes, and I tried to search her gaze. Then, before I could do anything, she moved forward, and suddenly her lips were crushing mine. I froze, not knowing what to do. My head told me to push her off, to get her away from all the fucking pollution

39

that was stuck on my body. Coating every inch. But something in my chest told me to keep her on me. Keep her rose smell and sweet taste there, removing all the bad.

Dolly pulled back, out of breath. Her eyes were wide as she stared into mine. "Rabbit . . ." she whispered and brought her hands up to touch her lips. "I just had to do that . . ." She swallowed. "I couldn't stand you being so sad anymore. And I just had to kiss you, Rabbit. I just had to . . ."

I didn't speak. Couldn't speak. Just felt Dolly all over my lips. Felt Dolly all over my skin. I wanted her back. Wanted her back in my arms. Rubbing her scent on me, letting it seep into my blood and bones.

I hooked my arm around her neck and pulled her into me. It wasn't long before I felt Dolly's tears running over the skin on my neck, and I leaned in toward her. She always felt whatever I felt. I always felt whatever she did. Fuck everyone else. It was me and her.

Dolly hugged me tighter, and I promised myself that *they* would never touch her. I would never let them. They would have me instead. As much of me as they could take. I'd take it to protect her. To keep her this pure. This innocent.

My little Alice in Wonderland.

But if they ever tried to hurt her, to take her from me, I'd kill them all. I didn't know how or when, but if they ever made her cry or took her the way they took me . . .

. . . I would fucking end them all.

And I knew that I'd enjoy it.

CHAPTER 3

Ellis

Six months later . . .

"Can you believe it's my birthday tomorrow, Mrs. Jenkins?" I asked as I came out of the shower. "Ten years old." I sat down at the vanity and let Mrs. Jenkins rub a towel over my wet hair.

She smiled at me in the mirror as she put the towel down and picked up a brush. "Well," she said, "it'll be your birthday in only one hour." I smiled in excitement. "Your papa has spoiled you tonight allowing you to stay up this late."

Mrs. Jenkins blow-dried my hair and smoothed it down my back with my brush. She fixed my black headband in place, the ends of my hair curling slightly against my shoulders. "Now, I take it you want to wear a blue dress again?" She shook her head.

"At least we have a new one. A special one for your birthday. One for older girls."

"Yes!" I said excitedly. I'd been desperate to wear that dress. I put my hand on her arm. "But now that I'm ten, am I allowed to wear the other socks?" I held my breath, crossing the fingers on my other hand, bouncing from foot to foot, praying she said yes.

Mrs. Jenkins leaned down and kissed my head. "Of course, young lady. You're a big girl now."

I shrieked and ran to my closet. I grabbed the black-and-white striped knee-high socks my papa had bought for me last year. They still smelled brand new. When he'd seen them after they arrived in the mail, he told me they were too old for me. But he said I could wear them on my birthday. When I turned ten. Because it would be a special day for me.

I'd be a *big* girl.

"Where are we going again?" I asked Mrs. Jenkins as I started getting ready in my dress and new socks. When I was dressed, I looked down at my new blue dress. It was tighter than my others had been. Shorter too, and the skirt puffed out off my thighs. There was even a black belt that went around my waist. I fastened it and looked at myself in the mirror. My eyes widened. I looked so grown up!

"It's a surprise." Mrs. Jenkins brought me a cup of tea. "Here, drink this." I took the steaming hot tea from her hand and sat down at my vanity. I brought the cup to my nose. I closed my eyes as I smelled the familiar scent of Earl Grey—my absolute favorite. I wouldn't drink anything else.

I took a sip, then another, and placed it down on the table. Mrs. Jenkins walked out of the door. When she came back, she was holding a box. "Keep drinking that tea, Ellis," she prompted and stopped before me.

I drank some more of the tea. "What's in the box?"

Mrs. Jenkins set it down on my lap. There was a blue ribbon tied around the lid. "It's from your papa."

Too excited to hold back, I opened the box and pushed back the blue tissue paper to reveal a black leather shoe. No, not a shoe, but a high ankle boot. I picked it up. It had four gold buckles up the side. But the best part was the small heel. Papa never ever let me wear heels; he said they were not for little girls.

But these had heels . . . because he had told me that at ten years old I was no longer little.

"They're beautiful," I whispered as I took out the second boot and stared at them together. A pair.

Mrs. Jenkins took the boots from my hand and kneeled down. "Let's get them on your feet." I lifted my foot. Mrs. Jenkins paused, the boot at my toe. "Tea," she said. "I want to see that cup empty before we go downstairs."

"Yes, ma'am." I drank the rest in one gulp.

Mrs. Jenkins smiled at me when I showed her the cup was empty. "Good girl," she crooned and carried on sliding my boots onto my feet.

When she was done, she stood and offered me her hand. "Come now, missy, let's see if you can stand in them." I played with my mummy's old high heels, so I knew that I could. But when I stood from the chair, I wobbled. I clutched onto Mrs. Jenkins. The room tilted a little to the right. I put my hand on my head. "Mrs. . . . Mrs. Jenkins . . . I don't . . . I don't feel so good." I rubbed my eyes. They'd gone blurry.

"You're fine, Ellis," she said and clutched at my hand. She looked at the clock on my wall. "It's midnight, Miss Earnshaw. You're officially ten years old." She smiled, but it looked lopsided to my eyes. "Happy birthday!"

"Mrs. . . . ." I tried to say again, but she pulled me forward by the hand, toward the door. I held on to her as tightly as I could. My breathing sounded funny in my ears. Like it was whooshing too fast, then too slow, and there was a ringing in the background.

Mrs. Jenkins led me to the elevator and pressed the button. She smiled at me again. I wanted to tell her I still didn't feel good, but my throat went all funny—it was too tight. I grabbed at my throat, and I felt tears building in my eyes. I closed my eyelids.

I wanted Rabbit.

He always made me feel better. But he kept getting taken from me. I never saw him much anymore. Only when he sneaked into my room at night, without anyone knowing. But when he came, he always acted strange. He always huddled against the wall, rocking back and forth, looking at his watch. *Tick tock, tick tock, tick tock . . .*

But he cuddled me. He always held me close. He never used to, but now he squeezed me so tight I sometimes couldn't breathe. And last week . . . last week he had even pressed his lips against my head. My heart had nearly exploded. Rabbit had kissed *me*. I had kissed him on his lips when he was sad. But I never dreamed that he would kiss me.

I wanted that cuddle again now. I wanted that kiss. Heathan always made me feel safe.

I flinched when the elevator door opened and the bright lights from the ceiling hurt my eyes. I tripped on the carpet as I followed Mrs. Jenkins. I glanced down at my hands, and I managed to breathe a little bit. I was still holding my doll, clutching her by her long blond hair.

It will protect you from bad people . . . I heard my mummy's voice say in my head.

The sound of footsteps made me look up. When I did, I saw Rabbit in the distance. Uncle Clive had his hand on Heathan's shoulder, and he was leading him to a room. I tried to call out for Heathan, but before I could, Uncle Clive led him into the room and shut the door. I still tried to open my mouth, to ask Mrs. Jenkins where Heathan and Uncle Clive were going, but I couldn't make my lips move. They were numb.

Was Heathan here for my birthday surprise too?

Was the surprise that I got him back after he had been kept from me for so long?

Mrs. Jenkins stopped outside of Papa's office door. She fixed my headband and smoothed out my hair. "Your papa is going to think you're so pretty, Miss Earnshaw. His perfect little girl."

My eyelids were lazy as I tried to blink. I opened my mouth to tell her I wanted to go back to bed, but my mouth felt too dry to make my tongue work. My lips felt too swollen to open, and I couldn't form words.

Mrs. Jenkins led me inside Papa's office. Her hand held mine a little tighter as she shut the door behind us. My papa rose from his chair with a huge smile on his face. "Ellis!" he said and came toward me with his arms held out. He hugged me and held me tightly. He kissed my cheek, making a loud smacking sound on my skin. "Happy birthday, baby." He stepped back and looked me up and down, holding my arms with his hands. "You look so beautiful." I swayed as I tried to see him better.

My uncles each give me a tight hug. By the time the last one had stepped back, I felt tears on my cheeks. *Help!* I wanted to scream, but I couldn't. *Something is wrong with me!*

"Come here, baby." Papa led me to the center of a circle of plush leather chairs. He moved to the side of the room, and the sound of "Dear Jessie," my favorite song in the world, filled the air. My uncles sat down on the chairs, as did my papa. "Dance for us, baby," Papa said, and suddenly the room stopped tipping to the side.

I tried to shake my head. Heathan had told me never to dance for them again. He told me that every night. He made me promise him, every night. And I hadn't danced for them, not since the first time he told me.

I didn't know if they had seen my head shake, but my papa didn't look happy with me. I gripped my doll's hair tighter in my fist. "Dance, baby," he said again. But when I didn't, he got to his feet. His hand touched my face, followed by his finger running down my cheek. "Did she drink it?" he asked someone over my head, behind me.

"All of it," Mrs. Jenkins replied. "I made sure of it." I heard the door open and close as she left the room.

My Uncle John stood and came over to us. He pulled my papa back by his arm and said, "I won the right to tonight, Jacob. I go first. It was a fair deal. I won that poker game fair and square."

My papa nodded and gestured toward the door. Uncle John

slipped his hand in mine then led me out of the room. I turned back to look at my papa, but he was already talking to my other uncles. They were shaking his hand and laughing. Uncle Samuel patted him on the back.

Uncle John yanked on my hand, pulling me forward. The movement caused my fist to open, and my doll fell to the floor. *No!* I tried to shout as Alice slumped to the carpet, but my mouth still wouldn't move. I watched her lying on the carpet as Uncle John led me down the hall. We stopped at a door opposite the one Heathan had gone through with Uncle Clive. I reached out and ran my fingers over the wood of Heathan's door. I tried to call his name. No sound came out. Before I could knock, to get my Rabbit to come to me, to tell Papa and my uncles that I was too sick for their birthday surprise, Uncle John took me inside the room.

He led me to a bed, and I sighed in relief. He could tell I was sick. He was going to let me sleep. He was going to take care of me.

He guided me to the edge of the bed. I sat down, closing my eyes to stop the room spinning, and I felt Uncle John's hands run over my new striped socks and up my thighs. He lifted my dress, and my eyes rolled open. I jumped, trying to move back as he took hold of the new frilly lace panties Mrs. Jenkins had given me as my present. Uncle John smiled at me, then leaned in and kissed me on my lips as he ran the panties down my legs. When he had taken them off my feet, he pushed them into his pants pocket.

"Lie down, baby girl." He smoothed his hand over my hair. My heart was beating fast. I shook my head, but he pushed on my shoulder, flattening me to the mattress. He crawled above me, and when I looked down, he was holding something in his hand. I couldn't tell what, but he was moving it back and forth. His cheeks were red, his breathing had gone funny, like he was out of breath, and he leaned down and kissed me again. "Happy happy birthday, baby girl," he whispered in my ear, then I felt his hand move. Move to a place I didn't want him to go.

No! I wanted to shout, but the light above me swayed and I couldn't move. I blinked and blinked again. Something hurt. It hurt so bad that tears fell from my eyes.

Alice, my doll, wasn't there. She wasn't there to protect me like my mummy had told me.

"Heathan," I tried to whisper, but my mouth didn't move. "Heathan," I tried again, but I think it only sounded in my head. "I don't . . . I don't like my birthday present, Rabbit . . . it . . . hurts . . . help me . . . take me away, down the rabbit hole, to Wonderland."

But Heathan never came.

Wonderland never came.

The rabbit hole could not be found.

So I just closed my eyes . . .

* * *

I WAS SO cold as I walked behind my uncle, back to the office. Goosebumps raced across my body, and my lips were shaking. They shook so badly I couldn't stop them.

I was limping. Between my legs hurt so much that tears still fell down my cheeks. But Uncle John ignored my pain, instead patting me on my head and telling me I was a good girl. He told me we were closer now. All of us. That all of my uncles wanted to get just as close as we had . . . because they loved me so much. That it was my birthday present.

I didn't think I wanted them that close. But I didn't dare say.

Uncle John pushed through the office door and led me back toward the circle. I saw my Alice doll on my papa's desk. I wanted to hug her. I wanted her to make me feel better, to protect me. Maybe if she was in my arms the pain between my legs wouldn't be so bad.

But then I heard a whispered "*No . . .*" come from the circle. I looked up. My heart fell and a big fat lump filled my throat when I saw Heathan in the middle. Another of my uncles was holding him, about to lead him past me out of the door. I shook my head to see him better. I wiped the tears from my eyes. But when I did, all I felt was sadness. He was getting thin. And his pretty silver-gray eyes looked different. They were red and had big dark circles under them. They no longer shone.

My bottom lip wobbled. I lifted my arms, holding them out, wanting to hug him. Rabbit always kept me safe and warm. And I felt so so cold. He would make me feel warm. And maybe . . . maybe I could make him feel better too.

Maybe we could have another kiss.

"No . . ." he said again, but this time his voice was louder and his mouth grew tight. "Dolly." He pushed Uncle Samuel's hand off his shoulder. Uncle Samuel slammed his hand down on Heathan's arm, but Heathan fought his grip and got away. He ran to me and threw his arms around me. I gripped him as hard as I could.

He was shaking.

His breathing was funny.

I inhaled deeply . . . Heathan. He might look different, but he still smelled like my Heathan.

Dark. The only way I could explain his scent was *dark*.

He stepped back and looked down. His eyes widened when he looked at my thighs, then his body shook even harder. He was so angry. I leaned against him and looked down at what he'd been looking at. All I could see was red. My socks were crumpled around my ankles, at the top of my new boots, but all my skin was red.

I gasped when I realized what I was seeing.

"Rabbit," I managed to whisper. "Is . . . is that blood?"

My head was woozy. Rabbit turned and pushed me back against my papa's desk. I sat on the edge, needing the rest. He stood in front of me. Blocking me from my papa and uncles. I peeked around his arm to see what was happening.

"I want them both," I heard Uncle Lester say. "I want them at the same time. Fuck the poker games, I'll pay whatever I have to to have them. Just look at them together . . . the way he loves her. Protects her. The way she gravitates to him. They are like magnets." He shook his head. "For years I watched them get closer. You can't create that kind of connection." He sucked in his bottom lip. "Imagine how explosive just ten minutes with them both would be . . . You know I like the fight. Ready, able and willing is so fucking boring."

Heathan made a choked noise in his throat. Then my papa came toward us. I ducked lower behind Heathan's shoulder. I tensed. I didn't like my papa much right now. He let Uncle John hurt me.

"Get back," Heathan snarled. "Fuck me all you want, but touch her again and I'll fucking kill you all. No one touches Dolly."

My papa paused, all of my uncles did . . . then they all started laughing. The loud laughter hurt my ears; their open, laughing mouths wounded my eyes. I wanted them to stop. Wanted them to stop laughing at my Rabbit. I pressed my hands over my ears and tried to stop the laughing.

"Move aside, Heathan. You're both going to have some fun with Uncle Lester."

"Take me. Leave her." Heathan moved so close to me that his back was flat against my chest. I didn't like the way Heathan's back smelled. It smelled of smoke again . . . like my uncles.

Like Uncle John had smelled.

"Last chance, boy," my papa warned Heathan. "Don't push me. This honorable shit is admirable, but futile."

Then suddenly, Uncle Eric rushed from the back of the room, right at Heathan. Heathan reached behind us and ran his hand along the desk. He took something in his hands. As Uncle Eric grabbed Heathan's black hair to pull him away from me, Heathan reached up and did something to Uncle Eric's neck.

My eyes snapped shut. They wouldn't let me see what Heathan had done. I heard a grunt, and a thud, and Heathan's body was no longer pressed against mine. I opened and rubbed my eyes, and when I lowered them to the ground, I saw Heathan stabbing Uncle Eric's throat . . . his chest . . . his stomach. Blood spat up and splashed my face, the warm liquid spilling down my cheeks.

Heathan's black clothes were covered in red, as were his face, his hands, every inch of bare skin.

My papa and Uncle Lester lurched forward and pulled Heathan off Uncle Eric. I let out a scream when they hit my Rabbit . . . they hit him and hit him again. Heathan dropped whatever he was holding, and I realized what the blood-covered object was. Papa's letter opener lay on the floor, the one engraved with a picture of the King of Hearts. Papa and my uncles loved to play poker. They always had cards lying about the house. Hearts was Papa's favorite suit.

I looked at Uncle Eric on the floor, studying him harder, and I cried out. He was so still, and his eyes were open and staring at the ceiling. He wasn't blinking. Blood poured from his neck.

"Rabbit!" I felt my tears coming faster. I needed him. I wanted to protect him. I wanted to make sure he wasn't hurt. "Rabbit . . ." I sobbed as he fought to get back to me. He punched out at my papa, at my uncles, but he couldn't get away.

"Dolly . . . Dol . . . ly . . ." he spat out as Uncle John wrapped his arm around Heathan's throat. Heathan couldn't speak, but his eyes never left mine. My hand reached out for him.

Papa ran to the phone beside me. He made a call, hung up and walked back to Heathan, who was still struggling against Uncle John's arm. "You've fucked up, boy."

"Leave her alone," Heathan snarled, turning his head from Uncle John's grip. My papa hit Heathan again. Heathan's lip split open, blood dripping down his chin. Papa kept hitting him. And hitting him until Heathan's teeth were coated in blood.

Heathan sneered at my papa, blood and spit dripping to the floor.

I couldn't stand it anymore.

I jumped off the desk and ran over to stop it. But Papa took hold of my arm and pushed me against his chest. Heathan looked me in the face. There was so much blood. My papa's mouth arrived at my ear. "Say goodbye to your little friend, baby." I stilled. "He's going away now . . . to a place he can't come back from."

"No!" Heathan and I shouted at the same time. Papa stroked my hair as I stared at Heathan. Heathan stared at me too. I was crying. Crying so hard because my heart was breaking. Heathan was my best friend. My most favorite person in the world. I didn't want him to go away.

He didn't have any other friends.

I was his Dolly.

He was my Rabbit.

I . . . I loved him . . .

Then I saw it. I looked into Heathan's silver eyes as a single tear slid out of one corner. I gasped, and my heart shattered into tiny pieces. Because Rabbit never cried. Never *ever* cried. Not even when his papa died did he shed a tear.

But he was crying now . . .

Because he was being taken away from me.

"Don't . . . don't cry, Rabbit," I whispered. My throat was closing up. I was so sad I could barely speak. I tried to reach out and push the falling tear from his cheek, but my papa hit my hand away.

I heard the door open behind me. "Take her to her room," my

papa said without looking around. Mrs. Jenkins's hand took hold of mine. I jerked it away. I needed to stay with Heathan. I was scared. Scared they were going to hurt him.

Papa tucked my hair behind my ear. "Say goodbye to Heathan, baby."

"No!" I shouted, shaking my head.

Heathan struggled to get out of my uncle's hold, but he couldn't. I pushed forward, escaping the invisible chains that seemed to have locked me in place, and wrapped my arms around Heathan's neck. I heard the sound of a car coming from outside and held him tighter. "Rabbit . . . I'm scared." I felt the tear from his cheek kiss my own.

"I'm coming back for you, Dolly," he whispered. "Wait for me. I'm gonna come back for you. To take you from this place . . . to Wonderland. Okay?"

My sob turned into a hiccup. "Okay." Then Heathan put his mouth to my ear and said, "My vest pocket. Take it."

I reached inside and pulled out his pocket watch. I clutched it in my palm, and then Mrs. Jenkins was dragging me from the room. "Heathan!" I screamed. I caught his eyes with my own and spoke what was in my heart. "I love you, Rabbit!" His eyes widened. "You're my best friend!"

I didn't hear Heathan's reply, because I tripped over something. I nearly threw up when I saw it was Uncle Eric.

"Rabbit!" Now I'd found the words again, I couldn't stop calling for Heathan, wanting my Rabbit to hold me. I cried his name over and over until Mrs. Jenkins threw me into my bedroom and slammed the door shut. I screamed and screamed, banging on the door, raking at the wood with my polished nails, but she didn't come back. She had locked me inside.

I heard car doors opening outside my room. I ran to the window and pressed my hand against the glass. A big black van was in front of the house. Papa came outside, followed by two of my uncles, who were holding Heathan. I shouted his name, slamming at the pane of glass, as they threw him in the back. And I screamed when the van pulled away, taking my heart with it.

I watched the van drive away until I could no longer see the taillights.

My papa and uncles walked back inside the house. I cried and cried for hours as I watched the driveway, but Heathan and the van never came back. My legs wobbled, no longer able to hold me up, and I slid down the wall. I crashed down to the floor, the pain between my legs making me moan. And I stared at the door. I didn't know if my papa or my uncles would return, so I just stared, praying they wouldn't come.

My lip trembled as I remembered that Heathan had said he was coming back for me. That I just had to wait until he did. I looked down at my hand. It was in a fist. Even though it was shaking, I opened my fingers. Blood covered my palm, but when I wiped the blood away, I saw Heathan's pocket watch in my hand. I stared at the cracked glass . . . at the two hands on the face. And I heard him in my head. *I'm coming back for you . . .*

My Rabbit was going to return and get me. Until then, I would count down the time. I gasped. The hands that had always been broken had jerked to life. They were moving! The hands were moving! I was seeing what Heathan always saw. It wasn't all pretend . . . I could see them tell the time!

Lifting the watch to my ear, I kept my eyes on the door, checking for movement from the hallway and anyone coming inside. I tapped at the watch—just like Heathan did—and whispered, "Tick tock." I swallowed, smiling as I heard the tick-tock of the clockwork hands. I knew Rabbit would never break his promise to me. "Tick tock . . . tick tock . . . tick tock . . ." I whispered to the rhythm of the watch, over and over again, until my voice no longer worked.

Tick tock . . . tick tock . . . tick tock.

I would count until my Rabbit came home.

CHAPTER 4

Heathan

Eleven years later . . .

I SWITCHED the stick shift down a gear as I arrived at a familiar set of gates. Only these gates were rusted and worn, hanging limply from their fragile hinges. Weeds wrapped like talons around the bars. They looked nothing like the imposing gates I remembered from my years spent living here. They were ruined and destroyed . . .

Just like anyone who had ever entered this fucking place had become.

Then again, maybe I was already different and altered when I first came here. But *she* wasn't.

I got out of the car and approached the gates. The hot sun

beamed down on me from above. I fixed my cravat, straightened my black shirt and vest, then smashed my foot against the gate's pitiful lock. The gate groaned under my force but then swung open, baring the vast hell that lay beyond. I stood, breathing slowly, deeply, trying to calm the voices spinning around my head. The ones that told me to leave no soul here alive, to take down every one of the fuckers and make them pay in blood and screams and torture . . . The voices that had kept me company all these years, never letting me forget the penance that must be paid.

"In time," I said out loud. Out of instinct, my hand ran over the pocket in my vest, searching for the pocket watch that had stayed by my side for so many years. Tick tock, tick tock, tick tock . . .

I'm in here, it seemed to call from the mansion that lay beyond the long driveway and wayward trees. The siren's call to the only two things that meant anything to my rotten core. My hand curled around the cane cradled in my palm. I glanced down, slipping my fingers down the black metal stick.

Rabbit, I heard Dolly's voice whisper, a distant echo from the past, as I stared down at the decorative head of the cane. A white rabbit's head, ears drawn back and teeth bared.

Rabbit.

Her rabbit.

Flicking my cane in a circle, I turned and got back into my car. I pulled forward, dust creating a smoky cloud behind me as my tires screeched on the now-dirt road. It was once paved and flat, but now it was bumped and degraded. I roared down the road, through the winding twists and turns. My hands tightened on the wheel when I approached the final bend.

The sprawling sight of the Earnshaw mansion lay just beyond. The house that birthed in me the beat that gave life, and the puncture that destroyed whatever semblance of a heart I once had.

My breath stalled as the edge of the brown-bricked building came into view. Moss and weeds crawled like a swarm of locusts up the once beautiful house, just like those spindling vines at the gates. The decay on the exterior reflected what had existed in the interior for too many years to count.

I knew those who had polluted this place with their poison were no longer here, but *she* was.

Finally, I was here to get her back.

As I pulled the car to a stop directly at the entrance, I looked at the stairs that led to the main doors. In my mind's eye, the weeds covering the large oak doors I'd been dragged through as a child rolled back, baring the expensive shining wood beneath. The brass from the knob, shed of its orange and brown rust, gleamed in the sun once again. The overgrown grass on the lawn shrank to reveal acres of manicured land, and the dead and depressed floral border that framed the house sprouted into color, rich reds and yellows chasing away the thorns of dark and night. In my mind, the Earnshaw estate was once again pristine.

Then I too was back there. The night I was taken away. Taken from my darling . . . my Dolly . . . my breath, my sails . . . my soul . . .

THE DOOR SWUNG OPEN. Mr. Earnshaw marched out, followed by the "uncles" dragging me behind. My teeth clenched so hard I thought they would shatter as they yanked me down the stairs and into a waiting van.

Only seconds after I was thrown inside, the van pulled away. I sat in darkness, slamming my bloodied fists against the walls, trying to find my way out. "Dolly!" I screamed. "DOLLY!" I screamed over and over again. I screamed until my voice failed. My legs gave out, and I ignored the pain that shot through my body at the memory of what they'd done to me. One after the other for months and months. No reprieve. No breaks. Just them behind me, grunting and panting, ripping into me, pressing their chests against my back.

What they'd now done to Dolly. My Dolly. Her eyes . . . her eyes when that fat fuck brought her back to the room. Limping, blood running down her thighs. Tearful, pale . . . fucking destroyed.

My delicate living doll ruined.

In my mind, I replayed plunging the letter opener into Uncle Eric's neck, his chest, his stomach. The blood that splattered onto my skin—hot and wet and strong in its metallic scent. The taste as it had hit my mouth, the flavor bursting on my tongue—the taste of his demise. The taste of my victorious kill. And I'd felt it, the power surging through me, as I'd felt his pulse slowing under my fingers. Saw his eyes draining of life.

I'd *done that.*

I'd *ripped the life from him. With my own hands.*

For Dolly. For my Dolly.

We drove for so long that I fell asleep. When I woke, it was dark outside again. A man dressed in black yanked me from the van and toward a tall water tower. It was white, but had no name painted on it. I looked around me: there was nothing but fields and fields. The man dragged me to the bottom of the tower, where a door opened. Pushed forward, I stumbled into the tower to see a set of stairs winding down below ground.

The man gripped the nape of my neck, forcing me to move. Down and down I walked, through the dark, until I came to an iron door. Bolts unlocked, metal ground, then the door opened and I was pushed inside. My eyes widened. Rows and rows of cells lay before me. Then a man stepped out from the shadows. An old man. The minute my eyes landed on him, my lip curled in warning. He smiled at me.

I envisioned his death in my mind. A bullet through his mouth would blast his brains out the back of his thick skull. Messy. Bloody. Brutal.

"You fucked with the wrong set of men, kid," he said. He shook his head. "Had some fucked-up people in here for years now, some have been here from their teens, but you've gotta be one of the youngest on record." The man behind me laughed and rubbed his hand down my back. I lurched forward and turned, staring at the fucker. I hated to be touched.

"Lotta my men gonna like that you're so young." I turned back to the older man and glared. "Oh, would you look at that? The little sadistic murderer's pissed." He put his hand over his heart. "Allow me to introduce myself. I'm the warden of this here establishment. The land of the forgotten. A place even the government don't know about. No police. No Child Protection Services. Just you and me, and my men, and a hundred other

twisted sick fucks that messed with the wrong people." He stepped forward. So close that I smelled the cigar smoke on his breath. Just like Mr. Earnshaw smelled. Just like the uncles. "No one's coming to save you. This is your new home. A secret Alcatraz funded by the filthy rich, the one percent who pay me very well to remove . . . problems . . . from their lives." He shrugged. "Rich men, you see. They like to commit crimes, but don't like to deal with the aftermath. That's where we come in. A cleanup service, if you will."

The warden looked at the man behind me. "The only cell left with any room is fifty-two."

"That wise?" the guard said. "Not sure we want anyone else in with them. They're bad enough without adding a third. Don't wanna make them any more dangerous."

The warden paused. "I see what you're saying. It'll be hard for the guards to get to him for pleasure, with those cellmates." He flicked his hand. "But there's no choice. He was a last-minute addition. It'll have to do. Anyway, he's just a kid. What harm can he do?"

The guard huffed in annoyance and shoved me forward. He led me up several sets of stairs. On every new level, I saw cells holding three or four men. Some licked at the bars. Some pointed at me, threatening to kill me. I felt no fear. I'd kill any of them who came close to me.

Sick fuck after sick fuck after sick fuck.

We came to a stop at a cell, and the guard took a gun from his holster. He held it out into the darkness of the cell. He quickly opened the door. When I didn't move, he shoved me inside, clanging the gate shut behind me, and immediately backed away.

I spun around, hands fisted, watching as he walked back down the steps.

A cold shiver ran down my back when I felt someone watching me from behind. "And who do we have here?" said a deep voice from the corner of the room.

I heard a rustle as someone else moved from another corner. I was surrounded. "A little Dapper Dan if his clothes are anything to go by. Slacks, shirt and vest. All black. Suave for someone so young . . . impressive."

I squinted into the darkness. A single dull lamp sat on the back wall, but whoever was in here with me was shrouded by the darkness. Then I saw a flash of white to my left. Someone stood. I held my ground, my hands grinding into fists, ready to fight.

"Look at this, Henry. The little Dapper Dan is ready to take me on."

"Good. He'll need that kind of strength in this place," a rougher voice said from my right.

Two footsteps sounded on the stone floor, and a man came into the light. A man with long blond hair down his back. He was dressed in black pants and a white shirt—both were filthy. He looked young. Maybe in his twenties. He put a hand on his chest and bowed dramatically. "The name's Chapel." He straightened, then smiled. He was handsome, with an accent I hadn't heard before. He sounded rich, like he had money . . . sophisticated. "Welcome to the Water Tower. The keeper of all things dark. Like the trophy chest of the most fucked-up collector of the underworld." He smiled wider. "I, as they might say, am a ripper of sorts." My brow creased as I tried to understand what he meant. "Too much for you to comprehend?" He nodded. "You're young.

You may not have come across stories of men like myself yet." He came even closer. "I have a, shall we say, unhealthy obsession with women of the night, and like to cut them open in the most delicious of ways."

I swallowed, but never let my eyes leave his. He laughed and fixed the gold cufflinks on his shirt. "Lawyer by trade. Something of a young hotshot, you might say. Ivy League–educated, years before my peers. But alas, I've been here two years now." Chapel looked into the far corner and flicked his head. He rolled his eyes when whoever was there didn't move. "Henry, we have a guest. Introductions must be made. That is proper etiquette." Chapel shook his head at me. "Yankees, you see. No manners, unlike my southern self."

There was silence from the darkened corner, and then someone moved. A tall, well-built, brown-haired man stepped into the light. His hair was long too, but his was brown. He had the lightest brown eyes I'd ever seen. They looked almost golden. He looked about Chapel's age. Maybe a bit younger? But a lot older than me. "This is Henry," Chapel explained. Henry glared at me but said nothing. He only pushed his hair back from his face. "Now, Henry here is a doctor." Chapel tapped his head. "Of the mind. A psychologist." He laughed. "Quite ironic, no?"

I was wondering what Henry was in this place for when Chapel added, "Henry here has never done anything wrong. He is an innocent." Suddenly, Henry's eyes closed, his teeth clenched, and a strained sound ripped from his throat. His long hair fell back over his face. His shoulders rolled forward, the muscles in his neck and shoulders bulging at the movement. The change in his frame made him look huge. Bigger and more intimidating than before.

When Henry's eyes reopened, he glared at me again. But this time he was different. His eyes were narrowed and tense. His nostrils flared and his hands rolled into fists.

"But this is Hyde," Chapel said. "He is . . . not so innocent. Let's just say he likes to watch people die . . . under his expert hand."

"I like to watch that too," I said.

Chapel smiled a surprised smile. "Splendid!" He winked.

"Though not as much as I like to kill them myself," I added. Hyde stood straighter, a flicker of a smirk pulling on his mouth.

"Henry and Hyde are two different people living in the same body," Chapel explained. "One always fighting for dominance over the other. A multiple personality disorder is the scientific diagnosis. Henry is a professional. A straightlaced man. Quiet. Reserved. Hyde . . . is quite the opposite."

"What is this place?" I asked, looking around me. I didn't care what these men were. I just needed to get out. I had to get back to my Dolly.

"Where those who want us gone have sent us." Chapel tipped his head to one side. "But you are so young that you have piqued my curiosity. How old are you, Dapper Dan?"

"Twelve," I replied. Chapel's eyebrows rose. He looked down at my hands and smiled.

"Blood on your hands? Literally? Young Dapper Dan . . ." He tutted, then laughed.

"They hurt Dolly. They touched her. Touched her like they fucking touched me. Her eyes . . ." I felt my hands shake. "They

65

made her cry. Her papa. Her uncles . . . they made her bleed . . ." I stopped when I felt like I would explode with rage.

"Then I would say you were justified in spilling that blood," Chapel remarked, his smile fading.

"I need to get back to her. I need to save her. Stop them from hurting her more. I'm not there to protect her. She's all alone. She—" I shook my head, thinking of Dolly. "She's too fragile. She won't be able to cope with what they'll do to her. I know it. She . . . she'll . . . they'll destroy her. Not only her body, but her mind. She's . . . different. Too delicate for this world." I turned to the barred door and shook the metal. It didn't move.

"We all have people to get back to, whether that be for revenge, protection or affection, but we have to bide our time . . ." Chapel said. "I just realized we did not learn your name."

I didn't turn around. I stared at the winding stairs that led back to the warden and his closed iron door. The door that led to the outside world. "Rabbit. My name's Rabbit. The White Rabbit."

"Well, Rabbit,*" Chapel said, moving beside me. "We all plan to get out someday. And someday that will happen. Until then we wait. You will soon realize that all we do in this tower is wait. We plan and we scheme. We plan for the day we once again see the sun and seek revenge on those who thought they could hide us from the world."*

THREE MONTHS AGO . . .

THE GUARDS never came close to our cell door.

Eleven years. Eleven years I had waited. I heard the guards, of course. Heard them enter the other prisoners' cells. Fuck them. Torture them. Do whatever the fuck they wanted to them.

But never ours.

Hyde and Chapel had made sure of that.

Hyde and Chapel had nearly escaped a year before I arrived. Hyde had ripped a guard's throat out when he had come too close to the bars. The guard was too cocky. He had taunted the monster within Henry. Until the monster was freed and killed him where he stood.

"We won't fail again," Chapel had told me shortly after I arrived all those years ago. "When the next opportunity arises, we will succeed."

So when a new guard started . . . a guard who couldn't keep his eyes off Chapel's good looks, opportunity burst in Chapel's eyes.

A smile here.

A wink there.

The closer the guard came.

A fly to his sticky trap.

I twirled the needle in my hand, the one that Chapel had used to draw my tattoos. The needle thrown into my cell when an infection had almost killed me. The infection was bad, but I wouldn't let myself die. I needed to get back to Dolly . . .

"Why are they helping me?" I asked Chapel through gritted teeth as I stabbed the needle into my leg.

"Those who paid a handsome sum to place us here want us to live. For living is punishment, Dapper Dan. A lifetime spent in a dank, dark cell. Most at some point have wished for death. It is easier than enduring this day after day."

My eyes were steel. "I haven't wished for death," I bit out as cold shivers accosted my body. "I won't die without Dolly."

Henry moved to sit beside me, throwing his shirt over my body for warmth. "And that is what makes you different. You and Chapel." He huffed a humorless laugh. "And Hyde. I would like nothing more than to be put out of my misery. I welcome the peace that death would bring. But Mr. Hyde within me won't ever let that be . . ."

I sat back in the dark. The pack of cards I had drawn was safely in my pocket. All but one. The one of my Dolly. The one Chapel had used to draw the tattoo on my back. Her perfect image and likeness. The picture that kept her alive in my head as every day in the Water Tower grew longer and darker.

I looked up as the new guard passed by our cell for the third time in the last thirty minutes. Chapel was already on his feet, waiting for him. His shirt was off, his chest and torso bare. The guard's eyes flared when they landed on Chapel. Chapel walked slowly to the bars, running his hand over his chest. Then his hand dropped further down to his cock. Hyde stifled a laugh beside me as the guard almost fell over himself at the sight.

When the guard moved away, Chapel came and sat beside me, waiting for him to return again. Every day, he amped up the seduction.

"You like him?" I asked, narrowing my eyes on Chapel. I owed him, Henry and Hyde everything. The guards never once

touched me, out of fear of them. Chapel taught me math and literature and art. As an artist himself, with only sharpened stones and walls for his tools and canvas, he had taught me everything he knew. Henry prepared me for what state I might find Dolly in.

Hyde had taught me how to kill.

All I needed now was to put it into practice.

Chapel rolled his head my way. "He is young and not too hard on the eyes." He smiled, then leaned in closer. "I can appreciate the male form, Dapper Dan, but I'm afraid cock does nothing for me. I am partial to a whore's hot, wet pussy . . . then her dying in my arms afterward, of course." He shrugged and sat back. "Though I am not opposed to using my . . . God-granted wiles to help our cause." His brushed back his long blond hair. "I am the quintessential narcissist, Dapper Dan. I believe my unrivaled looks can win anyone over."

He was right.

As the days passed, the guard came closer and closer to the bars. Over the months he had snuck us paper, card, pencils and pens. I had created my cards. Chapel had used the ink to draw my tattoos.

All at the request of Chapel. All because of his seductive efforts with the cock-hungry guard . . .

"You will not kill me for touching you, will you, Dapper Dan?" he asked as he hovered over my bare skin with the needle and ink.

"Just do it," I said through clenched teeth. As his hands touched my skin, I thought of Dolly. It was the only way I could stop myself from attacking the man that had kept me alive and untouched this far . . .

I awoke with the sound of something clattering against metal. I shot up, my eyes trying to see what was happening. Chapel was naked . . . and had the guard by his throat against the bars. Chapel's hand covered his mouth. The guard flailed, trying to get away. I jumped to my feet, but Hyde had charged to the bars, my needle in his hand, before I could even move. He stabbed the needle into the guard's neck.

Hyde held the guard as Chapel reached for the keys on his belt. In seconds, the door was open. I stared, fucking stared at the open door, heart slamming in my chest. Chapel seemed to be as shocked as me as he hovered on the invisible line that separated the cell and the freedom beyond.

Chapel glanced back at me, and a huge smile began to pull on his lips.

He stepped over the threshold and relieved the guard of his knife and gun. The guard's blood trickled from his neck wound and ran down his body. My breathing increased in speed at the sight of the blood. Unlike most people, blood didn't repulse me . . . it made my dick hard.

I walked to the falling blood like it was a magnet drawing me in. Hyde looked back as the guard's eyes began to drain of life. I was no longer paying attention to the open door, too focused on the seeping wound on the guard's neck.

Hyde smiled, showing all of his teeth. "End him," he instructed. His neck cracked as he rolled it from side to side. "Use the darkness that lives inside you. Think of the all the things I taught you... and finally use them."

A knife was suddenly in front of my face. I looked up. A still-naked Chapel was holding out the guard's blade for me to take. "We need to be quiet," he whispered. "Best not let the other guards know we are free. Surprise will be the key here, Dapper Dan."

I took the knife.

I stared into the guard's eyes.

And I plunged the blade right into his heart.

I twisted the knife, hot blood coating my tattooed hands. "I want more," I rasped, only removing the blade when the guard's eyes froze in eternal sleep.

"Then we should proceed," Chapel said and readied the guard's gun. Hyde lowered the guard to the floor, keeping hold of the needle. And we moved. One by one we took down the guards until there were none left.

We stopped at the door that led to the stairs that promised our freedom. All of us were silent as we stared at that fucking door. Eventually, Chapel threaded the key into the lock and clicked it open. Turning, he took all the keys he had gathered and threw them into the other cells. The sound of doors opening accompanied us as we raced up the stairs we had been led down so many years ago.

When we burst into the dark night, I gasped, the fresh air scalding my lungs. Hyde moved beside me, and I caught his hands clenching into fists from the corner of my eye. He broke into a sprint, heading for a house. "The Warden," Chapel said, then followed Hyde.

Feeling my blood thrashing through my veins, I let the adrenaline take hold and ran too. As I burst through the door, I heard the sound of screaming from upstairs. Chapel made it to the bedroom just a second before me.

The Warden and his wife were lying in bed, their blood seeping from the stab wounds Hyde had inflicted on them. Hyde was panting, out of breath, eyes lit with bloodlust.

Chapel walked to the closet and pulled out a shirt and pants. When dressed, he said, "We need money and a car. I'll get the keys for the car, you two find cash. There's no way this fucker kept what he was being paid in a bank."

Thirty minutes later, we were in a truck, Chapel in the driver's seat. Hyde called shotgun, and I took the back, bags of the Warden's money surrounding me. I stared out the window as we crossed states, driving to one of Chapel's secret houses. I thought of Dolly, and the plan I had concocted with the help of Chapel and Hyde.

For the next few months I planned my return, gathering the information I needed to make it all go without a hitch. I trained to kill with Hyde. I worked on my detailed plan with Chapel. Bought clothes. Had weapons made. Conversed with the corrupt private investigator Chapel knew from his days before the Water Tower.

After three months, I was ready.

Ready to come back for my girl.

Ready to lead her down the rabbit hole.

Ready to kill with her by my side.

CHAPTER 5

~~Heathan~~
Rabbit

I TOOK the box from the trunk and stood at the bottom of the stone stairs that led to the main door. My hand flexed around the rabbit head of my cane, my teeth gritted together and my jaw clenched.

Dolly, I reminded myself. *You're here for Dolly.*

Cracking my neck, I narrowed my eyes on the front door and took the first step. With every footstep taken, I smelled the smoke from their cigars. I heard their breath in my ear. But I kept going. I kept going even though I heard their grunts, their laughs . . . felt them above me, rocking back and forth.

"You're ready to get your darlin'?" Chapel had asked me several days ago.

"My Dolly," I had shot back.

"Your little Dolly darlin'". He had smiled and bowed like he always did. *"Then, young Dapper Dan, send her my loving regards, and Godspeed."* A slow smile. *"May the devil be firmly on your side . . ."*

"Dolly darlin'," I repeated under my breath, glancing up to the high windows I knew were hers. I turned the knob on the door, the old wood creaking loudly as it opened. A cloud of warm air hit my face. Air filled with a thick, stale dust. I stepped into the hallway, my eyes immediately relieved by the lack of light. My eyes didn't like the light after being in the dark for so long. I looked to my left and saw a mass of white sheets covering the dining furniture. The first living room was the same. Everything was covered. Hidden away, like they had never existed. Like this fucked-up house of hell didn't have secrets and screams trapped in its walls, pulsing as one passed. Didn't have the echo of kids' cries and pain.

Didn't vibrate with depravity.

Brow furrowing, I looked down at my hand on my cane. It was shaking. I hissed, my head tilting to the side at my body's rare display of emotion. I never felt anything. Nothing, save the urge to kill and destroy those who destroyed us.

But then there was Dolly . . . there were the memories of this damned place. The shadows that sought me out at night, forced me to constantly relive the feeling of violation. The demons of the past that made me replay each moment, every puff of breath on my ear, every sliver of sweat-soaked skin sliding against my own.

A noise from upstairs made me snap back into focus. I held

the box tighter in my other hand and made for the stairs. One step, two steps, three steps . . . I kept my eyes focused on the floor above. I moved my hand over the rabbit head, flicking my finger over the latch that would unleash its hell if needed.

When I reached the top, the carpets musty and stale beneath my feet, the red and gold of the walls faded and the wallpaper peeling, I caught the distant sound of footsteps withdrawing down the stairs to my right. I closed my eyes, listening to the sounds. My eyes snapped open and my lips curled back over my teeth.

I knew who those footsteps belonged to.

I walked forward, toward a door that was a beacon to everything I was. Stopping before the closed door, I stared at the wood. *Silly Rabbit*, I heard in my head, a voice from the past. A light smile, laughing blue eyes, a high-pitched giggle and a playful scold. *You're my most favorite person in the whole wide world, Rabbit. I hope you know that.*

Then . . . *I love you* . . . Three words never spoken to me before they were uttered from Dolly's mouth.

I love you . . .

I tucked my cane under my arm and entered the room. My breath hitched as I stepped across the familiar threshold. No smell of roses greeted me. No eighties music. No pink boombox. No tea set or laughter.

The room was dead.

Extinguished of life.

I placed the foot of my cane on the floor and looked to the left. The sound of light breathing came from around the corner. I made to move, but my heart slammed into a fast beat, stopping my feet in their tracks. My nostrils flared as I closed my eyes and tried to suck in deep breaths. I never did this, never had this kind of reaction to anything. Not in eleven years. Not when I was trapped in darkness. Not when we got out—bloodily, savagely, darkly. Especially not when my knife plunged into the guards' hearts and I watched the life fade from their eyes, the pure fascination of losing one's life essence occupying my mind.

But this was Dolly. The only person I'd ever given a shit about.

I had no idea what state I would find her in. Whether or not her fragile mind had been destroyed. Whether or not her glass heart had been shattered. No hope of salvation.

I had no idea if my only reason for living could be saved. I shook with venomous anger when I let my mind imagine the hell those sadistic cunts would have put her through in my absence. But Chapel's words rang in my ears . . . *Unleash the anger only on those who deserve it. Let it build within your heart like a well swelling with water . . . then unleash hell on those who took your freedom.*

Opening my eyes, I breathed through my rage and silently rounded the corner . . . I stopped. There she was, sitting in a chair. I sucked in a breath and heard it rattle in my ears. Her hair. Her hair was pulled back into a long braid, the woven strands falling to her lower back. And she was dressed in black. Long, baggy sleeves covered her arms.

Motherfucking black. Dolly didn't belong in black. Only color. Blue and white and gold and motherfucking pink.

I edged around the perimeter of the room until I faced her. My heart tore down the center and I had to hold back a loud snarl when I saw her curled up on the seat, a thick blanket over her thin legs and waist as she stared lifelessly out of the window. The window that overlooked the once-manicured lawns, now nothing but high-reaching weeds and too-bushy trees. I looked across at what she was watching, in the direction of what held her so captivated.

My heart was severed completely, the two parts of its flesh repelling the other, trying to escape the rage and pain and fucking consuming darkness.

She was staring at the spot where we used to play as kids. Where she had found me all those years ago, ripping the colorful butterfly apart in my hands. I moved into her line of sight, but her blue eyes didn't lift to meet mine, just stared through me as though I wasn't even there. I crouched down and studied her face. Porcelain skin. Full lips. Fucking perfection.

But there was no life left in her.

I had never felt fear before, but I imagined the sinking hole I felt dropping in my stomach was something like it. A sinking feeling that Dolly had gone to a place from which there was no escape, a prisoner in her own mind.

Fragility consumed.

"Dolly darlin,'" I rasped, my voice fucking breaking.

Twenty-one. She was twenty-one and more beautiful than I could ever have imagined. Perfection. My living doll.

A strand of hair lay over her face. My fingers clenched and unclenched as I tried to force myself to touch her. But I couldn't. Except for Chapel giving me my tattoos, I hadn't touched or been touched in years. I didn't know how to anymore. Allergic to human affection. Repulsed by the degrading feeling of touch.

I . . . I . . . I couldn't.

As I opened my mouth to speak to Dolly again, a loud gasp sailed through the air behind her. I straightened, gripping my cane, to see a familiar old face appear. I watched, the sinking hole quickly replaced by dark satisfaction as the blood drained from her face. "Good Lord," she whispered as I smoothed down my black cravat and vest.

I glared at the bitch. Leaning casually on my cane, I said, "More like Lucifer, I would think." I nodded in her direction "To you, anyhow."

Mrs. Jenkins swallowed and tried to back out of the room. "Ah-ah," I tutted and shook my head. She immediately stilled, eyes fixed on mine.

"He . . . Heathan James . . . it's . . . it's not possible . . ." she stammered and ran her eyes over me. Every inch of me.

"Rabbit." The bitch flinched at my correction. "I am Rabbit. The motherfucking White Rabbit. So never fucking utter that peasant name to me again."

Her skin paled, and her eyes fell to Dolly sitting on the chair. Dolly still hadn't moved. I shifted my grip on the box I had brought inside, about to hold it out to Mrs. Jenkins when she asked, "How are you here?"

I threw the box across the room. It landed right at her feet. "Dress her."

"Wh-what?" Mrs. Jenkins asked.

I pointed to the box at her feet. "Dress her. It wasn't a request." Mrs. Jenkins shook as she picked up the box and moved to where Dolly sat. Dolly didn't look at her either. Mrs. Jenkins opened the lid of the box and gasped again.

Her old, wrinkled eyes snapped up to mine. "No—"

Before she had even finished the sentence, I had reached into my pocket and pulled out my knife. I ran the flat side of the blade down my cheek. Slowly. Controlled. Watching her terrified gaze track my every move. "You'd best do as I ask, Mrs. Jenkins. My patience and tolerance for you appear to be at an all-time low."

She swallowed and, hands shaking like an earthquake, pulled out a blue dress, black waist belt, and black-and-white striped knee-high socks. Black ankle boots followed, along with a black silk headband adorned with a black bow.

Mrs. Jenkins straightened. "She hasn't worn these dresses since the day you left. She . . . she is no longer that person. She is no longer obsessed with that book . . ."

I vividly recalled the very day she referred to. The blood on the striped socks pooled at Dolly's ankles, the blood on the trim of her new, adult blue dress . . . "I'm back, bitch," I spat out. "Dolly will be in color once again. She'll be *my* Dolly, not the fuck-thing you all groomed her to be when you destroyed her innocent mind." I pointed the knife at the old woman's face. "Dress her. And make it quick."

Mrs. Jenkins reached her frail old hand out for Dolly. It took every ounce of my self-control not to rush forward and snap those bones in my hands. In many places, relishing each and every crack.

Mrs. Jenkins pulled Dolly to her feet and led her to the dressing room attached to the bedroom. Dolly followed her nanny without any semblance of awareness. Her black dress reached the floor, tenting her willowy body. Dolly was small. Maybe only five foot one.

Small, but all grown up.

As the door shut, my heart struggled to slow down at the thought of how she would look when she reappeared. Then I thought of her dead eyes and knew Henry had been right. Knew my biggest fear had been realized. I prayed that Henry's wise counsel would work.

"If she's been hurt as much as you believe, if her mind is as fragile and childish as you believe," Henry said, "she may not be the person you once knew."

"What do you mean?"

"Repression, probably; I worked primarily with repressed patients when I practiced psychology. Severe abuse or trauma can prompt timid fantastical personalities, such as Dolly, to shut down. Like a frightened child may hide under a bed when she is scared, a character with a fragile mind may find solace in a similar manner. But her safe place will not be under a bed, under her comforter or in a closet, but rather in the depths of her mind. Dolly may have locked herself behind a metaphorical mental door—no talking, no real living. Seek out her uniquely programmed protection mode. She may have adopted another personality to cope. A new personality, which to her way of thinking hasn't been touched or sullied. One that can face the world when her original self cannot."

"Like you," I asked. "Like you with Hyde?"

Henry's face clouded over at the mere mention of the other being lurking in his mind. "Hyde and I are . . . a unique case. Let's just leave it there." He leaned forward. "If you find your Dolly repressed, in repose from this world, you can attempt to lure her back to you with familiar but— most importantly—safe things. Things she loved, she adored, she liked. Things uniquely safe to her. Above all, things she recognized as belonging in her world." I listened to every morsel of advice Henry gave. "It may not work. Some minds, once cracked open, are lost forever, their prisons immune to breakthrough. But if there's a chance, that's how you bring your darlin' back to you from inside the panic room in her head. With things she loved."

As I leaned against the wall, resting my hand on my cane, the dressing room door opened and pulled me from the memory. This had to work. She must return.

There was no fucking way I was doing this alone.

Mrs. Jenkins led Dolly out of the dressing room. The minute Dolly appeared, I stood off the wall and felt that familiar, now completely underused flicker of a smirk pull on my lips.

Dolly.

My fucking Dolly darlin' . . . well, almost.

Mrs. Jenkins sat her back down in the chair. "Her hair," I said, pointing to the headband still in Mrs. Jenkins's hand. Mrs. Jenkins moved to the vanity, which was now chipped and clearly unused. She pulled out a brush, and in minutes Dolly's band was in place. I slowly moved before Dolly and crouched down to inspect her.

"Pink lipstick and perfume next. Her mama's perfume and lipstick," I ordered, the familiarity of Dolly returning minute by minute.

"R-Rabbit—" Mrs. Jenkins stuttered.

"I wasn't asking," I snapped. Mrs. Jenkins nervously opened a drawer in the vanity. Across the room, something pink on top of a set of drawers caught my eye. The boombox she used to love so much. I crossed the room and blew the dust from its top. I pressed the play button. The song that Dolly would always dance to came crackling through the speakers.

Her favorite song.

I looked behind me and felt my cold blood heat to boiling point as my gaze fell on Dolly. Pink lips . . . I closed my eyes. The scent of roses permeated the air, playfully chasing away the residual dankness of the Water Tower that lingered in my senses.

I opened my eyes. The music filled the room. Then my cheek twitched when I saw a flicker of movement come from Dolly. Her finger, resting on her thigh, lifted slightly. It was such a small movement, barely visible, but it was real.

She was still in there.

I knew it. Could sense it. I always could read her, and she me.

Mrs. Jenkins scurried out of my way as I crouched before Dolly again. "Darlin'," I whispered and lifted my hand up. Without touching her, I traced my finger over every inch of her perfect face, down her long blond hair, and down to her hand. Hovering, desperate but unable to feel the heat of her pumping blood under her pale skin.

Then I stopped. I fucking froze when I saw her bare forearms.

Rage and hatred like nothing I'd ever felt before surged into my body.

Scars.

Scar after scar after scar mottled her once-perfect arms. Raised white scars. Radiating the fury that was threatening to unleash within me, I stood up, stepping away from Dolly.

Mrs. Jenkins saw what had ignited my anger. She backed away from me toward the door. Her back slammed against the wood and small, frightened sounds slipped from her throat as her hand searched frantically for the knob. I walked forward and slowly crowded her space.

"He . . . he'll know you're out," she warned, the whites of her eyes shining bright with fear. I could smell its musty scent clogging the stale air between us.

"He won't." I raised my knife and ran the blunt side down her wrinkled cheek. Her breath hitched as the cold steel kissed her crepe-thin skin. "Tell me," I said, watching the light from the window reflect off the brushed steel blade. "Did you enjoy it?"

Her breathing stuttered.

"Did you enjoy taking the children into the den of wolves? Did you enjoy their screams? The sight of blood and cum running down their little legs as they staggered back into the office, only to be taken by another, then another, then another, night after night, year after year?" I moved my head closer to her face until the tip of my nose was just millimeters from her cheek. "Did you enjoy dressing my Dolly up in her favorite dress and presenting her like a shiny porcelain toy to her fucked-up daddy? Her uncles? Drugged and unable to fight them off?"

"P-please," Mrs. Jenkins begged.

"The money must have been real good to sacrifice your charge that way." I ran the blade down to Mrs. Jenkins's throbbing pulse. I paused, my mouth beside her ear. "I always wondered what your blood would look like gushing from your main vein. Running down your chest and soiling your clothes." Mrs. Jenkins whimpered again. I reared back, feigning surprise.

83

"Oh, did you actually entertain the thought that you would be allowed to live?" I shook my head slowly in disappointment. "None of you will, Mrs. Jenkins. Every one of you will pay in the most painful way possible. To me, and to my Dolly, my Wonderland darlin' . . . and there'll be your blood and all the others' blood pouring in rivers of penance, slipping through the cracks in houses' wooden floors all over my Lone Star State." I moved forward, my face just an inch from hers. "Mmm . . . I can just smell it now. Taste it. Savoring its warmth as it licks at my tongue." I bit my bottom lip and moaned. "My cock gets hard just thinking of it."

"You always were evil, child. From the moment your mother dropped you off at these gates, you polluted the air."

I pulled back a fraction. "You may well be right." I smiled coldly. "I always had a penchant for the dark." I shrugged. "And death . . . such sweet, messy, poetic deaths."

With a quick slice of my hand, I slashed the blade across her throat and stepped back as Mrs. Jenkins clutched at her neck. Blood seeped between her fingers as her eyes fixed on me in horror, and she gargled, drowning before my very eyes.

I tilted my head as I watched her in fascination. Her legs shook, until they finally gave way and she plummeted to the ground. I crouched beside her, studying the body draining of life. She watched me, eyes meeting mine.

I never once looked away.

She gasped. She choked. Then with a final gargle, she stilled. Hands falling to her sides, her eyes frozen in their deathly stare.

I sighed and wiped the blood from my blade onto her clothes. "Just as I expected . . . highly disappointing."

Getting to my feet, I reached into my vest pocket and pulled out the cards. "Queen of Hearts," I announced, running my thumb over the card I'd made by hand, the perfect likeness of her on one side—Mrs. Jenkins's pencil-drawn face staring up at me. My lip curled in disgust, then with a flick of my wrist, I sent the card sailing through the air to land on her bloodied chest. "One down, six to go."

I moved back to Dolly, who was still sitting on the chair. The boombox continued playing her mama's favorite tunes. I watched her fingers and saw them twitch again.

She was definitely in there.

Leaning forward, I placed my mouth at her ear. "Dolly, I've come back to get you, darlin'." I closed my eyes when her rose perfume filled my nose. "Like I said I would." I took a deep breath. "We're going on an adventure, darlin'. Your White Rabbit is here to take you to Wonderland. I found the rabbit hole in this house. All those years as kids we searched for it, with no luck. But I've found it, darlin'. And soon, down the rabbit hole we will go."

I closed my eyes and remembered those days . . .

"Today we'll try the east wing, Rabbit." Dolly pulled a hand-drawn map from the pink purse that crossed over her chest and laid it on the floor. "We'll start here and move through every room, searching every nook, every cranny, every crevice and every loose floorboard." She beamed at me in excitement. "Today's the day, Rabbit. I can feel it!" She said that every time we searched the house, and grew sad when we found nothing. After every unsuccessful search, she would put her arm around my waist, cuddling in, saying, "The way to Wonderland is here,

Rabbit. I know it . . . and one day we will find it. Find it and escape. You and me, Rabbit. We will have the greatest adventure of all. I just know it . . ."

Dolly's head twitched, pulling me from the past. And I smiled when I moved back and blue eyes switched from the direction of the window to clash with mine. There was no life yet. Little real sign of my darlin' beneath, but there was movement nonetheless.

She was hearing me.

There was a modicum of hope.

"Be right back, darlin'."

I ran down to my car. I took what I needed from the trunk and rushed back up the stairs. Kicking back the carpet in the back hallway, I began cutting a hole in the floorboards with the saw. It took me an hour to finish. Next, I went into Mrs. Jenkins's room. Predictably, her stash of cash was under her mattress: hundreds and hundreds of thousands of dollars. All for feeding the wolves, unable to be deposited in a bank lest she would have to explain the source of the payment. Abusers furtively sneaking around in the dark.

Leaving the rope from my trunk by the hole, I went back to Dolly. I packed her lipstick and perfume into a bag. Packed her favorite book, what was left of the old doll she used to love so much, and her boombox and put them in my car. In minutes I was standing before her again. I lifted her in her chair, stepping over Mrs. Jenkins's still-warm corpse and out of the door. I placed Dolly, still in her seat, by the hole and tied the rope around her waist. I guided the other end of the rope through the hole to the floor below, to exactly where I needed it to be. As I turned back to Dolly, I noticed her hand was clenched. It had been clenched the entire time. Looking into her downcast eyes, I reached forward and gently pulled her fingers from whatever they were clasping.

My breath slammed from my chest when I saw a familiar glint of metal. "Tick tock," I whispered automatically as my old pocket watch came into view. I swallowed, fighting the lump in my throat as Dolly's breathing changed from quiet to fast and loud. Her eyes were once again on me. I took the watch from her palm and, like I had always done, held it up to my ear and tapped the top. "We're gonna be late, Dolly darlin'. We're gonna be late." Her head turned toward me, tilting slightly. "Follow me down the rabbit hole, Alice."

I ran down the stairs to where the end of the rope dangled, and I took hold of it. Dolly's chair balanced on the edge of the hole above. I stared at her, my living doll, sitting frozen . . . until she glanced down. And just for a second, the merest hint of time, I saw her behind her eyes. The girl who was my entire life.

Dolly.

I yanked gently on the rope, and her thin body fell forward, plummeting down the hole and into my arms. The wooden chair crashed to the floor, the legs snapping off. I winced when I held her to my chest. I breathed heavily through my nose at her nearness. My head urged to me to drop her. To push her away.

She was close. So close against me. Her head was tucked into my neck, and I felt her warm breath against my skin. Shivers ran down my spine, so strong that I had to hold back a hiss. I breathed through the discomfort her touch caused.

It's Dolly, Rabbit. She isn't a threat. She's your world.

She weighed nothing in my arms. Her smell wrapped around me.

Roses.

Roses.

Roses.

Then she moved . . .

I held still as her head tipped back and I saw her face. My heart flipped in my chest when she blinked. Once, twice, three times, as though waking from a deep sleep. Her once pale cheeks were tinged with pink. Her lips were pouting in the way Dolly's lips always pouted.

Her eyes raked around the room, exploring all around us and up to the hole through which she had just fallen. A low gasp left her throat, then she slowly turned her face to mine. I held my breath as her blue eyes—no longer dull, but bright—looked into mine.

She rubbed at her eyes, clearing the sleep from them. When her hand dropped, her mouth opened into a small "o". She swallowed, never moving her gaze from mine, then she whispered dryly, "R-Rab . . . Rabbit?"

My eyes closed as the name left her mouth. Her voice, beneath the hoarseness, was just as sweet and soft as it had always been.

But gone was her Texas accent. In its place was her "tea party" accent. English. My Dolly had returned to me with a perfect English accent.

"Dolly darlin'." My voice was low and cut and fucking breaking.

She stilled, and a wide smile pulled on her mouth, the pink

lipstick shining on her cracked lips. "Rabbit," she said again, her voice still raw. "My Rabbit. My silly Rabbit. Come back for me." The minute the words were out of her mouth, the smile fell from her face just as quickly as she had tumbled down the hole.

"What is it, darlin'?" I asked, holding her closer. I wanted to push my hand through her hair. I wanted to kiss her head like I had done as a child. But . . . but I just . . . couldn't. Holding her this close was already causing me too much fucking pain.

But it was pain I'd take, for her.

"I was trapped, Rabbit," Dolly said, pulling my attention back to her. She had always commanded every part of me just by speaking, touching . . . breathing.

Tears built in her eyes, her long dark lashes fluttering to stem the drops from falling. It didn't work. "I was locked in a room full of doors, Rabbit, and I couldn't get out." Her breathing hitched. She shook her head and squeezed her eyes shut. "There were so many doors, and the room was dark. I tried every knob, but none would open." A pause. "Then the one that I had to leave through was too small and I was too big." Her eyes opened and slammed into mine. "I was stuck, Rabbit. For so long." Her bottom lip trembled, fucking eviscerating my heart and draining the blackness from my soul.

Light. She had always been the only light that ever got in.

"I was waiting for you, Rabbit. For so, so long." She shivered, goosebumps covering her scarred skin. "It was so cold and dark in there . . . but I waited, just like you told me to, huddled in the corner of the room. It was cold and damp, and the noises from outside made me afraid, but I tried to stay strong. Strong for you." She hiccupped. "Tick tock, Rabbit.

Tick tock, tick tock, tick tock. So many tick-tocks until you came back for me. It made me sadder and sadder each day that you did not come."

A single tear fell down her cheek. Shifting my hand, I caught the tear on my finger. Then just as I did as a child, I brought the drop to my mouth.

She still tasted the same.

Dolly's eyes searched the room, and she stiffened in my arms, eyes widening as she drank in the same fucking house of hell she had never escaped. "We're still here," she said, utter dread lacing her tone. "We're still in the room, Rabbit. There are so many doors. And I'm too tall." Her chest rose and fell erratically.

Her book. Her favorite story. Alice was too tall to leave the room of doors. Dolly thought she was too. Too tall to leave this goddamn house.

If you find your Dolly repressed . . . lure her back to you with familiar but—most importantly—safe things. Things she loved, she adored, she liked. Things uniquely safe to her . . . things she recognized as belonging in her world . . .

Henry's words repeated in my head. I placed Dolly down in front of me. She was too thin, but still so fucking beautiful. She took a frantic but small step back, never taking her attention from my face. Leaning toward me but never touching . . . as though she couldn't bear to touch me either.

They'd done this to her.

To *us.*

Reaching into my vest pocket, I pulled out a small glass vial . . . identical to the one in her favorite book. The vial of blue liquid had a label on the front reading "Drink Me." I'd tied a black ribbon to it to create a necklace.

"Rabbit? Is . . . is that what I think it is?" Her blue eyes widened, their striking color matching the liquid in the vial.

Sugar water, dyed blue.

"It'll shrink you, darlin'. So you can follow me through the door and out into Wonderland . . . at last." I resisted touching her hair. It looked like spun-gold silk. "We have an adventure to start, and I need to get you out of this room of doors."

"Yes," she said and laughed the laugh that had echoed in my mind for eleven years. A blinding smile pulled on her lips.

She reached for the vial.

"Just a sip. We may need it again on our adventure," I said.

"Okay," she whispered breathlessly and took the vial in her palm. Staring at the necklace like it was the most precious thing in the world, she gently removed the cork from the top and brought the mixture to her lips. She swallowed the tiniest amount, then reattached the cork and hung the ribbon around her neck.

Her arms suddenly spread wide, and a shocked inhale sounded around the stale, empty room. "It's working, Rabbit!" She stared down at her feet. "I'm shrinking! Can you see? I'm really shrinking!"

I smiled at my girl and the fucking beautiful look on her face. I crossed my arms over my chest and let the sound of her laughter fill my ears, my mind and my veins. "I see, darlin'. I always see you."

A few seconds later, Dolly lifted her head, an excited gleam in her eyes. "The door!" She whipped her head in the direction of the main entrance. She ran, her long slim legs carrying her across the wooden floorboards. Her hand reached out and pulled on the knob. The door opened, and Dolly staggered back as the sunlight filtered into the dusty foyer. I stood back and watched as her hands flew to her mouth. I flinched as the bright light flooded in, but I ignored the pain it caused my eyes so I could watch her take her first steps over the threshold.

Then she turned and glanced down at my hand. She looked at the pocket watch in my palm, and she fucking smiled. I slowly stepped forward and stopped an inch behind her. I drank in her scent and raised my watch to my ear. Her cheeks flushed with excitement as she waited . . . and waited . . . and waited . . . then . . . I tapped the side of the watch. "We're gonna be late, darlin' . . ." My nose flared when her eyes widened to the size of the moon. "Tick tock."

I brushed past her, rushing out of the door and down to my Mustang. I heard a high-pitched giggle of excitement from behind me and the sound of Dolly's heels clicking on the stairs as she ran down each step. I threw the passenger door open for her to get inside, then took my seat in the driver's side.

I put my sunglasses on and turned on the engine.

Hearing the passenger door close, I looked over to the girl sitting beside me. "You ready for Wonderland, darlin'?"

"Wonderland," Dolly whispered in awe. "I don't think I've ever been outside of these gates, have I, Rabbit? The final barrier before we enter Wonderland."

"No."

"And Wonderland definitely commences just beyond?"

"Wonderland and our adventure, darlin'. Our great adventure, the one we have been waiting all these years to start."

Dolly pressed her delicate hands into her lap and took a long deep breath. "I'm ready." She threw me a big smile, one that eleven years of hell couldn't dim. "Ready for whatever Wonderland has in store for us."

The blood pumped faster through my veins as her words trickled into my ears. As we pulled away from the house that had held so much darkness for us both, I thought of the journey ahead. Thought of the blood we would shed, the hearts we would stop and the lives we would steal. And all the time, a smile threatened to grace my lips when I thought of my Dolly beside me, slitting throats, slicing flesh—her tainted blood guiding our revenge.

Dolly killing, a laugh pouring from her pink lips and crimson blood coating her fragile hands . . .

. . . I could imagine nothing more beautiful in this or any other world.

CHAPTER 6

~~Ellis~~

Dolly

SQUINTING AGAINST THE BRIGHT SUN, I tipped my head back and stared at the sky. It was so blue. So bold—I had never before seen colors so vivid. In the room of doors, I inhabited a world of shade. Spindling shadows danced menacingly on the walls, their tentacles straining to reach me in my corner, where I crouched in trepidation of them touching me. If they reached me, I instinctively knew everything was lost. Rabbit would never, ever find me. So I would block them out, close my eyes and live in the dark.

Night. Eternal night.

Down the rabbit hole, there was *so* much light. So much color, as if a rainbow had bathed the world in its beautiful rays. I ran my hands down my dress. My blue dress, so striking and pretty.

The prettiest dress you ever did see.

Tipping my head back again, I watched the fat, fluffy white clouds as they drifted across the sky, and let excitement fill my heart.

It was beating so fast.

I lowered my head and looked out of the window at the long driveway. The car's tires crunched the road beneath us.

Then I glanced across at Rabbit.

My breath was trapped in my throat. He stared straight ahead at the road, one hand on the wheel and the other resting on the car door. The roof was down, and the wind blew over us like a comforter of feathers. Unlike the rest of the world, Rabbit wasn't bathed in color. He was clothed in darkness . . . save for his eyes.

Silver orbs . . . just like the moon.

He wore a strange thimble on the index finger of his left hand. It was gold and gleamed in the light. Curiously, it wasn't blunt like a traditional thimble, but sharpened, like a talon. I had no idea why he wore it.

Rabbit turned his head, and those silver eyes landed on me. "You good, darlin'?" I shivered at the sound of his voice. It was deeper than I remembered. Rougher and lower.

I felt my cheeks blaze red. He raised an eyebrow. "You sound different," I said. "Your voice is deeper." My gaze fell on his body. He was bigger too, taller and wider. His clothes were similar, but his shirt sleeves were rolled up to his elbows and the skin below was marked with drawings. Black and gray clocks. Clocks and watches of all kinds covered every inch of his skin—on his arms and all the way up to the top of his neck. On his cheek, just next to his left eye, was a single black drawing.

A spade, from a deck of cards.

"You look different." I tapped my head. "In here, I remember you differently." I smiled when I looked up at his hair. "But your hair is still the same . . . and your eyes. I could never forget those eyes." I smiled and whispered, "*My* Rabbit." I wasn't sure if he heard or if the wind had carried my whisper away to the sky.

He didn't say anything for a while, then ventured, "You look the same too. But different. Grown." He raked his teeth over his bottom lip, and his nose flared. "Like a living doll." His lip twitched. His hand tightened on the wheel. "My little Dolly, all grown up." Rabbit's voice was raspier than just a minute before, for some reason. Confused, I was about to ask him why when he stopped the car and took a deep breath. "Look ahead, darlin'." He pointed through the windshield.

I followed his hand and looked straight ahead. My heart fired into a sprint. We had stopped at the gates. They were broken and open, and my eyes could not help but focus on the road beyond.

"Wonderland," I whispered.

"You ready?"

I dropped my head and played with my fingers on my lap. "I . . . I have never been out of these gates before, Rabbit. I've never been to Wonderland."

"I have," he said. I lifted my eyes to meet his. He was staring through the windshield. He turned slowly to face me. "It's different, and it will be scary to you at times, but I'm here to lead you, Dolly." He lifted his pocket watch to beside his face. "This is my job, remember? I'm here to guide you on the adventure." He put his watch back in his pocket. "Do you trust me?"

I stared into those silver eyes and immediately knew the answer. Smiling, I shook my head and laughed. "Silly Rabbit. Of course I do."

"Then we go," Rabbit said. "We have places to go and people to meet. We have to fulfill our destiny."

I sucked in a deep breath and sat back in my seat. "I'm ready, Rabbit." I reached up and clutched the vial around my neck. "I'm ready to see this new world."

Rabbit drove the car forward, and I gasped as we flew past the broken gates. I glanced behind us at the house where I had been trapped. I frowned as I remembered my friend who used to live beyond the room of doors. I would speak to her sometimes. She was on the other side of one particular door, but it wasn't a good door. It wasn't the one that led to a nice part of Wonderland. It was a bad door, one where she got hurt. I didn't want to ever end up in that part of Wonderland.

I hoped she was okay. I hoped that she would one day get out and away from the people who had hurt her.

"You good, darlin'?" Rabbit inquired. I turned my head to face forward and felt the wind slap at my cheeks. When I lifted my hand, I realized my cheeks were wet with tears.

"Dolly?" Rabbit pulled the car to a sudden stop. I looked around. There were bright green fields all around us. They were so pretty. "Why're you crying?" Rabbit asked. I faced him and saw his jaw clenching.

"I . . ." I sniffed and wiped another tear from my face. "I had a friend in that house, Rabbit. One who I just realized I will never speak to again. If I leave . . . she will be all alone."

"A friend?" Rabbit asked. His eyes seemed to darken. "Eddie?" he said through gritted teeth. "Eddie fucking Smith? Is that your friend?"

"Eddie?" I asked in confusion. "I don't know an Eddie."

"You don't?" Rabbit sat back in his seat, and his dark eyebrows pulled down. "You don't know an Eddie?"

"No." I shook my head. "Should I?"

He paused. Then, "No . . . it doesn't matter." He looked away. When he faced me again, he said, "Then who?" He still seemed tense, and a bit confused.

My heart dropped in sadness. "Her name was Ellis."

Rabbit froze. His skin seemed to drain to white. "Ellis?" he said, half whispering.

I nodded, fighting back tears when I thought of her soft frightened voice. "She . . . she was trapped behind one of the doors. She spoke to me sometimes." My lip trembled. "She didn't have a nice life, Rabbit. There were some men in her home that . . . hurt her. They hurt her so much." Rabbit made a noise in his throat, as if he was in pain too. "She was so lonely. She would cry a lot." I sniffed. "I tried to make her feel better by talking to her, but nothing worked. Then one day she stopped coming to the door. I . . . I don't know what happened to her. I never heard from her again." I blinked away my tears and looked at Rabbit. His face looked stricken. I knew he was sad for my friend too. "Do you think Ellis is okay?" I whispered, my voice getting trapped in my throat. "I don't want to leave her there alone, if she's still there, behind the door.

Alone, afraid, scared of the men that come for her every night."

Rabbit cleared his throat and dropped his eyes. When he looked up several seconds later, he said, "Ellis . . . your friend . . . I think she'll be okay. In time."

I nodded, heaving a sigh of relief. Rabbit knew Wonderland. He knew if she would be okay or not. I stared at him. "Ellis had a friend, too. Like I have you. She would talk to me about him. He's called Heathan."

A moan slipped from Rabbit's mouth, and I frowned in panic. "Are you hurt, Rabbit?" He breathed hard and slammed his hand against the wheel. "Rabbit?"

"What happened to . . . Heathan?" His voice sounded strained. He was speaking through gritted teeth once again.

"He was sent away from her, and she never saw him again. She would cry when she told me about him. She was waiting for him to come back. But every day, when he didn't return, she grew sadder and sadder. Her voice grew quieter and quieter until she spoke no more." I swallowed the lump in my throat. "She told me she loved him . . . and that he had been hurt badly too, by the bad men, then they sent him away. She was left all alone. No hope and no Heathan."

Rabbit stared out across the fields. "They're so green. The trees," I remarked. Rabbit nodded. He didn't speak for quite a few minutes. Eventually he turned around, and I thought he looked . . . upset? I was used to him looking angry and sad, but not upset.

"Rabbit—?" I went to speak, but he started the car, cutting me off.

"We're going to be late," he said in a gravelly voice, then raised his pocket watch to his ear and tapped on the metal. I frowned when I saw that his hand was shaking. I didn't say anything though, because sometimes my hands shook too.

Looking straight ahead, I said, "I'm ready." A long deep breath. "Ready for our adventure, in Wonderland."

* * *

I HAD NEVER SEEN anything like it. Tall trees were scattered around the roads, and vehicles of all shapes and sizes whizzed past us—the people of Wonderland going about their business. I watched with bated breath as we passed buildings and bright lights. As we passed fields that rolled in greens and yellows for such a long time that I struggled to see where they ended.

The wind blew through my hair, ruffling my curls. As he drove, Rabbit glanced over to me from time to time. I smiled, but he still looked confused, as if I were a puzzle he was trying to work out. I had no idea why, but I was too focused on the strange sights to ask.

So much time passed that the sun began to set. Just as it touched the horizon, Rabbit turned off the country road we were on and pulled onto a dirt path. Bushy tree branches curled above us to create a tunnel. I leaned my head back and caught the last rays of sun slicing through the leaves. When I lifted my head I saw a building up ahead. A house made from wood stood before us.

Rabbit pulled the car to a halt. There were no sounds coming from this house. No screams or crying. Everything was just . . . silent.

Rabbit's hands slid from the wheel, and without looking at me, he said, "This is where we'll be staying for the next several days."

I leaned forward and looked out of the window. "Your home?"

He shook his head. "The first stop on our adventure." I looked at him and found his silver eyes were already on me. "We have many stops to go."

My heart fluttered in nervous excitement. "And this is number one . . ." I whispered, more to myself than Rabbit.

Rabbit opened his door. I was still staring at the woods surrounding this place when my car door opened too. Rabbit stood, rabbit-headed cane in hand, waiting for me to leave the car. I swallowed back the nerves that were creeping up my throat and stepped out. The ground crunched beneath my shoes.

"This way." Rabbit held his arm out toward the house. I fell into step beside him. I glanced all around us, searching for any sign of people. As if reading my mind, Rabbit said, "There is just you and I here for now. We will meet more people when our journey truly begins."

"It has not begun?"

Rabbit led us to a wooden door and paused. Gripping the head of his cane tighter, he faced me and said, "Soon, darlin'. Before we go, we must prepare." He opened the door. "But first . . . tea."

My breath caught in my throat. Beyond the threshold lay the

most perfect tea-party spread one ever did see. "Rabbit!" I gasped. My hands flew to my mouth. I took a step forward into the house and onward into the magical room just beyond. As I passed Rabbit, I looked up to see him watching me. I moved swiftly to the long table in the center of the wooden-paneled room, and my eyes widened as I beheld the spread. A white tablecloth lay over the table. Tall seats were positioned around it—eight to be exact —and at each seat was set a plate, a teacup and a saucer. I ran my hand over the cloth and smiled at the silver-domed dishes in the center of the table. I looked behind me to find Rabbit, but he was nowhere in sight. Turning back to the table, I lifted the first silver dome to peek at what was underneath. My mouth watered when I saw strawberry tarts. Smiling in excitement, I skipped to the next. Victoria sponge. Desperate to see them all, I removed each cover —cucumber sandwiches, Bakewell tarts, Battenberg cake, carrot cake . . . so much cake! All of England's finest delicacies.

My favorites.

A floorboard creaked behind me, and I turned to see Rabbit walking back into the room. I opened my mouth to ask him where everything came from, but then I spotted what he held in his hands.

"Tea?" I asked as Rabbit placed the silver tray, which held a teapot, a jug of milk and a bowl of sugar, on the table. I walked closer and closed my eyes as I inhaled deeply. "Earl Grey," I whispered, smelling my absolute favorite tea in the entire world.

"Only ever Earl Grey for my little Dolly," Rabbit confirmed and pulled out a chair for me. I sat down, and Rabbit tucked me in. He took the seat a few places down and gestured to the food. "Help yourself. After all, this tea party is in your honor."

A giddy laugh escaped my throat as I reached forward and carefully selected a variety of cakes and sandwiches. When I had filled my plate, I took the teapot and poured myself a cup. Rabbit watched me with a peculiar look on his face. His lip was hooked at the corner, and his eyes were . . . soft. His eyes were never soft, always hard and focused, but as he looked at me now, they were almost gentle.

I swallowed, unsure what this strange feeling in my stomach was. I pressed my free hand to my stomach as a comfort against the strange tingling sensations inside. "Tea?" I offered, my voice barely above a whisper.

Rabbit nodded; not a word escaped his mouth. His gaze became more intense as I moved beside him and poured the steaming liquid into his cup. As my arm neared him, I felt him stiffen in his seat. Only a sliver of air prevented our limbs touching. His breathing grew labored as he watched me pour.

But we didn't touch.

Clearing my throat, I placed the teapot back on the tray and moved to take my seat once again. Just as I took a step, an image floated into my head. Of me and Rabbit. Lips touching. My entire body tensed.

I heard Rabbit's ragged breathing behind me. Goosebumps broke out along my body, chasing one another up my arms and up to the back of my neck. Shaking my head clear of the image, I sat back down.

I raised my eyes and found Rabbit watching me intensely. I lifted my teacup toward my lips. Rabbit did the same, but just as the lip of the teacup almost reached his mouth, I shouted, "Rabbit!" He froze. "Your little finger!" I scolded. I lowered my cup and shook my head. "You cannot drink tea without raising your little finger, silly!"

Rabbit exhaled, then bowed his head. "You're right, darlin'. How could I forget?"

His little finger lifted and, never taking his eyes from mine, he took a sip of his tea. He raised his eyebrow as he placed his cup back on the saucer. I couldn't help it. I laughed. I laughed some more, then took a sip of my own.

"Mmm." I placed my tea back on my saucer. I ate a strawberry tart, and then said, "My first tea party in Wonderland, Rabbit. I have waited my whole life for this very moment!"

"I know, darlin'."

I ran my eyes along the spare chairs. "Will anyone else be joining us? The Mad Hatter? The Dormouse? Maybe even the March Hare?"

Rabbit sat back on his chair, gripping the cane that rested near his side. A curl of black hair fell lazily across his left eye, leaving only the inked spade visible. He made no effort to move it. "Wonderland ain't all it seems, darlin'."

I frowned. "It's not?"

He shook his head. "Not everyone is . . . good."

"I don't understand." I took another sip of my tea.

Rabbit leaned forward and looked me straight in the eye. He went to say something, but then he turned away. His pressed his lips together and turned back to me. "There was a reason I was sent for you." Rabbit reached into his pocket and pulled out a pack of playing cards. My eyes widened. He spun the pack in his hands. "Dolly darlin'," he said. He placed the pack on the tabletop. My eyes snapped to his. Rabbit's

104

nostrils flared. "I . . ." His lips pursed, tongue running over his teeth. "I was sent for you because Wonderland is in trouble."

My breath hitched. "It is?" I whispered, dread filling my heart.

He nodded slowly and leaned further forward. He paused, and I wondered why. Rabbit's cheek twitched, and then he said, "Your friend . . . Ellis . . ." He stopped speaking. My heart stopped beating. The jam sandwich I was holding slipped from my hand, falling messily to my plate. He watched me closely. I said nothing. "She's . . . lost," he said, his voice hoarse. "She's . . . in trouble . . . here in Wonderland."

I looked down at my hand. It was shaking. My eyes closed, and a slice of pain dashed through my chest. Blackness engulfed me, blotting out the bright room, and I found myself back in the room of doors. I crouched in the corner, eyes shut, curled against the wall. Then I heard the soft voice from behind the bad door, the one I never wanted to open. "Help . . . me . . . Heathan . . . Help me . . ."

I gasped for breath as I opened my eyes. The room was blurred, and I felt tears run down my cheeks. "Ellis . . ." I whispered, "is trapped here? In Wonderland?"

Rabbit nodded, and the corners of his eyes tightened. A sob escaped my throat and my stomach turned. Rabbit inched his chair closer to mine. I held my breath for what he might say. "Dolly darlin'." He paused and rubbed his lips together. "Ellis's friend . . . Heathan?"

I stilled.

"He . . . he was the one that sent me to get you."

"You know him?" I asked, shocked. And this Heathan knew me? How?

Rabbit nodded and sat back in his chair. He took another sip of his tea and picked up the pack of cards off the tabletop. He spun them in his hands again, and I stared, mesmerized, as the box danced between his fingers. "Heathan . . ." Rabbit said the name through clenched teeth, as if he couldn't stand to say it. "He is . . . unavailable at this time. He asked me to help him."

"You know him?" I asked again, still in shock.

Rabbit nodded once more. His face paled again, but before I had a chance to ask why, he said, "He wants his girl back. He wants his Ellis back." Rabbit coughed. "He wants to free her. Free her from the bad place she's been left in for too many years. From the bad men who captured her . . . the men who hurt her and caused her to fade away, trapped behind the locked door where you found her."

"How?" I whispered. *How could she ever be saved?*

Rabbit tapped the cards on the table and opened the box. The cards fell to the table, all upside down. I narrowed my eyes in confusion. "There are only five cards," I said.

"There were six once. One has been fulfilled." I didn't know what he meant. Rabbit ran his fingers over the red-backed cards. "Ellis needs a champion, darlin'. A brave warrior to find her and save her." My heart began to race.

I shook my head. "I cannot . . . I do not know how to fight—"

"That is why Heathan sent me to you. I will teach you. I will come with you on your journey. I will guide you. I am the White Rabbit, after all." Rabbit took his pocket watch from his waistcoat and ran his finger over the glass. "Heathan knew that Ellis knew you. He . . . he knew that she trusted you. You . . ." He breathed deeply. "He knew you were her friend." He shook his head. "There is no one more worthy of bringing the men responsible for her pain to justice than you."

I looked down at the abandoned cakes on my plate. At my once hot tea that had now gone cold. "And . . . and if we succeed in rescuing her . . ." I looked up. Silver eyes were watching. "Will Ellis be free? Will she be . . . okay again?"

Rabbit swallowed hard. "We hope so . . . We can always hope." Rabbit ran his finger over the first card and flipped it over. On it was a picture of a man, drawn in pencil. "The Caterpillar." Rabbit's face fell, and anger consumed his silver eyes. "He's first." He turned over the second, third, fourth, the fifth card. "The Cheshire Cat, Tweedledum and Tweedledee, the Jabberwock, and finally . . . the King of Hearts."

"The King of Hearts? Not the Queen?"

"The Queen has already been taken care of," he said quickly and sat back. He stared at me . . . waiting.

I closed my eyes. Immediately, I was in the room of doors, accompanied by the sound of Ellis crying. My chest clenched in sorrow as the echo of her cries seeped into my bones. A deep coldness took hold of me. My muscles tightened as Ellis's cries grew louder and louder . . . Suddenly they disappeared, never to be heard again.

"I'll do it." I slowly opened my eyes. "But I don't know how."

Rabbit's lip hooked up at one side. Not a smile, but the whisper of one to come. A promise.

He got to his feet, cane in hand. "Come with me." He walked

through a door at the end of the room. I followed, down a hallway and out through a back door. We crossed the yard to a building at the back. Rabbit opened the door, his ink-marked arms tensing as he held open the door for me. I walked through and was hit by a surge of freezing-cold air. I yelped and rubbed my arms, and then I felt Rabbit come up behind me. I shivered again, but this time it was prompted by Rabbit's warm breath on the back of my bare neck. He was behind me, crowding me.

I wanted him there . . . yet I wanted him to keep far away.

My eyes closed as I waited for him to speak. It was several seconds before he said huskily, "To be a champion, my little Dolly, you must learn how to defeat the bad men." He paused. "You must learn how to kill, darlin'. Kill and kill and kill." I inhaled quickly through my nose at his words. "Blood, you see?" he carried on. His hand ghosted along my arm but remained always an inch away. As though he was practicing touching me, but not allowing himself to actually do it. "Blood . . . it is a fascinating thing. The way it smells when it's fresh from the vein. How it spurts when you slice a spot of flesh just right." He hissed through his teeth, his breath kicking up my hair. My eyes closed and my legs clenched together as a strange feeling settled within my stomach and the apex of my thighs. "It's a sight like no other." A step closer. His breath reaching my scalp. "To feel someone's life drain from their body by your hands . . . bad, bad people who need to be plucked from this earth like the fleas they are . . . It is . . . a taste of the divine."

My breathing was heavy; my chest was heaving. His words stirred a want . . . a need I'd never felt before within me. "You were born for this, little Dolly." I sucked in a sharp breath as

Rabbit pushed a blond curl off my shoulder. His body was so close I could hear his heart. It was racing. "You were born to stand by my side in Wonderland." The force of his breath increased until I knew his mouth was a mere inch from my ear. "Born to kill, by my side." He took two more deep breaths. "Come." Rabbit walked around me and headed to the right.

I followed. His voice my master.

When I rounded the corner, I found him at a long table filled with . . . "Weapons," he said when I stopped and stared. "Come," he ordered again.

I followed once more.

I walked up to the table and saw knives and blades and guns. Rabbit leaned on his cane and picked up a large knife with his free hand. The blade was decorated with filigree patterns. My eyes widened at its beauty. "I had some things designed for you," he said. "This is the first." Rabbit held out the ivory handle of the knife, and I took it in my palm.

"It's beautiful!" I felt a smile pull on my lips. I twisted the blade in the air and thought of Ellis. Thought of the bad men drawn on those cards in Rabbit's pocket. Thought of what the bad men had done to my friend. What she had told me they had done to her every night since she had been a little girl. My stomach tightened as I thought of each man on the cards . . . as I envisioned blood falling down their faces, their chests, to pool on the floor.

It is a taste of the divine . . .

"I want this," I whispered and glanced up at Rabbit. He ran his hand through his black hair and nodded slowly. I could see the triumph in his silver gaze.

You were born to kill at my side . . .

Rabbit reached for something else, something out of my line of sight. When he turned, in his hand I saw a flash of blue . . . the same shade of blue as my dress.

"Rabbit?" I stepped forward, placing my blade on the table, to better see what he was holding out. "Rabbit . . ." I said softly as I absorbed the sight of the gun in his hand. A blue gun, with writing on the side. I tried to read it. But I could only make out some of the letters and only one word. I ran the tip of my finger along the engraved words. "What does it say?"

"I had it made just for you." Rabbit stepped closer. His voice had softened at my question. I wasn't able to read or write much. Never had been.

I inhaled his scent and momentarily lost my breath. I looked up at Rabbit hovering over me. He was so tall. I stared into his silver eyes, swallowing when the strange feeling from before set in my stomach and thighs once more.

"It matches the blue of your dress," he said in a low voice. I nodded in agreement. His fingers almost touched mine on the side of the gun, but when they were just a hairsbreadth away, he moved.

He couldn't be touched either.

Just like me.

"It says 'Time For Tea.'"

My eyes snapped to the writing, then back to him. A laugh bubbled up my throat and sprang from my mouth. I laughed in pure excitement as he dropped the gun into my hand and I held it tightly. I reached for the knife he had also gifted me, holding my new weapons in my grip.

"Time for tea!" I shouted, spinning around. "Time for tea, time for tea, time for tea!" I danced around Rabbit until I was breathless and my voice was hoarse from laughing.

I stopped dead, then stepped back, raising both the gun and blade in the air, like I thought a champion would. Rabbit watched me with wide eyes and a heaving chest. I parted my feet and lifted my chin. I wanted to look strong.

"This is our Wonderland, darlin'. And we cannot allow these bad men to live. Until all of them have been destroyed . . . Ellis won't be safe." He rolled his neck. "You don't want that, do you, little Dolly?"

"No." I tightened my grip on the gun and the blade. Then, looking Rabbit square in the eyes, I said, "Train me, Rabbit. Train me to destroy the bad men who hurt my friend Ellis. Teach me to make blood drip down their faces, to their feet and to the floor . . .

"Teach me to kill. Teach me to kill them all."

CHAPTER 7

Dolly

"This way."

I followed Rabbit as he stepped backward toward a wooden door. He turned the knob. A cold blast of air, even colder than before, muscled through and blanketed my skin. I shivered, but Rabbit didn't react. He turned his head toward me. "Down we go," he said and descended the stairs. The foot of his cane tapped on each step. I followed him down—following my Rabbit, my guide.

When we reached the bottom step, my eyes widened. I gripped my knife and gun tighter. "Pigs?" I said as I looked across the freezing-cold room at a mass of dead pigs hanging upside down on strange hooks.

"A pig's flesh and skin are the closest to an actual human's.

We will train you here." He shrugged, both hands on the top of his cane. "When you are ready, we move to the next part of our journey."

"The killing?"

Rabbit nodded slowly. He leaned forward, his face close to mine. "The best part . . . the most fun you will ever have."

My heart raced with excitement. I looked around the room. When I turned back around, Rabbit was watching me. I looked down his body, at his clothes and cane. "Where are your weapons?"

The corner of Rabbit's mouth kicked up. In a flash, he had spun the cane in his hand. In a move almost too quick for my eyes to take in, he split the cane in two. The bottom half was in his left hand, the top—owning the rabbit head—in his right. Rabbit held both hands out in front of him and charged toward the nearest pigs. I only realized that the bottom of the cane had become a blade when he plunged it into the stomach of a pig to his left, severing it in two. Before I could say anything, a loud bang fired from the cane in his right hand. I watched as bullet after bullet, so many bullets, sliced through the pig on the right. Flesh splattered to the floor and onto the walls of the room.

Rabbit turned, his black hair mussed from the show, and lifted his eyes to face me. "My weapons, darlin'," he said and reattached the cane pieces. He swung the foot of the cane back to the floor and placed his hands over the rabbit head once more.

I stared, lips parted. "I would never have known . . ." I whispered, trying to study the cane. I lifted my gaze to his. "I want to fight like that." Something glittered in Rabbit's silver eyes.

He stepped aside, clearing a path to a space beside him.

"Then by all means." He nodded to the spot to his right. Ignoring the cold, I moved beside him, my heels clicking on the stone floor. I tipped my head back and looked at the pigs. They were hanging from long silver hooks.

"This place belongs to my . . . friend." He said the word as though it were a question. "Chapel. He has secret places like this all over the South."

"He uses these hooks for pigs?"

Rabbit waved his hand dismissively. "No. Not pigs."

"Rabbit?" I asked. "How far into Wonderland are we right now?"

"Just at the start, little Dolly. The bad men don't know we're coming. We're safe." I released a long breath. "Now . . ." Rabbit moved beside me. Just like before, my heart beat faster. I held my weapons tighter. "First the knife," Rabbit instructed. "Raise your hand." I did as he said. "Now stab it into a pig." I drew my hand back and, rushing forward, sliced the blade through the stomach of the first pig. My knife slipped through like butter. "I did it, Rabbit! I did it!" I shouted excitedly.

"Feel it," he commanded.

"What?"

"Push the knife in and out. Feel what it's like to cut through flesh." I pushed and pulled on the knife, and the tip hit something hard. I rammed the knife in harder and harder, until something snapped. I whipped my head to Rabbit. "Your first bone." He nodded. "Snapped successfully. Watch out for those when we get to our kills."

I nodded and pulled out the knife. I plunged it into the pig again. And again and again, until only scraps of the pig remained on the strange hook. Sweat fell from my brow. I brushed my hair back from my face with my forearm and turned. Rabbit was watching me, his pupils blown. Something about the way he was looking at me—intensely and . . . maybe proud?—brought strange feelings to my chest. "Was that good, Rabbit?" I gasped, as I caught my breath.

Rabbit's fingers tightened around the cane's head. He shifted on his feet, bringing the cane closer to his body. Like he was hiding something. His skin was flushed, and his Adam's apple bobbed in his throat. "You liked that?" he asked in a raspy voice.

I looked back at the massacred flesh on the floor and felt a spike in my pulse. "Yes." I smiled.

It was a *big* smile.

Rabbit edged closer, never taking his eyes from me. He stopped right before me. His head tipped back and he hissed through his teeth, before lowering his gaze back to me. "Born to kill," he announced in a low, graveled voice. "To kill by my side." He lifted one of his hands from his cane. He tried to reach out for my face, but at the last minute he curled his fingers into a fist and pulled back his hand with a low snarl. "Thirsty for blood. Little Dolly. My champion of Wonderland."

"I want more," I said, closing my eyes, imagining the feel of his fingers on my face. Imagining him praising me. Petting me. Telling me I was his good little Dolly. "Teach me more," I begged.

I opened my eyes. Rabbit reached up and loosened his black cravat, exposing more inked markings on his neck. Clocks and clocks and even more clocks. He threw the cravat into his back pocket, leaving his black shirt collar open, his waistcoat buttoned, still pristine.

"Gun," he ordered. I held it up. Rabbit looked along the pigs. "That one." He pointed to one at the back and moved behind me. My eyes closed, his close presence holding me in its thrall. "Raise the gun." I did as directed, my hands trembling a little. "Push away the fear," he said, his lips a fraction of an inch from the shell of my ear. I focused on what he said and imagined Ellis in my head.

Rabbit breathed in and out, warm air heating my face from the chill. His fingers touched the parts of the gun I wasn't touching. "Safety." He clicked off a white part on the top of the gun. "Trigger," he said, ghosting over the blue latch where my finger rested. "Now squeeze." I did as he said and jerked back as a loud bang echoed around the room. A small cry left my throat as I saw the bullet burrow through the pig.

"Hit," Rabbit said, directly into my ear. I froze, and then let out a giggle when I saw what I'd done.

"Hit!" I rushed forward and looked at the bullet wound. Whipping back toward Rabbit, I held up my gun and sang, "Time for tea!" Rabbit nodded proudly, and a surge of something shot through my veins. Something exciting. Something . . . addictive . . .

"Again." I clacked my heels against the stone floor as I made my way back to Rabbit. He stepped back to give me space. I raised my weapons again. I slashed my blade into the flesh of one pig. I sent a shaky bullet into the other.

"Again," Rabbit said behind me. I didn't even turn. I just struck and shot. Again and again, until my arms ached.

Breathless and hot-skinned, I lowered my weapons, still needing to use them again. Needing to feel flesh and muscle submitting to my blade, and the piercing of skin, gristle and bone by my bullet, I turned to Rabbit, who had never stopped watching. "Together."

Rabbit's nostrils flared, and I nodded to the empty spot beside me. His lips formed a dark smirk, and then he unsheathed the blade from his cane and lifted the head to make the gun. He moved beside me, looked down at me and said, "Tick tock."

Laughing, I struck. I shot. He stabbed. He fired.

Side by side.

Piling up the flesh.

Over and over again, until all the ammunition was spent.

When the echoes of the final bullet had rung out, both of us breathless yet energized, I turned my head to Rabbit. He was already watching me. Lifting my blade—now dripping in blood —I brought it in front of my face and studied the filigree steel. "I like this," I said, my heart pounding in my chest.

"The blade?" Rabbit prompted, voice husky.

Smiling, I raised my eyebrows. "Using them." A dash of crimson slid down the handle. "The sight of blood." The drop splattered onto my dress. "Though the color clashes with my pretty dress." I pouted, realizing that my dress was now ruined. My favorite dress ever.

"Don't worry, darlin'," Rabbit assured me. "I got plenty more dresses for you. All that design. Your favorite."

"Silly Rabbit," I whispered, feeling my chest burst with warmth.

"Enough for tonight. We have days to practice." He turned and gestured for me to climb the stairs. I kept my weapons in my hands. I never wanted to let them go.

As I climbed the stairs, I stared down at my gun. "Time for tea," I sang to myself on every new step. "Time for tea," When we reached the top, I saw the sky outside had grown dark.

Rabbit came up beside me. "Time for a bath and bed, little Dolly," he said softly. I wanted to argue that I wasn't tired, but I saw in his eyes that he meant it. I wanted to obey.

"Okay." I let him lead me back into the house and to the bedroom. The bed was large and covered in white lace. A white nightgown lay on the bed. Rabbit had disappeared to an adjoining room. I guessed it must be the bathroom by the sound of running water. I wandered around the room until I reached the closet. When I opened the door, I smiled in delight to see racks and racks of my favorite blue dress. My black-and-white socks were piled high in drawers, and lots of black headbands were laid out on a velvet-covered shelf. Finally, there were five pairs of my boots on the closet floor.

"Have your bath, darlin'." I peeked around the closet door to see Rabbit on the other side. I blinked up at him and momentarily lost my breath. His cheeks were flushed, and in the bedroom's bright light I could see every part of his face.

My Rabbit was very handsome.

He inched closer until his chest pressed against the wooden door. Swallowing, I pressed against it from the other side. It was as if we touched. My breathing became heavier the more I pressed against the wood. Rabbit's became heavier too. And he never broke my stare.

Eventually, he said, "Go have your bath, darlin'. I got some surprises for you when you get out."

"Okay." I forced myself to move away from the door. I took the nightgown off the bed on my way.

"You can wash yourself, can't you, darlin'?" Rabbit asked just before I reached the bathroom door. His nostrils flared and his eyes darkened.

Shaking my head, I laughed lightly. "Silly Rabbit! Of course I can."

I couldn't help but think that he looked disappointed.

In the bathroom, I undressed and sank into the warm bubbly water. I tipped my head back and thought of Rabbit. Thought of his silver eyes watching me. Thought of his deep voice speaking to me. And thought of him fighting beside me, wielding his cane without even breaking a sweat. My thighs began to clench, and a deep pressure built so greatly between my legs that I slipped my hand in between them and over my private parts just to try and find some relief. I gasped as a burst of heat shot up my spine. I snapped my hand away and sat up, wondering what it was.

But when I thought of Rabbit again—the way he watched me, the way he looked at me, the way he cared for me—that feeling came back. My cheeks blazed with heat. I wasn't sure if it was due to the temperature of the bathwater or my thoughts of Rabbit.

The feeling between my thighs wouldn't go away.

My eyes fluttered closed, and I slipped down the tub. My fingers walked down my stomach and settled back between my thighs. My fingertips ran over my private parts, and I moaned low in my throat when the ache lessened some. I kept going, thinking of Rabbit. Thinking of his inked skin—clocks. So many clocks . . . My lips parted and another moan slipped out when I pictured us fighting side by side. The way his eyes found mine as I had sliced my blade into the flesh of the pig. The way he stepped so close to me that I could feel his breath on my face when we had finished. Like he had wanted to touch me.

My fingers worked faster between my thighs, and my back arched as the pressure there grew. My feet flicked the water out of the tub when a feeling so addictive flushed over every inch of my skin. "Rabbit . . ." I whispered, not wanting this feeling to end. I groaned low as something big began stirring in my stomach. Sounds fled my mouth as my fingers searched for something I couldn't describe. And then my back arched, my head fell back and my mouth dropped as a wash of pure light engulfed my body. My breathing was stuttered. My skin flushed, and a long cry fell from my throat as I became nothing but sensation.

I calmed as the crest of the wave peaked and I began to come down. My eyes fluttered open, and my legs flopped around the water with a splash. I drew in slow breaths and stared up at the ceiling.

Shock and surprise ran through me. I swallowed hard. I lifted my hand and stared at my fingers, wondering what they had just made me feel. As I lowered my hand, I heard a creak outside of the bathroom. I washed quickly, then got out of the tub and ran a towel over my body and through my hair.

I pulled the nightgown over me and brushed my long hair. I

glanced in the mirror, then, pleased with how I looked, opened the door to the bedroom.

And I paused, breath held in my throat, when I saw Rabbit on the floor, shirtless, repeatedly curling his body up from his torso. He must have heard me because he stopped, abdominals tensed, holding his body still, and met my gaze.

I swallowed as I ran my eyes over his body. His muscles were tight. Not large, but not a single layer of fat marred them. And his skin—not an inch of bare flesh could be seen. Tattoos ran over his arms, his chest, his torso and his neck.

I . . . liked them.

Clock after clock after clock.

Tick tock, tick tock, tick tock.

Without saying a word, Rabbit got to his feet, covered in a light sheen of sweat. He was wearing dark sleep pants on his legs. As he stood, my eyes were drawn to his crotch. A large bulge lay underneath, obvious under the thin material. Rabbit moved his arm, and my eyes snapped to his. He was watching me, cheeks flushed and lips parted. His breathing seemed as unsteady as my own.

But I didn't understand what was happening.

He turned abruptly, and a louder gasp fell from my lips at the sight of his back. My hand covered my mouth in shock, and Rabbit's shoulders tightened. His neck stiffened, then he slowly looked over his shoulder at me.

"Rabbit . . ." I murmured and dropped my hand from my mouth. My feet dragged me forward, my eyes once again focused on his back.

The tattoo . . . the tattoo on his back, was . . .

"Me," I whispered as I stopped just a hairsbreadth from Rabbit's back. My hand rose of its own accord, yet it did not touch his skin. It did not touch the familiar pair of blue eyes, the long blond hair I knew so well, nor the pink lips, coated in the lipstick that my lips were never seen without.

"Rabbit." I traced—from a distance of half an inch—every bit of my face . . . right down to the shoulders that wore a dress made of blue.

That of Alice.

That of me.

Rabbit's head turned away and fell forward, showing me only the ends of his black hair and the large pocket watch design that graced the back of his neck. "You were all I thought about," he said, his voice barely above a whisper. "I knew I had to come and get you. Find you, rescue you."

"Rescue me . . ." I echoed. "From the room of doors?"

Rabbit tensed again and turned to face me. I had to tilt my head up to look at his impressive height. I inhaled his scent, the musky aroma filling my nose. The muscles in his chest twitched as I stared at his magnificent body. His cheeks flushed.

"Yes," he eventually replied. His hand started to rise, but it clenched into a fist and lowered back down to his side. "All I saw was your face . . . where I was being kept. All I saw were these blue eyes. This blond hair . . . those pink-painted lips." I lifted my fingers to my lips and traced the flesh. "You were the prophecy. You were always meant to come to Wonderland and defeat the bad men, ending with the King of Hearts."

"You marked your skin with my image to remind you of your

mission. To lead me through this challenge to defeat the king and his men," I said knowingly.

Rabbit stalled for a second, then nodded. "Exactly that." His lip twitched. "And now I have found you. My little champion."

I smiled, liking the sound of that. "My guide," I offered in return.

We did not speak for many seconds. We just stared into one another's eyes. Then my eyes drifted to his body, as though they were being pulled by an invisible force. I wanted to run my finger along his stomach. My gaze dipped lower.

I wanted to run my hand over the bulge at his crotch.

I began to tingle between my legs again, and my face blazed as I recalled how touching myself there made me feel.

"Little Dolly," Rabbit growled, and my eyes snapped to his. When I glanced down, the bulge in his pants increased in size. My eyes widened. Rabbit hissed, thrust his hands through his hair and stumbled backward.

He turned away, his hands fisted at his sides. He stopped at the wall and let his forehead drop to the brick. I heard his heavy breathing, heard him whisper "Tick tock, tick tock, tick tock" under his breath.

I didn't move, glued to the spot. Rabbit stepped back and, without looking at me, stormed from the room.

I watched him go. My heart sank, until Rabbit came back with a box in his hands. He placed the box on the bed.

He paused, eyes closed, and sucked in deep breaths. Then his eyes opened and fixed straight on me. I couldn't speak, wondering what was wrong, what was in the box . . .

"Presents . . . for you." His voice broke on the last word, but he stepped aside and gestured with his hand for me to take a look.

I stared at him harder, and I saw whatever was bothering him filter away as he gazed upon me. I smiled when his shoulders relaxed and he gestured again to the box.

"More presents?" I asked, anticipation filling my bones. "But I already had my tea party, my gun and my blade!" I gave him a small smile. "You spoil me."

"You deserve to be spoiled," he said immediately.

Shaking my head, I said, "Silly Rabbit."

I walked to the box, my heart beating fast as I opened the box. When I saw what was inside, I stumbled back, shock zipping through me like a bolt of electricity. I snapped my eyes to Rabbit. "My favorite things . . ." I whispered.

A sweet lightness bubbled inside me. It bubbled and bubbled until a giggle erupted from my mouth. I launched forward, opening the box completely. I reached inside and felt something cold . . . hard. I pulled, and a familiar face appeared.

"Alice!" I said, amazed. I studied my old china-faced doll.

"All that's left is her head and a few strands of her hair. Her face is cracked, and I couldn't find her body, but I thought you would like to see your old friend nonetheless."

I held up Alice's head by the few strands of yellow hair that remained. And I smiled. I smiled so wide I feared my face would crack. "I love her . . ." I whispered as I stared at my very favorite toy. "She may be broken and parts missing, but I love her all the same."

Rabbit made a small sound. When I looked up, he seemed sad. It made me sad too. Keeping Alice's hair gripped in my hand, her cracked head hanging by my side, I stepped toward Rabbit and looked into his silver eyes. "It's okay, Rabbit. Alice may be damaged, but I love her all the same." I smiled. "I'll take good care of her from now on."

Rabbit nodded, but I thought he still looked sad. "There's something else in there," he said, tilting his head toward the box.

I rushed to the box, Alice's head in hand. I looked inside and — "No," I exclaimed, my pulse kicking into a sprint. I laid Alice down on the bed, as gentle as can be, and lifted the next surprise from the box. When the pink plastic was in my hands, I felt so ridiculously happy.

"My boombox," I said, staring at the loveheart stickers covering the speakers. "Rabbit . . ."

"Open it up," he said. His arms were crossed over his chest as he observed me.

I pressed the eject button . . . and inside was a cassette. I pulled it out. "No-o-o," I said quietly, slowly. I looked at Rabbit, who had moved in front of me. He slid his fingers along a strip of white that ran across the cassette. It had writing along the front.

"Dolly's Mix Tape," he said, his fingers tracing the letters. I couldn't read them all.

"My mix tape?" Suddenly, I felt my heart get heavy. I closed my eyes. The image of a pretty woman with blond hair and a kind smile filled my mind. She had a cup in her hand, drinking tea—"*Earl Grey*," she whispered. "*Nothing else will do.*"

Then we were dancing. Dancing, hand in hand, to the songs on this tape . . . dancing to one song in particular.

Opening my eyes, I scrambled to insert the tape and press

play. That song . . . the one that had played in my head, my favorite song to dance to, emerged from the speakers.

"Rabbit," I cooed as he stepped back and sat on the edge of the bed. I moved past him and placed the boombox on the nightstand. Taking Alice by the hair, I held her tightly. In my other hand I gathered the side of my nightgown, and I let the music fill my ears. Closing my eyes, I began to twirl. My lips stretched into a smile and I sang the words. Releasing my nightgown, I put my hand in the air and opened my eyes. I held Alice out in front of me and spun her around by the sides of her face.

I looked up. Rabbit was watching me, eyes glittering. Like they always did when he watched me. Holding his stare, I dipped my shoulder in his direction, dancing for him. Rabbit always liked me dancing for him.

No one else. He once told me that I wasn't allowed to dance for someone else, but I couldn't remember who that was.

Only for him.

Dolly's dance for Rabbit.

So I danced and danced until my legs grew tired. Song after song played, each one a favorite. When the tape clicked off, needing to be turned over, Rabbit got to his feet. He came to where I stood, my hair now almost dry and sticking to my face. "Enough for tonight, my little Dolly. Your small body is tired and needs to rest." He stroked Alice's cracked face. For a moment, I wished he had stroked mine. "It's time for bed. We have a big week ahead of us. You must train to fight the bad men. It will be hard work."

"But there'll be time for dancing?" I asked, yawning wide. I cradled Alice to me as I followed Rabbit to bed. He pulled back the comforter and I climbed inside. He pulled the cover over me.

He lowered his face close to mine. "There'll always be time for dancing, darlin'," he assured, his voice quiet yet rough. "Always time for dancing."

I smiled at his words and felt them warm my heart. "Goodnight," he whispered, and then moved to the corner and sat on the floor. He rested his back against the hard wall and met my eyes.

I sat up, my brow creased in confusion. "You're not sleeping in a bed?"

Rabbit shook his head. Angry that he was sleeping on the floor, I reached over to the other side of my bed and pulled back the comforter. I looked at Rabbit again. "Climb in." Rabbit looked like he was about to say no. I rolled my eyes. "We always shared a bed when we were young. We're best friends; we can do it again." I waited for him to move. Eventually he did. I pulled the comforter over us and laid my head on the pillow. He did the same. His shoulders were stiff at first, but then he relaxed. "Silly Rabbit," I whispered, hearing him exhale a long deep breath as I did.

My eyelids began to feel heavy as I thought of the week ahead. I couldn't wait to get back to the basement and use my blade and gun. I wanted to be the best champion of Wonderland I could be. I thought of Rabbit as he'd watched me stab the pig and fire my bullets, such happiness in his silver eyes. I wanted to make him proud. I wanted to kill the bad men that made our world so unsafe.

Then I thought of Ellis, trapped behind that door in the darkness of Wonderland. And most of all, I wanted to destroy the bad men for her. I didn't want her to cry anymore. I wanted her to be free and safe.

"I'll win, Ellis," I whispered as I fell asleep. "Me and Rabbit, we will set you free."

CHAPTER 8

THE CATERPILLAR

Rabbit

One week later . . .

THE WIND RUSHED through our hair as I watched her pointing the gun out of the corner of my eye. "Time for tea." She aimed the gun at the windshield. "Time for tea," she announced, in a different tone. She shook her head, exasperated.

"Darlin'?" I questioned. Her hands fell to her knees, the blue gun lying on her lap.

Her bottom lip was pouting. It was painted bright pink, her favorite lipstick safe in her pocket. The wind ruffled her mass of blond curls, a black headband the only thing keeping it in any sort of place. She was wearing a clean blue dress, her black-and-white striped thigh-high socks and her polished ankle boots.

Beautiful.

"I haven't decided what to say to the Caterpillar when we get to him. Can't decide how to say what I want." She looked up at me, and her shoulders slumped. Her finger ran over the engraving on her gun. "I want to say this, 'Time for Tea,' before I shoot him, because it's on my gun and I think it sounds *so* good. Because I *love* tea." Her face clouded over. "But only Earl Grey; nothing else will do."

My chest tightened. She'd always said that when we were kids. And she would get real pissy if anyone around her tried to drink anything but Earl Grey, never mind if they tried to serve it to her. If they dared drink Darjeeling, she would completely lose her shit.

"Try them out on me," I prompted, and her face brightened. Dolly shifted in her seat and pointed the gun at my face. I smirked.

"Time for *tea*," she said. "*Time* for tea." After she'd offered me five different ways of saying it, she asked, "Well?"

"Number one, darlin'. It's perfect."

"Yes!" she trilled, victorious, and faced forward in her seat again. "Time for tea," she said, trying to look menacing. She didn't do such a great job. She was too fucking beautiful for that. A corrupt angel . . . corrupted by me, agent of the devil himself.

The perfect pairing.

Dolly lowered her gun just as we passed the sign—Amarillo. The minute we hit the city limits, I felt the blood in my veins heat up and my flesh begin to twitch. The smell of hashish filled my nose even though there was none present. Just the thought of this fucker made me smell him, hear his grunt from behind me. I glanced across at Dolly, now brushing her doll-head's raggedy hair, singing to herself. I wondered what the fat fucker did to her when I'd been gone. I could still hear his words echo through time from that night. *I want them both together. I want to have them both at the same time.*

Uncle Lester, the fat piece of shit who liked raping kids in pairs, gender not an issue. Well, the fucker was going to get his wish.

We'd been driving for a while to reach the Caterpillar's hidden home. The Caterpillar, named from Wonderland because of his love of hashish—smoked from his treasured hookah.

Dolly had trained hard this past week. And she was a sight. Hit her mark with perfect aim, sliced her target with venom in her heart.

Killing perfection.

I'd never been so turned on as watching her fight. I wasn't sure how I'd contain myself watching her make real kills.

Especially this pedophilic fucker, and any other cunts he had protecting him.

"How long now, Rabbit?" Dolly asked from the passenger seat. I saw our exit just ahead and drove onto the inconspicuous dirt road.

"No time at all." I reached into my vest for my pocket watch. I ran my thumb over its face as we followed the road. When I saw the house in the distance, I pulled the Mustang into the cover of trees and killed the engine.

Dolly sat up in her seat, her eyes bright, her breathing fast.

"Is this it, Rabbit?" She pointed at the terracotta roof up ahead. "Is this the home of the Caterpillar?"

"It is," I confirmed through gritted teeth. I could feel the need to kill beginning to take its hold over me. I glanced at Dolly. She was looking at the house. Again, I thought of that fucker hurting her. I thought of how he hurt me.

And I really needed this fucker to die . . . in great pain.

I closed my eyes and visualized what I'd found out about "Uncle Lester" when I'd researched them all at Chapel's home. "They're all dispersed throughout Texas," Chapel had said after receiving the intel from the private detective he'd hired. He wasn't a normal PI, Chapel had informed me. But one that had worked for him for years. In not so . . . legal ways.

Uncle Lester had run to Amarillo after a kid they'd abused started to talk. The talk hit some ears that the "uncles" and Mr. Earnshaw had not wanted to reach. Some corrupt cop friend of theirs had buried the allegation as best he could. But they fled, separating, hiding away from those who might find out the truth and come looking . . .

Yet not one of the fuckers had stopped their fucked-up extracurricular activities. They had a shit-ton of money. They had many contacts with similar tastes. They could still do whatever and whoever the fuck they wanted.

Until I escaped the Water Tower and set in motion my plan to fuck with their idyllic lives. Me and my little Dolly. Blasts from their pasts they would never see coming.

Their worst nightmares made flesh.

"Are you ready, darlin'?" I asked. Dolly nodded her head, clutching her blue gun tightly.

I got out of the car and took my cane from the trunk. I straightened my cravat, rolled my shirt sleeves down my arms and put my suit jacket on. I fastened the buttons and turned to see Dolly watching me.

"So handsome." I fought back a growl at those words coming from her lips. As she walked toward me, I couldn't help but admire what she was wearing.

Perfection . . . until I saw those scars on her arms. The ones that she had given herself, in her deepest despair. Because of those assholes.

Because of the asshole inside this fucking terracotta-roofed house.

"Get your blade, darlin'," I said and stepped back from the trunk. Dolly pulled it from her waist belt. She gripped the handle and met my eyes.

"I'm ready," she declared and nodded for emphasis. She was small, but in that moment she was a fucking warrior. The champion of Wonderland.

"Stay by my side," I said as we fell into step. I walked us through the trees. The recon on the Caterpillar showed that he had hired help. Bodyguards to protect him from anyone who might want to seek revenge for being fucked as a kid.

I welcomed bringing death to him. To *all* of them. I didn't care who I killed. I never cared.

As we walked through the high grass, Dolly hummed under her breath. It was her favorite song. And she hummed it like she had no cares in the world. I looked down at her. She looked up.

Then she fucking smiled.

Her bright pink lips standing out against her pale skin and

blue eyes. My Alice in Wonderland about to start her adventure. I held out my arm, stopping her in her tracks when we reached the edge of the line of trees.

The house was silent.

I pointed to the front door. "We walk right through." I felt the familiar rush of adrenaline at the thought of taking lives.

"Right through the door," Dolly repeated, nodding her agreement. I almost smirked at the look that took over her expression —total hardass determination.

I sucked in a deep breath and straightened. Looking down at Dolly, I took my watch from my pocket, raised it to my ear and announced, "Tick tock."

Her eyes shone. She lifted her gun and stroked the engraved barrel. "Time for tea."

My dick hardened, and the need to kill pounded even harder through me. The three always turned me on: blood, and death, and Dolly.

And better yet . . . *Killer* Dolly.

Breaking from the cover of the grass and trees, we walked toward the front door, weapons in hand. I scoured the area, waiting for the first guard to make his appearance. None came as we reached the door. I silently tried the knob. The door was locked. I felt Dolly's eyes on mine, waiting for instruction on what to do next. I stepped back and charged at the door, kicking at the lock. The door flew open. I recovered quickly, ready to storm in when Dolly stood in my path. She looked at me over her shoulder and said, "Ladies first."

Fuck, this girl was everything.

Dolly rushed forward, blade at her side and her gun held out in her right hand. I followed close behind, ready to defend her against anyone who came to confront us. We had traveled halfway down the hallway when I heard the sound of floorboards creaking. A guard dressed all in black came running around the corner. I lifted my cane, unsheathing the blade from the gun, and aimed to shoot. But before I could, Dolly charged forward, heels clacking on the wooden floor, gun held high. My breath locked in my throat as the guard raised his gun, but before he could even get his finger on the trigger, Dolly shrilled, "Time for tea!" and sent a bullet roaring into his chest.

The guard fell back, dropping to the floor. Blood poured out and his eyes ceased blinking.

Dead.

One down.

Dolly stopped, looking over the corpse. A gasp fell from her lips and her head whipped to me. Her chest was heaving, her breathing fast. "I did it!" A single laugh. "Rabbit! I killed one! I killed one of the bad men!"

"Sure did, darlin'."

Her back straightened with pride. Then her eyes darkened, the pupils dilating. "I want more," she demanded and looked around. "I want more blood." She took off at a sprint; I followed in her wake. Dolly took to the staircase. Seconds later, another guard ran down the stairs, shooting first. His bullet hit behind Dolly, chipping plaster from the stairwell's red-painted wall. Dolly fired back, again screaming "Time for tea!". Her bullet sliced through the guard's leg. But I saw him lift his gun . . .

aiming at her head. I pulled my rabbit's-head trigger before he even had a chance to see me coming up behind her. My bullet tunneled straight through his forehead, ending him.

His body flopped over the stairs. Dolly ran to his limp corpse and whirled to face me. Her full hands hit her hips, and her bottom lip stuck out in a pout. "Rabbit!" she admonished. "I wanted to kill him!"

I fought a smile. "My apologies, darlin'." She huffed out a breath as I stopped before her. "You can have the next one. I promise."

Dolly kicked the body, but eventually dropped her arms and looked up at me with a pissed-off glare. "Fine." She stepped closer still. A spatter of blood had stained the collar of her dress. I'd never been so turned on in my whole fucking life. She pressed the tip of her blade against my chest. "And I want the Caterpillar too."

Scratch that. *Now* I was the most turned on I'd ever been. That fucking commanding, demanding voice . . .

I bowed, the blade pressing deeper against my chest. "As the lady wishes."

"Good!" she sang, all her moodiness forgotten. "Now," she said, racing up the next two steps. "Who's next?"

I knew we had one more guard left from this shift. And he'd be guarding the Caterpillar. The final barrier to the reason we were here. We searched left and right but found no one. Until we found a back staircase. "Here," I said. Dolly immediately pushed past me. I ran up the stairs behind her. I had barely made it to the top when a bullet fired into the stairwell. My heart stopped, needing it to not have hit Dolly, when suddenly I heard Dolly tutting and witnessed her plunging her blade into the barrel chest of the guard. As he slumped against the wall, slowly sliding down, his blood smearing the white paint, Dolly pulled her blade from the wound. "Naughty boy!"

She left the blood dripping from the filigree-patterned blade and stared at the door. I joined her. I knew what she was smelling —I was smelling it too.

Hashish.

"The Caterpillar," Dolly said under her breath.

"The Caterpillar," I repeated. "I'll get to him first." Dolly turned to argue, but I held up my hand, stopping her mid-breath. "I'll secure him so he can't move." I reached down and stroked along the wet blood on her blade—up and down and up and down . . . stroking. Her cheeks flushed as my fingers almost touched hers. I brought my finger to my mouth and sucked the blood. My teeth ran over my bottom lip, and I closed my eyes. When I opened them again, Dolly was watching me with blatant hunger in her gaze. I bent down, placing my mouth at her ear, and said, "Then he's all yours."

Dolly moaned, causing my already hard dick to twitch. I slammed my shoulder against the door. The wood gave way, and I wasted no time in rushing in. I followed the scent of tobacco, letting it guide me to a large desk. A gun sounded from somewhere behind it, but the aim was pitiful and lacked precision. I looked down . . . and there he was.

A red mist descended.

The Caterpillar's fat body was quivering in the corner, his

hookah by his side. His head was down and his eyes were closed . . . until they opened and landed straight on me. I let him stare. I let him piece together exactly who stood before him.

I waited—*tick tock*—waited—*tick tock*—waited—*tick . . .* until . . . "Heathan . . ." He shook his head in disbelief, double chin wobbling. His lips pulled back from his stained yellow teeth. "Impossible . . . you were locked away."

I bent down and kicked away the gun he had dropped after his piss-poor shot. "That's the thing about a prison full of psycho killers." I unsheathed my cane and brought the spiked blade to hover at his throat. "We can manipulate an escape and kill those who stupidly kept us all captive."

He blanched. "H-he'll . . . h-he'll know you've got out. He'll know."

I tilted my head, not breaking his terrified gaze. "I'm counting on it."

"Rabbit?" Dolly's voice called from the doorway. "Do you have him yet?" The Caterpillar's face paled even further. "I'm bored. I want to have some fun!"

"Coming, darlin'." I smiled as the Caterpillar locked eyes on me. "My Dolly has joined me. You remember her, don't you?" My face hardened. "Get the fuck up."

The Caterpillar shook his head. I pushed the tip of my blade into his shoulder. He screamed. I smiled. "I wasn't requesting. I was *insisting*."

The Caterpillar cried out in pain but scurried to his feet. Using the blade in his shoulder as my leash, I guided him out from behind the desk, kicking the wheeled office chair behind him. I pushed harder on the blade, and he sat down. I reached into my pocket for the duct tape and began securing him to the chair.

When I finished, I saw a flash of blue in the door. "Rabbit . . . I said I'm *bored!*" The Caterpillar turned his head toward the doorway.

"Ellis," he murmured, and Dolly's blue eyes snapped to his. Her lip curled in fury as he uttered that name.

She raised her blood-soaked blade and stormed to where he sat, her head dipped and her expression like fucking thunder. She sliced across his cheek with the flat side of the blade. Blood painted his face—not his, but the guard's. "Don't you dare say her name!" she hissed. The Caterpillar faced her again, eyebrows drawn down.

"*Her* name . . .?" He looked to me. Like I would fucking help. Clear things up.

Wrong.

"Yes. *Her* name." Dolly narrowed her eyes and moved directly in front of him. She traced down his sweating cheek with the barrel of her gun. "You touched her when you weren't supposed to." She shook her head, clicking her tongue. "She didn't want you to." The Caterpillar swallowed, and Dolly backed up. She studied him, tied to the chair, duct tape around his middle. Her head tipped from side to side.

"Darlin'?" I asked. Dolly blew out a breath and turned to me, shoulders sagging. "What's wrong?" I unbuttoned my jacket and shrugged it from my shoulders. I rolled up my sleeves and checked the time on my pocket watch. We had plenty left until the next guard shift.

"Is it time to go?"

I shook my head. "No. Plenty of time." Her shoulders sagged again.

"It's smashed," the Caterpillar said. Dolly and I turned to face him. "The watch. It's broken. It was broken back then and it's broken now. You're fucking insane! Always were." He shook his head. "And why is she speaking with an English accent? She's from Dallas!"

I glanced down at my watch and saw the hands ticking around. Dolly did too. She shrugged and tapped her head with the barrel of her gun. "He's crazy! It works just fine."

Ignoring his smart mouth, I asked again, "What's wrong?"

Dolly kicked the tip of her boot along the wooden floor. She sighed. "I thought I would know what to do when I got here." She lifted her eyes to meet mine. "But now I'm here I'm spoiled for choice. I have all of these ways to kill him, and I just can't pick one!" She began pacing. "Do I stab him? Shoot him? Both?" Her hands, holding her weapons, lifted in frustration. "Do I do it quickly or slowly?" She stopped, and her face looked beautifully sad. "I practiced saying 'Time for tea' so much that I never gave much thought to this bit." Her bottom lip stuck out. "I should have. I don't want to screw up."

"You could never," I said. The sound of the chair moving on the floor made Dolly turn around. He'd only moved a little. But just as I was about to counsel her again, her head whipped up and she gasped in excitement. She ran across the room and stopped in front of an old record player.

"How pretty!" she declared in awe. Putting her gun on the table, she moved the needle and the player crackled to life. Dolly squealed as the opening bars of the record played. "'My Boy Lollipop'!" she shouted and began to sing along. Taking hold of her doll's head, which she had tied to her belt by its hair, she danced around the room, her blade in her other hand.

I smirked as she danced with her doll, Alice, singing each and every word. When the song ended, Dolly ran back to the record player and played it again. "You're fucking insane!" the Caterpillar said as she danced past him.

Dolly stopped dead and whirled to face him. I held my breath, waiting for her reaction, braced to watch the beauty of her wrath unleash. Instead she got right in his face and said, "Didn't you know? All the best people are!"

He shook his head, but his words had been enough for Dolly to stop dancing and focus on the task at hand. She studied his tied-up form like he was a puzzle she was trying to solve. I could hear her murmuring to herself: "I could push the blade through his heart. Or I could stab his legs one at a time, then his arms and his chest. Or I could stab his skull . . . No, I might hit too much bone . . ."

I walked to the record player, placing the needle just so, to repeat the song again and again. As I turned, I spotted one of the Caterpillar's hands breaking free from the restraints. Before I could act, he brought his hand up in a quick movement and slapped it across Dolly's face. In mere seconds I had drawn my cane, ready to stab him in the back of his neck, when Dolly whipped around, her lipstick all over her cheek from the slap. I paused, seeing something new in her expression. Pure rage.

Darkness.

Cruelty.

Murderous intent.

Dolly touched her cheek. She met my eyes as I grabbed the Caterpillar's arm and re-tied him. Her eyes looked to the side . . . where she found herself staring back. Dolly walked to the mirror hanging on the wall and inspected her reflection.

She turned to me and spat, "He smeared my lipstick!"

Dolly's emotions seemed to boil, anger causing her body to shake and her skin to blaze red. Gripping the blade tighter, she charged at the Caterpillar and stabbed his shoulder. She yelled as she did so, piercing him over and over again in new spots—his shoulders, his thighs . . . his stomach. She drew back, out of breath, eyes ablaze with pleasure. It was then that I realized more lurked inside my Dolly than innocence and light. Darkness dwelled in her too. A malevolent presence lurking in the shadows, waiting for its chance to feed. My Dolly, sinister and cruel. Thirsting for the kill. I took a deep breath. She was my living, breathing doll. She wore the face of the purest angel, masking such evil living within.

My soul's perfectly fucked-up counterpart.

The Caterpillar began to choke on his blood. Dolly's eyes never wavered from his as she watched him try to fight his inevitable death. He spluttered, he coughed, then he hissed, "You're sick"—cough, splutter, spit—"You're just a couple of sick fucks."

Dolly stilled, then looked at me. "Sick fucks . . . We're just a couple of sick fucks!" Then she was moving, circling the Caterpillar, dancing in rings around him as he shuffled off this mortal coil. "Sick fucks, sick fucks, we're the sick fucks!" I walked to stand behind him, and Dolly circled me too. As I smiled, watching the most beautiful creature ever to grace this earth smile and dance and laugh so free, I bent and whispered in the abusive cunt's ear, "You said, years ago, you didn't care what you had to pay to have us both . . ." I pushed my own blade into his spine, severing his ability to walk. Not that he'd survive to walk again anyway. "You've now had us both . . ." I sucked in a breath through my teeth as I watched Dolly singing along to the song, twirling her doll's head in her blood-soaked hands, discoloring the spindly yellow strands of what was left of its hair. "I hope it was everything you craved."

He spluttered his final breaths. His head fell forward, and I knew he was gone. I felt only satisfaction.

I stood straight. Dolly stopped dancing. Her eyes lit up. "He's gone? I defeated him?" she asked, holding her breath.

"You sure did, darlin'." I moved around to where she was standing. Her lipstick was still spread over her cheek from the Caterpillar's slap. I narrowed my eyes. "He hurt you."

Dolly brought her hand to her cheek. Her face clouded with anger. "No. But he smudged my favorite shade." She pulled out her lipstick from her pocket and walked to the mirror. She wiped away the smeared lipstick and reapplied it to her lips. "Rabbit? What's a sick fuck?"

I saw the confusion on her face. "People who kill bad men," I said, picking up my jacket. "People like us."

"Sick fucks," she repeated. She looked down at her lipstick, then lifted her head again with a gleam in her eyes. She twisted up the lipstick, ran to the wall and began to write. I stared, breath held, as her uneducated hand tried to write . . . tried to spell. The pink lipstick stood starkly against the white wall. When she had finished, I exhaled, and a smile edged on my lips.

"There!" She jumped back to admire her work. "Sick fucks!" She stared proudly at the wall, but when she turned back to me, I saw concern, even apprehension, on her face. "Is it correct, Rabbit? Did I spell it okay?" She worried her bottom lip with her teeth. I glanced over her head and read her untidy writing. No education except what I had taught her. Educational neglect, deprived of her absolute right to learn by that cunt of a father and his predatory friends.

Yet she was still the fucking brightest star in my sky.

I read her writing, the misspelled word shining like a beacon . . .

SICK FUX

"Well, Rabbit? Did I do well?" Her voice was weak and nervous. I walked to where she stood with her head bent and eyes wary.

"You did perfect, darlin'. 'Sick Fux.' That's us, written in your lipstick. Your favorite shade, as always."

Dolly looked down at her lipstick, now completely ruined, and whimpered. I clenched and unclenched my fist until my finger found its way, found its strength, to touch her chin. Dolly gasped at the contact and lifted her huge blue eyes. "We'll get you another. We'll get you all the fucking makeup you'll ever need."

"Now?" she asked, seeming to forget I was touching her.

"Now."

Dolly darted across the room for her gun. I made my way to the exit. But Dolly stopped and turned to face the Caterpillar's dead body. She placed her weapons on the floor and ran to his chair. Pushing on the backrest, she rolled him toward the wall where she had written "Sick Fux." She placed him directly underneath. She stepped back to admire her work. "Now all the bad men will know who destroyed him." She smiled, and what I saw was malice through the beauty. "And they'll know who is coming for them too. Wonderland's Sick Fux."

Dolly picked up her weapons and ran out of the door, gun and blade and doll's head in hand. I took one look at the room, at what my girl had achieved, and I felt the black hole in my chest begin to fill.

Fill with the inky black tar that only Dolly could bring. Fill with the confirmation that we had met as children for a reason.

That she had been designed solely for me.

As evil as me, and all mine to control.

My Dolly.

My darlin'.

My fellow Sick Fuck.

I took the pack of cards from my pocket and fanned them in my hand. When I found the one I wanted, I strolled to the body, mesmerized by the expression of death on his face, and held the card up high. I studied the likeness of my drawing and the face of this asshole, the one that was etched into my mind just as sure as if a blade had sliced into my brain. The two were similar, but nothing could come close to the real face of this prick: a man with an insatiable craving to touch and fuck kids.

I cleared my throat and spat at the bloodied cheek of the Caterpillar, watching the spit merge with the fresh-spilled blood. Flicking my fingers, I sent the card falling to his chest.

I smiled, triumphant at the kill.

The Three of Hearts was dead.

* * *

"It's a treasure trove," she whispered as she looked around the store. My trunk was filled with more cash than I could carry —the latest bounty found in the Caterpillar's safe.

Now it belonged to us, inadequate compensation for the years of hell Dolly had been subjected to. It had joined the stash I had from under the Warden's and Mrs. Jenkins's mattresses. I had more money than I knew what to do with.

Spending it on what Dolly loved most seemed a fitting way to blow it.

I leaned on my cane as I looked around the store that held my little Dolly so captive. Makeup, stretching from the front of the store to the back. I glanced down at my girl and felt something like warmth fill my cold dead heart.

"I've never seen anything so beautiful in my life," she said in awe. She looked up at me, her long lashes batting against her cheek. We'd cleaned up at the motel and then come straight here.

"Can I help y'all?" a female voice asked from in front of us. I immediately shifted next to Dolly, protecting her, making sure no one fucked with us.

I glared at the tall, slim brunette before us, dressed all in black. Dolly gasped and stepped closer to her, her eyes fixed on the woman's face. "Your face," she said, her English accent sounding all proper and thick. "I want to look like that. How do I look like you?"

The woman's eyebrows pulled down, and then her gaze roved first over Dolly, then me. Her eyes widened. "Oh my God! Are you cosplayers?" She stepped back to assess Dolly. "Alice in Wonderland, right? Steampunk?"

I had no idea what the fuck she was talking about, but I stepped even closer to Dolly, ready to pull her back. But Dolly's eyes lit up at the mention of her favorite book. "Alice, yes! We're in Wonderland. We're on an adventure."

The woman laughed, but before she had a chance to say anything else, Dolly pulled out her tube of ruined lipstick. "I need more of this. It's all gone."

The woman took the lipstick and studied it. "Vintage Chanel?" She shook her head. "You should keep hold of this. The tube alone will be worth something. Lucky for you, the shade still exists, just a newer formula and design." She waved her hand. "Come on. If you're cosplaying Alice, we need to make you look the part."

Dolly looked back at me. I nodded, giving her permission to go. The woman led Dolly around the store, filling a basket with shit I had no idea about. But I didn't care as I watched Dolly's smile grow wider and wider with each new item added. This was what I had waited eleven years to see. Her face. Her body. My fucking girl killing so fucking beautifully it was like watching one of Chapel's poems come to life. A damn symphony in motion—a slice here, a stab there, and so much deliciously warm blood spilling to the floor.

Death had a smell.

I had always imagined it smelled of roses, like Dolly.

I hadn't been wrong.

As we walked through the store, people stared; stared, until I glared back at them. They must have sensed how much I wanted to see them robbed of life, because they looked away quickly, most fleeing the shop as if they could sense I was a predator stalking my prey.

I paid for the makeup, Dolly bouncing behind me in excitement. "You see all this, Alice?" she said to her bodiless doll as she held it up to the register. "All these pretties are for us. We're going to be the two prettiest girls in all of Wonderland."

My lip twitched as she took the bag from the cashier and turned my way. "Can we go back to the room? I really want to try all of this on."

"Sure thing, darlin'."

Just before we left, the cashier asked, "Where's the cosplay event being held?" I stared at the woman blankly. Dolly did the same. The cashier pointed at the bag. "What will you be wearing all that makeup for?"

Dolly smiled. "For the killing . . ." She looked to me, confusion on her face. "Who's next, Rabbit? I cannot remember." She blinked, all big blue eyes and pink lips. I could still envisage the red blood staining her neck and cheeks. I had to stop from growling out loud at the thoughts those images evoked.

"The Cheshire Cat."

Dolly's eyes glittered, and she turned back to the cashier. "For when we kill the Cheshire Cat." She held up the bag. "Now I will look my absolute best!"

Dolly turned, and I saw the cashier try to make sense of what Dolly had said. *Non-killers*, I thought. So fucking boring, living their mundane little lives.

"Rabbit!" Dolly called from the doorway. I turned to see her arms crossed and foot tapping impatiently on the floor. "We're going to be late!" A cheeky smile formed behind her pursed lips, and her dimples caved in her cheeks. "Tick tock." I couldn't fight back a laugh as I walked toward her, shaking my head as she stole my lines. "Silly Rabbit," she whispered when I joined her. I tapped her leg with the top of my cane, the mildest of punishment.

Then we went back to the hotel, so my darlin' could paint herself into a doll.

I WATCHED her from the bed as she sat at the tired, old vanity across the room, putting on all the makeup she had bought. I sharpened the blade in my cane, never taking my eyes from her reflection as she painted her eyelids blue, coated her lashes in black. As her pale skin became porcelain with some liquid she brushed over every inch of her face. Her cheeks were pink and, of course, her lips were bright pink.

She hummed and sang along to her boombox as her tape played the familiar songs. Her shoulders shook as she danced on her seat, her long blond curls bouncing with the movement. And all the time I watched her, I grew hard. As she transformed into a living, breathing doll before me, I became so hard that my teeth gritted together.

I had always envisioned her this way. At my side. Fully made up like a doll. Sharing in my ways. Killing. Stopping hearts. Not giving one fuck about anyone else but one another.

I slipped my blade back into the shaft of my cane, just as

Dolly attached something to her lashes. When I stood, she turned.

I was still. Rooted to the fucking spot. Big, long lashes had been placed on her eyes, and the bottom ones were styled into sections, making her look precisely like a doll. Only the fact that she breathed and blinked made me aware that she was alive.

"Darlin' . . ." I hushed out, my throat close to sealing shut.

She smoothed her hands down the front of her dress, then lifted her arms out and curtsied. She looked up at me through her fake lashes. "Well? Am I more your little Dolly now, Rabbit?"

I nodded without blinking. Without fucking breathing. I was too hot under my shirt, vest and cravat. "Yeah," I rasped, running my teeth so hard over my lip that blood trickled into my mouth.

It only served to make me harder.

Dolly's face changed from her usual smile to a serious expression, hunger in her gaze. "I did it for you, Rabbit," she whispered and stepped closer to me. My heart slammed in my chest with every step she took.

The closer she came, the more I smelled roses. She had bought the perfume she had always worn as a child, the one that originally belonged to her mother. She stopped right before me. Her hand reached out, and my every muscle froze. My nose flared as I thought she might touch me. I felt the usual sickness that rose whenever someone tried to lay a hand on me. On skin tarnished by the deeply invasive touch of men who had no fucking place touching it. The men who pushed inside me, filling me with their filth.

But then she touched my cravat, pulling it from my vest and running it through her fingers. She looked up at me, and I was breathless at the sight of her beautiful face. At her makeup. At my Alice in Wonderland brought to life, standing before me. "I want to look good for you, Rabbit. But only for you." She batted her eyelashes three times. "Do I look pretty, Rabbit? Am I beautiful for you?"

"Yes," I confirmed in a rough voice. Dolly began to wrap the length of my cravat around her hand, just like she was wrapping me around her little finger. She always had. "Am I your pretty pretty champion? Am I your painted champion of Wonderland?" Dolly leaned around me, looking at my back as if she could see through the clothes I wore. "Like the picture on your back?"

"More than her." I freed my unsteady hand to stroke a strand of her long hair between my fingers. It was so soft. Dolly sucked in a breath.

"This Dolly . . ." She lowered her eyes, and I hardened further as I saw her notice my want for her. Every part of me ached to take hold of her and possess her, smother her and drown her in my flesh. She whimpered. The very cells of my skin were dominoes of coldness. I staggered back, a sheen of icy sweat covering my face.

"Rabbit," Dolly whispered. Her bottom lip began to quiver. Blushing, she lifted her hands to her breasts and cupped them in her palms. "I keep feeling all these sensations . . ." She shook her head and began walking toward the bed . . . toward me. As I watched her, she became my prey once again. Darkness stirred within me. I stared at her neck with its racing pulse. I wondered what it would look like if I sliced open one of her veins with the tip of my thimble and let the blood pour. Not a main vein, but one where I could watch the vivid red render her pale skin into a sadistic artist's masterpiece. I imagined lapping at the blood. Then in turn, her opening a vein in my neck and feeding from me just the same.

Joining in more than just the physical. In every way.

My legs hit the bed at the vision and I slammed my hand over my cock. My eyes rolled back as my head hit the pillow.

"Rabbit," she called. I heard the desperation in her voice. I heard the hitch of her breath. When my eyes opened, I saw her opposite me, at the bottom of the bed. Her back rested against the railing at the foot of the bed. Her legs were open, and her hand was underneath her dress.

"Dolly." I stroked along the length of my dick over my pants.

"I want to touch you, Rabbit," she said as the heel of her boot scraped at the comforter. "I want to feel your hand do this to me. I want you to make me feel the shivers that break out inside of me when I simply think of your face. I want to feel you above me." A whimper fell from her lips. "Little Dolly wants her Rabbit."

"Dolly darlin'," I growled as I shifted my back against the headrest. We were face to face, just a few feet between us. And then her hand came to the top of her dress. Never taking her eyes from mine, she began unthreading the lace that kept the bodice of her dress together, exposing her white skin inch by inch . . .

Until the material parted at her waist and the two sides opened, baring her breasts. White breasts that would fit neatly into the palms of my hands. Hard pink nipples, almost as pink as the lipstick that graced her lips, begging for my mouth.

"There's nothing like it, Dapper Dan," Chapel had told me one night when I had asked him about women. "Their taste, their

feel, their breasts in your palms . . ." He'd nodded. "You'll get this with your little dolly darlin'. One day, when the dam that keeps your abusers' touch living within you breaks, you'll both get it from the other . . . and there'll be nothing quite like it ever again. Synergy, Dapper Dan. Complete synergy."

But that dam had not broken . . . yet.

So I watched from a distance. I watched as Dolly closed her legs and pulled down her panties. The frilly white panties I had bought her came sliding down her legs. I snarled as her slim, pale legs parted again, wide and bent at the knee, heels digging into the white comforter beneath us. Then her fingers were moving to the hem of her dress. My gaze flitted between the blue satin that was now shifting up her thighs and her eyes as they remained locked on me. Her lips were pursed and her pupils were blown.

"Rabbit," she whispered as she lifted her dress to her waist. I swallowed, still looking at her face, until I had no other choice but to look down. A groan clawed from my chest at the sight of her exposed pussy, the blond hair enticing me in.

"Dolly," I growled. She lowered her hand and ran her fingertips over herself. Her eyes rolled back as she moved her fingers back and forth. Slowly. Painfully fucking slowly.

I couldn't take it. I couldn't take any more, couldn't take my cock being trapped behind my pants. Ripping open the button, then the zipper, I reached inside my pants and pulled out my dick. My hand wrapped around its thick length and I jerked it back and forth. I hissed as I saw Dolly's hand freeze. She watched me. She never took her eyes off me as I kneeled up on the bed. I let go of my cock just long enough to pull off my shirt and vest. Bare-chested, pants wide open, I inched closer to where

TILLIE COLE

she lay. I stopped only a foot from her. Stopped close enough to watch her eyes glaze over as her fingers entered her hole, and to hear her cry softly and whisper, "Wider, bitch."

Every fucking part of me turned to solid granite as I heard the cry, the echo of Ellis's past pouring from her lips. "You're so fucking tight, tiny bitch." She was being pulled back from our Wonderland into the Earnshaw estate. Into the years void of me. Void of my protection.

A surge of fury swept through me watching my Dolly come apart, so broken from what those cunts had done. What they'd done when I had been locked in their prison. Her lips trembled as her eyes filled with tears. "You like that, don't you, baby whore? You like me filling you? You fucking love it."

I threw my head back and screamed as a tear fell down her newly made-up cheek. When I lowered my head to face her, her big blue eyes were lost . . . alone. She was lonely. Lost in the hopeless isolation of her past.

Her fingers continued to trace down. With my shaking hand, I slid my palm along my still-hard cock and hushed out, "Take it, boy . . ." I swallowed, pumping my dick, and let forth the words I heard whenever I closed my eyes, whenever I tried to sleep . . . whenever I took a motherfucking breath. "Take it, boy. You were meant for this. You are mine. This ass is mine."

Dolly cried, her tears flowing freely down her cheeks, slipping down her bare firm breasts. "Look at this smooth, pretty skin," she said.

"Look at this pretty back," I said in return.

"You're so fucking tight, baby whore."

"You're so fucking tight, little boy."

"You clutch me so damn tight."

"You love this. Lap it up."

"Faster, little girl."

"Faster, little boy."

Breaths were faster. Hands worked harder. Tears fell from our eyes.

"I'm gonna come, little girl."

"I'm gonna come, little boy."

Dolly broke apart, her ass lifting off the comforter as her back arched and her head fell back to rest on the top of the railing of the bed. Her hand circled her pussy faster until her body jerked. The sight alone caused me to stiffen and then burst apart. I fell forward, my hand slamming onto the railing beside Dolly's head. I groaned as I came and came, my cum lashing Dolly's pussy, dripping down onto the bed.

My hand shook on the railing, sweat coating my forehead as I stared down at Dolly. Her huge blue eyes were staring up at me, makeup smudged from all of her tears. "Darlin' . . ." I said, my voice gritty from exertion. From my fucking tears.

"You too?" she asked, and for a moment I wasn't speaking to Dolly. It was Ellis. I was speaking to my girl, my best friend; my need for her had endured what we had been through.

"Me too," I replied, seeing both pain and relief in her eyes. Pain for what I went through at the hands of those bastards. And relief. Relief that she wasn't the only one. That someone else knew her pain.

Just like she knew mine.

Yet it was my biggest failure. I'd left her alone. I'd let those fuckers hurt her—the King of Hearts and his men.

We never took our gazes off one another as we caught our breath. Then, needing to feel something but the remembered touch of the one who hurt me most, I took my free hand and brought it to hover over her cheek. Dolly swallowed, and then, after a gentle nod of her head, I forced myself to touch the skin of her cheek. I gritted my teeth; she held her breath.

Her skin was so soft. "Darlin . . ." I whispered and suddenly felt water on my finger. I looked into her eyes and saw a tear had fallen. But a smile had formed on her mouth.

She had liked it.

So had I.

When I lifted my hand, the tear was still on my finger. With Dolly's attention still on me, I sucked the tear into my mouth. It tasted of her.

I swallowed it down. Seconds passed by, and then a wider grin spread on Dolly's mouth. She shook her head. "Silly Rabbit."

The residual ice in my veins melted in an instant.

Taking that same finger, I ran it down her cheek again, more than curious at how it felt. "Get bathed and ready for bed," I ordered. Dolly's eyes closed under my touch.

"Okay, Rabbit." She moved off the bed and into the bathroom.

I lay back on the bed and stared at the ceiling until she came out. I thought about the next kill. Thought about the next "uncle" we would defeat. The one who had kept me under his thumb. The one who had come for me and come in me night after night. The one who had dared call me his "little boy." The one who always smiled. Smiled at me, like him sticking his dick in me was all that I wanted in life.

Uncle Clive. The Cheshire Cat. The Four of Hearts.

The bathroom door opened and Dolly stepped out, freshly washed and wearing her white nightgown. Like this, she looked so young. She was beautiful either way.

Dolly walked to her side of the bed, and I pulled back the comforter like I had done for her every night. She climbed in, and I drew the comforter back over her, keeping her warm. Just as I went to lie on my back, like I did every night, Dolly asked, "Do you think . . . if it is at all possible . . . you could put your arm around me as I sleep?"

My eyes widened in the dim glow of the lamp beside the bed. Without turning, without moving, Dolly said, "Like you once held me as I slept." She paused. "I do not think I have ever slept as well as I did then . . . I . . . I loved it, Rabbit."

I ran my hand through my hair, then, rolling to my side, threaded my arm under hers on top of the covers. I breathed deeply at the discomfort the action brought, but also at the familiarity it delivered too.

No one but Dolly could ever do this for me.

Dolly sighed. "Do you remember the film we would watch as children, Rabbit?" I stilled. "*Chitty Chitty Bang Bang?*"

I searched my memory to pinpoint the one she was talking about. She insisted I watch a movie with her every night. "Films" she called them, using one of the British words that her "mummy" had instilled in her vocabulary.

"The one with the song 'Truly Scrumptious.' The doll that sang.

I never really understood what the song was about. But when I would hear it, I would always think it was about a doll who wanted to be free, always spinning and spinning but never being able to move from her music box. Stuck. I always felt sad as nobody ever helped her. So she stayed trapped there forever." I closed my eyes at the sad tone of her voice. Dolly was always happy. Never sad. I fucking hated the sound of her being sad. I suddenly felt something on my hand that made me go stock still. It was her finger. Her fingertip, softly circling the back of my hand wrapped over her waist. She laughed once, but the laugh was sad too. "You used to say I was the doll on the box, because of her makeup." A pause. "But now I think I'm like her in different ways."

I got what she was saying. She was trapped like the doll appeared to be. Trapped in her room of doors, and no one came to let her out. All she wanted was to be saved. To be free.

"She . . . the doll . . . I always felt like she wanted to be kissed too. Felt she wanted to be loved. I think she wanted her true love to return from wherever he was to save her." Her finger stopped moving on my hand, then I felt her fingers wrap around mine and grip me tightly. "She was under a spell, and only her love's first kiss could set her free." My jaw clenched as she spoke. I knew she was telling me what her life was like when I left. How she'd waited for me to return.

She was the doll. Her words right now had nothing to do with the damn movie.

I'd taken too fucking long to return. The damage had already been done.

Then she started singing. In her soft, gentle voice, she started singing that song. The one sung by the woman dressed as a doll in the movie . . . and it fucking shattered my black heart. Her hand gripped mine tighter and tighter as she sang each line. And I heard all the pain. Heard it all come pouring from her mouth through that damn song. My vision blurred, and I blinked when I felt my cheeks get wet. I lifted my hand to my face and felt tears.

I hadn't cried in eleven years. The last time was when I'd been taken from Dolly. And now, when I'd gotten her back . . . but gotten her back in pieces, with her heart now made of fragile glass.

Dolly finished her song, and the room was plunged into silence. I held her tightly, and then even tighter as her sleepy voice said, "One day we will kiss, Rabbit. One day we will kiss, and then this adventure will be so impossibly perfect . . ."

It wasn't long before Dolly's breath evened out.

But I didn't sleep. With every hour that passed I replayed the image of her splayed in front of me, those words pouring from her lips. Words her fucked-up "uncles," one in particular, had spoken to her as he raped her as a kid. I thought of her innocent voice singing that song. I mulled over what she wanted, what she had wanted for too long.

Freedom.

Love.

Then I thought of the kills yet to come. I thought of how we would take each one down. Because what I had planned before was no longer painful enough. No longer bloody enough. No longer violent enough.

The cunts deserved more. They deserved all that our fucked-up minds could conjure up. And they would get it. They would incur the full force of our revenge, and they wouldn't see us coming.

I closed my eyes, a smile on my face.

I smiled at all the blood yet to come.

Carnage: courtesy of the Sick Fux.

CHAPTER 9

Eddie

Earnshaw Estate
Dallas, Texas

Slowly, I approached the door. The old hinges were broken and the wooden door smashed. Someone had kicked them through. I reached into my back pocket and pulled out my gun. I fixed my hat so I could see the whole hallway as I crossed the threshold.

The second I did, a vile smell assaulted my nose. "Shit!" I hissed as I covered my nose and mouth with my forearm. Standing as still as a stone, I listened for any sounds. There were none. Moving as quietly as possible, I checked the first-floor rooms. They smelled musty; the furniture had been covered with sheets for years.

They still looked exactly the same.

My heart sank as I reached the bottom of the stairs. "Ellis . . ." I said under my breath. I raced up the stairs two at a time. The closer I got to the room where she had been holed up for years, the stronger the putrid smell became. "Ellis!" I called out. I felt an increasing sense of dread as I approached the door. It was open. No noise came from within.

I raised my gun and stopped beside the wall. I took a deep breath. Relying on the intensive Ranger training I'd been through in recent months, I crept slowly into the bedroom—Ellis's bedroom—heart in mouth. My breathing seemed to stop as I paused before turning the corner to look at her spot, the place she always sat. I closed my eyes for a second, then counted to five and turned to face the rest of the room. I froze. Ellis's chair was missing. Her dark clothes, the clothes she always wore, were in a heap on the wooden floor . . . and then I felt the blood drain from my face. A pair of feet poked out of the shadows, near the bathroom. I forced my feet to move, one reluctant step after the other, until I felt something beneath my shoe. I looked down and saw a pool of congealed blood, now nearly black in color. "Ellis," I whispered, feeling the muscles in my chest tear in two, only to freeze when an older body came into view.

I tiptoed closer and closer still until I saw the blank, death-masked face of Mrs. Jenkins. It seemed as if she was staring toward the window Ellis used to sit and stare out of. I crouched down, making to check for a pulse, when I spotted the deep gash across her throat. The wound was a faded red, the skin split wide open, revealing the flesh beneath. But the blood was dried and cold, caking her skin and the floor around her.

Heart pounding, I kicked into action. I tore through the house. "Ellis!" I roared, gun held out before me, searching for anyone who remained alive. Where was my oldest, best friend? "Ellis!" I zipped through back hallways, hallways I hadn't even known existed. I ran up stairs and through rooms, dread seeping into the very marrow of my bones, until I came to a stop.

A total dead stop.

There was a hole in the wooden floor before me. It was uneven, the edges hard, clearly carved with a saw.

What the hell . . . ?

Carefully, I shuffled forward and looked down. A rope lay pooled on the floor below, surrounded by fragments of wood, the remains of a chair. I looked closer and recognized it instantly. "Ellis," I said softly, my eyes widening as I realized what must have happened.

Someone had taken her.

"Ellis!" I instinctively called again and reached into my pocket for my cell. I pressed the number for the third person on my speed dial. "Uncle," I wheezed, out of breath, as I ran back to Ellis's room and the rotting body of Mrs. Jenkins. "You've got to get to the Earnshaw estate now. We have a kidnapping on our hands."

* * *

"WHERE'S EARNSHAW?" my uncle asked as the forensic team took samples from the room and the folks from the mortuary began removing Mrs. Jenkins's body.

I ran my hand through my hair, gripping my Ranger hat in

my free hand. "Left years ago. He ran his business from here, with his associates, for decades. I used to come here to play with Ellis when we were kids. They all left years ago when there was some kind of problem with the business." I shrugged. "No idea where they went. It was . . . weird."

My uncle's brow furrowed in concentration. "And Ellis?"

My chest tightened. "She had a breakdown years ago, when she was in her mid-teens." I looked at the spot where she would always sit. I had visited her every week since I found out she was sick. I talked to her. But she never said a thing. Just stared out of the window, silent, eyes completely devoid of life. I thought back to when we were kids. "She was never allowed off her property when we were young. I once asked my mama why. She told me that Ellis had some issues." I shrugged. "Anxiety and such about leaving her home. It's why she was homeschooled. Her papa told my mama that it only got worse when her mama died." I shook my head in sadness. "Don't think she ever left this place . . . then she had her breakdown. Guess she always had a fragile mind."

"Then she could have snapped and killed the nanny herself, perhaps?" my uncle mused.

Vehemently, I shook my head. "No, you don't understand," I snapped. "She was practically a zombie. And even if she had somehow found a way back to herself, there's no way she would do something like this." I looked around the tired pink room. "Ellis Earnshaw is the sweetest, most innocent person on this earth." My stomach flipped when I thought of how, as a kid, she would dress up as Alice in Wonderland and pretend she was drinking tea. "She's delicate." My heart broke for the shell she'd become. "She was almost too fragile for the world. Easily manipulated. Too vulnerable." My mouth, which had a formed a nostalgic smile, fell. Only one person came to mind. The prick who had taken her from me. Took away my best friend and molded her into his lap dog . . .

Heathan fucking James.

But he was dead. Or at least presumed dead. Disappeared when we were kids, leaving Ellis heartbroken. He was always selfish. I'd tried to see her once, months after he had left, when I found out from my mama that he'd left her all alone. But it was the start of Ellis's spiral into darkness. Heathan fucking James left her and ruined her goddamn life.

That dick was better off dead and gone. There was always something weird about him. As if he lived with evil in his veins. And the minute he set his sights on Ellis, he did nothing but corrupt her, and devour her spirit and grace.

The ringing of my uncle's cell cut through my smoldering anger. I blinked away the image of Heathan, with his strange clothes and eerie gray eyes. I focused instead on my uncle's eyes, which had fallen on me.

"I'm on my way." My uncle ended the call and tucked his cell back into his pocket.

"What is it?"

"Murder," he replied. "Amarillo."

My heart started racing. My uncle was pretty high up in the Texas Rangers. From being a kid, I had wanted to be him. I started training the minute I turned eighteen. At twenty-two, I was now truly learning my craft. Even when I was officially on leave, I didn't take the day off. Instead I shadowed him, the best. Yeah, it was a blatant case of nepotism, but my uncle let me. He could see how much I wanted it. I had two weeks of vacation time. For me, it translated into two weeks' worth of the most important cases to observe and understand.

"When are we leaving?" I followed him as he turned and raced from the room.

"Now."

* * *

"HOLY SHIT," I whispered under my breath as I drank in the scene before me. We'd passed bodies on our route to an office in the secluded house we'd been called to. Guards. When the next shift of guards had started, they'd immediately called in the murders.

It was carnage.

I followed my uncle into the office. And I had barely taken one step inside when I stopped in my tracks. A man, stabbed to death, slumped in his office chair against the wall. I tore my eyes from the bloody sight of his corpse and up to the writing above. The scrawl was messy, almost childlike. I squinted to make out what it said. Just as it swam into focus, my uncle gave it voice: "Sick Fux."

He stepped up to the writing and ran his finger over the edge of one of the letters. He brought the pink stuff it had been written in to his nose, then rubbed it between his fingers. "Lipstick?" Eyebrows pulled down, he drew a handkerchief from his pocket and wiped his fingers.

On closer inspection of the writing, I saw he was right. "Lipstick?" I asked. "And what the hell is Sick Fux?"

My uncle put his hands in his pockets. "I'm gonna say the person, or persons, responsible." He crouched down beside the body and gazed over the wounds. "They toyed with him." He studied the tape around the man's wrists. "Tied him down and played with him like he was a piece of meat."

Without looking behind him to the deputies assigned to the case, he asked, "We have a name?"

A deputy flicked his notepad open. "A Mr. Lester Knowles."

That name sounded familiar. I racked my brain trying to work out why. I moved to the desk and searched through some of the papers, his name playing over and over again in my head. *Lester Knowles . . . why do I know your name?*

My blood cooled when the answer hit me. I spun on my heels to look at my uncle. "Lester Knowles was one of Mr. Earnshaw's colleagues. An associate in his business."

My uncle came toward me. "Earnshaw? The missing girl?"

"Ellis," I said and felt everything inside of me frost over in trepidation. "She called him her uncle. He wasn't by blood. But that"—I pointed to the corpse—"was one of her father's best friends. He practically helped raise Ellis." My face blanched. "Do you think they're connected?" I heard the fear lacing my voice. "Ellis's kidnapping, Mrs. Jenkins's and his deaths . . . Do you think they're linked?"

My uncle gazed around the room. I knew he was thinking. I had seen him do this over the years. "Perhaps," he said out loud. "You said 'they'—the so-called uncles and the girl's father—dispersed from their properties?" I nodded. "Why?"

"They had to move when their business went elsewhere. That's all I know. One day they were all there; the next, they were gone, leaving Ellis behind for Mrs. Jenkins to care for. Mrs. Jenkins claimed Ellis couldn't be moved, needing to be close to her doctors. For her mental breakdown."

"How many of these uncles were there?"

I blew out a breath. "Five, six maybe? I was young when I knew them. They talked to me, quite a lot, even asked me to stay for dinner and such. But you know how mama is about family dinners. She never let me miss one, so I never got to see Mr. Earnshaw and Ellis's uncles much beyond those passing comments."

My uncle looked over my shoulder at one of his Rangers. "We need to find out who all the associates of Earnshaw were and where they live." He glanced to me, then back to his deputy. "We also need a missing person's notice put out for Ellis Earnshaw."

"You *do* think they're connected," I said. I looked at Uncle Lester sprawled on the chair, bathed in his own blood. I thought of Mrs. Jenkins, also murdered brutally . . . then I thought of Ellis. If they had her . . . if they hurt her . . .

My fists clenched.

"The Sick Fux," my uncle said as he stared at the scruffy pink-lipstick scrawl. "It implies more than one person, maybe a group?"

"A group responsible for several dead bodies and a kidnapping," I added.

My uncle shook his head. "They've only tagged this one murder as theirs. Maybe they are connected to the Earnshaw case, but right now we don't know."

"So what's next?" I followed my uncle from the room, breathing in the fresh air as soon as we walked outside.

"We try to get camera footage—security, mainly. Hope they haven't destroyed it. Then we work out who these people are."

I nodded. "You think they'll strike again?"

My uncle pulled a smoke from his pocket and lit it up. He stared across the fields surrounding the quiet property. "We'll see." He tipped his head to the sky. "I want to speak to all of these 'uncles' and Earnshaw himself. Could be an isolated incident. Might be linked. But regardless, we need to tell Earnshaw his daughter is missing."

Ellis, I thought as I stared out across the fields too. *I'm gonna find you, I promise. And we'll get you better. Get you better help.*

Resolve settled in my gut, and I fixed my hat in place. I wouldn't let anyone hurt her again.

Not after that walking demon Heathan ripped out her heart and vaporized it.

It was my second chance to save her. To bring back to life the sweetest girl I'd ever known.

I promise.

CHAPTER 10

THE CHESHIRE CAT

Dolly

I LOWERED the kohl liner and sat back in my seat. Staring at the reflection in the vanity's mirror, I smiled in satisfaction. Now I looked just like him.

The sound of the bathroom door opening prompted me to turn and face Rabbit. He walked out of the door, head down. My stomach squeezed. My Rabbit had been acting strange all morning. We had traveled to another place. And the whole way, Rabbit had been quiet. In our motel room, I danced and I sang, but he didn't smile like he usually did. Instead, he sat on the end of the bed, sharpening the blade that lived in his cane. He took the gun apart and cleaned the pieces.

I tried to think of ways to make him happy. This was the only thing I thought could work. I had played with my new makeup every single day. I wore blue on my eyes, pink on my cheeks and lots of mascara on my lashes. I stuck fake ones on top so I looked extra doll-like. Rabbit liked me as a doll. He especially liked my big pink lips. He stared at them often. He licked his lips when he did.

It made me wet between my legs. It made me want to touch myself, like I had in the bath . . . and on the bed with Rabbit. But Rabbit had kept his distance from me after that night. He hadn't stroked my cheek. He hadn't held me as I slept. He had slept on the floor beside the bed, if he slept at all. Most nights he just sat against the wall, staring into space. His nose would flare, his hands would fist, and my heart would break. I didn't know what I'd done to upset him. I didn't want to displease him. I only ever wanted to make him happy. He was the most important thing in my life.

Rabbit swung his long coat on, his back to me. He hadn't looked at me sitting very prettily on my seat. My eyebrows pulled down when he reached for his cane, then the car keys. Everything but my makeup and doll were in the car ready to go.

I smoothed down my dress and cleared my throat. Rabbit's shoulders bunched. I got to my feet, feeling the heat from outside kiss the bare skin on my thighs. Then Rabbit turned. As he did, I flicked the hair hanging over my left shoulder away from my face.

Stormy eyes fixed on me. My gaze dropped to his tattooed hand gripping his rabbit-headed cane. If that poor rabbit on his cane had been alive, its skull would have been cracked open like an egg. Rabbit gripped his cane so hard his knuckles turned white.

Grabbing the hem of my dress at both sides, I swung from side to side, looking up at him from under my eyelashes. "Do you like it, Rabbit?"

His nostrils flared, as did his eyes. His teeth ran over his bottom lip, and I saw his naughty parts swell under his trousers. "Mmm," I murmured and stepped closer to Rabbit. He stayed still, yet watched my every step. As I walked, his pupils dilated and my heart began to beat fast. A tingling sprouted between my thighs; I knew I'd pleased him with what I'd done.

"Do you like it, Rabbit?" I asked again and stopped right before him. I couldn't tear my eyes away from the way he watched me. Rabbit always watched me this way. He stared and stared and stared. Then his gaze would drop, and he would stare at the throbbing pulse in my neck. "*Your vein . . .*" he would whisper to me when he thought I was asleep. "*Your vein . . . so thick . . . so full . . .*"

My breath would hitch as I kept my eyes closed, playing possum. I'd keep them shut because I knew what would come next: his mouth, hovering just above that vein. His sharp thimble, like a feather, touching my pulse. Warm breath would fan my skin, shooting shivers down my spine. Then came the tip of his tongue. Its wet tip tracing the vein so completely, never straying from its path. Rabbit groaning low in his throat as he touched his shaft between his legs. As he stroked his hand back and forth, faster and faster, lapping at my throat until he stilled and choked on his breath.

I would spy through my almost-closed eyes as he sat back

against the wall, his shaft hanging from his pants, large and long, making me squirm. I'd watch his eyes close and the sharp-tipped thimble dig into his skin. Dig into the vein in his wrist . . . right on the tattooed clock that looked just like the pocket watch on his vest. Blood would sprout and he would rub it along his lips. Plump flesh, red and raw; his tongue would run slowly and gently over the blood—tasting and . . . enjoying.

I wanted that blood to be mine.

I wanted him to taste me that way.

I wanted to meld with him like that—blood and blood.

Merged.

"Fucking Dolly," Rabbit rasped, hauling me back to the here and now. I tried to calm my flushing cheeks. But his silver stare just made them hotter. He reached out, his hand freezing just before it touched my left eye. "Roman numerals,' he whispered. I nodded, smiling even though my legs shook at the intensity of his glare.

"I drew them on for you." I pointed to the clocks branding his skin. "We're the Sick Fux. Tick tock, Rabbit. Now we match. Rabbit and Dolly . . . hunting the bad men on borrowed time." I tapped the clock drawn in black eyeliner around my left eye. "Tick tock, Rabbit. Always and forever, tick tock."

He didn't speak after that, just stared. I wanted him to say something. Wanted him to touch my cheek, my lips, the clock around my eye. But when he didn't, I felt my heart deflate.

"We need to go," he said as he walked past me. I fought back tears as I gathered my makeup from the vanity. I placed my lipstick in my pocket and took hold of Alice's hair. I closed the door to the motel and stepped into the bright sun, keeping my head down as I walked to the car. Alice's cracked china face knocked into my leg with each step.

I climbed into the car. As Rabbit pulled out of the car park, I pressed play on the tape player. Just as one of my eighties songs began to play, Rabbit snapped his hand forward and slammed the music to silence. "No music today," he said coldly, and I felt the icy chill from his dark tone seep into my bones. Even though the hot sun blazed down on my painted pink cheeks, I felt as though I had been plunged into a freezer.

Rabbit made me warm.

He was the only thing that ever did.

I didn't like this side of Rabbit. He made my heart hurt.

Fighting the tears in my eyes, I took out my lipstick, pulled down the mirror in my visor and began to draw. I circled my lips, and then pulled the lipstick down at the corners.

I sat back and studied my reflection.

Dolly now had a sad face.

I didn't know if Rabbit saw. He didn't say anything as we drove along the empty roads. No cars passed us as we chased the sun across the sky. I hugged Alice to my chest, sniffing back my sadness when it became too much for me to take.

As more and more time passed, with Rabbit still not looking my way, I took my blade from the teapot-shaped white purse Rabbit had bought for me. "We're the Sick Fux," I whispered, practicing for the kill. "You, the Cheshire Cat, will never smile again . . ." My lip hooked at the corner, proud of what I had said. Suddenly, Rabbit yanked the car to the side of the road and slammed on the brakes. I was flung forward, my blade slipping from my hands and landing beside my boots.

"He's mine," Rabbit growled, his hands gripping the wheel so tightly I feared it would break.

"W-what?" I whispered, feeling my heart pound as Rabbit's tattooed neck corded and bulged with venomous veins.

My eyebrows pulled down, and a fire flared in my stomach. I turned, Rabbit's face only an inch from mine. Gritting my teeth, I met his eyes and said, "I am the champion of Wonderland. Charged with destroying the bad men." I narrowed my gaze. "The Cheshire Cat is *mine*."

A sound like a groan mixed with a vicious snarl poured from Rabbit's mouth, and I saw his lip flick up at the corner. He shifted in his seat. When I looked down, the bulge in his trousers was back. But he was harder than ever before. The shape of his shaft was visible through his black pants. Rabbit shook his head slowly. He tutted at me. "My sweet little Dolly," he said quietly . . . menacingly . . . *lovingly*. "You just tread carefully, pushing me this way." He raised his left hand, and I felt the tip of the long, sharp-nailed thimble creep up my neck, along my vein. The vein he liked to lick when I was asleep.

The tip of the thimble traveled up my neck and over my chin until it reached my mouth. Rabbit's eyes flared as he concentrated on my lipstick, a frame to the frown that now curved my bright pink lips. His head tipped to the side, and his eyes followed the path of the lipstick. He sucked in a quick breath. "You will do as I command, little Dolly. *I* am the White Rabbit. *I* lead you . . ." His head straightened. "*I* control you in Wonderland."

I was breathless, my eyes fluttering slowly to a close, as if his words, his commands, were a string on my heart. Plucking and pulling, holding me in its grip. His thimble traveled downward as his heavy breath played across my face. It traveled down until it ran over the swell of my breasts. Dancing with the top of my corseted blue dress, back and forth . . . back and forth . . .

"You will obey, *darlin'*," he ordered curtly, and I shifted on my seat. I cupped myself between my legs and arched toward him; a magnet, a pull of need as my moan traveled into the balmy air. A bird up above caught it and it rode away on its feathered back. I rocked forward and back as Rabbit's thimble held me in its thrall. "Today, you will stand back and watch."

"Yes," I said, breathlessly, passively.

"Today, you will watch your master at work."

"Yes . . ." My fingers moved faster.

Tingling. Heat. Pressure . . . so much pressure . . . building . . . building . . . building . . .

"Today you will watch me. You will watch the killer you belong to. You will watch as he takes back what he lost to the Cheshire Cat." He leaned forward, and my mouth parted as a crest, a high wave, began to surge through my body.

"Yes!" I shouted.

"Today," Rabbit whispered directly into my ear, moving forward until I felt the smoothness of his cravat slip against the tops of my breasts. "Today you will watch your master shred a man. You will watch me stab and cut and bathe in his tarnished blood . . . over and over and over and . . ."

"Yes!" I screamed, my legs parting as I was swept away by bliss, a heat so intense I was incinerated, only to return to a pile of pathetic bones and skin and flesh. "Yes . . ." I slumped against the seat. "Yes . . . Rabbit . . . *yes* . . ."

The thimble that had stilled on my breasts retreated, but his masterly hand patted my head. I opened my eyes to see black eyes watching me, only a sliver of gray coating their edges. "Good Dolly."

I smiled. I had pleased my Rabbit.

I caught my breath as Rabbit pulled the car back onto the road. It wasn't long before we made a right turn to travel down a dirt road. Rabbit stopped at an old wooden house and tucked the car out of sight. Bushes hid us, just like with the Caterpillar. I turned to Rabbit, about to speak, but he held his hand in the air. I slammed my mouth shut and looked through the gap in the bushes. A man came out of the wooden home.

My eyes narrowed—the Cheshire Cat.

Rabbit's gaze followed him as he walked to a barn at the back of his property. Rabbit reached for his cane and flicked the trigger of his rabbit's head over and over. The Cheshire Cat disappeared into the barn.

The air thickened around us. "Rabbit?"

"He's mine," he hissed, glaring me into submission.

I nodded dutifully. "Yes, Rabbit."

So vicious a veil of darkness descended over Rabbit's face that I waited a long second before exiting the car. Rabbit never took his eyes from that barn.

Then we were moving.

I followed Rabbit, Alice in hand, gun tucked into my waist belt, blade in my right hand. As Rabbit picked up speed, so did I.

Then we were at the doors of the barn.

Rabbit stopped. I watched his back as it froze, solid and

tense. He rolled his neck from side to side. It cracked, the crunching sound ricocheting off the walls of the wooden barn.

Rabbit split his cane in two, one weapon in each hand. I stayed behind, waiting for him to lead the way. My heart swelled with anticipation.

Rabbit lunged forward and slid the barn doors open. He charged in. I followed behind. But all that greeted us was . . . an empty barn.

Rabbit's head whipped from side to side. I felt the rage pulsing off him in waves. I scoured the barn, but there was nothing. Rabbit took off, searching the walls. I did too. Then he stopped. I ran to where he crouched and looked down at a door in the floor.

"Another rabbit hole?" I whispered.

Rabbit glanced up at me through his fallen hair. "Not a good one," he said, and then paused. "Or maybe it is . . ." He smiled a dangerous smile. "It depends. If ripping someone apart can be classed as good . . ."

I smiled, turning my lipstick-painted frown upside down.

"It's good," I replied. "Really, very, very good." I bent down. "Maybe even as good as a strawberry tart."

Rabbit glanced down, and the smile fell from his lips. He quietly lifted the heavy wood and climbed down the ladder underneath. I followed, my palms twitching as the call for blood lured us further down.

When we reached the bottom, a sliver of light shone from the end of a narrow hallway. Rabbit placed his finger over his lips. "Shh," he whispered. I nodded obediently. My pulse was aflame as I followed Rabbit further down the hole.

Suddenly Rabbit stopped. An ice-cold feeling shot down my spine when I heard a familiar sound seeping from the room at the end of the hallway. My eyes slammed shut.

Echoes of Ellis's tales of the bad men came back to taunt me . . .

He would take me by my hand and lead me to his room. I would be forced to stand before a bed, Dolly. He would turn me around and touch me between my legs. He would play with me, Dolly . . . and then he would put himself inside me. And I would scream . . . I would scream and scream and scream . . . and I'd want Heathan. I would cry and scream for Heathan . . . over and over and over again . . . but he never stopped . . .

I shook my head, body shivering, as I blinked myself back into the hallway. I was sweating, Ellis's story making me feel sick . . . making me feel rage . . . making me feel . . . *There!* That sound. The sound coming from the room . . . it was the same. It sounded the same as Ellis had described, it was—

Rabbit roared and ran forward. He burst into the room. With a shrill cry, I followed. A bare lightbulb hanging above bathed us in brightness as we took in the scene.

The Cheshire Cat . . . the Cheshire Cat over . . . a boy. My body vibrated with rage as I saw a boy, no more than ten, bending over a dirty old cot at the side of the room. His dark, sunken eyes snapped around and fixed on mine.

I heard a whimper from behind me. When I turned, I saw a cage. I took a step forward, my blade readied to draw blood, and I saw a pair of blue eyes. A young girl with long blond hair looked back at me.

"Ellis?" I whispered Her eyes darted behind me . . . so I turned too.

"Guess who?" Rabbit taunted as he grabbed hold of the Cheshire Cat's hair and yanked him off the boy. The boy fell forward, hands in the dirt, his pants around his ankles. Rabbit spun the Cheshire Cat around and slammed him into the nearest wall.

The little boy ran to the cage. I opened the door. The girl and the boy watched me with huge eyes. "Run. Run, little ones," I urged. The boy reached inside for the girl, dragging her to her feet. As they ran past, I stood in the girl's way and asked, "Ellis? Are you Ellis?" My head cocked to the side. I thought she looked familiar, perhaps someone I knew long ago, with her long blond hair and her big blue eyes. She could only have been about ten years old.

She shook her head, folding her arms around her stomach. "She's called Helena," the boy said.

"Helena," I repeated. Such a nice name. "Run." I smiled and waved my blade. "Unless, of course, you want to see some blood spilled?" I added in excitement. I knew it would be such fun to watch.

The children ran. I laughed. The little ones had no idea what a show they would be missing! "Run, run, little ones. The little kitty-cat is about to purr and purr!"

Spinning, I gripped the Alice doll-head at my side by her hair.

"Impossible," the kitty-cat hissed at Rabbit, who was holding him by the neck, glaring.

Rabbit ran his blade down the kitty-cat's face. "Possible."

Then the kitty-cat looked my way.

His eyes squinted. "Ellis? Ellis Earnshaw?" He blinked. "You're better?"

I shook my head and tapped my skull with my blade. *That* name cut through me. "Ellis, Ellis, Ellis. Why does everyone keep calling me Ellis?" I walked forward, but stopped when Rabbit turned his furious face to me. I nodded, then peeking from around Rabbit's shoulder, I said, "What's new, pussycat?"

Kitty-cat's eyes widened. I smiled and hummed a teasing tune under my breath. "Poor, poor kitty-cat. My rabid Rabbit has come for you." I skipped to the edge of the room and sat on the edge one of the tables there. Kitty's eyes tracked me the entire way. "Naughty, naughty kitty—time to pay the price."

"What the fuck?" Kitty-cat asked, just as Rabbit lifted his blade and sliced it across his mouth. Kitty screamed. I giggled, clapping my hands. Rabbit grabbed Kitty's hair and wrenched him back up. Kitty's flesh was cut, his cheeks. I screwed my eyes up to see better, and I suddenly realized what Rabbit had done.

"The Cheshire Cat!" I danced my bottom on the table in happiness. "You gave him a smile, Rabbit, a wide Cheshire Cat smile!"

But my happiness evaporated when I looked to the wall behind me and saw lots and lots of pictures. I jumped up as Rabbit dragged Kitty to a table in the corner of the room. Rabbit grabbed some ropes that were hanging on the wall beside him.

I focused my attention on the pictures. I didn't like them. In fact, I hated them. Hated them so much I shook my head and closed my eyes to block out the images. "Rabbit!" I shouted as a sob escaped my throat.

I felt him beside me in moments. When I looked around, I saw Kitty tied to the table by the rope. I pointed to the wall. "The pictures, Rabbit."

Rabbit faced the wall and studied the nasty pictures. I saw him squirm at the sight of the Cheshire Cat putting himself inside all the children of Wonderland, defenseless girls and helpless boys. He looked at them crying, screaming . . . and bad Kitty just laughing. Laughing, laughing for the camera . . . nasty, smiling Cheshire Cat.

A harsh cry thundered from Rabbit's throat. Slowly, he put his cane back together. He rested it against the table I had been sitting at. I sat on a seat next to it. I looked on, blinking the sad tears from my eyes, as Rabbit unbuttoned his coat and slipped it from his shoulders. He placed it carefully on the table beside me. He undid his cufflinks and rolled his shirt sleeves up to his elbows. He reached for his cane once more and walked over to naughty Kitty, who was staring at him with big eyes.

I didn't like those eyes.

"Dolly darlin'," Rabbit said as he stood behind the kitty.

"Yes, Rabbit?"

"Come here."

I stood up from the chair and skipped over to my Rabbit. I looked up at him, waiting for him to speak. Rabbit ran his lips over his teeth, then ordered, "Pull his pants down."

Kitty made a sound in his throat. But he didn't speak. I wasn't sure he *could* now that Rabbit had given him such a pretty smile—new, bloody, and wide. I looked at the Kitty's trousers. They were already open from when he had bent over the little boy.

I walked behind him and pulled down his black slacks. They fell to the floor and pooled at his ankles. My hands covered my mouth as a laugh escaped me. I shook my head and stuck out my tongue in disgust. "Eww!" I said as I stared at his ugly, hairy bottom and the limp shaft hanging between his legs.

I looked at Rabbit, and my hands fell from my mouth. My stomach turned and my heart sank at the look on Rabbit's face as he stared at Kitty's bare bottom. His hand tightened on his cane.

"Take it, boy," Rabbit said, so low that I almost didn't catch it. But naughty Kitty did. His face went white. Rabbit lifted his cane and unsheathed his blade and gun. "Suck it, boy." He began to circle Kitty. My stomach swam. But I didn't dare move. I couldn't take my eyes from Rabbit's face. I wasn't laughing anymore.

He was hurting.

My Rabbit . . . he was hurting so badly.

My Rabbit was feeling intense pain.

"Feel my cock." Rabbit lifted his blade into the air. He studied the blade as his rough voice got even rougher . . . as it began to break. His hand shook. "Take my big fat cock, little boy," he said, choking on the words.

Then he stopped dead. He closed his eyes, and in a high voice, like a child's, he called out, "Don't touch me. No one touches me but Dolly . . ." He hissed, and then cried out as if he was in agony. "You made it so I can't be touched . . . I CAN'T FUCKING BE TOUCHED!" Rabbit spun around, blade held high, and sliced down hard between Kitty's legs. The Cheshire Cat howled as his shaft dropped from between his legs to the floor.

But Rabbit wasn't done. As though nothing had just happened, Rabbit began to pace back and forth. "Your scent. Your touch. Your fingers. Your cock. Your cum. Your fucking spit. Your fucking breath! Your breath on my face, on my neck, my body, my dick . . . all fucking over me!" Rabbit slashed and slashed again at Kitty's back. Kitty screamed, but it was drowned out by Rabbit's roars.

Rabbit lurched forward and cut the ropes that held Kitty down. Rabbit grabbed him by the neck and threw him down hard to the dirt-strewn floor. Rabbit glanced around the room. He darted to the back of the cellar and grabbed something in his hand. As he came back into the light, I saw it was a big spade. Rabbit turned and dropped on top of Kitty, one leg on either side of his torso. He glared at Kitty and held up the spade in his hands. He rose on one knee. Gripping the spade tightly, he slammed it down over his strong thigh. The spade snapped in two, leaving a long stick, jagged and sharp. Rabbit threw the half with the metal to the side. I watched it skid past me as I sat on the table, entranced by the master at work.

He was magnificent.

"You took me when I was a kid," he hissed and held the stick in the air. Kitty stared, eyes wide, waiting for the inevitable. He tried to speak, but his cheeks flapped too much. Blood from his back leaked into the dirt beneath him. But my Rabbit wasn't done. His wide back was taut, his shirt and vest pulled tight. My heart beat so fast.

My Rabbit was so handsome.

My Rabbit was such a beautiful, pretty, pretty killer.

"You fucked me. Fucked me so hard I couldn't walk."

Rabbit's head tipped back. I couldn't see his face, but I imagined his eyes were closed. Imagined his red lips pulled over his teeth. Imagined his black hair fallen over his eyes.

I squirmed on the table.

My Rabbit was formidable.

Rabbit crouched down and ran the edge of the stick down Kitty's face. Kitty tried to scream, but he choked on his blood. Rabbit sliced down Kitty's chest and stomach with the sharp end of the stick.

Rabbit's head twitched. "Tick tock . . ." he muttered under his breath. "Tick tock." His hand tightened on the stick.

"Kill him," I whispered to myself. "Kill the bad Kitty." My hands gripped the edge of the table. "Kill him, Rabbit," I said quietly. "Make the pussycat pay for his sins."

My eyes were fixed on Rabbit as he straightened, silently. He reached into his vest pocket with his free hand and pulled out his pocket watch. He fisted it in his hand, and then placed it back in his vest for safekeeping.

I knew my Rabbit so well.

He was ready to play.

"I would stare at my watch," he informed the Cheshire Cat. "I would watch the hands ticking by, waiting for you to finish. Fighting the whiskey you poured down my throat so I couldn't fight back." He rolled his neck and the bones cracked. "But the hands just kept on turning as you kept on spreading your scent all over me. Thrusting your putrid cock into my ass, time and time again." Rabbit growled. I could see by the set of his shoulders that he was losing patience.

My pulse began to race.

"You tattooed your smell and touch all over me. Your grunts were branded onto my mind." He shuddered. "When I close my eyes I feel you. I see you. I taste you. Salt and sweat and grime." Rabbit raised the stick into the air. I held my breath, waiting for what he would do next. "I would imagine you dead. I would imagine what I would do to you when I found you again. I have waited eleven long years for this moment." Kitty's eyes clashed with Rabbit's. "Tick tock." Rabbit slammed the stick down, sending the jagged, sharp edge straight into Kitty's torso. The Cheshire Cat meowed loudly, and then screamed as the wood drove through flesh and fat and flaccid muscles and bone, right into his vital organs.

My nostrils flared in excitement as bloodlust darted through my veins. "Get him, Rabbit!" I cheered from my place at the table. But I didn't move. Rabbit had ordered me not to move.

Kitty began spluttering, and I leaned to the side to watch as lots and lots of blood spilled from his wounds. It was bright red, contrasting and then mixing with the brown dirt beneath him.

Rabbit didn't move. He stood above him, watching. My Rabbit watched as Kitty tried to beg for help, as he bled from his back, his face, his chopped-off shaft and the stick in his torso.

But it wasn't enough. The naughty Kitty needed more.

"More," I called quietly. I wasn't sure if Rabbit heard me, so I shouted, "More, Rabbit. More!"

Rabbit stayed as still as a statue. Suddenly he turned his head my way. I froze as our gazes clashed . . . then a slow grin pulled on his lips. A flutter batted in my chest, and my corset suddenly felt too tight under his watchful eye.

Rabbit bowed and placed a hand on his chest. "As my lady

wishes." I squeezed my thighs together as Rabbit faced Kitty again. I stilled. His hands clenched and unclenched into fists. I wondered why . . . but I didn't have to wait too long to find out. Rabbit bent down and gripped one of Kitty's arms. The Cheshire Cat uttered a low pained sound, but Rabbit didn't care. Rabbit shuddered as he held Kitty's arm. He lifted it into the air, then snapped the bone in two. The Cheshire Cat screamed. He screamed so loudly that it echoed off the walls. I clapped as Rabbit moved to his other arm and did exactly the same.

Rabbit jumped up and moved to the back of the cellar, where he'd found the spade. He returned a second later holding a paintbrush. He dipped the brush into the pooling blood and began to draw a circle around Kitty. Kitty's eyes were closed now, his face losing its color.

The naughty Kitty was dying.

Rabbit dipped and dipped and dipped his brush again and again into the blood. He painted a big pocket watch on the floor. Roman numerals, like the ones I'd drawn on my face, surrounded Kitty. The stick in his torso became the center of the watch. Rabbit stood, his hands and arms coated in Kitty's blood. He walked back to Kitty and took hold of one of his arms. "Dolly," he said without looking my way. "My cane, please."

I grabbed the cane at my side and jumped off the table, rushing to where he stood. "Yuck!" I shook my head in disgust when my pretty black boots stood in Kitty's gooey blood.

I handed Rabbit the cane, and obeyed the silent flick of his head that told me to go back to the table. Rabbit unsheathed the blade and struck down. I gasped as one of Kitty's arms came free from his body. Rabbit did the same to the other, then put his cane back together and tossed it aside. He stared down at Kitty, whose eyes had long since stopped blinking. At Kitty, whose lungs had stopped breathing.

At the Cheshire Cat, whose heart had stopped beating.

Rabbit took the severed arms and placed them on the opposite sides to where they belonged. He placed them at the numbers, the clock reading a time. I didn't know what; I was never taught to read the time.

When Rabbit stepped back from Kitty, from the watch he had created on the cellar's dirt floor, he was drenched in Kitty's blood. Only his face was showing any clean skin. Even then it was splattered with bloody drops, on his cheeks, forehead and chin.

"Tick tock." Rabbit stared down at his handiwork. His fists were clenched at his sides again. "Tick tock." His body started shaking, and he dove for the discarded paintbrush. My heart was in my mouth, a lump in my throat, as I watched him screaming "Tick tock" as he painted something at the base of the clock.

I didn't know what to do.

He shook his head. "No," he whispered, his voice cracking. His hand ran up his opposite arm, over the blood that had coated him. "No!" He clawed at his skin. At all the skin that was bare. That had been splattered with blood. "Get off me! Get the fuck off me! I can't have you on me!"

Rabbit backed away from the Cheshire Cat. He ripped the buttons off his vest. He yanked it off him and threw it to the ground. His shirt was next, uncovering his tattooed chest and rock-like stomach beneath. But the blood had soaked through.

An agonized cry ripped from his throat. "Can't have his

scent. Can't have his blood. Can't have his cum. Can't have him on me. Get off me. Get the fuck off me!"

I rushed forward. I had no plan in my mind as I crossed the dirt floor in a manic rush to save him. To save my Rabbit, just like he had saved me.

I didn't think as I stood in his path and slammed my hands on his cheeks. I didn't think as I stood on my tiptoes and stared him in the eyes. And I didn't think as I leaned forward and captured his mouth with my own.

I froze, my lips sealed on his, as I ate his cries and swallowed his pain. Rabbit was soft under my lips. His skin was hot. Rabbit groaned. His lips moved, as if they were fighting my touch. But then they gave in. He made a tortured noise in the back of his throat and gave himself to my mouth. Gave himself to *my* touch.

My heart seemed to swell in my chest as his mouth began to work against mine. Images from the back of my mind flashed through me. Me, as a child in my bedroom. Rabbit on the floor, hurting, crying . . . against my bedroom wall.

And I was kissing him. I kissed him to take away his pain. My eyes flew open in confusion at the vision. I didn't know when it was from. I didn't know if it was real. But before I could think any more about it, Rabbit snarled, "Dolly," against my mouth and pushed me backward. My hands slipped from his cheeks and ran down the muscles on his chest as his lips devoured my mouth.

"Rabbit," I whispered, and my eyes collided with his. His pupils were dilated and wide.

"His smell," he said as his arms caged me against the wall. "His fucking smell . . . his breath. It's all over me. It's fucking all over me!" He pushed a hand through his hair and down through the blood on his neck. "I need it gone. I need to get it off me. Need his smell and breath to get the fuck off my body and my head."

More tears fled from my eyes. I ran my hands down his chest. "Dolly," he growled. He bared his teeth, and his wild eyes slammed on mine. "Get the fuck off me. Get the motherfuck off me!" But I didn't. I tipped my chin and stared him down. I worked my hands faster. Running *my* scent, breathing *my* breath, over his skin.

"Mine," I spat as my hands moved to his hips. As my hands dipped lower and brushed over his crotch. "My smell," I said, tearing at the button on his pants. Rabbit moved closer to me, his left hand dropping to my throat. His sharp-tipped thimble ran over my skin as his breath floated over my ear. His teeth scraped against my shoulder. I slammed my hand on the back of his head and pulled him closer. "My breath on your neck."

I parted his pants and pushed them to the floor. Rabbit snapped his head back and pressed his forehead against mine.

I reached forward, gripped his shaft in my hand and placed my mouth at his ear. "My cock," I said. Rabbit smacked his fist against the wall above me and burrowed his face into my neck. "Rub my scent all over you." He thrust against my hand, his cock swollen and hard. "Take my breath. Take my touch." I bit my lip and said, "Take my pussy."

Rabbit snapped. On a low growl, he reached down and yanked up my skirt. His searching hands found my lace knickers, sodden from watching the beauty of his kill. He rubbed his cheek and his lips all over my neck, my face, the tops of my breasts, as he pushed the panties down and dropped them to the floor. His fingers ran along my folds, and I tipped my head back against the wall. "Rabbit," I moaned as I ran my hands through his black hair and gripped the strands.

I smiled when his breath hitched against my skin. "You're touching me." He groaned loudly and thrust his crotch against me. "You're taking away his smell and breath."

Rabbit reared back his head, and his eyes clashed with mine. He froze. I froze. Kitty's blood was smeared across his face. When his eyes flared, I knew that the blood was now on my face too. Then he was on me. He reached forward and split apart the laces of my corset. My breasts spilled out, and he let out a roar and wrapped his strong arms around my thighs. With a strength only my Rabbit could possess, he lifted me off the floor and pulled my legs around his waist. I cried out as he pushed the skirt of my dress away and put himself at my entrance. He looked me in the face, and his jaw clenched. I shook my head when I heard Ellis's voice inside my mind. *They would tie me down. They would push into me when I didn't want to be pushed into. Between my legs would hurt. I can't stop feeling them between my thighs . . .*

"Be gone," I whispered and clenched my eyes shut. I didn't like hearing Ellis's voice in my head. I wanted to take away the bad men's touch for her. I wanted Rabbit to take away the bad men between my thighs. "Your smell," I said and felt Rabbit still. "Your breath, Rabbit. Give me your touch . . . take them from my skin . . . Ellis's," I corrected. "Take them from Ellis's body."

"Dolly." Rabbit pushed inside me. I screamed out, clawing at Rabbit's bare back as he filled me with his erect shaft. He pounded the wall with one hand and squeezed the flesh of my thigh with his other. "Dolly . . ." he shouted again as he thrust all the way inside.

I screamed. I screamed as I shut my eyes and fought away the touch of that man . . . the man who would always take Ellis. The man who would always hurt her. The one who would always say—

"Fuck me," I commanded, taking back that bad man's demand as my own. "Fuck me, Rabbit. Take away their scents." I licked along the side of his neck. "Take back the power."

Rabbit pressed his chest against me with a pained roar. He pressed his skin against my skin as his cock moved inside me. He rubbed his cheek against my cheek, his lips against my lips. He breathed me in as I breathed him in, and then he began to thrust. He snapped his hips back and forth and filled me with his shaft. Ellis's bad man's shaft being replaced.

My nails dug into his back. "Rabbit," I murmured as the flutters of bliss that took over my body whenever I touched between my legs began to accost my arms and legs.

"Dolly," Rabbit said into my neck. "My Dolly . . . mine. Her smell. Her taste. Her breath. Her pussy." He increased his speed. Increased his speed so much that my eyes rolled back into my head as I broke apart, my limbs so light I felt like I was floating.

Rabbit growled long and deep and rough, then he spilled inside me, filling me with himself. All Rabbit. My Rabbit. My Rabbit; his Dolly.

Rabbit held me tightly, sandwiched against his body and the wall. I clung to his slick skin, a smile pulling on my lips. He pulled back his head and looked right into my eyes. "My cum," he said in a whisper. Shivers ran down my spine as he reached between us and pulled his shaft from within me. I moaned at the loss. His fingers ran along the space he'd just occupied. "Your cum."

"Rabbit," I said softly and shuffled my legs until my unsteady feet hit the floor. As slowly as possible, I ran my hands up his blood-and-sweat-slicked chest. "I'm touching you."

Rabbit exhaled a long, pained breath. "I'm touching you, little Dolly," he said, reaching out and cupping my breasts.

Tears welled up in my eyes. Touching me. My Rabbit was finally touching me. I had waited a very long time for this, trapped in the room of doors, too big to enter Wonderland, to be with him. To follow his lead.

"We need to go," Rabbit said, but he never stopped running his hands over my flesh. I couldn't keep my hands off him either. He placed a kiss in the center of my palm. When he pulled back, he said firmly, "We must go." He raised his eyebrow. "We have more kills to make. More bad men to destroy."

Heat swirled in my stomach and darted to the apex of my thighs. "Yes." I slid my hand up to his pocket and pulled out the pack of cards he kept there. "Ah-ha!" I called when I found the pencil-drawn face of the Cheshire Cat.

I stepped back from Rabbit. I reached into the pocket of my dress with my free hand, sliding the Cheshire Cat's card across Rabbit's cheeks as he watched me with transfixed eyes. Uncapping my lipstick with my teeth, I walked over to the kitty on the floor and stepped into the mess of blood.

I wiped away the blood from Kitty's forehead and positioned

my lipstick against his graying skin. Tongue at the side of my mouth in concentration, I wrote "SICK FUX" right on his face.

"Bad, bad pussycat," I chided. Admiring the smile Rabbit had carved on Kitty's face, I slid the card between his teeth. "The Four of Hearts." I straightened to see Rabbit watching me. He had gathered his clothes, but I knew his eyes had been on me the entire time.

They always were.

Just like I needed.

I turned to face him. "I liked touching you, Rabbit."

His eyes grazed down my now bloodstained body, then crept back up to my eyes. "I liked touching you too, Dolly darlin'."

I smiled and walked toward him. I ran my hand down his arm until my fingers entwined with his. I stared at our joined hands, as did he.

"I think we should always touch, Rabbit."

"Yeah," he agreed, his voice broken and graveled.

"This way neither of us will get lost in Wonderland."

Slowly, he brought our joined hands to his lips, kissed my fingers, and said, "As my lady commands."

A laugh bubbled up my throat and sailed into the stale air of the cellar. He released my hand and tied up the ribbons on my corset. When they were taut, he took hold of my chin and brought his mouth to mine for a kiss. He winced as our lips joined, but then he relaxed.

He broke away and tapped the roman numerals still painted on my face. "Time to go. We don't want to be late."

CHAPTER 11

Dolly

"POLICE REPORTS CLAIM that this is the second of two apparently linked murders. Sources close to the police tell us that detectives refer to the killer or killers as the 'Sick Fux'. It seems to be the killer's signature, found written in pink lipstick at the scenes. Both victims are Caucasian men in their fifties. Another murder, of an elderly female in Dallas, and the abduction of a young woman, also from Dallas, may also be linked. At this time there are no leads on the identity of the killer. Police ask the public to be vigilant and immediately report any unusual activity in their area. More after this break."

I squealed at the television and bounced up and down on the couch. "Rabbit!" I called. Rabbit pounded from the bathroom. He had a towel wrapped around his waist, his skin still glistening wet from the shower. My eyes traveled down his skin. I had knowledge of it now, how it felt and how it tasted.

He walked over and stood behind the couch, and his hand found its way to the nape of my neck, holding me in place. Ever since we had left the Cheshire Cat's home, he found a way to touch me whenever he could. And I found a way to touch him too.

He stroked the nape of my neck as the woman on the TV began to speak again.

"Besides the killer's name, sources tell us that hand-drawn playing cards have been left with each body. The first victim, in Dallas, was the Queen of Hearts; the second, in Amarillo, the Three of Hearts; and the latest killing, the Four of Hearts. We will bring you more as the story develops."

"See, Rabbit?" I looked up at Rabbit, whose eyes were glued to the TV. He nodded but said nothing. He just kept stroking the nape of my neck.

Rabbit had called the police after our last kill. He wanted the police of Wonderland to know that the Cheshire Cat, our Four of Hearts, was dead.

"They know us, Rabbit!" I yelled in excitement. "They know our name!"

Rabbit straightened, took the remote from my hand and turned off the TV. I pouted. "I was watching that!"

"You need to shower." Rabbit looked down at my dress, and his lip curled in disgust. I was still in the clothes from Kitty's death. I still had his blood on my skin.

"Okay." I jumped up, swaying my hips as I walked. I knew

my Rabbit would be watching. I heard him growl low in his throat as I entered the bathroom.

I showered quickly, the blood running to the shower tray, mixed with the makeup that had survived the kill and being taken by Rabbit. When I stepped out of the shower, I wrapped myself in a towel and combed my long blond hair. My skin was fresh and clean. I slipped a nightgown over my head and stepped out of the bathroom. Rabbit was sitting on the bed, wearing a pair of sleep pants. He held my knife in his hand . . . and there were cuts all over his chest, blood dripping down his fresh clean skin, marring it once again.

"Rabbit." I lurched forward. He lifted his head. His mouth was closed and his lips were tight. He continued slicing into his chest as he stared at me. "Rabbit . . . what are you doing?" I asked as his blood spilled onto the white linen of the bed.

Rabbit said nothing. Instead he picked up a pen from the table next to the bed. He snapped the pen in his hands, and as the ink spilled from inside, he spread it over his cuts, rubbing the ink into his wounds. I rushed forward and jumped onto the bed. "Rabbit! What are you doing?" My heart beat wildly with worry.

Rabbit hissed as the ink sank in. Using the towel that had been around his waist, he wiped the blood and ink from his tattooed chest. As he pulled the towel away, my mouth dropped open and I gasped. "Rabbit . . ." I whispered. "Sick Fux." My hand reached out and hovered over the words carved on his chest —words, for once, I recognized easily. Drops of blood sprouted from the letters. Without thinking, I ran my fingers through the warm liquid.

Rabbit stopped breathing as I did so. His pupils grew wide as his eyes tracked my fingertips. I froze, fingers in midair, as his nostrils flared and his breathing began to quicken. I glanced down and saw him hardening under his sleep pants.

He liked his blood on my fingers.

Holding his attention, I rubbed my fingertips together, feeling his blood soak them. He groaned. As my fingers rubbed together, more blood escaped, ran down the side of my hand and onto my wrist. I brought my hand to my mouth and licked at the falling drop.

Rabbit hissed. My eyes snapped to his. Rabbit's neck was taut. His hands were fisted on the comforter. Breathless, I took another drop and circled it around my lips. His chest rose and fell. Leaning forward, I stayed just an inch from his face and licked my lips. My eyes fluttered closed. I now held a part of Rabbit in my mouth. I was taking his blood, his life force, into my soul.

I felt a sharp object run down my face and a hand wrap around my neck. Smiling, my eyes rolled open. Rabbit was before me, his hard chest smeared with blood and ink. He tilted his head as his eyes locked on to my neck . . . on to my pounding pulse.

"Little Dolly," he said, voice so low I felt it all the way down to my bones. The tip of his thimble ran over my vein and traced across the front of my throat. My breasts ached as the cold metal touched my my skin. "So easily split open," he whispered. His tongue licked around the shell of my ear.

"I can see your veins, little Dolly. I can see how blue they are against your pale skin. I can see your pulse pounding, throbbing in your neck." He breathed in the scent from my freshly washed skin. "It's calling my name." He smiled against my neck. "It's telling me to taste you as you have tasted me."

"Yes," I whispered and arched into his body. I felt the heat from his skin as soon as we made contact.

His thimble dug into the side of my throat. His eyes narrowed as he studied my skin. "You're tempting me, darlin'," he drawled, as his nose gently followed the path of the thimble. His tongue lapped at my skin. I moaned at the feel of having him so close . . . wanting my blood.

Blood he wanted to taste.

"I have always wanted your blood in my mouth, running down my throat." He pressed a soft kiss on my pulse. I shivered. "You held me mesmerized from the first moment I met you. Not by your smile, not by your eyes, but by your throat and your veins. By your pulse and the paleness of your skin. My little Dolly. My painted Alice from Wonderland."

"Rabbit," I said hoarsely, my back arching as his other hand wrapped around my throat and began to squeeze.

"When I apply pressure like this, your veins bulge. They beg to be opened." He tightened his grip. "Your blood sings to me. Begs for me to take you how I want. How I have always wanted to."

"Do it," I urged, tilting my head to offer him my neck.

"Mmm," Rabbit murmured. He released my neck from his grip and unfastened the buttons at the front of my nightgown. The humid air in the room stuck to my skin. I rubbed my lips together as my body was bared. As the material parted, he guided me down to the bed. He swung above me, his legs straddling my waist. His arms were braced on either side my head. As Rabbit's silver eyes roved over my body, I watched a stray droplet of blood run from the "X" carved into his chest. It rolled forward to the bottom of his neck. I lifted my chest and caught the drop in my mouth. Rabbit groaned above me, and using the hand on my throat, he slammed me back to the mattress. I locked on to his stare, moaning as his eyes moved from hungry to completely wild.

"Taste me." I pushed my breasts up to rub against his chest. "Taste me . . . make me completely yours. Own me." I looked him square in the eye. "Your Dolly. Own your Dolly." I smiled. "Rabbit and Dolly . . . forever."

Rabbit growled. He dragged the tip of his thimble carefully along my throat, over the vein. I held back my cry when the cold metal sliced gently into my flesh. Warm blood trickled down my neck. I glanced at Rabbit. He was watching my blood like it was the tastiest treat he ever did see.

"Dolly," he rasped and ran his hand gently through my hair. He gazed into my eyes. His hand ghosted down my cheek, making me breathless.

I wanted to give him my blood.

Dolly's lifeblood.

Rabbit's deepest need.

Rabbit's eyes got heavy. Then, as I felt a drop fall to my shoulder, Rabbit bent forward and ran the tip of his tongue over the escaping droplets. I moaned at the feeling of his hot tongue as it climbed up my shoulder, over the bottom of my neck, eventually hovering over the tiny cut he had made.

His tongue flicked back and forth over my vein. My legs moved restlessly on the bed as his hand wrapped around my throat and held me down. My eyes flickered open, only to collide into Rabbit's, watching me as he fed on my blood. Watching as I arched my body into his chest, breasts catching the blood from his newly cut tattoo.

I moaned as he sucked on my skin, crying out at the brief sting of pain it caused. My hands rakcd through his hair. Rabbit groaned. Then he pulled back, releasing me from his lips. I fixed my gaze on his mouth. His lips were bloodstained, bright red. And he smiled. I swept my finger along his mouth, and my own blood gathered on it. I held his attention captive as I brought the finger to my lips.

Rabbit's grip pulsed on my throat. My tongue flicked out and I tasted the blood. That was all it took to make Rabbit crash his mouth to mine and kiss me hard. His tongue plunged into my mouth, and I cried out at the shock of it. Rabbit was kissing me. He was kissing me back. He meant it. I felt his need for me through our joined mouths.

"Dolly," he whispered against my lips. His mouth moved along my cheek, rubbing my blood into my skin with his lips. And he was kissing me. Moving down my neck and over my opened skin, his thimble traced down my chest to my breasts. I felt a pinch as he pushed the tip into the nipple on my left breast. His hand slipped from my throat and cupped my breast as he squeezed the flesh, causing a fleck of blood to bud on the tip. Rabbit growled as he wrapped his lips around me. His tongue flicked over my nipple as he took more of my blood.

He moved to my other breast and did the same. He shifted to my torso and tracked prick after prick along my stomach and down across my hips. His mouth took from each small cut.

Lapping.

Licking.

Drinking me down.

He shifted his body between my legs and ran the tip of the thimble along the flesh of my inner thigh. My breath got trapped in my throat as I looked down at him. His bottom lip was caught between his teeth, his intense gaze focused on me. I whimpered as I felt his warm breath ghost over my core.

"Blood is the color of the heart," he said, his voice raspy and raw. His thimble moved closer and closer to the apex of my thighs. He looked down at the slow movement of the thimble as it drew white lines along my delicate skin, threatening to break through. He lowered his mouth to the very top of my right thigh, his cheek brushing along my folds. He nipped at the flesh with his teeth, then let go, licking the tender spot he had bitten. "Red, the color of blood." He moved across to my other thigh and bit me again, his tongue soothing the pain his teeth had caused. "Red means stop. Red means danger." He looked up at me, a stunning, sinister smile on his face. "It is the liquid that both delivers and takes life." Rabbit smudged the blood he had drawn and caressed it into my pale skin.

His breathing hitched as he watched my skin stain red. "It is the covenant one makes with the devil himself." He lifted his head, eyes locked on mine. "A covenant you are making with me." Rabbit's thimble climbed north. The sharp tip balanced on a precipice, forcing me to trust him.

I did. I would always trust my Rabbit.

"The devil will lie." He kissed my inner thigh. "He will cheat." He edged closer to my core, his mouth moving up and sideways until his cheek brushed the spot between my legs that made me fall apart. "And he will trick." He moved ever closer, and I shifted on the bed, needing him to take me. Needing him to relieve me of the pressure building at his touch. His eyes softened. "And he will kill, and travel miles to get to the one who holds his fucked-up black heart in her palm."

"Rabbit . . ." I whispered as tears filled my eyes.

"He'd kill anyone who hurt her, just to make her his. He would punish anyone who got in his way." His eyes flared with something so dark it seemed to blot out the dim light of the lamp. "He will awaken, through blood, what lies dormant in her soul. The darkness that had lurked hidden for years, sleepily waiting for the time to strike. To be born." I yelped as he pierced the skin on my upper thigh. I looked down and saw blood between my legs.

Rabbit flicked out his tongue. In one long swipe, he licked my core from the bottom to the top.

"Rabbit!" I screamed as his touch sent a wave of pleasure soaring through my bones.

My eyes closed, only for Rabbit to command, "Open!" My eyes snapped open. He licked his lips. "Watch. Watch me as I drink from you. As you split apart from my touch, with your blood staining my mouth."

I remained silent, need and incessant want stealing my voice. Rabbit's eyes darkened. "Answer me, little Dolly. Answer the devil who is taking your freedom with the pact of blood."

"Yes, Rabbit." My skin burned, waiting for him to bring me to the light that only my Rabbit could show me.

With a savage growl, his head plunged between my legs and

he licked me. He licked and licked, taking my blood into his mouth, down his throat. And I screamed. I screamed and cried out as he took from me.

I gripped his hair as tightly as I could. I moaned as his tongue moved faster, as he took and took from me. My skin flushed—the blood under my skin rushing faster than the blood that escaped through the pinholes and slices Rabbit had made.

"Take it . . ." I felt my cheeks blaze with heat, as the shivers that brought the pleasure zipped around every inch of my skin. "Take it," I ordered. Rabbit snarled, his mouth against my core, tongue sliding more and more deeply into me. With every slash of his sharp thimble, my pleasure built and built like a storm on a scorching day, ready to thrash the skies and bring the relief of thunder, lightning and rain.

Rabbit moved his thimble to the bud that broke me apart. He pushed the tip so slightly that it barely touched me, but it was enough to splinter my body in two. A scream ripped from my heart as I yanked on his hair and my eyes squeezed shut. Rabbit sucked and pulled at the new piercing, and I shook my head as the pleasure surged through me. It came and came like a rainstorm sweeping through dry lands. He licked and licked until I could take no more.

I pushed his head away. I fought for breath as my back hit the mattress and sweat dripped between my breasts. The beads of sweat mixed with a drop of blood and fell down my stomach. Rabbit lurched forward, as if in attack, and his mouth landed over the pink drop. I stilled, gasping as his eyes met mine and he swallowed.

And we didn't move. We stayed that way, frozen. Rabbit's

breathing was uneven as he stared at me, full from feasting on my blood.

I'd left my life in his hands.

Gave over to him the power of life or death.

He exhaled a long breath. "You gave me your blood." He blinked, as if he couldn't believe I had let him have me that way. My hand was shaking as I ran it down his face. My fingertip stroked across his spade tattoo, drawing a groan from Rabbit's mouth.

He waited, breath held, for me to speak. When I did, I said, "Now it's my turn." Rabbit's lips parted, and his eyes widened then hooded as my words sank in. A low rumble sounded in his chest, and he crawled up my body. His eyes never broke from mine. My heart slammed in my chest. Rabbit's face met mine, his lips, cheeks and chin covered in crimson. His teeth were coated with blood.

Rabbit's head tipped from side to side as he studied my face. I lifted my fingers to his chest and walked them along his raw tattoo. "Sick Fux," I whispered, reading the words aloud. Words I could read. Words I had drawn in pink on the Cheshire Cat's head.

Words now forever etched into Rabbit's flesh.

My fingers kept trekking north until they stopped on the beating pulse in his throat. My fingertip tapped on his pulse, in time with its beat. Rabbit's eyes darkened. "What you gonna do, little Dolly?"

Naughty Rabbit was taunting me, and my core throbbed at his tone. Narrowing my eyes, I reached out beside me to the side table. Without looking, my hand found the familiar ivory handle.

Rabbit's nostrils flared as I brought my blade to hover in the small space between us. I placed the tip over his heart. A grin pulled on my lips as I listened to its beat and sang, "Tick tock . . . tick tock . . . tick tock . . ."

Rabbit's eyes rolled back. Then I was moving the blade upwards. I scraped his skin, the tip dragging cold steel over the raw flesh of his new tattoo. Rabbit's eyes snapped open and told me without words that he wanted the pain.

My Rabbit loved the pain.

My blade stopped where my finger still hovered over his pulse. Rabbit's lip curled as he waited. When I ever-so-gently dug the tip of the knife into his skin, right into his clock tattoo, I watched as his blood pumped to the surface and trickled down his neck. I was mesmerized as it tiptoed over ink until it could hold on to Rabbit's skin no longer and dropped on to my breast. His shaft grew harder against my thigh. Knowing he was watching, I scooped up the drop on my finger and brought it to my mouth.

"Mmm," I murmured. Rabbit's cheeks were flushed, and his breathing was out of control. His hips began to thrust his shaft against my thigh in short, slow movements. Using my free hand to push my upper body off the bed, I rose until my face was a mere inch from Rabbit's.

"Delicious."

Rabbit wrapped his hand around the nape of my neck. Holding my head captive, and with a tight mouth and harsh eyes, he ordered, "Drink . . ." He forced my head to his neck. "Drink from me."

Smiling, victorious at getting the response I wanted, I inhaled his scent, then flicked out my tongue and tasted his blood. Rabbit groaned and pushed my mouth closer to his neck. I let him control me, fixing my lips over the cut and sucking.

I liked it when he controlled me.

Blood dripped onto my tongue and trickled down my throat. Rabbit's shaft rubbed against my leg, faster and faster, as I drank and drank. Then I stopped. I fought Rabbit's grip and tilted my head to the side.

I knew my Rabit liked it when I tried to resist.

In a heartbeat, his hot mouth had latched on to the slit on my throat, and he took from me as I took from him. I dropped my hand between us and under the waist of his pants. Without breaking away, I took hold of his shaft, Rabbit snarling at my touch as I pumped his length. I groaned and groaned as we took and took. In seconds, Rabbit snapped his head back and roared out his release. He spilled into my hand, and I stroked him until he pulled back his hips.

I drew my head back to find Rabbit watching me. Suddenly, he was off the bed and retrieving something from his bag. When he came back, he was holding a vial just like the one around my neck. I gasped and gripped the vial I never took off. The one that held the potion that made me small. The one labeled "Drink Me."

Rabbit kneeled on the bed and removed the cork from the vial. Without speaking, he brought the vial to my neck and filled it with my blood. My heart raced and my breasts ached at the thought that he wanted my blood near him at all times.

He pulled back and met my eyes. I lifted the black ribbon attached to the vial and secured it around his neck. "Rabbit," I whispered as he reached around my neck to untie the ribbon keeping my vial in place. He uncorked the cork and poured the blue liquid onto the floor. "Rabbit!" I called frantically. I reached out in panic, but Rabbit grabbed my hand and thrust the vial into it.

"You don't need that now, little Dolly. My blood is all you'll ever need."

I swallowed and searched his face. "Really?"

He nodded. "It'll make you tall if you need it. It'll make you small if you need it too." He leaned forward, mouth at my ear. "And it'll give you strength when you're weak."

My eyes widened. It was better than the blue drink? I snatched the vial to my chest, then pushed the glass to the dripping cut on his neck. Excitement grew inside me as the blood filled up the vial. When it was done, Rabbit took the glass bottle from me, secured the cork and tied the ribbon back around my neck. I reached up and felt the bottle—it was warm.

Rabbit took my blade from the mattress, and with one quick swipe, he slashed the knife across his palm. He made a fist, and blood dripped to the linen. "Hand," he said. Immediately, I held out mine. Rabbit stared at me. With an equally quick swipe, he sliced the steel across my palm. I hissed at the sharp, stinging pain.

Rabbit leaned forward and stroked my cheek with his bloodied hand. His lip hooked as though he would smile. Then he grabbed my hand. He slammed our palms together and brought them up high. My eyes locked on the sight, and I felt the warmth from his blood mixing with mine. Rabbit moved his head closer and ran his nose over my forehead. "A pact, signed in blood," he said and inhaled the mint shampoo scent from my freshly washed hair. "Your contract with me . . . telling me that you belong to me now. My little Dolly darlin', your blood merged with mine. Your blood running with mine, through my veins, bringing me your light." His nose ran down my cheek, and he smiled in victory. "And my blood now runs in yours. My darkness . . . my blackened soul polluting yours, bringing you over to my side. My Dolly . . . after all these years, mine. Succumbing to my will."

"Yes," I said dreamily, as I swayed, seduced by his words, by him being so close, skin on skin, sharing our blood.

I smiled and looked up at Rabbit looking down at me. "Always one." I pulled him down to the bed, facing him, our hands still joined.

My eyes wandered to the blood on my hands, and my stomach suddenly fell. I squeezed my eyes shut when images began assaulting my mind. I shook my head when I saw things I didn't want to see . . .

"Tie her down. Do it before she makes a fucking show and draws unwanted attention."

A hand hit my face and my head spun. The taste of blood sprouted in my mouth. I blinked and looked to my left, and then to the right; the same face stared at me from both sides. Two identical sets of hands held my wrists. Uncle Jeffrey and Uncle Samuel. My identical twin uncles were pinning me down. I tried to see what room I was in. I didn't recognize it. A door opened behind me, and I heard footsteps approach. But my head was foggy. My papa had given me a cup of tea. But the tea made me feel dizzy. It made my head all fuzzy and my eyes struggle to focus.

"Keep hold of her." I looked down at my feet and saw my papa standing there.

Then I saw him. *Uncle John moved beside me, and I shuddered. I didn't like Uncle John. He came for me every night. I didn't like what he did to me in the room opposite where Heathan used to be taken.*

Before he left me.

My eyes filled with tears as I thought of his face. As I thought of his eyes. As I thought of—

"I thought you said she was on a shot or some shit?" Uncle John said to my papa. His hand came out and stroked my head. I hated his touch. I wanted to pull away. I tried, but Uncle John's face snapped my way and his fingers wrapped in my hair. He yanked my head back to face him. He bent down. He made it so our noses were touching. Then he kissed me.

His free hand slid down to my stomach. I felt his hand on my bare skin. I was naked. My heart raced as I looked at my twin uncles pinning me down. At my papa talking to a man in white at the side of the room . . . at Uncle John petting my stomach.

"Too bad you can't keep this, Ellis," he said and smoothed his hand over my hair. "She would have been just as pretty as you. Blond hair. Blue eyes . . . pale skin." He closed his eyes and smiled. My stomach rolled. "And she would have been mine. Mine to have. Mine to raise. My pretty half, Ellis."

I didn't know what he was talking about. I tried to think through the fog in my mind, but I couldn't. "Don't worry," Uncle John soothed as he kissed my cheek. "The doctor is here to make it all go away." He shushed me when I tried to open my mouth to speak. Panic filled me. There was a doctor? Why was there a doctor here?

Uncle John shook his head and pressed a finger over my lips. "You'll only be asleep for a while. And when you wake up, things like this won't be able to happen anymore." He kissed my lips, and I tried to fight the grip of my twin uncles, but Uncle Jeffrey struck my face again, and the back of my head smacked against the table I was on.

I cried out as they tightened their grips on my wrists. "Think of all the fun we can have afterwards," Uncle John said. My papa moved beside him and pulled him away by the arm.

A woman came from behind me, and I looked up into her eyes. They were brown. She had a green mask over her mouth and rubbery gloves on her hands.

"Help me," I managed to whisper, ignoring the tears that fell down my lips. My mouth was dry. My tongue felt too fat in my mouth. But she looked away, took something in her hand. Then I saw a mask coming toward me. She pushed it over my mouth . . . the room began to spin as I breathed . . . then everything went black.

When I woke I was in my room. I tried to move, my body trying to get out of my bed. Confusion filled my head. But when I tried to move, a slicing pain from my stomach made it impossible.

"Ellis," a soft voice called from the doorway. My bottom lip shook at the amount of pain I felt. Mrs. Jenkins came toward me with a cup of tea in her hand. She sat next to me on the bed. "Shh, sweetie," she soothed. I cried harder.

"Mrs. Jenkins . . ." I rasped, my voice dry and my throat sore. "What happened? My stomach hurts. Everything hurts."

Mrs. Jenkins brought the tea to my mouth. "It's Earl Grey, sweetie. Your favorite." I didn't want the tea. I always wanted tea, but not right now. Mrs. Jenkins didn't give me a choice. She tipped the liquid into my mouth. She made me drink it all. My throat felt better as the hot tea spilled down it.

When all the tea had been drunk, my eyes began to close. Mrs. Jenkins's hand pressed against my forehead. I was nearly asleep, but I still heard Mrs. Jenkins place the china cup on my nightstand. Still felt her move my comforter down my body and touch something around the place my stomach pained me most.

Still heard her say, "A scar is a small price to pay for the comfort that you'll never have babies, Ellis. That baby was better off not entering this world. It was the best thing for you both . . . best you can never get pregnant again . . ."

I gasped and ripped my hand from Rabbit's. "I can't breathe," I cried. My hand flew to my chest and rubbed. But it didn't help. So I clawed. I clawed at the place over my heart. It was beating too fast.

"Dolly." Rabbit sat up next to me. But I needed to be off the bed. I jumped off the mattress, my nightgown hanging open. But I still couldn't breathe.

" . . .you'll never have babies, Ellis . . ."

Scar . . . scar . . . scar . . .

I closed my eyes and propped my hand against the wall. I smacked at the side of my skull with my hand when I couldn't get the nasty thoughts from my head. When I couldn't get the voices out of my ears.

Ellis . . . Ellis . . . Ellis . . .Why were they calling me Ellis?

Sweat ran down my chest. I pushed off the wall and walked in circles, but the voices just kept getting louder. Uncle John . . . Uncle John . . . Uncle John's voice . . .

Who was Uncle John?

"No." I opened my eyes. I shook my head, backing against the wall. My nails moved down to my wrists and to my arms, clawing at the flesh. I clawed and clawed until the blood began to pour. I was covered in blood. So much blood. Mine. Rabbit's . . . *a baby's . . .*

"No!" I screamed and slumped to the ground. I threw my hands on the side of my head and began to rock. Why were they calling me Ellis? Ellis had a scar.

She had a scar!

I ripped my hands from my head and looked down. I wiped away the blood on my stomach with the material of my night-gown, soaking the white material with red. But then I saw it. I would never have noticed it if I wasn't looking. It was almost not there. But I saw it.

I had the scar . . .

But Ellis . . . Ellis had the scar. Not Dolly. Dolly didn't have the scar. The bad men had hurt Ellis. Her twin uncles and Uncle John . . . her Uncle John, the nastiest man of all.

Ellis . . . her name started to sound different in my head. Ellis . . . I closed my eyes as I heard different voices call that name in my head. *"Ellis . . . baby girl . . ."* her papa had said. *"Ellis . . ."* Mrs. Jenkins. *"Ellis . . ."* A boy, a boy wearing a hat. Then, *"Ellis . . . that's a stupid name . . ."* Heathan.

Heathan?

My eyes snapped open. Heathan sounded like my Rabbit.

Rabbit . . . Rabbit . . . my Rabbit . . .

Two hands grabbed my arms, and I looked up. "Ellis . . ." I blurted, and Rabbit's face paled. "Ellis can't have babies." A sob tore from my throat. "She had one, in her belly. But they took it out. They took it all out. No more place to keep a baby. No more blood every month. They took it all." I choked on a cry. "They gave Ellis a scar . . ."

Rabbit didn't say anything, but his hands shook on my arms. His face turned from white to bright red.

My hands raked across the scar on my stomach. "I have a scar, Rabbit. It's there! I see it. Can you see it?" My head shook and too many images sprang into my head. A hallway . . . an office . . . a bed . . . Uncle John . . . Uncle John . . . Uncle John . . . Papa . . .

I clawed at my scar, but Rabbit threw my hand out of my way and looked down. A growl ripped from his throat, so venomous that I flinched away. "Rabbit, why do I have a scar? Why were people calling me Ellis? Why do I have a scar like Ellis . . .?"

Rabbit went dead still and locked his eyes on mine. His jaw was still tight, but he released one of my arms and lifted his thimble into the air. "I gave it to you," he said. I didn't like the sound of his voice. It was frightening. He hissed, eyes closing for a second. "I gave it to you years ago." He tilted his head to the side, searching my eyes. "Don't you remember?"

I shook my head and uncurled my body some from its place against the wall. "When? Why?"

"When we were little." He swallowed, and a drop of blood fell from the cut on his neck. "We were having afternoon tea with the Mad Hatter, the Dormouse and the March Hare. I accidently dropped the teapot on the ground. You tripped and fell. A piece of the teapot cut your stomach."

I racked my brain to remember. But I couldn't. I couldn't remember the faces of the Dormouse, the March Hare or the Mad Hatter. But I did like my afternoon tea . . .

"I don't remember," I whispered and felt my bottom lip quiver.

Rabbit's angry silver eyes softened, and the hand holding the thimble moved to my cheek. His hand was shaking. I didn't know why. "You hit your head," Rabbit whispered back. He tapped my temple. "You lost some of your memory." My heart felt sad at how sad he sounded.

I reached up and covered his hand on my cheek. "Don't feel bad, Rabbit. I don't remember, but I know you didn't mean to hurt me." I smiled, but it felt strange on my face because my heart still wanted me to cry. I fought against it. I was a champion, after all. "I am not mad at you, Rabbit. I could never be mad at my Rabbit."

His eyes closed, and he inhaled quickly through his nose. When his eyes opened again, I sighed. "Rabbit . . . did all of that happen to Ellis? Did she have her baby taken from her? Did they take away the place in her tummy where babies live? Did they do that to her, even though she cried?"

Rabbit made a strange choking sound in his throat. But he nodded. His lips shook, still stained with blood. "I think it did," he said, his voice catching. He cleared his throat. "Ellis was hurt real bad."

I nodded and looked down. Tears fell from my eyes and splashed on the floor. "My Ellis . . . I am sad for my friend Ellis."

"I am too." He stroked his thumb across my neck. "Do you want some tea, darlin'? Will tea help you feel better?"

I smiled, even though it hurt my lips. "Yes please, Rabbit. Tea always helps."

He stared at me without words, then my heart flipped in my chest when he leaned forward and kissed my forehead. His lips were soft, and they stayed, branding my skin for so many seconds that my cold skin began to warm. My hurting heart began to feel warm.

Rabbit never kissed me so gently . . . It confused me so.

But I loved it. I loved his softened eyes. They were like a bright sunbreak on a gloomy day. They made my heart flutter in my chest.

I watched him cross the motel room to the tea station I had set up as soon as we arrived. I watched him boil the kettle and place the Earl Grey teabag in the teapot and set out two china cups, one for me and one for him.

As the teabag steeped, he turned to me, and his eyes met mine. He paused only for a moment, then bent down and lifted me up in his arms. My head rested against his shoulder as he placed me on the bed and pulled the comforter over my legs.

He retrieved the tea and brought it to the bed. I smiled when I looked at the cake dish. "Strawberry tarts," I proclaimed tiredly. My voice was husky from crying . . . from my sadness for my sweet friend Ellis.

"Your favorite." He poured the tea. My legs were cold, but as soon as I tasted the sweet milky tea on my tongue, I felt warm. I closed my eyes, and I saw a blond woman in my mind. I saw her sitting on a chair in a pretty room, drinking tea with a blanket over her legs. She had dark circles under her eyes, but a little girl sat on her knee. Even though the woman was sick, she still smiled at the girl on her lap. The little girl was drinking tea too. I smiled at how happy the little girl was. I smiled at how nice the woman was.

She made me feel warm all over. She was so kind.

Then the little girl turned her head my way. Her blue eyes met mine. My heart skipped a beat. Tears filled my eyes, and my throat closed up. Because the little girl was . . .

"Ellis?"

Ellis smiled as I whispered her name. I had found Ellis. She was so young. No older than ten. Long blond hair. Big blue eyes . . . just a little girl.

Finding the strength to move, I waved, and Ellis waved back. She slipped off her mummy's lap and came toward me. A lump clogged my throat. I had finally seen her. Finally knew what she looked like. After all these years . . .

I thought she looked a little like me.

"Dolly," she said and smiled. She reached down and touched my hand.

I smiled at the tea she had just left behind. "You like afternoon tea too?"

She laughed, and I couldn't help but laugh too. "Yes, so very much!"

"Only Earl Grey," we said in unison. We laughed even harder.

Her smile fell. "Thank you for destroying the bad men." She

brought her hand to her stomach. Right where I knew the scar was. I forced myself to hold back my tears.

"I haven't finished." I reached for her hand. It was soft as I held it in mine. Her nails were painted bright pink too.

"No," she said and worried her lip. She glanced back to her mummy. "My mummy is not here anymore." I looked up and watched as her mummy disappeared before my eyes. "The tea," she said. I watched as the walls of the bright, pretty room began to run with black paint. "I think the tea was making her sick." Ellis turned to me. The blue dress she wore also began to turn black. "The men you will face next hurt me badly, Dolly."

I nodded, now knowing how they did.

"You must make them pay." Her hand slipped from mine as something unseen dragged her backward. A dark forest sprang up around us, and she faded away. "Only then can I be free," she said, before she was gone . . . her sweet little voice was gone too.

I blinked and found Rabbit searching my face, his hand under my chin. "Dolly . . . Dolly, are you okay?"

I nodded and gripped the handle of my teacup. "I . . . I was talking to Ellis, Rabbit."

Swallowing, he asked, "What did she say?"

"That I have to defeat the rest of the bad men." My eyelids fell. "Because they hurt her the most. Only then can she be free."

He nodded, then gently pulled me back to lie down, placing my teacup on the side table. His hand was wrapped around mine, and he watched me as I began to fall asleep. I heard the sound of card hitting card and opened my eyes. Rabbit was holding three cards in his hand. The three cards we had left. I sat up when I caught sight of one in particular.

"The men who held Ellis down," I said, seeing the drawings of the twin uncles. "The ones who hit her face when they hurt her belly."

"Tweedledum and Tweedledee," Rabbit announced, his voice returned to its dark tone. He laid the card between us, and my lip curled, anger building inside of me at how they had made my friend Ellis feel. "They're yours." He placed the card on my lap.

"Destroy them."

"What?" I exclaimed. Rabbit's eyebrows pulled down.

"I didn't say anything," he said.

"Destroy them, Dolly. For me . . . for us . . ." the voice said again.

I breathed deeply when I realized who had spoken. My head tipped to the side as she spoke. I nodded in understanding. Looking at Rabbit, I explained, "It was Ellis." I tapped my head. "She spoke to me in here."

"Wh-what did she say?"

I stared down at the card. At the drawing of Tweedledum and Tweedledee. And I smiled, tasting the remaining blood in my mouth. "To destroy them. To destroy them both . . . painfully."

Rabbit's nostrils flared, and he put the card on the side table. Gripping my hand, he faced me. "Then you shall destroy them, little Dolly. You shall have them all to yourself."

I closed my eyes and sighed in relief.

Rabbit kissed my hand, and I drifted to sleep. *I shall break them apart piece by piece, Ellis. I promise. Just hold on. You'll be free soon . . . please.*

Just hold on.

CHAPTER 12

TWEEDLEDEE & TWEEDLEDUM

Rabbit

SUNSET HAD DRAWN in as we arrived in El Paso. Dolly was asleep, her head resting on her arm on the Mustang's door. My hands tightened on the wheel as her confession about Ellis, about the scar I hadn't even seen on her lower stomach, played in my mind. My stupid fucking eyes had been blind, enraptured by bloodlust, enraptured by at last having my little Dolly in the way I had always wanted her. I hadn't noticed the fucking faint white scar that marred her perfect skin. Hadn't picked up the evidence of what those dicks had done to her. It had been so much worse than what they'd inflicted on me.

Those cunts had knocked her up as a kid.

Those cunts had aborted a baby . . .

Those cunts had ripped Dolly's womb from her immature body. They had made it so she could never have kids again. All so they could keep fucking her, against her will, coming inside her as much as they wanted without ever having the worry of impregnating her. Stealing from her every piece of her rational mind, until it had shattered and she retreated into her shell. The vegetative state in which I had found her, sealed off from the real world.

Their crimes, of which I was finally aware, loosed the volcano of rage they had planted inside me; it erupted into a molten sea of lava intent on destroying everything in its path. The people who tied her down on the operating table. The twin "uncles" we were en route to see. Add to the list the pricks most responsible for abusing her body and her mind: Uncle John and her papa. Her papa, the very person who was meant to protect her. Instead, he had pimped her pussy to his "colleagues" on a silver platter, poisoned teacup in hand.

El Paso's country roads gave way to town lights as I drove toward our destination. A property on the farthest edge of town, a nice little hacienda. Secluded. Private . . . perfect for a spot of light massacre by Wonderland's finest.

"Fancy fucking dinner parties," Hyde had said as he came up beside me in Chapel's secret Louisiana home. Hyde was looking at the photographs in my hand, the usual snarl on his lips. Henry was currently "asleep."

Chapel walked to where I stood reading the research on Uncles Jeffrey and Samuel. He whistled as he looked at one of the photographs the PI had taken at one such party. Strings of lights hung across the outside terrace. A number of people sat around a long table. All interesting characters in themselves; more kid abusers, no doubt. A couple of rapists, and some stupid whores who got turned on by the twisted tastes of the abusers— pieces of pussy that got high watching their men force themselves on others . . . age not a problem. "Oh, what fun one could have wreaking havoc on that little crowd." Chapel sat beside me and ran his hand over the photo of the women sitting beside the built middle-aged men. "Paid whores?" he inquired, firelight in his eyes.

I checked the PI's information. "Yes. But ones that like the darker side of fucking."

Chapel sucked in a hungry breath. "Oh . . . what possibilities they could offer . . . what relations we all could have," he murmured, his pupils dilated.

"Make them all fucking hurt," Hyde growled. "Tear out their fucking throats." He left the table and made his way back to his rooms. No doubt Henry would be back soon.

Chapel stood too and brushed the long blond hair from his face. "Yes, young Dapper Dan. I can only imagine the beautiful, poetic deaths our local blood enthusiast will conjure up." He pointed his finger in the air and smiled. "You must write down these adventures for the sake of your friends." He placed his hand over his chest. "I do quite enjoy a good murderous novel, my fine young sir. One such as this violent tea party would be quite the spectacle."

He walked away, leaving me to stare at the photographs, imagining Dolly's face lighting up at the fare of cakes and tea.

Imagining her bathing in their blood, a lightly toasted buttered crumpet in her delicate little hand . . .

Dolly stirred, pulling me from my reverie. I glanced over just as her eyes opened. Her makeup was perfectly in place. I got hard just seeing the clock drawn around her left eye. But not as hard as I got seeing the vial of my blood dangle from the ribbon around her neck. The label "Drink Me" had never been so apt.

Dolly gasped and sat up. I turned my head to see what she was looking at. Bright lights lay ahead. Parked limousines lined a road that led to a large building, from which music was blaring. Kids, no older than seventeen or eighteen, were scattered around the grounds.

"What's happening, Rabbit?" she asked as I slowed to a stop, allowing her to see more. Kids stared in at Dolly as they passed the Mustang. "Wow," she murmured as she watched girls dressed in big poufy dresses and thick makeup to rival her own—except for the clock around her eye—linking arms with boys in tuxes.

I couldn't take my eyes off Dolly as she watched them, wide eyed. Her leg bounced up and down in excitement. She turned to me and asked, "What is it, Rabbit? Why are all the girls dressed so prettily? Why are the boys dressed so handsomely?"

I looked at the banner above the building: "Senior Prom." Dolly was gazing at the kids entering the school grounds. But I only watched her. I watched as she was mesmerized by the girls in dresses. Long, fancy dresses.

As if reading my mind, she said, "Their dresses, Rabbit . . ." Her voice was laced with awe. She glanced down at her own bare thighs. "Mine is nothing like theirs." She gave me the saddest fucking smile I had ever seen. "But where would I wear one so pretty? Surely not to destroy the bad men. I wouldn't waste something so beautiful on people so ugly."

My heart—if I even had one—cracked right down the fucking middle. She was right. She never did anything. Even as a kid she lived most of her life in her head, imagination fueling her tea parties, her adventures around the property. She danced every minute she got. Imagined a life outside the walls of the estate. I never danced, much to her chagrin. I was happy to watch. But fuck . . . Dolly deserved something fucking better in her life.

"It's a prom," I said. Dolly's brow creased in confusion. I knew she wouldn't have been able to read the banner above the doors. "The kids of . . . *Wonderland* go to one when they finish school." I shrugged. "They dance or some shit. Dress like this and dance."

"They dance . . . ?" she whispered as more limos pulled into the drive. "What fun they must have." She smiled at two more girls walking past. They looked inside the car, and their eyes fell on Dolly. They paused, then laughed. Right in her fucking face.

My lip curled. As if hearing the growl that rumbled under my breath, they snapped their eyes my way. I causally lifted the throat-slitting thimble on my finger and motioned across my neck. By the paling of their faces, I knew they had gotten the message to shut their fucking slut mouths. If not, I'd slit their fucking slut throats right here, right now.

No one slighted my Dolly.

"You both look so pretty!" Dolly said to the ungrateful bitches, oblivious to the fact that they had dared to sneer at her. Laugh at her clothes and makeup. They had no idea she could end their pathetic lives with one graceful sweep of her knife.

I wished she would teach these stuck-up whores a lesson.

I narrowed my eyes, staring at them, daring the sluts to

ignore her. "Th-thank you," one of them eventually blurted out, and they scurried across the road.

Dolly turned to me, a huge smile upon her face. "They spoke to me, Rabbit! The pretty princesses spoke to me!"

I nodded, but Dolly was already lost to the music coming from the school. "I do not know these songs. They are not on my tape." Dolly frowned. "What else happens at proms, Rabbit?"

I racked my brain, trying to remember. I'd never been to one before I went to the Earnshaw estate, but I obviously knew what one was. I seethed at the stark reality that it wasn't obvious to her. Her papa had never even taught her how to read, let alone allowed her go to a school where she could have made friends, gone to proms and whatever the fuck preppy girls would have done. For a second I was almost glad her papa didn't; Dolly would have never been friends with a freak like me. A freak who thought about death and murder twenty-four-seven, not football games and baseball.

"Rabbit?"

"They dance, drink punch, then they crown a king and queen."

Her eyes widened. "They do?" Her mouth dropped open. "Do they get to wear a crown?" I nodded. Dolly sighed. "I should very much like to wear a crown," she said. "To be crowned a queen . . ."

My gut clenched at the fucking sad smile on her face.

What she didn't realize was that she *was* a fucking queen.

My blood-soaked queen.

Checking my watch, I saw it was time to go if we wanted to crash the party. I put the car in gear and pulled away from the prom. Dolly's neck stretched as she watched the school until it was completely out of sight. When she sat back in her seat, she flicked the card of Tweedledee and Tweedledum back and forth in her hands. Her face fell from happy to furious in an instant.

I smirked, seeing my little Dolly mentally preparing for what came next. Each of these cunt's deaths was such a treat. The Cheshire Cat's death ended the vendetta I had held closest to my chest. The next four kills meant so much more after the revelations about her scar.

I couldn't wait for Dolly to unleash her rage on the fucks who had tied her down when they took her womb away. I was counting the seconds until she appeared like a fucking demon from their past.

We arrived at the hacienda, miles from anyone and anything, just like the rest. The news outlets still hadn't released the names of those we had killed. Months ago, Chapel's PI had told us that the uncles hadn't communicated in years. I shook my head, loving the fact that none of these fuckers knew we were coming. Surprise kills always felt that much more gratifying.

Off the radar, and oblivious to the specters coming to haunt them from the past . . . It made their blood taste all the sweeter.

Dolly stood and placed her hand on the frame of the windshield. "Rabbit! They are having a party!" Before I could stop her, Dolly jumped from the car, Alice doll-head in one hand and her knife in the other. Her gun was in the belt around her waist. I pounded over the driveway to catch up with her.

Dolly rushed through the door of the hacienda. I followed behind, searching the house for anyone near. The sound of clattering dishes rang out from the backyard.

Dolly turned to me, a smile on her face. "No . . ." She let out a high-pitched giggle, covering her mouth with the hand holding the doll-head. "Rabbit, are they having a tea party?" Without waiting for a reply, Dolly ran forward, then stopped in the center of the doorway that led to the veranda. I strolled up behind her, and my eyes fell to the table before us. Just like the PI's pictures, the table was long and filled with that odd mix of unsavory characters. Kid abusers. Rapists . . . and whores who got turned on by watching these fucks carry out their depraved acts.

Dolly gasped and clapped her hands. A loud, shrill giggle soared from her mouth, cutting through the loud music. Eight heads turned, and eight pairs of inquiring eyes landed on us. Dolly dropped her hands from her mouth. A maid had laid teapot after teapot on the table, and a cake tray boasting a wide selection of treats.

We'd interrupted dessert.

"You're having a tea party!" Dolly sang and rushed forward to the table. I casually swung my cane in my hand, eyes scouring the guests at the table. They all stared at us in confusion. But there were only two guests I gave a fuck about. The two identical fat shits at the end of the table. Matching suits. Matching swept-over balding hairstyles . . . matching death countdowns branded on their heads.

Dolly pulled a chair from the side of the terrace and pushed it between a rapist and a whore. She placed her doll's head on the table. The whore screeched and leaned away.

From the corner of my eye, I saw the maid try to escape. Just as she tried to run past me, I slammed my cane against the wall and created a barrier that she could not cross. Her startled blue eyes landed on me. I shook my head, tutting. "No leaving, dearie." I flicked my head at a bench at the side of the terrace. "Why don't you take a nice little seat over there?" I pointed. The maid had frozen, eyes deer-like, caught in the headlights, but I cracked the bones in my neck as my head rolled from side to side. "I wasn't asking . . . I was *insisting*."

She scurried to the bench, just as one of twins—Tweedledum, I decided to name him—stood up. "Who the fuck are you two? What the hell are you doing in my house?"

My eyes snapped to his flushed face, and an insatiable rage built up inside. I opened my mouth, ready to speak, when Dolly slammed her hand on the table. Her furious eyes latched onto Tweedledum's bloated face. "Where are your manners?" she hissed, her English accent more pronounced than ever before. Dolly shook her head, displeased, and pulled the gun from her waist belt. Tweedledum's eyes fell on the blue-and-white Glock. Dolly ran her finger over the inscription. Her head tilted to the side as she looked at the "uncles." "Time for tea." She spun the pistol in her hand and held it like the proficient gun handler she had become. She pointed the gun around the table, aiming its barrel at each of the guests in turn. They were staring at her, their faces rapidly draining of color. When her gaze landed on Tweedledum, he froze.

"We are guests here." She glanced at the woman next to her and ordered, "Rabbit needs a chair." The woman hesitated, only for Dolly to spin around and aim the gun at her head. "Don't tell me your mummy never taught you manners?"

The woman scrambled off her seat and retrieved a chair for me. She brought it back, hesitating when she clearly didn't know where to place it. Dolly gave me a stunning smile and lifted one shoulder.

My pretty, fucked-up doll.

"Opposite me, I think," Dolly said, and the woman placed the chair where Dolly indicated. I moved slowly, assessing them all as they flicked their gaze between me and my girl. When I sat down, Dolly looked at me. "A tea party, Rabbit! Can you believe it?"

I leaned casually back in my seat. "I can't believe it, my little Dolly." My right hand rested on my cane, and I ran my left index finger around my lips. With my sharp thimble, I pierced the flesh, and I felt the blood gather in my mouth and run down my chin.

I let it pour.

I let them all stare.

"You know, Rabbit? You know what really ticks me off?" Dolly asked as she sat down.

"What, darlin'?"

She lifted her knife and began sticking the tip into the wood of the linen-covered table. Her gun remained in her other hand, finger braced on the trigger. Her shoulders sagged, and a disappointed expression engulfed her pretty face. "I really don't like rude people."

I nodded in agreement, spreading the blood over my teeth with the tip of my tongue. I felt the tension radiating from the guests. The heavenly smell of fear permeated the humid air. Dolly sighed and shook her head. Her eyes flicked to the side, staring at nothing. Her head tilted like she was listening to someone. "Ellis doesn't like it either. She says it really makes her mad."

I smiled.

My little Ellis never had liked ill manners.

Sitting forward, I let the blood from my lips drop onto the tablecloth. Then I smiled. Rubbing the rabbit head of my cane, I shrugged and quoted, "Manners maketh man."

Dolly turned on the twins, who had turned a rather fetching whiter shade of pale. Their deathly pallor did nothing but excite me. I knew they had heard Dolly mention Ellis.

It teased them, foreshadowed what was to come. Pain. Lots of lovely, addictive pain.

"You invite us here, to your hacienda, and then treat us with such blatant disrespect?" Dolly's eyes saddened, and her dimples popped out as her pink lips pouted in disappointment. "We have traveled so very far to be here tonight." She paused, darkness flickering in her gaze. "To see you both . . . In fact, we could scarcely contain our excitement." A sinister smile tugged on her lips, and then it returned to a pout. "You put on this beautiful spread, and then make us feel so very unwelcome." She sniffed. "It is most upsetting."

The man on Dolly's left whispered something to the whore beside him. I studied his face. My blood boiled when I remembered he was a child abuser. She was the bitch that liked to watch him fuck kids.

He dared fucking speak when my Dolly had the floor? Dolly quieted, spun, knife in hand, and plunged its blade directly into the side of his skull. The whore, his fellow sick and twisted fuck-piece, screamed as his blood spurted over her. His hands scrunched the white table linen as he began a slow descent to death and the waiting hands of the devil himself. "I told you I hated bad manners!" Dolly said in her loudest, most commanding voice.

Dolly took a deep breath and closed her eyes. I heard her count to ten under her breath. I had to shift in my seat; my dick was so hard it was painful.

She was glorious.

When she opened her eyes, she smiled in relief, put her hand over her chest, and said quietly, "I am calm now." Her smile fell as she swept her gaze around the table. Our hosts were all staring at her in abject fear. Pissing themselves at the titan of darkness she had become. She brushed her hair back from her face and fixed her headband.

Suddenly, the whore who had just been covered in blood leaped to her feet. She fled for the door. She had only made it three steps before Dolly pulled her gun from the belt around her waist and fired a bullet straight into the back of the slut's skull. The slut's body slumped to the floor. The hooker beside me screamed in horror. I looked around the table. The rest of the fuckers were clearly too terrified to move.

"Anyone else?" Dolly asked, facing the rest of the guests, arms spread wide. She shook her head in disappointment. "You are all trying my patience!"

When no one uttered a single word, she placed her gun back into her waist belt. Turning to the prick she had murdered, now slumped on the tabletop, she grabbed the knife handle and unceremoniously yanked it from his skull. Blood spattered her dress; she tittered in embarrassment and reached for the napkin he had around his neck. She took it and dusted at the bloody spots on her clothes. Unfortunately, that only made it worse; blood oozed from his broken head and onto the napkin, spreading even more crimson stains onto Dolly's dress.

"There we go!" She looked at her knife. "Ugh," she said, grimacing at the blood and brain residue clinging to the filigree steel. Shrugging, she looked around for something to wipe it on, before turning to the prostitute to her right. "Excuse me," Dolly said politely, and wiped the blood on the silk scarf around the whore's neck. Dolly cast her a grateful smile. "Thank you so much, lovely lady."

Dolly shook her head in response to something. "What?" she said as she sat down, staring off to the side again. The people around the table looked at one another, fear and confusion haunting their expressions. "Who?" Her gaze wandered to Tweedledee and Tweedledum, who were sitting motionless, casting frequent, worried glances at one another. Their hands twitched in unison on the table's edge.

I smirked. They were piss-scared of my little Dolly darlin'.

"These two?" Dolly pointed to Tweedledee and then Tweedledum. She shook her head, an incredulous look on her face. "They wouldn't do that to you, Ellis. I am sure of it . . . they are our hosts. Hosts could never offend in such a manner." Dolly sighed, and then shook her head again, slowly, sadly. "They wouldn't hold you down while you were cut open and your insides removed. Surely they could not have taken your baby from your belly, and slapped you around your face when you tried to cry and fight them off." The twins choked on a shocked breath. Tweedledee's mouth dropped open. "They look too nice for that."

She sat down and got comfortable back on her seat. Tweedledum and Tweedledee couldn't tear their eyes from her.

Because they knew her.

Remembered her.

Feared her.

Then they looked at me.

They looked at the blood coating my mouth . . . and I saw it. I saw it in their frightened eyes the moment they realized who also sat before them . . .

"Heathan," they mouthed to each other and shifted their chairs back. I shook my head, slowly, warning them without words to stay the fuck down.

And I saw the moment they realized that they wouldn't be leaving this here tea party alive.

Dolly gasped suddenly, her inhale of air drawing all eyes back to her. "Are we celebrating my unbirthday?" She giggled. Her eyes landed on the cakes and tea before her. On the china teacups and the teapot that steamed with freshly brewed tea.

She looked to Tweedledum and Tweedledee. "Well . . . is it?"

They looked at each other. Tweedledee cleared his throat. "Wh-what is an unbirthday?"

Dolly batted her hand and rested her elbow on the table. "Just a bit of nonsense, really. Yet *sooo* much fun!" She surveyed the contents of the table and picked up a small plate. She stood and leaned over to the three-tiered cake stand. "So much choice!" Dolly began picking cakes and placing them on her plate. "Carrot cake," she said excitedly, licking a smear of cream-cheese frosting that had fallen onto her hand. "Fondant fancies . . . and . . . Rabbit!" she squealed. "Scones with strawberry jam and clotted cream!" She veritably hummed with excited happiness as she sat down. She danced in her seat as she put the "scone" into her mouth. It wasn't a scone, of course. The cakes were none of the ones she had said. This was America. Dolly lived in England in her head.

Dolly wiped a crumb of cake from her mouth as I observed the people watching her. Looking at her as if she was mad. She was, of course. But so was I.

It was what I loved most about us.

"Rabbit?" Dolly asked. I turned my attention to her. "Would you be a sweetie and pour the tea?"

"My pleasure, darlin'." I rose from my seat, picked up the teapot nearest to her and poured some into her cup. Dolly waited with a huge smile on her face. She pulled the cup close to her and lifted the milk jug beside her. She froze. When she looked up, everyone became a statue, all eyes fixed on her. "Drink your tea, please," she said kindly. She poured the milk into her tea. The walking corpses did nothing. "I said, drink your tea!"

The pricks scrambled for the teapots in front of them. I poured a cup for myself. Dolly reached for the sugar lumps in the center of the table. "One lump or two, Rabbit?"

"Two, darlin'."

Dolly plopped two sugar lumps into my tea, then did the same to her own. She lifted her cup, and then she looked at me. I mimicked her movement, but I saw her eyes narrow. Winking at her, I stuck out my little finger. She giggled. Without looking around, she said, "You had all better have your pinkies in the air. I do not drink tea with people who do not. It's so uncouth!"

Dolly flicked her eyes up, and everyone, in unison, lifted up their pinky fingers. Dolly sighed in relief and brought her cup to her lips. What happened next seemed to flow in slow motion. Dolly, eyes closed, took a sip of tea. The instant the tea touched her lips, her eyes snapped open and she spat the tea onto the table.

Everyone froze, backs bunched in fear, as Dolly dropped the teacup, the fine china smashing on the tiled floor. Dolly's head remained down, her thick blanket of blond hair hiding her face. Her hands were flat on the table, but I could see them shaking. Her fingers scrunched into tight fists.

She made a noise under her breath. A snarl. A grumble . . . a fucking ascending roar. Suddenly, Dolly reached for the gun at her waist and fixed her eyes on the whore to my right. Without hesitation, she pulled the trigger and, with a deafening bellow, sent a fucking metal slug straight between the bitch's eyes. Her blood splattered across my face. Our hosts screamed. Dolly seethed, her eyes wide with rage, shoulders tight with the need to kill. I wiped a drop of blood from my face and brought it to my mouth. My lips curled in disgust.

The whore tasted as fucked-up as her choice in men.

"Darjeeling . . ." Dolly said under her breath. The screams around us began to fade. "Darjeeling . . ." she repeated, louder this time. Dolly's eyes shut tight as her body began to shake. She grabbed her knife off the table. Not a sound could be heard. Dolly snapped her head up, her face bright red. "Darjeeling . . ." The word cracked from the rage lacing her voice. "I don't drink

Darjeeling." Her pursed lips pulled back and she screamed, "I ONLY DRINK FUCKING EARL GREY!"

Dolly spun to the whore to her right and swiped her knife clean across her throat, slicing apart her silk scarf in the process. But she wasn't finished. As the whore grabbed her throat, spluttering as she choked on her blood, Dolly's eyes collided with Tweedledum and Tweedledee. "Who was responsible for this?" she asked, picking up the teapot in front of her. She tipped the teapot and poured the now lukewarm tea on the tabletop. She released the teapot from a height, the china smashing when it hit the table.

Tweedledee, panicked, pointed to a man two seats down to my right. I rolled my attention his way and watched as the blood visibly drained from his face. I recognized him from the pictures —another child abuser. I focused on the pulse in his neck. It was beating so fast. I wanted to take my thimble and pluck it from his throat. "I . . .I . . .I . . ." he stuttered. His hands flew into the air. Dolly glared, positively vibrating with anger. "I . . . I have shares in a tea company . . . it's my favorite. I brought it as a gift to the hosts."

Dolly stilled, and her head slowly tipped to the side. She never took her eyes off him. "It's your favorite," she repeated his words quietly, without emotion. The kid-rapist searched the table. All his friends on the opoosite side were dead. He nodded, answering her question. "It's your favorite . . ." Dolly continued, her tone lifting slightly at the end. She closed her eyes and brought the heel of her hand to her forehead. "It's his favorite, he says," she said to herself. "Darjeeling is his *favorite* tea. He has *shares* in a tea company." Her eyes opened, but they were glazed. Her head dipped again.

She was listening to Ellis.

"I know," she agreed and began turning her head slowly. Her eyes returned to the kid-rapist. I pushed the dead whore beside me to the floor, then turned in my seat to better see him too. I didn't want to miss whatever my Dolly was about to do. "We like Earl Grey." She nodded in response to something Ellis had said. "Its light tone. Its flavor, bergamot. It is the superior blend." She nodded again and raised her top lip in disgust. "And he had the audacity, the gall, to serve Darjeeling to us. Because it was *his* favorite . . ." I held my breath as Dolly stopped speaking. Then she moved. In a flash, Dolly had scrambled onto the table, smashing the food and cakes and tea under her feet. She rushed for the dick two seats down from me and slumped to her knees. Lifting her knife in both hands, she plunged it into his chest. She plunged and plunged, again and again and again. I groaned, my cock hardening to the point of agony as she sliced into his chest cavity until his ribs began to show. The dick's body slumped in his chair. But Dolly only stopped stabbing him when she was out of breath.

Leaning forward, she took hold of his collar and brought his still-open eyes to meet hers. Hissing, breathless, she spat in his face, then said quietly, "Only Earl Grey will ever do."

I couldn't help it. I couldn't not fucking touch her as she sat on the table, bathed in blood, eyes blazing with fury from her kills. I launched up, dropped my cane and wrapped my hands around her throat. I dragged her to me and slammed my mouth over hers. My tongue swirled in her mouth. Dolly moaned and pulled at my hair. I bent her backward on the table, eating at her mouth, before ripping myself away and staring down at her— blue-dressed, drenched in blood, eyes and hair wild.

"End them," I demanded through gritted teeth. I felt their fear wrap around me, and it brought a smile to my face. I slammed my mouth on hers again, needing one more taste of her lips, before breaking away to suck the skin on her throat. "Fucking end them all," I growled into her ear. I stepped back, taking hold of my cane and kicking my chair the fuck out of my way.

I palmed my cock under my pants as Dolly shifted to the end of the table, legs open, giving me a perfect view of her "frilly knickers," as she called them. "Wanna have some fun, Rabbit?" she teased, a sparkle in her blue eyes.

"Always, darlin'." I held out my hand and guided her off the table.

She dusted invisible lint off my coat and purred, "My Rabbit . . . such a gentleman."

Dolly skipped toward Tweedledee and Tweedledum. She stopped behind them and threw her arms around their shoulders. "Now it's your turn," she announced. Looking to me, she said, "Would you be a dear and help me, Rabbit?"

I bowed and walked her way, twirling my cane. I met the eyes of the fucker left alive at the table and the maid. They were both shell-shocked, immobilized by fear. When I reached Dolly's side, she ordered, "Pull out their chairs." Smirking, I dragged the twins' chairs out until they sat away from the table, further out on the veranda.

Dolly skipped around them until she faced them. She turned to the maid, who was still sitting on the bench. "I shall require two knives, of equal size." The maid's eyes widened. Dolly shooed her with her hand. "Chop-chop," Dolly said, sounding so, so fucking English. The maid scurried into the house. I followed. As I filled the doorway, her eyes widened and she backed away to the kitchen drawers.

"Make sure they're sharp," I called. The maid took two knives from the drawer and held them out to me. "To her," I said, pointing at Dolly, who was busy pressing kisses on her Alice doll's lips. The maid crept past me, never taking her eyes off mine, and handed Dolly the knives. Dolly placed her doll's head on the table and took the knives. She had tucked her blade and her gun in the waist belt of her dress.

I strolled over to where she stood. I held my cane close as she offered Tweedledum and Tweedledee the knives. They stared at her, not moving. Dolly sighed. "Okay. I can see you are confused, so I'll explain." She bent down, like she was speaking to recalcitrant children, and said, "Only one of you will survive tonight." She brandished the knives in her hands. "You are going to have a fight. One of you will kill the other." She shrugged. "Whosoever survives shall be freed." A smile. Another shrug. "Simple."

Tweedledee and Tweedledum shook their heads as Dolly offered them the knives again. Sick of their shit, I unsheathed my own blade and held it across both of their throats. Their blood-shot eyes landed on me. "The lady wasn't giving you a choice." I smiled a bloody smile. "She was *insisting*." My smile disappeared. "Now get the fuck up." Dolly clapped loudly from behind me. I used my blade to gently guide them to their feet. "Take the knives." They looked at me, ready to refuse, but I pressed my blade harder against their throats. Panic on their faces, they grabbed the knives. I guided them backward. Suddenly, Dum broke away and lunged for Dolly. Before he could reach her, I sliced my blade through his side, and he bowled over in pain. The second of the twins, Dee, looked at me with shocked eyes. Shrugging, I awarded him the exact same injury. As he fell to the floor, I looked at Dolly. "Thought we had better make the fight even."

She tapped her finger to her head. "Good thinking, Rabbit."

Dolly turned to the lone man left at the table and the maid. "Get to your feet and come here." They did. They stood around the twins on the floor. "Place your bets, people," Dolly sang, circling the rapist and maid. "Who will win tonight? Will it be Tweedledee, the man who held Ellis down and fucked her while she cried? Or will it be Tweedledum, the man who slapped Ellis around the face as he pinned her down and robbed her of the place where babies grow?"

Dolly stopped at maid. "Place your bet. Tweedledum"—she pointed at one of the twins—"Or Tweedledee?"

The maid's bottom lip quivered. "Tw-Tweedledee," she whispered. Dolly nodded in acknowledgment. She turned to the man. "Tweedledee," he echoed shakily.

Standing between the twins, she put her arms in the air. "Tweedledum will face the favorite, Tweedledee, in a death match. On my command, let battle commence!" She looked to me and smiled. "Ready, set . . . tick tock!" Dolly jumped aside, but neither of the twins moved. "Fight!" Dolly commanded, hands on her hips, but they stubbornly refused to move. She looked at me and sighed. "I suppose we will just have to do it ourselves."

My cock throbbed as Dolly dropped to her knees behind Tweedledee and took hold of the hand holding his knife. Before he even had a chance to fight her off, Dolly guided the knife straight into the shoulder of Tweedledum. Dolly gasped. "The first strike goes to Tweedledee!" She looked over his shoulder at me, then asked, "Question is, will his opponent respond?"

"No!" Tweedledum shouted, holding his bleeding side. He tried to scurry away, but I held him by the hair and grabbed the hand holding his knife. I easily overpowered him, plunging his knife deep into his brother's stomach. Both twins screamed, and Dolly laughed.

"You're sick!" Tweedledum shouted.

"Yes!" Dolly replied excitedly. "The Sick Fux!"

Growing tired of these fuckers being alive, I drove the knife into Tweedledee's heart. His eyes glanced up in shock, then slowly frosted with the glaze of imminent death.

"No!" Tweedledum shouted again as his brother slumped to the floor.

Dolly got to her feet and put her hands on her hips. "No fair!" She stuck out her bottom lip.

"Dolly," I said, and she begrudgingly turned to me. I threw Tweedledum to the floor and pinned his wrists behind his head, leaving his stomach free. "Would I ever deprive you of anything so delicious, darlin'?"

Dolly scuffed her boot on the floor, but reluctantly shook her head. "No."

"Now," I said and nudged my head in the direction of Tweedledum's stomach. "Wouldn't you like to do to him what he did to Ellis? Wouldn't little Ellis like that too?"

Dolly stared off, listening to the voice in her head, then she turned back to me and a slow grin sprouted on her lips. "Yes. We both agree we would."

Dolly ran to Tweedledum's feet and took out her knife. Tweedledum flailed around in my arms. "No!" he cried, trying to break free. "Get the fuck off!"

Dolly's eyes clouded over. She sliced the back of her hand across his face. "Shut it!" she shouted and did it again. "You shut your mouth!"

Dolly lifted his shirt and slashed her knife across his stomach. But she didn't stop. She did it again and again, and again. She scarred him like he had scarred her, but he got so much more. He got so many scars that his skin was no longer visible. Tweedledum slumped in my arms, and Dolly drew back, blade held in the air. She locked eyes with me. I could see the hunger in her gaze.

My cock twitched, and I knew her pussy would be flooding too.

Tossing the body to the floor, I stood up, turned on the remaining male guest and unsheathed my cane. "You lost the bet," I said, before shooting the fucker in the head.

But just as I aimed at the maid, who had closed her eyes in readiness for the blow, Dolly yanked on my arm. "No, Rabbit!" she shouted and looked at the maid. She was blond with blue eyes. Dolly stood before her and got on her tiptoes to stroke the woman's face. "She's far too pretty to die." Dolly stroked her hand down the maid's face and over her lips. "She looks like a doll." She smiled. "She looks like me."

She didn't. Not a fucking patch on my Dolly, but I didn't burst her bubble by disagreeing.

"We can leave her alive," Dolly said, and the maid's eyes widened. I snarled, wanting to kill the bitch stone dead, but Dolly turned and presented me with a stern face. Reluctantly, I nodded and put my cane back together. Dolly turned back to the maid. "Put out your hand," Dolly ordered sternly. The maid did. Dolly lifted her own hand and smacked it hard across the back of the maid's. The maid cried out, but stayed still. She was too scared to move. "You worked for very bad men," Dolly scolded and shook her head. "Next time," Dolly said, pointing in the maid's face, "make better choices!"

Dolly ran to the white wall of the veranda, a contrasting backdrop to the pile of bodies on the floor, and pulled out her lipstick. After scrawling a Chanel-pink "SICK FUX," on the wall, she collected her doll's head from the table. Just as she went to turn back, she grabbed two doughnuts from an untouched plate. "A doughnut each for the road?"

I nodded. Dolly took my hand. As we walked out of the hacienda, blood-soaked and needing to fuck, I knew it wouldn't be long until I pulled over and took her body under mine.

Unclean.

Covered in their blood.

Hot.

Wet.

Fucking perfection.

* * *

My jaw clenched as Dolly's hands ran up and down my thigh. Her tits were pushed up against my side, and her teeth played with my earlobe. I gripped the steering wheel so tightly I thought I might rip it clean off.

"Rabbit," she whispered and stroked my arm. Her hand covered one of mine and she pulled it from the wheel, over the stick shift and across to her thigh. She sucked in a breath when I touched her bare skin.

"I need you to touch me," Dolly whispered into my ear. "Only you. No one else. No one else can touch. Just my Rabbit. Because my Rabbit makes me feel sooo good." I growled low in my throat. "And your Dolly is the only one who can touch you." She guided my hand closer to her pussy. I could feel the heat of it under the hem of her skirt. "No bad men can hurt us anymore. Because Dolly and Rabbit take their touch away with each other's hands and mouths and naughty parts." She moaned and slipped my hand into her frilly knickers. The minute my fingers felt her pussy, hot and wet, I hissed and turned my head to ravage her mouth with my own.

Dolly moaned against my mouth, then bit down hard. Her teeth sank into my lip, piercing the flesh. She smashed her mouth against mine again, sipping at the blood from my lip. The car swerved, and I pulled my mouth away. I straightened the car before we plunged into a tree. But Dolly's lips licked down my cheek and neck as she moved closer and closer to me.

I was about to pull the car over and fuck her on the side of the road, when spots of rain began pelting our skin. Dolly gasped as a raindrop hit her cheek, and she looked to the sky. She closed her eyes as a deep rumble of thunder sounded. The spots of rain gave way to a torrential downpour. Fork lightning struck the tree-lined pastures in the near distance. Dolly's loud laughter drowned out the music from her cassette. When I looked over at her, her head was tipped back, eyes closed as slews of water ran down her skin, washing the blood onto my leather seats. Her hands shot into the air as the rain cleansed her of the fuckers' blood.

I was so entranced, watching her mascara and the clock around her left eye track down her cheeks, that I almost missed the sirens blaring in the distance.

Police.

Growling under my breath, I took Dolly's arm and yanked her down to the seat. She snapped her head my way, a scowl on her beautiful face. The makeup she had so perfectly applied before the hacienda was now smudged, black lining her eyes and pink smearing her lips.

She looked wild. Wild, and so fucking beautiful.

"Police," I spat as I stamped my foot on the gas. The Mustang roared as I redlined her. I flicked off the lights and plunged us into darkness.

The maid, I thought as Dolly searched behind us for any sign of blue lights.

"No matter what you do, never leave any witnesses alive," Hyde insisted before I left.

Chapel nodded in agreement. "No matter if they are inno-cent, kill them quick. Leave no eyes open that have seen your face."

But I'd fucked up. Failed on the number-one rule of killing, all because my little Dolly thought the maid looked pretty. Like a fucking doll.

I checked the rearview mirror—no hint of blue lights. I raced down the deserted country roads as fast as I could. The sirens grew faint, but I knew there would be more coming. Rain pelted the windshield; I was driving blind.

"Run, run, Rabbit," Dolly sang beside me. "Run, run as fast as you can!" I glanced at her from the side of my eye. She was bouncing on her seat in sheer excitement.

She had no fucking idea what would happen if they caught us.

I thought back to the state she was in when I found her. She would revert to that. Dolly ripped from Wonderland, plunged back into the room of doors. Too big to fit through any door that gave her back her life . . . her sane mind.

I didn't want her sane mind. I wanted her like this: fucked up, and dark perfection.

I pushed the gas pedal so hard the car shook at the effort. I drove for hours and hours, until we arrived at a small town. We were both drenched, and I could no longer see through the raging storm. Spotting a building up ahead, set back from the road and surrounded by thick trees, I turned right and headed that way. The car skidded on the rough gravel as I turned in and parked us around back, under the cover of trees and darkness. We would wait out the cops before moving to our next destination.

I cut the engine, the rain lessening some due to the shelter of the thick leaves of the trees. Dolly leaned over the console and, looking up at the bright neon lights dancing on the building's roof, asked, "What does it say, Rabbit?"

I looked over at her. With her clothes wet, she looked so young. All big blue eyes and pink lips. Her dress clung to her body, her tits wet and glistening. The blood now only stained her dress and socks. "Rabbit?" she said, stroking the rain-slick hair from my face.

I looked up at the sign, and my eyebrow rose in interest. "Girls," I said, watching the neon woman dance on the roof.

"Girls . . ." Dolly said in awe. She sat forward in her seat and imitated the dancing woman. Even with the worry of the police and not knowing what the fuck this place really was, I couldn't help but stare at my girl. My eyes were always fixed on her. I could never look away. Nothing else in the firmament—stars, sun or sea—was enough to pull my gaze from her.

Taking out my cell, I texted Chapel.

ME: Call the cops. Tell them you saw us heading east. Throw them off our track.

CHAPEL: Well, how lovely to hear from you, young squire. I am, as they say, "on it."

Another reply followed almost immediately.

CHAPEL: How many to go?

I glanced at Dolly, who was still dancing as she listened to her cassette, staring at the neon dancer in rapt fascination.

ME: Two.

CHAPEL: Exciting times, Dapper Dan. Good luck. Hyde sends his regards . . . so does Henry, though he has not been around so much lately.

I frowned, wondering why Henry had been absent, when

another crack of thunder sounded above us. It was getting closer. I got out of the car and opened Dolly's side. "Let's go, darlin'." She took my proffered hand, and we walked to the entrance of the building. A muscled man stood in the doorway. His eyes narrowed as we approached. He crossed his arms over his chest.

"ID," he said. I raised my eyebrow at him.

"Wow . . ." Dolly peeked around me. "You're huge!" She reached out and pressed one of his arms. I ripped her hand away. She narrowed her eyes at me, pissed, but I didn't care. She didn't fucking touch anyone else but me.

I reached into my pocket and pulled out wads of hundred-dollar bills. I edged forward and stuffed them into the giant's jacket pocket. His eyes were wide as he saw how much I had put in there. Cash, courtesy of Tweedledee and Tweedledum's secret office stash, that I had taken, for safekeeping, before we left.

I stepped back and rested my hands on my cane. "No questions. No ID. A private room. And if the police come, you didn't see us."

The meathead stared at me. I smirked, waiting for him to challenge me. In fact, I invited it. But the meathead stepped out of our way and opened the door. Taking Dolly's hand, I entered the building. The stench of smoke clogged the air. Music shook the walls as the meathead led us down a hallway. My feet stuck to the carpet. And I tightened my grip on Dolly as men walked past us, looking her up and down as she smiled wide at them and waved, dancing to the music as she walked.

Meathead led us through a red curtain . . . and my eyes widened at the scene before us. I yanked Dolly to my side. Her jaw dropped as she looked up at a stage. Women, naked women, and women divesting themselves of their clothes to music, drew our gaze. Men loitered around the side of the stage. One woman dropped to a crouch, a solitary string posing as panties on her oily body. A man slipped cash into the string, and then she got back up and danced away to the other side of the stage.

It wasn't dancing like Dolly did for me. These whores fucked men with their eyes as they paraded around the stage in high heels. They rocked their bodies and touched themselves.

"Rabbit . . ." Dolly whispered, loud enough for me to hear. She was transfixed by the women. She never took her eyes off them. I didn't take my eyes off her, so I didn't feel a whore touch my back. I didn't see the half-naked whore reach her hand around me and put her mouth at my ear. "Hello, handsome," she said. "Come here to play?"

Unable to stand her fucking touch on me, I spun around and grabbed her by her throat. I slammed her back into the wall and braced my cane at the side of her head, gun side, ready to fire. "Don't fucking touch me!" I thundered as her eyes widened in shock. I squeezed my hand tighter around her throat, watching her eyes turn red.

Bitch was going to die.

A hand on my shoulder wrenched me from her. I turned, teeth gritted, ready to fucking slit some throat. The meathead stood there. "Don't touch the talent," he said, then backed off, arms in the air, when he saw my murderous face.

I rolled my head back to the whore, just in time to see the bitch run away to a back room. Rage built inside me, until Dolly slid her arms around my waist. She flattened her breasts and body against my stomach. I quickly inhaled the scent of her hair. Of the perfume that she always wore—roses.

Roses, roses, roses.

Dolly looked up at me and smiled. I exhaled the long breath I held imprisoned in my chest. But I could still feel that bitch. I could still feel her, until . . .

Dolly threaded her arms around to my back and began to rub the spot the whore had dared to touch. I breathed. I breathed and breathed as Dolly's touch started to replace that of the whore. But I needed more. As my anger lingered, as I watched the pulse in Dolly's neck throb, and as her hands touched me, igniting my blood, I needed so much fucking more.

"Room," I demanded, knowing the meathead remained standing behind me. "Private room. Now. Or consider the money I gave you your funeral costs."

The meathead walked to the right and down another hallway. Moans and groans emerged from the under the doors. But we kept on walking, my hand braced at the back of Dolly's neck. The meathead stopped at a door and handed me a key. "It locks. There's a back entrance too, just in case." I nodded. Clearly we weren't the first people they'd harbored for cash.

Just as I was about to enter the room, a text came through on my cell.

CHAPEL: Done. Took the bait. Wait an hour before you leave. Godspeed.

I slid the cell back in my pocket and walked through the door. Dolly followed, pushing past me when she saw what was in the center. "A stage . . ." she whispered and edged closer. She reached up, stroking the metal pole in the center of the black stage.

"It's what the women out there were using to dance." I shut the door, locking us inside. The lights were dim, only a red glow coming from the ceiling light. Music pumped through the speakers. Facing the stage was a large couch.

I walked past Dolly, anger still ripping through me like a hurricane. My cock hardened as I felt my pulse pounding and my blood rushing through my veins. As I passed Dolly, I reached out and brushed my fingers over the back of her neck. My sharp thimble scraped at the wet skin. Dolly turned, eyes leaden, and curved her spine into me. I kept going to the couch. Without looking back, I shed my jacket and tossed it to the corner of the room. I sat down and rested my hands on the rabbit head on my cane.

I leaned against the back of the couch. Then I looked up. Looked up to see Dolly watching me from beside the stage. Her hair was wet. Her eyes were wide. Pupils dilated.

I knew she'd be wet too.

I knew she'd liked seeing me slam that whore up against that wall for touching what was hers. Her pussy leaked at the fact that it was only her touch I could ever stand.

Her tits pushed against the corset of her dress. Chapel would rip into me for calling them "tits." *Breasts*, he had told me. *Dapper Dan, one must never sound like an uneducated, classless heathen. Even if the shoe fits.*

But right now, with the heat from the kill and the need to slaughter the whore who touched me, I *was* a fucking heathen. And I was staring at Dolly's *tits*.

Red flushed over her pale skin and crawled like wildfire up her neck and to her cheeks. Dolly rocked from side to side, her tight thighs trying to stave off the pressure; I knew my stare was feeding her pussy.

She bit her lip. Her hands fell to her sides, and her fingers began to creep up the hem of her dress. I watched those fingers, gripping my cane with increasing force.

Then, "Dance."

Dolly's eyes snapped to mine as I stared at her through unyielding, commanding eyes.

I didn't move a muscle as Dolly asked, "What?"

My eyes flicked to the stage, then back to her. "Dance."

Dolly's eyes grew hooded then wandered to the black stage lit by a flood of red light. The silver pole shone in the glow. The music filled the room with a heavy beat, so loud one could feel it through one's chest.

"I always dance for you, Rabbit." She turned back to me, a teasing smirk building on her pink lips. She knew exactly what she was doing. She knew she was the snake tamer, rousing my cock with her innocent act.

"Not like that," I said, stroking my thimble over the back of the hand resting on my cane. I leaned forward. "Like the whores out there." Dolly sucked in a sharp breath and squirmed some more. I tipped my head to the side, keeping her locked in my stare. "I saw you watching them, darlin'. I saw you wanting to climb on that stage. I saw you wanting to grind around the pole, coveting the attention they got, performing naked." I smirked. "I saw you wanting to strip for me." My eyes darkened. "Only me . . . And you want to dance. You want to use the adrenaline from tonight's kills to dance." I sat back, hands still resting on my cane. "I know you want to tease, then fuck away your pent-up energy. The victory of ridding the world of Tweedledee and Tweedledum."

Dolly was breathless, her cheeks bright red. I raised an eyebrow and casually flicked my finger. "So dance . . . and this isn't a request," I emphasized, knowing she knew what I would say next. Dropping all niceties, I adopted the dark tone I knew she would obey. "I am *insisting*."

Dolly exhaled, her body moving to the stage, honoring my command. My puppet, on my string.

Teeth clenched, I watched her as she climbed the stairs leading to the stage. My cock throbbed as she walked to the center and stroked the metal pole. Her blue dress was soaked through, ripped and stained with blood. Her blond hair was a mass of curls, wild, as if I'd just taken her up against the wall, ruining my perfect little dolly. Her eyes were rimmed with black, and her lips were pink-stained from her lipstick. Her socks were bloodstained but intact, the black and white stripes like a ladder, leading me to the spot where we both wanted me to go.

A new song drifted through the speakers, a deep bass shaking the walls of the room. The singer sang of a woman turning him into a savage. The song was apt. Around my little Dolly darlin', I fucking lost my mind.

What little sanity remained.

I sat back, tried to relax, but that was shot to hell as Dolly began to move. Her hips swayed as she gripped the pole. Her gaze locked on mine as her fingers danced up and down the metal. They were slow and seductive. I knew how they felt tracking up and down my dick. She knew that too. Smiling, she stroked the pole like she stroked me.

"Faster," I ordered, knowing she could hear me just fine over the music. Dolly walked around the pole until she stood with her back to it, facing me. She rocked against it, eyes closing as her ass hit the hard metal. She reached above her, holding the pole above her head. Then she began to descend, dropping slowly down the pole. Her thighs were squeezed together, until she reached the bottom, where they opened. Slowly.

Painfully . . . fucking . . . slowly.

I growled under my breath when her milky thighs spread to reveal her "knickers." Dolly's back arched, then she released one hand from the pole and stroked it up her thigh until she reached the edge of her knickers. My breath held in my throat and I stilled, motionless, as she pushed the white fabric aside . . . and her blond pussy came into view.

I snarled loudly, Dolly's eyes snapping open at the sound. Then she let go, her knickers sliding back in place.

I glared at her, my cock desperate to be released, but then she climbed up the pole, spinning so her back was facing me. Her hands slid down the pole. My eyes remained glued to the long socks covering her slim legs. My gaze moved north until it reached her milky thighs. Dolly flicked her hair and slowly looked back toward me. My attention snapped to her face. To her eyes as they smiled, knowingly. My hand dropped to my crotch and I righted the rock-hard cock in my pants.

A loud, victorious giggle burst from Dolly's throat. She spun, facing me, spine resting against the metal pole. Her wide smile dropped as her gaze landed on me. Her pupils dilated, and she circled her lips with her tongue. Her eyes scanned me from head to toe, tits pushing against her tight corset.

"Rabbit, Rabbit, Rabbit . . ." Her face changed in an instant. Gone was the innocent Dolly I knew. In her place was Dolly the whore. Dolly the pole dancer, thrusting her hips forward to the beat.

Dolly the woman, not the innocent little girl I grew up with.

With this version of Dolly, I was pretty sure we weren't in Wonderland anymore.

Pushing off the pole, Dolly walked forward two steps, and then stopped. She lifted the ribbons on her corset. Looking up at me with hooded eyes, she began unthreading them, her hips rolling around and around in time with the heavy bass filling the room. My jaw clenched as the tight corset began to part. The scalding blood in my veins rushed south. Inch by inch, my cock grew so hard that I growled at the ache induced by Dolly's seductive act.

My lips rolled over my teeth when the ribbon fell to the floor at Dolly's heeled ankle boots. "Oops!" Doe-eyed, she covered her mouth with her hand. She looked down at the ribbon and then back up. A slow grin pulled on her lips, and her hand fell away. She walked forward again, and her slim fingers pulled the corset apart.

I groaned, the sound masked by the music as her tits were bared—a perfect handful, as if they'd been devil-designed solely for me. She rocked on her feet, hips swinging from side to side as her corset slipped slowly to her waist.

Dolly's eyes closed as if she were overcome by the savage rhythm of the song. She ran her hands up her sides, over her bare skin. My focus stayed glued on her as her hands climbed and climbed until they cupped her tits. Her head rolled back, lips parting as she flicked her thumbs over her hard nipples.

I gripped my cane-head tighter. I tested the metal under my palm as I struggled to keep a leash on my need for my girl. In my mind, I threw the cane to the side and marched to the stage. In my mind, I took hold of her throat and slammed her back against the pole. I ducked my head and licked my way over her damp skin to her nipples, where I sucked one into my mouth. Dolly would fight against me, but I would hold her in place. Controlling her, making it impossible for her to do anything but submit to me.

Her lord, her king.

My hand would fall lower, pushing up the skirt of her dress and ripping off her panties. Her pussy would be slick and wet, and my fingers would slip inside. Dolly would scream as I held my hand on her throat, then moved it to her hair. I'd wrap the strands around it—three times—and I'd make her lock eyes with me. And I'd take from her. I'd take all her moans and screams and swallow them down deep. I'd snap open my pants and, lifting her thigh up, with the leverage of the pole, slam inside her. I'd make her scream louder and louder into my ear as I held her in place, a flush rising to her face. And she'd come. She'd come, shaking in my grasp as I refused to let her move. As I took every ounce of her pleasure until she couldn't stand on her own.

Then I'd fill her with my cum. I'd fill her so deep that I'd feel it against my thighs. "My Dolly . . ." I'd whisper in her ear as she panted into mine. "All. Fucking. Mine."

My eyes blinked away the fantasy and refocused on the stage.

Dolly's hands were on the waist of her dress. Thumbs hooking into the blue material, she pushed it down over her stomach, her hips, and then finally, her thighs. Dolly bit her lip as the material fell to the floor, leaving her in her frilly panties and thigh-high socks. I pushed the heel of my hand over my dick, trying to tame it for now. I forced my muscles to remain seated.

This was Dolly's moment.

This was Dolly seducing me. After all of these years . . . she was coming for *me*.

As the next song began, Dolly dropped to her knees. Leaning forward, she flattened her palms on the stage surface. On all fours, and with a smirk on her lips, she moved toward me. I stayed completely still as she reached the edge of the stage. Close enough for me to touch her if I wanted. Close enough for me to reach up and force her mouth onto my lips . . . close enough for me to swipe my thimble across her throat and watch her blood drip as she danced.

As if reading my mind, Dolly tipped her head to the side, exposing the milky skin of her neck. Her hand tickled down her stomach and disappeared into her panties. Her eyes fluttered closed as she toyed with her clit. A deep red blush burst on her cheeks, and her throat bobbed as she swallowed in pleasure.

Licking my lips, hungry at the invitation, I shifted to the end of the seat. I lifted my hand and ran my thimble over her slender white neck and carefully pierced the skin. It took everything I had to sit back as the scarlet droplet descended over her paleness. Dolly moaned so loudly it rang out over the pounding music. Her hand lifted from her pussy, and her wet fingers rubbed over the blood on her neck, mixing the juices. My mouth watered, desperate for a taste. But I stayed still. Watched as she teased and brought me closer and closer to the edge of losing control.

She had no idea what would befall her if I did.

I could only be pushed so far . . . even by Dolly. Could I contain the darkness that always walked with me, beneath my skin, ever ready to be freed? The monster that *they* made me.

"Conditioning," Henry said when I had asked him about it one night. The thoughts I had, the ones that only ever involved Dolly. "It is the way you gain the most pleasure." He shrugged. "Typical with abuse cases." He sat forward from the darkness of his corner of our cell. "She may be the same, when you find her. She may gain the most pleasure from the way you wish to deliver it." Henry sighed. "You are both victims of circumstance, Rabbit. It does not make you wrong. Simply . . . different. It is known as edgeplay. Role-playing what in real life would be an unthinkable act. Between two consenting adults, who both gain gratification from the act. It is simply a form of sexual expression."

"Taste." Dolly's voice sailed into my ear, dragging me from my thoughts. I stared at my girl, braced on the edge of the stage, her pussy's wetness and throat's blood waiting on her neck, offered like a feast for me to take. My lips parted in need.

"Taste," Dolly said, sterner this time.

Placing her hand under my chin, she guided me forward. Her eyes never left mine as I approached. Her eyelids hooded as I snarled, and I wondered if Henry had been right. If she would be able to take it. If she would gain the utmost pleasure from me that way.

When she whimpered as I flicked out the tip of my tongue and swiped at the blood and juice, I thought maybe she would.

Spurred on by that thought, I dove back in for more. Slamming my lips on her skin, I sucked hard, the intoxicating flavor of the blood cocktail bursting on my tongue. Then, losing the little control I had, I bit. I sank my teeth into her skin.

Dolly stiffened under me, then released a moan so loud that I almost came right there. Her hand slammed into my hair. Her nails raked over my scalp, ripping a snarl from my throat. She pushed me closer. I bit her harder. She screamed louder. Her nipples hardened further against my chest.

Then Dolly pushed me away. I fought. I overpowered her, pushing against her, refusing to go. But then she pushed back . . . and I fucking smiled wide. Her hands clawed at me, pushing me away.

I reared back, needing to look into her eyes. Needing to read her, to see if Henry was right. When I pulled back an inch, Dolly's fierce gaze met mine. She shifted, then a hand came sailing across my face. My head snapped back, but I swung it back to see her. She was breathing heavily as my eyes dropped to the bite mark on her neck. I looked into her eyes again, and my heart thundered as I saw what was in them . . . need. Want.

Desperation.

In a second, Dolly had her arm around my neck, and she smashed her lips against mine. We were all teeth and tongues as we bit and lapped at each other's mouths. The she pushed me backward. My elbows slipped from where they rested on the edge of the stage. The heel of Dolly's boot was on my chest. She kicked out, warning me to get back on my seat. My lip curled into a smirk as I felt my blood spark from her challenge.

Our gazes locked, a battle of wills . . . until I sat down, legs spread, and unzipped my pants. Dolly's eyes glazed as she watched. Watched as I reached inside my pants and pulled out my cock. The cock that was going to take her before we left this place.

The one I knew she craved just as much as I craved the pussy that was soon to be mine.

Dolly's gaze narrowed, and she shifted to her knees. Her hands roamed her body, landing on the waistband of her panties. She rolled them down her hips, her blond pussy immediately on show. She sat down and kicked her legs into the air. She mimicked the whores she'd seen outside as she worked the panties slowly over her legs. Reaching into my vest pocket, I pulled out some cash, and as her eyes met mine, I threw the notes at her. Fire sparked in Dolly's eyes as her panties hooked on the tip of her boot. With a quick flick, the panties flew my way and landed on my chest. I tucked them into my pocket.

And then I choked on a breath as Dolly stood and faced me. Naked, but for her socks and boots. Her wet hair was wild as it haloed her face. Her hands moved to rest on her hips. I drank in the view —tits and stomach and thighs and that blond pussy, all calling my name.

Dolly bit her lip as she crouched down and moved to take off her socks. I brought my cane onto her thigh. Dolly's eyes snapped to mine. "They stay on."

Dolly's expression changed, like she was about to challenge me. My heart beat faster, knowing I would have to *insist* . . . but her lip hooked into a ghost of a smirk and she stood up. Black-and-white thigh-high socks and black leather ankle boots were all I could see.

Then Dolly began to move. She swayed and swung her hips to the music as she moved to the stairs of the stage. I stroked my cock harder as she began to walk toward me. Her eyes didn't break from mine as she skirted around the stage, her white skin red in the soft lighting.

She stopped before me, her head tilting as she regarded me on the couch. As her blue eyes dropped to my busy hand. Her lips parted and she sucked in a sharp breath.

Dolly edged closer still. She placed her knees on either side of the couch, straddling me. She didn't touch me. Instead she swayed over me. Her arms moved either side of my head, gripping the backrest of the couch. Her hips began to grind to the beat, her tits a mere inch from my face. My cheeks heated, my body boiling with the need to grab her by the wrists and slam her down on the couch. To ravage her mouth and slam my dick inside her.

But I stayed still as she sat over my thigh. I released my cock, and she stared at it with hunger. But she resisted, torturing me where I sat as she rolled her back, her tits coming toward my face, her hard nipple scraping past my lips. I groaned as they circled and came back again and again. Then Dolly dropped down, her naked pussy against my clothed thigh. The tip of my cock rested against her stomach as she rocked back and forth. Her cheek brushed past my cheek, and her mouth landed at my ear. I heard her breathing—fast and out of control. It hitched as her clit swelled against my lap.

My hands were fists at my sides. I stared up at Dolly's face, lost in rapture. Then she looked down, and all her movement stopped. Her eyes flared, and a slow smile pulled on her mouth.

Her tongue lapped around her moist lips, then it came. The whispered sentence that broke me.

That brought out the darkness I had fought to keep back . . .

"Rabbit belongs to Dolly now."

I jumped forward, wrapping my hands around her neck. Dolly cried out as I swung her off my lap and slammed her down onto the couch. Dolly's hands raked at my arms, her nails clawing at my skin. But I couldn't feel it. Sitting up, moving my knee to Dolly's chest to keep her pinned down, I ripped at the buttons of my vest and shirt. I threw them off my body and across the room. My chest was tight with anticipation. I closed my eyes and rolled my head, only to open them and see Dolly fighting for freedom beneath me. I smiled and lowered my head down until my mouth was at her ear. "There's no getting away from me, little Dolly," I whispered. Dolly thrashed under me. Her hands slapped onto my back, and I hissed with pleasure as I felt her nails slice into my skin. She clawed like a wildcat, but I kept her pinned down. I moved my body as I felt her draw blood. Shifted until my cock was braced between her legs. Her pussy was drenched as I held her down. As she fought to be free . . . as she tried to throw me off.

I drew back and met her eyes. They were ecstatic. Furied. Wide with violent bliss.

My heart fucking exploded in my chest.

My Dolly liked to play.

I gripped her shoulders, keeping her in place. "Get off me," she cried. My mouth tightened when I saw her smile. When I felt her slap at my face, rake at the skin on my arms and chest and neck with her nails. "Don't touch me!" Dolly was panting, her breath labored and thick.

So I gave it back.

Leaning down, I moved one of my hands to take hold of her face. "I'm gonna fuck you," I told her. Heat rose to Dolly's eyes as they fluttered closed. My blood rushed faster and faster as Dolly's hips lifted off the couch, her pussy rubbing against the tip of my cock.

She worked her hips harder and harder until she was squirming under my tight hold. Until her eyes fixed on mine and she hissed through gritted teeth, "Get off!"

Smiling darkly, knowing what she really wanted, I forced her thighs apart with my knees and brought her wrists above her head. Dolly fought me the whole way, kicking and thrashing, all the time causing me to harden even more. I added more pressure until she was locked beneath me.

I ran the tip of my nose up her cheek and across to her lips. I caught her bottom lip in my teeth and nibbled. Dolly's moans filled my ears, then she tried to buck me off.

I saw red.

Taking her wrists in one hand, I moved my free hand to her throat. Dolly's eyes grew leaden, her lust feeding off my violent touch. I squeezed, watched her face redden and her cheeks fill with heat. Then, cock braced and ready, I slammed inside her. Dolly cried out as I filled her to the hilt.

And I didn't stop. I didn't give her time to adjust. Didn't give her time to catch her breath. I unleashed my darkness on her, wrists locked and throat captured; I slammed inside her, relentless, harsh and hard, and so fucking good.

Her lips tried to work as I held her down. But her voice was unable to make a sound, my hand on her throat holding it in check. "No words," I demanded and hovered my face just above hers. Her gaze lit with challenge as she tried to speak again. I lifted her wrists and smacked them back down off the couch. But Dolly's lips kept working. My jaw tensed as her pussy clenched around my dick.

I growled on seeing the victory in Dolly's eyes. She fought to get her wrists free, but I held them like a vise. "Don't push me," I warned and squeezed her throat as a reminder.

In response, Dolly thrust her hips against mine, drawing a groan from my throat. Sweat ran over our slick skin as I pounded into her. Her pussy clenched tighter and tighter in time with the choked sounds of her impending orgasm.

"Submit," I ordered and increased my speed. Dolly struggled harder, one final attempt to fight me off. My balls tightened as she did, giving me the resistance I craved so fucking badly.

"Submit!" I bellowed with a final thrust. Dolly's scream joined the music vibrating in the air. She arched into my chest, before her body went limp under my touch. Seeing her flop to the couch, wrists weak and throat vulnerable to my hand, heat swept through me and I came. I gritted my teeth together as a feeling I'd never felt before, a release so strong that I snarled and growled, took me over, incinerating me from the inside.

I thrust and thrust until Dolly's tight pussy ceased gripping my cock. Her legs collapsed to the side, her body completely spent.

Breathless, I rested my forehead in the crook of her neck and shoulder. Her body shook and shivered under mine. Heat filled my chest when I knew who caused those jerky movements—me. My roughness. Her fight. Our perfect fucked-up-ness.

Needing to see her, I raised my head and looked down. Dolly's eyes were closed as she took in deep breaths through her nose. Her hair was slicked to her face, her cheeks flushed red. The cut on her neck was red from my thimble's stroke. Blood stained her flesh, and my fresh bite mark branded her skin.

I groaned, liking that most of all. It announced to everyone that Dolly belonged to me. She was branded with my mark.

Dolly's tits rose and fell as she came down from her high. My cock twitched at the sight of one of my hands holding her wrists above her head. My balls ached at the sight of my hand over her throat.

As if feeling my stare, Dolly opened her eyes, long false lashes now the only bit of makeup that remained on her face. She blinked, clearing the fog from her sight. I held my breath, waiting for her to say something. To react.

Then she smiled.

Exhaling, I released her wrists and pulled my hand from her throat.

Dolly's hands slowly slid from above her head. Her eyes never left mine as she pushed her hands behind my neck. I dropped my forehead to hers and just breathed.

She didn't speak until I went to pull out from between her legs. "No," she said, wrapping her thighs around my waist. I could have easily overpowered her and withdrawn, but I liked that she wanted me to stay inside her. My cock began to wake as I met her eyes and she shook her head. "I want to keep you there."

I sat up, taking Dolly with me, and rested my back against the couch. Dolly was plastered to my front, her head tucked into my neck. I ran my hands down her back. Dolly practically purred into my ears as her hips rolled slightly at my touch.

I stared straight ahead, replaying her cries and moans in my head. I stared at the pole and stage, seeing again my Dolly strip for me. Seeing her offer me her vein. I dropped a kiss on her shoulder and wondered if anyone had ever done this before. Wondered if any fucker out there had this with his girl. A woman who was handcrafted for him.

Perfection, forged in hell.

Dolly sighed and slowly drew back her head. Her arms stayed loosely looped around my neck. "Darlin," I greeted her, seeing her eyes dip and a flush set on her cheeks. She looked up at me from below her lashes and bit her lip.

What a beautiful sight.

Dolly stroked a piece of hair back from my forehead. Her finger dropped to the spade tattoo on the side of my face. Then she looked right at me. "Do you think other people in Wonderland, people like us, Rabbit and Dolly, find pleasure just like that?"

I narrowed my eyes. "Meaning?"

Dolly ran her hand down to my chest and over the welts that her clawing and scratching had brought to my tattooed skin. I fixed my attention on the bite mark on her neck.

Dolly held me tighter. "I was watching TV the other night. There was a film on."

I waited for her to continue.

"The people . . . the people like us, they were doing what we do. What we just did." She paused again. I placed my hand under her chin and lifted her head until she met my eyes. I raised my brow in question. Dolly sighed. "They didn't do what we do. It was different."

"Different . . .?" I trailed off, wondering how else people were when they fucked.

Dolly nodded her head. "They were on a blanket. In a field under the stars." A whisper of a smile ghosted her lips. She shrugged. "There was no fighting. There was no blood being shared." My eyebrows pulled down, imagining what that even looked like.

Dolly's finger went down to my chest. She traced the Sick Fux tattoo. "The man was on top of the woman. She was holding him close. Soft . . ." Dolly's voice seemed just as confused as I was. "It was slow. It was gentle." She smiled and tipped her head up, reaching her arm into the air. "It was under the stars. The moon was so big. And . . . and he told her she had his heart. He told her he loved her."

She shook her head and brought her hand back to my chest. "The people of Wonderland lead strange lives. They go to balls, wear princess dresses and crowns to celebrate leaving school. They join their bodies under the stars, quiet and soft, only a blanket beneath them." She shook her head and then, smiling at me, said, "They are all entirely bonkers, Rabbit! Completely off their rockers! What strange creatures they all are!"

I nodded in agreement, but inside my head was thick with a heavy fog. Dolly's smile fell, and I saw straight through her charade. She was sad about the way the other people were. How they were different to us.

Placing my hands on her cheeks, I pulled her to my mouth. Before our lips touched, I met her eyes. She blinked, but I saw the tears building regardless. Tears for something she had never had. The dresses. The stars. The declaration of . . . love? That perplexed me most of all.

Clearing my mind, I pressed my lips against hers. But this time I did it softly. Gently . . .

When I pulled back, Dolly sighed and her eyes flickered open. She stared at me, wordlessly, regarding me strangely.

"We must go," I said.

"Okay." Dolly climbed from my lap. I put on my shirt and vest, and zipped up my pants. I stared at Dolly as she dressed, her ruined, blood-soiled blue dress back on her body. When she turned to me, my breath was swept from within me.

She was mine.

She was all fucking mine.

I held out my hand. Dolly walked to me and slipped her hand into mine. I led her through the back door the guard had told us about. The skies were clear, save for a sea of stars, as we got into the car and pulled back out onto the country roads. I had placed my jacket over Dolly to keep her warm. Her responding smile seared my black heart. Another brand on the tally of how many times she made my chest ache.

I left the lights off as I drove. A ballad came through the speakers as we sailed through the silent night. Dolly's words spun in my head. About the man and woman in the movie. About the stars and the blanket. The lack of blood and roughness . . .

Glancing across at Dolly, I saw she was fast asleep. A small smile was on her lips as she dreamed, wrapped up in my coat.

Black covering color. Exactly how we were. My darkness polluting her light.

But there was no other way. I couldn't be without her. I would never let that happen. It was just the way it now was.

Taking my cell from the console, I brought up Chapel's number. He answered on the third ring.

"Young Dapper Dan," he said. "To what do I owe this unexpected pleasure?"

"How do people fuck?" I asked, careful not to wake Dolly from her sleep.

Silence greeted me. Then, "Mostly not as you do, I would hazard a guess." I frowned. Chapel sighed. "Romantic gestures, young squire. Most intimacies are born from romance. Soft touches. Kisses. Gentle strokes of hair." I listened in silence. "One would start by gifting the lady with a present, something that will make her happy. Bring out a smile. Then romance—a meal, a night out . . . a slow dance." I looked at Dolly again as I turned right onto another road. Onto the path of the man who hurt my girl most of all. "Clothes would be removed by the other, savoring each touch from their lover. They would take it to their bed, or some other place that was comfortable for what was to come." I swallowed as Chapel continued. "Then they would make love, Dapper Dan. Not fuck. No aggression. Nothing untoward, just him and her. Joined. Intimate. Slow. Sweet kisses and sensuous strokes until they are brought to climax." My hand tightened on the wheel as I tried to imagine how that could be. I couldn't even conjure up the image.

"Then the man, being the gentleman that he is, would hold

her close in the aftermath. And if his heart so felt it, tell her that he loves her."

I froze, completely froze.

"Dapper Dan?" Chapel said. When I didn't speak, he asked, "You do love your little Dolly darlin', do you not?"

"Love?" I questioned.

"Cannot imagine your life without her in it? Would kill if anyone hurt her? Would die if you ever lost her? Can't breathe or sleep without seeing her face?"

My pulse thundered in my neck as I looked at her again. All of them. I had all of those. What was Rabbit without his Dolly?

Chapel spoke. "You should tell her, young squire. That is something young women tend to enjoy hearing." A pause. "You are on your way to the penultimate kill?"

"Yes," I replied.

"The ace in the pack, if I remember correctly?"

My lip lifted in disgust. "Yes."

"Then, if memory serves, a declaration of love may be welcomed after Dolly darlin' takes him on. Meeting the ghosts of the past, especially one that was more than instrumental in your demise, can play havoc with one's emotions." He exhaled heavily. "Just a thought."

I hung up without saying goodbye. Chapel's explanation of fucking throbbed in my brain. I looked up at the stars above. *It was under the stars. The moon was so big. And . . . and he told her she had his heart. He told her he loved her . . .*

Fuck the stars, I thought when my eyes fell back to the girl beside me. The only one worthy of my attention. Of my eyes.

They are all entirely bonkers! she had said on a strained

laugh. But I knew my little Dolly. If they were "bonkers," she wanted to be bonkers too.

The ballad ended, so I rewound the cassette and played it again. *Romance.* The slow, soft song playing seemed appropriate to Dolly's wants. To how I felt about her.

I drove until the sun began to rise, cresting over the horizon, the word "love" still playing havoc with my mind.

Cannot imagine your life without her in it? Would kill if anyone hurt her? Would die if you ever lost her? Can't breathe or sleep without seeing her face?

Love, I thought. A word so alien to my vocabulary, yet it seemed I had lived with it in me since the age of nine. *Love.* Not deep enough to describe my feelings for Dolly.

But it would have to do.

I had no other word as mighty or as strong.

CHAPTER 13

Eddie

"JESUS CHRIST," I muttered as I walked over to the pile of bodies. The maid was shaking, wrapped in a blanket.

"They just walked in?" my uncle asked her.

She nodded. "Walked in like they were invited. The woman —no, more a girl—sat down there"—she pointed to a chair in the center of the table—"and started pouring tea and eating cakes." She shook her head. "They were insane. They were both insane."

My uncle rested his hand on her shoulder, and then allowed the sketch artist to sit beside her and draw the killers from her descriptions. My uncle came over to me. "Male and female. Seem to be in their early twenties."

I nodded and moved away from the bodies as forensics began

their work. The same tag had been written on the wall in the same pink lipstick.

My uncle put his hands in his pockets and shook his head. "They're escalating. Each kill more deadly than the last." He leaned his head closer to mine. "I have a lead I want you to follow up on."

I raised my eyebrow in question.

"What we found with Clive, the third body . . . the children he'd abused. I decided to dig deeper." He looked around to make sure no one was listening. "I found out that the former chief of the Rangers was a close friend of Earnshaw." Shivers ran down my spine. Something just didn't feel right. "Turns out, several years ago a complaint was brought to him. A young man who claimed he had been abused when he was a kid. A kid in foster care. Claimed he was taken to the Earnshaw estate, along with others, and raped. That his social worker got money from Earnshaw and his associates to fuck him, and others in the same situation." I felt the blood trickle from my face, drop by drop.

My eyes widened and I shook my head. "Not possible," I said, imagining Mr. Earnshaw in my head. He wasn't that kind of man.

My uncle shrugged. "The case, for whatever reason, was squashed. Classed as a false report and filed away so deep you would never know it had ever been made, unless you were looking . . . hard." He clapped a hand on my shoulder. "When I get it through here, I'll have you look it over. Could be nothing, but the guy could be worth talking to."

"Smith?" The sketch artist's voice cut through our silence. I followed my uncle back to the maid and the artist. He held out a piece of paper. My focus had drifted again to the tag on the white wall. The lines were getting neater. It suggested their confidence was growing. By the acceleration of their kills, and the manner in which the murders were carried out, that much was obvious.

"What the hell?" my uncle remarked as he studied the picture. He turned to the maid. "They were dressed like this?"

She nodded slowly.

I took the picture from my uncle and looked down at it . . . If my blood had trickled from my face on hearing about the false report of Earnshaw's abuse, it positively drained in slews on seeing the faces staring back at me. And not just their faces. Their style of dress.

Outfits and faces I knew very well.

"Eddie?" My uncle's voice burrowed into my ears. His hand hit my shoulder and squeezed. "What is it, son?"

Swallowing to lubricate my dry throat, I whispered, "Ellis."

The paper shook. I realized my hand was trembling. My finger ran over her face. Her painted face, a hand-drawn clock circling her left eye. Then my gaze fell on the man beside her. The one who caused my blood to ignite. The one who took my best friend from me.

The one obsessed with death and corrupting Ellis's goodness.

"Heathan James," I said, my voice betraying my dislike. Shock soon replaced dislike. Heathan was alive? After all of these years he had surfaced. From where? And how?

"Son? You care to explain?" my uncle probed.

Slowly lowering the paper, I faced him. "Heathan James."

Recognition sparked in my uncle's face. "The kid you knew

when you were young? The runaway? The one never found, presumed dead?"

I nodded and glanced down to see those eyes looking straight back at me, taunting me. Mocking me . . . laughing at me. They were gray and cold. Like steel bullets. No life in their depths. No soul.

And he had my Ellis.

He had corrupted her. Forced her to do evil things.

"He took Ellis. He is forcing her against her will." Anger took hold of me. "He is making her watch him kill."

My uncle ran his hand over his forehead. He was about to say something when the maid got to her feet. "No," she said, head shaking profusely.

"What, dear?" my uncle asked.

She pointed at the picture of Ellis. "You're wrong."

"About what?" I asked.

"The girl." The maid pulled her blanket tighter over her shoulders. She visibly shivered, although the night was hot and sticky. She was shivering at the memory of what she witnessed . . . at the killers.

The killers, who I knew personally.

The maid cleared her throat. "The girl is not innocent." My breath became trapped in my lungs. Her blue eyes met mine. "She was the one who led them." Her face drained of color. "The things she did . . ." She tapped her head. "She is insane. They both are. He is dark." She choked on a sob. "He wanted to kill me. She spared me . . ." She shook her head, eyes closed. When they reopened, she said, "He does not control her. She is as much to blame for these murders as he is. More, in fact."

275

"Ellis wouldn't do this," I argued, imploring my uncle to understand. "It will be Heathan. He will have brainwashed her, somehow."

"Those weren't their names," the maid cut in. I stared at her. "They were called Dolly and Rabbit. I heard that loud and clear." She pointed at the twin men on the floor. Men I had also known when growing up. "They called them Tweedledum and Twee-dledee. You know, the characters from—"

"*Alice in Wonderland,*" I finished and closed my eyes, inhaling deeply through my nose. When I opened them again, my uncle was watching me. He wore a questioning expression on his face. "When we were kids . . . Ellis loved that book. She . . ." I imagined her blue dress. Glancing down at the drawing, I saw she wore one similar to the one she'd had as a child. But this one was more provocative. Much more revealing. I breathed deeply. "She used to pretend she lived in Wonderland." A memory from our youth came back to me. "She christened Heathan James 'Rabbit.' She claimed he was the White Rabbit from Wonder-land, come to take her on an adventure."

"And?" my uncle said.

I fixed my Stetson. "She said I wasn't one of them. That I was too clean-cut. Not 'insane enough.' That was when I lost her to him."

I could still remember every part of that day . . .

"You can't be the Mad Hatter, Eddie. It just doesn't suit. You don't belong in Wonderland . . ."

I looked over at the table. "A tea party." I shook my head. "Ellis always loved tea parties." I realized everyone was looking at me strangely. I hit the sketch. "This is all Heathan. He'll be the mastermind behind this. He always was too smart for his own good. Manipulative. A true Machiavellian. Ellis was bewitched from the minute she met him. He had the ability to bend her to his every whim. She hung on his every word." I clenched my jaw. "This is him. He came to get her, to rope her into this murder spree."

"Son. I know you've always had a soft spot for this girl, but maybe you didn't know her so well after all."

"I did!" I argued. "She isn't capable of this—"

"She's evil," the maid asserted, interrupting me. Her face was stone. "That girl is evil. Pretty, disgusting, a demon." She shuddered. "She laughed as she killed. She welcomed their blood on her flesh." The maid sat down, overcome by the memory. "That girl is made by the devil . . . they both are."

My uncle pulled me away. "What do we know about this Heathan James?"

"All I know is that his mama dropped him off to live with his papa at the Earnshaw estate when he was nine." I cupped the nape of my neck. I was getting a headache. "She said he scared her. She couldn't be tracked down after that. When his papa died in an accident on the estate, Ellis's papa took him in."

My uncle's face was impassive. "Then maybe we need to find Mrs. James and ask her a few questions."

I nodded. Just as my uncle went to move away, I said, "There are two more left." I picked up the playing card that had been put in an evidence bag. "There's her 'Uncle John' and her papa." I blew out a breath. "And we have no idea where either of them are. But they have to be going for them next. They are systematically eliminating anyone who lived on the estate." I added a fact

I didn't want to face. "And the kills are getting more gruesome. Emotion is playing a part. And by the way their killing is escalating in its intensity, the worst is yet to come."

"We have everyone we can muster tracking them down. But one thing intrigues me," my uncle said. "Why would such formidable businessmen seemingly go into hiding?" He stepped closer and lowered his voice. "Right about the time they were accused of abusing a child." His eyebrow rose. "We must not rule out any possibility."

When he walked off, I stared at the card in my hand. The drawing of the twins was so accurate I got chills. Then I remembered Heathan's drawings as he sat with Ellis on the lawn. Sick and twisted pictures. Pictures of them killing.

I closed my eyes. *Ellis . . . what the fuck has he made you do?*

* * *

"HEATHAN?"

Mrs. James—now Mrs. Lockwood—paled as she uttered her son's name.

"We just want to know more about him."

Mrs. Lockwood's gray eyes—Heathan's eyes—fell on my uncle, and her hands twisted in her lap. Her husband took her hand. She cast him a grateful smile.

Mrs. Lockwood was a petite woman. Seemingly timid and weak. I couldn't imagine Heathan being her son. But then, I was sure Heathan's evil was innate, not learned.

Her husband rubbed her back and encouraged her to speak.

Mrs. Lockwood brushed a piece of black hair from her face and said, "Heathan, from being very young, always displayed some . . . tendencies." Her eyes grew distant. "He was always a quiet child. Lived in his head most of the time. Didn't like to be touched." She took a drink of water. Placing it down, she said, "To cut a long story short, I couldn't cope with him anymore." She inhaled deeply. "He . . . he scared me. Heathan was always a tall child. Well-built for his age. By the time he was nine, he was the same height as me." She worried her lip. "There . . . there was an incident, and I knew I couldn't have him around anymore." Her head fell to her hands, and a sob ripped from her throat. "I feared that he would kill me." She wiped at her tearful eyes, and said, "He told me he would. Told me that if I ever crossed him, he would kill me." She sniffed. "My own son. My nine-year-old son. I was alone. A single mother, with a son I believed would do as he threatened. I feared for my life."

"Why was he like that?" my uncle asked. "Was there a particular moment you can pinpoint?"

Mrs. Lockwood drained her glass of water, and her husband handed her a tissue. She nodded. "I was very young when I had Heathan. I foolishly believed his father loved me. He didn't. Soon after Heathan was born, he left us." She looked out of the window, eyes unfocused. "With no money, I had no choice but to move back in with my father. My mother had died years before from cancer." Her husband gripped her hand more tightly.

"My father was a hard man. A taskmaster. With Heathan, he was particularly strict. Heathan never said anything, but I knew he hated him."

I was tense as I listened to the story.

"One day, I came back from work to find my father on the floor of our kitchen." She squeezed her eyes shut. "Heathan was sitting beside him, soaked in blood." She hiccupped. "There had been a break-in. The men were caught. But those men had come in and tried to take money from my father. All he had was a pocket watch, a family heirloom that he refused to give up. They later confessed everything to the police. My father was stabbed, ten times, right in front of my little boy, for not handing over that damn pocket watch."

My blood cooled when I remembered that watch. *Tick tock . . . tick tock . . . tick tock . . .*

Mrs. Lockwood became lost to her tears. "I knew Heathan would be affected by the murder. What six-year-old child wouldn't? Only he wasn't affected like I expected. No"—she shook her head—"Heathan wasn't scarred by the memory. He seemed . . . *inspired.*" The hairs on the back of my neck stood up. "The pocket watch vanished after the murder. We all thought the murderers had taken it or thrown it away. It turned out Heathan had it. It had been damaged, ruined beyond repair. I found him with it when I caught him sitting beside next door's dog on the side of the road. It had been run over by a car. Heathan was braced over that poor dog, his eyes wide with wonder as he studied its dead body, holding that watch, repeating 'Tick tock, tick tock, tick tock.' The boy believed the watch was working. Seemed to associate that watch with anything death-related. Always uttering 'Tick tock'. I realized in that moment that seeing the murder of my father had altered him permanently. All he did after that was read about death, murders, serial killers and ways to kill.

"I couldn't afford any specialists to look at him. And then things only seemed to get worse. His obsession spiraled. He burned insects. Destroyed butterflies. He was fascinated by their demise, by their deaths caused by his own hands.

"One day, when he was nine, I came home to find him sitting on the kitchen floor. Heathan was covered in blood. There was a knife on the floor beside him and he had cuts all over his body, wounds he had clearly inflicted upon himself. He was rubbing his blood into the skin on his arms and face, only to stop and write 'Tick tock' on the kitchen floor with his finger, using his own blood as the ink. I snapped, and I tried to take that cursed watch from his hands." Her cheeks paled. "That boy of mine. He . . . he shot to his feet, put his hand on my throat, and forced me back against the wall. He threatened that if I came near him again, that if I dared take the watch, he would kill me in my sleep." She stared at my uncle. "And he would have." She straightened her back. "That was the day I drove him to the Earnshaw estate and gave him to his father. I couldn't take it anymore."

My uncle shook Mrs. and Mr. Lockwood's hands and got to his feet when the interview had finished. I followed. As we left, Mrs. Lockwood put her hand on my uncle's arm and said, "I don't know what he's done, but that boy is trouble. Nothing or no one will ever get through to him. He will never let anyone in to try."

That was where she was wrong. Because the girl he let in once belonged to me. An extroverted blond, five foot one and weighing no more than one hundred pounds, now had the full attention of one Heathan James. She returned the favor.

The most fucked-up pairing I'd ever seen.

We drove back to the Ranger base in silence. I couldn't stop thinking about what Heathan's mother had said. How even as a child he would kill. Hours passed as I worked at my desk. Just as I had signed off on my last report concerning the tea-party massacre, another file landed on my desk. I groaned and looked up at the junior officer.

"Don't blame me. Your uncle told me to get this to you as soon as it came through."

Turning my lamp back on, I picked up the file. "Earnshaw," the label said. I ran my hand over the file. It was old.

The false report.

I turned the page and began to read . . . and I didn't stop until I reached the last page. I sat back in my seat and ran my hand through my hair, feeling sick to my bones. The clock on the wall struck three, the loud chimes reverberating around the deserted office.

Yet I remained, eyes closed, knowing that what I had just read was real. And it had mentioned Ellis. Little Ellis. Innocent, fragile, little Ellis.

And Heathan.

It had mentioned Heathan James too.

I squeezed my eyes shut tighter, fighting the bile that had risen to my throat. And to no one and everyone, I opened my mouth and whispered, "Jesus Christ."

CHAPTER 14

THE JABBERWOCK

Dolly

"DID YOU LIKE YOUR PICTURE?" I asked Rabbit as we drove down another new road.

Rabbit shrugged. "I don't care about the picture."

I leaned back in my seat and thought of the picture in my head. As soon as I switched on the TV this morning, I had seen a picture of me and my Rabbit. It was drawn in pencil. "SICK FUX" was displayed along the bottom of the screen. I couldn't read the rest so good; the words went by too fast. But Rabbit told me it had said we were "Serial Killers." It had said we were on the loose. It described what we wore, and told people to watch out for us.

I didn't care about all of that. I just liked the picture of me and my Rabbit. I wanted a copy. I wanted to put it in a frame. "You looked so handsome," I told him and turned to give him a smile.

Rabbit raised his eyebrow. I laughed at his moody face. "You're the most handsome boy I ever did see." Rabbit glanced at me from the corner of his eye and smirked.

I turned up the music. My mummy's music blasted at us. I thought of what was coming up. I hugged my doll to my chest when my stomach began to drop and shivers broke out all over my body . . .

The Jabberwock.

I swallowed, feeling something I had never encountered before when facing the bad men. Fear. I felt fear as I looked down at his card. Rabbit had given me the card this morning. He had told me that the Jabberwock was mine to kill.

The Jabberwock was the fiercest bad man of all.

He was the evil one who hurt little Ellis the most.

He was the one who put a baby in her stomach . . . then ripped it all away.

I ran my hand over the Jabberwock's face. I shuddered at the eyes staring back at me.

Nasty, nasty, wicked eyes.

Rabbit's hand landed on my thigh. Taking a deep breath, I looked at him. I had worn my extra-long false lashes today. I had put my lipstick on extra thick. I needed their protection. The Jabberwock was a good fighter, a very good fighter.

He was my biggest challenge yet.

"You can defeat him," Rabbit assured me, reading my mind.

I nodded, but my doll shook in my trembling hands. "I . . ." I sucked in a deep breath. "I am scared, Rabbit. The Jabber-wock . . . he scares me so."

Rabbit's jaw clenched. He looked over at me, and for a moment, I got lost in his silver eyes. They were pretty moons. Their beauty made me feel slightly better. "You can defeat him," Rabbit repeated. His voice was low and hard. I knew Rabbit was annoyed. I knew he was angry. He was acting like he had done when we went for the Cheshire Cat. Only today, he had not once left me alone. Wherever I went, so did he. When I showered, he was with me, touching my face and stroking my hair. When I put on my makeup, I sat on his lap. And now, his hand remained firmly on my thigh.

If I didn't know better, I would think my Rabbit was scared too.

"You have your knife and your gun," he continued. "I'll be there every step of the way." His nostrils flared. "I won't let him hurt you."

I didn't know why, but my bottom lip began to quiver. My eyesight blurred as I looked at Rabbit's hand on my knee. And then I looked again at the card in my hands. He was no different to the other men we had killed. But at the same time, he was completely different. Because he was the man who hurt Ellis the most.

Beyond all doubt, I knew she feared him most of all.

Ellis had gone quiet in my mind. Ever since I told her that we were coming but first we had to defeat the Jabberwock, she'd stopped speaking to me. But I felt her; she was hiding in my mind. And she was in darkness. Scared and hiding in a place where the Jabberwock could not find her again.

Because he wanted to hurt Ellis. He always wanted to really hurt her. Just like when Ellis was younger, he would hurt her . . . then hurt her some more. Again and again, not caring that she cried. Not caring that she wanted her Heathan to make her feel better. The Jabberwock kept taking and taking from her until Ellis became trapped behind the door . . . trapped in a dark forest full of vicious beasts and mind-numbing nightmares.

Rabbit took my hand. A tear from my eye fell on the back of his hand. Without speaking, Rabbit lifted my hand to his lips. I held my breath, shocked that he could be so soft and gentle with me.

And then he kissed me. His lips, so soft and plump, kissed the back of my hand. Warmth replaced the ice in my chest as his precious breath ghosted over my skin. When he lowered our hands, he kept them on my lap. He didn't utter a word, but then I was sure that the moment would have been spoiled by idle chit-chat.

The silence told me everything. My Rabbit loved me. He never said so, but I felt it. And that would be enough for now.

I gripped his hand all the way to the place where the Jabberwock stayed. As we pulled into the town that protected him, I smelled salt in the air. I could see the sea as we drove along the quiet streets.

"Where are we?" I asked.

"Del Rio," Rabbit replied and fell silent once more.

We traveled a long way, then Rabbit turned off the road. We drove down a country road until we came to a large stretch of water. I gasped at its beauty. I didn't get chance to say so before Rabbit asked, "How do you intend to kill him?"

I looked down at our joined hands. "I . . . I don't know." I gazed out over the water, glistening blue in the light of the sun. "I want to make him pay." A deep breath. "The Jabberwock is the worst of all the men. Worse even than the King of Hearts, because he hurt Ellis the most. Locked her behind the door and left her all alone for a very long time."

I blinked as the tears built again in my eyes. "Ellis told me he was the one who helped send her Heathan away." Rabbit stilled. His hand tightened around mine, so much that it almost hurt me. "He did so many bad things that I feel, and Ellis feels, the Jabberwock should die in the worst way possible. But . . ."

"But what?"

"But I just can't think. For some reason, with the Jabberwock, my head can't think. I don't know why. There is this big fog in my brain."

Rabbit gently stroked my cheek. My eyebrows furrowed. That was the second gentle touch I had received from Rabbit. "Rabbit?" I asked, unsure what I was really asking.

"You just kill him," he said. "No messing around. You go in there. You choose your weapon, and you slaughter him. Don't let him hurt you. Just kill him. Then . . ." He closed his eyes.

"There is only one more left," I finished for him.

He opened his eyes and nodded.

"Rabbit?" I held his hand tighter and looked back over the water. It was so quiet. "We are nearly at his home, aren't we?"

Rabbit tensed, but nodded again. "It is about ten minutes down this road."

I breathed in through my mouth, then out through my nose. I wasn't sure how long we sat in the car, looking out over the water, but as a bird swooped high in the sky, I turned to Rabbit. "I'm ready," I declared, hearing a shaking in my voice.

Rabbit, in his third act of unexpected chivalry, closed the distance between us and kissed me on my lips. My heart skipped a beat at the feel of his lips against mine, so gentle and kind. There was no blood. No biting nor harshness, simply peace and softness.

It stole my heart.

As he pulled away, he left his hand on my cheek. "Rabbit," I whispered breathlessly and fluttered my eyes open. Rabbit swallowed, his cheeks flushed. There was a strange look in his eyes. One I couldn't decipher. But if I had to guess, I would venture it looked like . . . some kind of . . . happiness.

Rabbit slid back over to his side and pulled the car onto the dirt road. As we passed the water's edge, I clutched my knife in my hand. I closed my eyes and let the awful things he had done to Ellis fill my mind. Not only had Ellis told me what he had done to her, she had also shown me. So I replayed the images one after the other. I let Ellis's cries fill my ears until they rang with pain. And I let myself feel the Jabberwock between my legs, thrusting and making Ellis scream.

Anger, more anger than I had ever experienced before, began to fill my body. I felt it like quickfire, shooting down my arms, my legs and my chest. It reached my fingers, which tightened their grip on the knife. I embraced the anger, so much that when we pulled up to the house, surrounded by dark trees . . . a dark forest, like the one that imprisoned Ellis . . . I didn't think, I acted.

Guided by the rage bubbling in my stomach, I burst from the

car. And I ran and I ran. I ran over the lawn and straight up to the house. I raced up the steps and slammed my way through the front door.

I didn't wait to see if Rabbit was behind me. A red mist had coated my vision. I had to follow my anger's path to the source: the Jabberwock.

I ran down the hallway, searching all the rooms for any sign of movement. Someone jumped out at me from the third door. I plunged my knife into his chest . . . and I kept running. I didn't even stop to see who I had killed. I just knew it wasn't *him*. I instinctively knew I would recognize him when we found him. I could never forget the ugly, evil face that Ellis had etched on my mind.

Another person caught me by the hair as I ran by them, wrenching me back. When I turned, a man, dressed in black, stood before me. I stabbed my knife upward through his throat into his brain. Blood immediately hit my face, and his hands fell from my hair.

I turned, searching the large house for my next kill . . . and then I heard it.

"Ellis!" A voice called out from the top of the stairs. "Ellis!" My blood cooled. I knew that voice. Ellis had let me know how that voice sounded . . . and worse . . . he was calling her name.

The Jabberwock, the nastiest of them all, was calling Ellis's name. Taunting me. Mocking me . . .

He was going to die.

I ran up the stairs two at a time. I raised my knife above my shoulder, ready to strike. When I reached the top, I heard footsteps. Whipping my head to the right, I set off at a sprint. I chased the sound of the footsteps until I entered a darkened room. I narrowed my eyes, searching for the monster, when he called her name again. The Jabberwock was across the room, standing in the shadows.

He stood right before me.

I shook with rage. I shook as anger-driven energy surged through me, and my legs propelled me forward. I had only taken three steps before my footing faltered. Suddenly I was falling. I screamed as I fell . . . down and down. Until I hit something beneath me. Something soft broke my fall. I looked up, dread and absolute terror holding me captive.

A hole . . . a hole above me . . . a rabbit hole.

"No," I whispered and searched around me. I was in a room: a room with three doors. Jumping from whatever I was sitting on —I looked back to find it was a bed—I ran to the first door. It was locked. I ran to the second. It too was locked. "No!" I called louder, my voice cracking in my throat. I approached the third door, dragging my feet. I reached out . . . It was locked.

I shook my head. I shook my head so fast that I became dizzy. Something clattered on the floor. When I looked down, I saw that my knife was on the hard wood. I backed away. I backed away until my legs hit the mattress.

My bottom lip shook as I took in the four walls surrounding me. The three doors . . . it was a replica of the room I had been trapped in for years.

I was back in the room of doors.

A sob crept up my throat. Strength seeped from my body, like blood draining from a wound. My body automatically curled on the bed, arms wrapped around my waist for protection. I closed my eyes, trying to fight the dark and the sinking pit that was forming in my stomach.

Suddenly the door to my right opened. My eyes snapped open, ice-cold fear freezing my bones. I watched as a man walked through. I stared at his feet, at his polished black leather shoes . . . That was all I needed to know who had trapped me.

His legs were in my vision as he reached the bed. I closed my eyes when a hand pushed through my hair. I wanted to move, I wanted to run away, but the room of doors kept me trapped. My body wouldn't move. My hand wouldn't slap his touch away.

"Ellis . . ." he whispered. I felt his voice slice down to my soul. Felt its talons scrape the fragile glass that was my heart, tapping at the weak spots, until it shattered apart, finally draining all my courage and hope.

The Jabberwock's hand stroked roughly down my face, replacing the sensuous path that Rabbit's had traced a short while ago. I wanted Rabbit's touch. I wanted his gentle touch caressing my skin.

I wanted Rabbit, full stop. I wanted Rabbit. But he wouldn't find me in this room. He wouldn't be able to get it in—all the doors were locked. Only the Jabberwock had the keys.

"My Ellis," the Jabberwock whispered. The bed dipped at the side. I felt the Jabberwock's body move closer. I smelled his scent—whiskey and smoke.

I hated the smell of whiskey and smoke.

"You think I didn't know you were coming?" He chuckled. The sound hurt my ears. "As soon as I heard the victims' names, as soon as I saw the picture on the news, I knew you'd be coming for me." A finger slid under my chin. He forced my head to the side. "Open your eyes."

Unable to resist his command, I did as ordered. The instant I saw his face, I felt the makeup Rabbit had bought me fall from my face. I felt my dress fade from blue to black. I felt Dolly disappearing. Felt her bravery and courage evaporating into the dank air. I shook with fear.

"Ellis Earnshaw," the Jabberwock said. Only when I looked into his eyes, I saw that he wasn't the Jabberwock. Instead Uncle John sat beside me, holding my face.

"Uncle John," I whispered. He grinned.

"There she is," he said and traced his hand down my side until it rested on my bare thigh. "My little Ellis. With an English accent, no less." His eyes flared when they fell on my dress. "You always did like to play, didn't you?" And then he began to lift it. My breathing quivered as his calloused hand crept up my thigh toward my bottom. I choked down a sob when he pushed my knickers aside and flattened his palm on my buttock. I squeezed my eyes shut as he moved to kneel beside me.

Uncle John rolled me onto my back. I opened my eyes and stared at the ceiling as he lifted my dress. Lifted my dress until it bunched around my waist. His hands hooked into the waistband of my knickers, and he rolled them down my legs, slid them over my boots and tossed them on the floor.

He got up off his knees and crawled over me. My eyes glazed over as I pictured Rabbit in my mind. I pictured his silver eyes. I pictured his tattoos and his jet-black hair. But most of all, I pictured the kiss he had given me today, by the water. Soft and gentle, and so very loving.

I pictured loving my Rabbit.

Fingers tiptoed up my legs until they reached my stomach. Uncle John's fingertips traced my scar. He blew out a breath. "I remember this." I heard the triumphant smile in his voice. "We had so much more fun after this cut was made, didn't we, Ellis?" His head dipped and he kissed my stomach. Vomit clogged my throat. I swallowed it back down. "You were always my favorite, Ellis. Out of all that I schooled, you were my favorite." He sighed. "But then you faded on me, lost your spark. It was a sad time, Ellis, when you left me, when the light in your eyes dimmed to nothing." He ran a fingertip over my eyebrow. I wanted to fight him off, but my body was paralyzed. My body never could fight off Uncle John.

Uncle John owned me. He always had. He'd won me years ago in a game of poker.

"I hated leaving you, Ellis. But now here you are, back again, back with that spark in your eye." His hand drifted to the inside of my thigh.

My heart slammed into an erratic beat. It called for him to leave me alone. But the call was not answered. The call wasn't strong enough. So I closed my eyes and tried to block out the sounds. Tried to block out the feel of his hand slipping between my legs.

I blocked it all out.

I welcomed the return of the blackness.

Back in my room of doors.

Back to being all alone.

CHAPTER 15

Rabbit

"Fuck!" I shouted as I looked through one of the windows. Two men lay dead at my feet, throats slit and stomachs slashed. Dolly had disappeared through a door upstairs.

She had disappeared from sight.

And then she'd fucking screamed.

I raked my hands through my hair as I paced back and forth. There were guards inside. Guards the fucker hadn't had before.

The news. The TV news had shown our pictures. Revealed the names of the victims. Now they both knew we were coming for them.

Clearly, if these new guards were anything to go by.

I raced back to my car. Opening the trunk, I searched through all the shit I had in there. The shit I had bought last night while Dolly slept in the back seat.

I found the AK-47 and took it in hand. I slammed the trunk shut, and then froze. I glared at the house. And then my heart fucking sank.

What if she was gone?

What if that fucker had killed her?

She'd run off.

Disappeared, before I could get to her.

Pain split my chest and stole all my fucking breath. I fought to breathe through the thought of losing Dolly. Of not having her by my side. Killing. Understanding.

Having her beneath me.

Hands shaking, I reached for my cell. I pressed the only number I had logged.

"Dapper Dan!" Chapel said.

"He has her!" I hissed and felt my heart start to crumble. I couldn't fucking breathe at the thought of her in there, bleeding . . . dead. Not Dolly. She was the only person I couldn't have dead.

"Breathe." Another voice came on the line. Henry.

"He has her! In his fucking house!" My legs weakened, and I leaned against the side of the car. "She ran off. I couldn't get to her before the door shut and he locked her inside." I swallowed, startled when I felt a teardrop fall from my eye.

My jaw clenched. "He has her . . ."

"Then get her." I froze as Hyde's familiar gruff voice came through the speaker. "Man the fuck up and go get your girl." My hands tightened around my cane and the AK-47.

"She screamed . . . what if . . . what if he killed her?" I almost choked on the words.

"Then you kill them all. Whoever is left inside that house, you end them. You take them all out. And if you go too, then at least you won't be away from your Dolly for long."

"He also might not have killed her, Dapper Dan," Chapel's calming voice said. "He might simply have her in captivity." He paused. "And she will be waiting for her White Rabbit to rescue her."

I lowered my head and took a deep breath at his words. When I lifted my head, I stared straight ahead and let my anger toward this fucker infuse my veins.

"Gotta go," I shouted into the phone and dropped it into the car.

I had the house in my sight. Fixing my crooked cravat, I palmed my cane and held my AK-47 in firing position. I walked at first, and then I pounded over the lawn, sheer determination pushing me forward as I burst through the front door. I unsheathed my cane and held the blade tightly. One guard came at me, then a second, then a third. I cut them all down. Shots were fired, but I took the shooters out before they could hit me.

Then I was walking up the staircase. I turned right and glared at the door that held my Dolly inside. I picked the lock with the pin from my cravat. The lock turned, and the wooden door opened. As quietly as possible, I snuck into the room, gun and blade braced for whoever was beyond. An empty room greeted me.

I walked lightly over the wooden floor, then I suddenly heard a voice coming from below. "You always were so eager, little Ellis. Always ready for Uncle John."

White-hot rage surged through me as his voice assaulted my ears, spewing his fucked-up shit to my Dolly. I searched the floor for its origin . . . and my stomach fell.

A hole in the floor?

A rabbit hole.

Dolly had fallen through a rabbit hole.

My eyes widened at what that meant. What that would mean to her, how she would perceive that fall in her damaged mind . . .

She would no longer be in Wonderland. Which would mean . . .

"No," I whispered. I circled the hole, only to freeze. Dolly lay on a bed in the center of the room. I shook with rage at what I saw next.

That fucker. The Jabberwock hovered above her. Dolly's eyes were lost, staring at nothing. A catatonic body on the bed.

My broken little doll.

I backed away from the hole. I searched the room, looking for another way to get to her. There was a door in the corner. I moved as quickly as I could and pulled it open. A narrow stairway lay beyond, leading to the room below.

I crept down the stairs to a door at the end. I breathed, trying to keep calm. *He's her kill*, I reminded myself. *When she comes back—because she* will *come back to you— Dolly will have the Jabberwock's head on a platter.*

I counted to five and kicked through the door. The wood gave way easily under my wrath. The Jabberwock looked up.

Him and me, both here for the doll. Vying for ownership.

She was mine.

And he was as good as dead.

The Jabberwock leaped from the bed. His eyes widened, and then he spoke. "Heathan James." He shook his head. "I never thought I'd see *you* again. In fact, I paid a lot of money to make sure I wouldn't."

My lips curled in disgust. This prick didn't even deserve a conversation. All I could see was *him* pinning my girl down on this bed. All I imagined in my mind's eye was this prick holding her down, raping her, then ripping her baby from her stomach. I seethed, my anger inflaming my senses from the inside out.

Bursting into the room, I fired a shot from my AK-47 straight into his leg. He reached for the gun holstered at his waist. I fired another round into his wrist. Blood spurted to the floor as he screamed.

My dick twitched at the heavenly sound.

The Jabberwock fell to the floor. Head up, he began scrambling for something. I glanced down and saw Dolly's knife near my feet. Slinging the strap of my AK-47 over my shoulder, I bent down and retrieved the knife. The Jabberwock was a tenacious bastard. Slowly, he crawled forward, murderous fury illuminating his eyes.

I let him crawl to my feet—right where he belonged. "Fucker," he spat, spraying my shoes with his bloody saliva.

I tipped my head to the side as I surveyed his pitiful form. "Sick Fux, apparently," I replied with a hint of sarcasm. I smirked. "You seemed so much more frightening when I was a child." I bent down until I was mere inches from his face. His cheeks were mottled red, no doubt a result of the pain my bullets were inflicting on his body. I looked over at the bed and saw my Dolly staring up at the ceiling. My breath hitched as I watched her chest. Then I exhaled, relief like nothing I had ever felt before settling over me, when I saw it lifting up and down, slowly.

Then my eyes dropped lower . . . and this time I became a fucking inferno. I shook uncontrollably as I saw Dolly's dress bunched around her waist. As I saw her panties on the floor . . . and as I saw her legs parted. Her limbs were paralyzed. The Jabberwock had forced Dolly out of Wonderland, back into the room of doors to which he had exiled her for all those lost years.

I tore my eyes away from Dolly and focused them on the rapist at my feet. My hands wrapped tighter around Dolly's blade.

Her kill, I sternly reminded myself when my blackened soul tried to usurp control and finish off the fucker. I looked at the bed again. At the catatonic state she had so easily entered under his touch. His mind games had again ensnared my Dolly. After the years of turning her innocent mind to mush, just so he could take her every night, fuck her until she became a mindless automaton, doing whatever he commanded.

He was the one who had banished Ellis.

He was the one who had torn us apart.

He was the one who had financed my years in the Water Tower. I had found that out from the Warden's records when I escaped.

This prick at my feet, the cunt spluttering for breath, gritting his teeth in pain, was the reason I had lost my girl for all those empty years.

I jumped to my feet. Unable to resist any longer, I drove my foot into the Jabberwock's stomach. He curled up, coughing on my leather shoes. I snarled in disgust, and then flipped him onto his back with the toe of my shoe. I paced back and forth as he lay on his back, his whiskey-induced gut rolling up and down like the swell on the ocean. I shook my head, talking myself down from slitting him navel to nose.

I turned again to Dolly, staring at the mascara that had tracked down her face.

He'd made her cry.

This pathetic motherfucker had made her cry.

He was her kill. His last heartbeat had to be delivered by Dolly's hand. Flipping my blade in one hand, the steel so comfortable in my grip, and Dolly's in the other, I spun and slid both blades into his shoulders. The Jabberwock screamed. I smiled as I peered down at him. The steel blades had sunk into the wood beneath his shoulders.

He was stuck fast.

He was now the prey, waiting for Dolly to rouse from her slumber. He flailed, trying to move, but he wasn't going anywhere. His eyes met mine. I saw in that moment his realization that he had lost.

Then his eyes looked to Dolly . . . and he smiled a small smile of victory. Because he had reduced Dolly to this, lying there, on the bed. To the girl I found all those weeks ago sitting in the chair, staring, unseeing, out of a dirty window.

The lost girl dressed in black.

But no more. She was lost temporarily, because she was

without me. The Jabberwock was no fucking match for her Rabbit.

And I'd show him.

I climbed onto the bed. My hand settled gently on Dolly's face. She felt stone cold. Her eyes looked past me to the ceiling. They didn't acknowledge my presence.

"Dolly," I whispered into her ear. There wasn't a sound. Not even a flicker of movement. I pushed her dress down over her pussy, then moved back to look at her face.

"Wonderland," I whispered, thinking of Henry's advice from our discussion months ago. I had to bring her back.

I had to take her through a rabbit hole.

I looked up at the hole in the ceiling. There was no way I was using it. Scooping her in my arms, I raced from the bed to one of the locked doors. I kicked and kicked at the door until the lock gave way. A closet. I rushed to the next door and kicked at the wood. This one was stronger. Eventually, the wood splintered. When the door flew open, a bathroom lay beyond. It was vast, all fine finishes, with a shower and bath.

I ran to the bath and laid Dolly on the floor. I turned on the faucet and put in the plug. Water rose, filling the tub. I sat down and dragged the lifeless Dolly in my arms. I rocked her back and forth in my lap. I stroked back her hair and kissed her face. "Come back to me, darlin'," I implored and rocked faster. "Come back to me, little Dolly." My voice was husky and cracked.

I checked the water, willing it to fill faster. Dolly's eyes were fixed on the towel rail behind us. No life. No spark.

No Dolly in their blue depths.

"Stay with me!" I pulled her higher, biting gently at her neck.

"Come back," I commanded and slit my thimble across my throat. My blood fell onto my shirt, and I placed Dolly's mouth at my neck. "Drink," I ordered. "Feel me. Feel our bond." Setting her down, I sliced my thimble across my hand. I did the same to hers and clasped our palms together. I squeezed them tight, but Dolly's hands were limp.

Repression. I heard Henry's warning in my mind. *Sometimes the repressed are lost forever. Forever imprisoned in the deepest, most inaccessible reaches of their minds.*

"I brought you back once," I said as I dropped our parted hands. The tub was full. I picked up her light body and plunged her into the water. Dolly's makeup ran as the water washed over her face. Lightly gripping her throat, I moved her head so she was looking at me. Forcing her eyes to meet mine, I rasped, throat tight and heart shattered, "I'm the White Rabbit . . . I have come to lead you to Wonderland. There was a mission. You got lost." I swallowed and squeezed my eyes shut. "But now we need you back." I coughed and fought for breath. "*I* need you back." Taking the pocket watch from my vest pocket, I brought it to my ear, directly in her line of sight, and whispered, "Tick tock."

Then I pushed her under the surface.

I grasped her throat with two hands and kept her under the water. Bubbles came from her nose, but she remained still . . .

Until her leg began to twitch. My eyes snapped to it. I squeezed her throat harder, keeping her down. "Come down the rabbit hole."

Dolly's arm moved. Her legs began to kick. At first there were only slight movements, then her hand gripped mine. My eyes flared as I saw life seeping back into her body. "Go down the rabbit hole!" I shouted, as her hands covered mine and she clawed at my skin. I pushed even harder, until Dolly's head touched the bottom of the tub.

She began to thrash wildly. Full-body thrashes, fighting the black hole she had to travel down to come back to me. My eyes filled with tears, blurring my vision, as she fought me.

"Let go!" I shouted. "Let go! Come back to me!"

But Dolly fought the whole way, until her limbs began to tire. Until her hands, gripping and cutting into mine, loosened . . . until they slipped to her side.

Lifeless again, the bubbles from Dolly's nose stopped.

I wrenched Dolly out of the tub and onto the tiled floor. I breathed into her mouth and began compressions on her chest. I pumped and pumped her chest, using my breath to breathe life into hers. Her skin was pale and her hair was slicked to her face.

"Come back!" I repeated, slamming my hands against her chest. "Come the fuck back! That's a fucking order!"

Dolly shot up from the floor, spluttering and coughing up bathwater. "Dolly!" I exclaimed and moved the hair back from her face. Her eyes snapped open.

"Rabbit," she cried in a panicked voice. Then she looked down at her body and screamed. She began hitting at her arms and legs. "I'm too tall!" she shouted, eyes wide and wild. Her head whipped around the room. "The doors! I can't get through the doors!"

I snapped the vial of my blood from around her neck and bit off the cork. "Drink," I ordered. I tipped her head back and poured the blood down her throat.

Stray drops fell from the side of her mouth. She swallowed,

and then she sat up. She stared down at her arms and legs. "It's working!" she yelled, just like the first time I brought her back to me. "It's working!" she said again, but her eyes clouded over with darkness. Her short-lived joy fled their depths, only to be replaced by the most vicious of looks.

"The Jabberwock," she said coldly. "He did this to me." Dolly scrambled to her feet. She was dripping wet, blood trickling down her chin. "Where is he?"

"Through there," I replied, pointing to the other room. I got to my feet, watching the beauty that was Dolly consumed with wrath, ready to make the man pay for destroying her life.

Dolly stormed out of the room, her blond hair swinging as she moved. I quickly followed, not wanting to miss one second of this kill.

Dolly looked down at the Jabberwock, part-crucified on the floor. I watched as his eyes landed on her. His mouth moved to speak, but before he could, Dolly rushed to him, straddled his waist and ripped her blade from his shoulder. She didn't pause. Didn't even take one single breath as she struck. She stabbed and stabbed and stabbed, never pausing. Never missing a beat, she hacked him as he lay on the floor, nothing but the lust for death in her eyes.

She struck and struck until she began to lose strength and her frantically flailing arms finally failed her. She had reached more than fifty strikes.

Drenched in blood, Dolly fell back from the Jabberwock, now dead by his former victim's hand, his lifeblood draining to the floor.

Dolly gasped for breath, her arms clawing her backward.

Sobs began to cut through the gasps, and soon they were all that could be heard. Chest racking, her entire body shook. Tears cascaded down her cheeks.

Then she saw me. She scurried to my feet and clung to my legs. "Rabbit . . . you came for me." She cried as she gripped me tightly. Her head fell forward, resting on my knee. "Thank you," she whispered, voice now completely cut and raw. "Rabbit . . . you came for me. Rescued me from the room of doors . . . Thank you . . . thank you . . . thank you . . ."

She was worshipping at my feet. Me, her god, her master . . . the one to whom she now finally belonged. She sobbed and sobbed, slumped on the floor. But I couldn't fucking take it. Couldn't see her lowly and down.

My little Dolly wasn't my fucking slave.

She was my goddess, a fucking titan.

Leaning down, I placed my finger under her chin, which I nudged up, commanding her to look at me. Her eyes were lowered, submissive to my touch. I shook my head. Dolly waited, patiently waited for me to speak, hooked on my every move.

"A queen bows to no one," I said, and Dolly's face transformed. It lit with light and color.

Dolly always belonged in color.

Bending down, level with her eyes, I said, "Especially to her king."

Dolly gasped and jumped into my arms. Her mouth smothered mine as she kissed me. She kissed me and kissed me, throwing her arms around my head. She held on as she took from me what she needed.

My doll queen dressed in blue.

I held her back until she pulled away. Her eyes were dilated and her breath came fast. She let go of me and got to her feet. Dolly walked, silently, to the slain Jabberwock, spread-eagled on the floor. Taking the tie he wore around his neck, she dipped the fabric into the blood pooling around him and began writing on the wall behind. "SICK FUX," this time written in crimson, written in his blood. His blood in payment for the crimes he had committed over the years. Dolly moved to his shoulder and pulled out my blade. She pulled a sodden playing card from her corset. She placed the card on his forehead.

The Ace of Hearts.

Dolly stared down at his face, now his death mask. She stood there for many minutes. Then she turned back to face me. "For you," she said and handed me my blade. I sheathed it in my cane, not bothering to clean it.

I wanted to keep the Jabberwock's blood on my steel for a while longer.

"I'm tired," Dolly announced suddenly, a new kind of sadness edging into her sweet voice. She took my hand in hers. Her fingers were still freezing cold. "Let's go, Rabbit. I no longer wish to be here."

Dolly pulled me through the doorway, but I guided her through the house. We showered quickly in a bathroom we found, ridding our skin of the Jabberwock's tainted blood. We washed our clothes, not caring that they were wet afterward. It was hot outside. We would quickly dry.

Once finished, I led her to the car. No music played as we pulled away. Dolly curled up on the backseat, wrapped in my jacket. Only minutes passed before her exhausted body succumbed to sleep.

I looked more at her than the road as I drove. She had asked to go straight to a motel. But we were going somewhere else. Dolly had deserved what I was going to do for her anyway. But after tonight, I would make sure she adored it.

She would never adore it as much as I adored her.

My gut twisted as I saw her shift in her sleep, delicate hands clinging to my jacket for dear life. She brought my jacket to her nose and inhaled. My heart completely crumbled when her lips formed a small smile.

As she breathed deeply in her sleep, all I could think about was tonight. How I had nearly lost her. I knew, beyond a shadow of a doubt, that if she died, I would surely follow.

There was no Rabbit without Dolly.

There was no Dolly without Rabbit.

As I drove to our destination, my eyes barely strayed from her. My little doll, broken, but not so much that she couldn't be repaired.

And I was the only doll master sufficiently skilled to perform those repairs.

* * *

I STOOD BACK and surveyed the scene before me. I drew in a deep breath and ran my hands through my hair. Straightened my fresh suit and cravat that I'd taken from my case in the trunk. I shook my head, laughing a quick laugh at what the fuck I was doing.

Then I glanced at the Mustang. My eyes fell on the sleeping blonde in the backseat. And I knew.

Her.

This was all for her.

My brave little champion.

I opened the trunk. The boombox was at the front. I pressed play, knowing the songs would be perfect for this moment. Slow music filled the air. I paused, hidden by the trunk's open lid. I rolled up the sleeves of my shirt and tipped my head back. I took in the sky above . . . and I smiled.

She would get exactly what she wanted.

Moving to the backseat, I leaned in and stroked Dolly's cheek. She shifted with a soft moan, but did not wake. Smiling at her stubbornness, I stroked her cheek again, this time whispering, "Dolly?"

She pulled my jacket higher over her shoulders. So I tried again. "Little Dolly darlin'," I said, louder this time. Dolly's eyes blinked open. She stretched out her arms. I watched her, mesmerized, and then she turned to look at me.

A small smile pulled on her lips. "Rabbit . . ." she said, her voice still weak from the experience of hours before. Her hair had dried on the journey, and her clothes were no longer soaked. "I'm tired," she said and curled back in to go back to sleep.

I shook my head, my chest feeling light, for once, at how cute she could be. "But I have a surprise," I announced and watched her eyes slowly open.

Dolly turned to face me. Her eyebrows were lifted. She turned her head again, this time in the direction of the music. "Is that my boombox playing?"

I nodded, then held out my hand. "Come."

With a confused smile, Dolly took my hand, and I helped her rise from the backseat. Needing to feel her against me, I wrapped my arms around her. Dolly squealed lightly as I lifted her from the car. She met my eyes, and I swallowed, nervous about what she would think of all this. It wasn't me. I didn't think like this. I didn't operate this way.

It was the most nervous I'd been about anything in my life.

And I never felt nervous. It was strange to feel the emotion. It had taken me a while, when she was sleeping, to label it.

I was nervous she would hate it.

I was nervous that I couldn't do it.

I placed Dolly on the ground, and a blush burst on the apples of her cheeks. That blush destroyed me where I stood. Always had; that, and her dimples, which caved when she smiled.

Dolly slipped her hand in mine, and I stared at our joined hands. Remembering she had liked it before, I brought her hand to my lips and pressed a soft kiss on it.

Dolly gasped. Her breathing increased in speed.

"Come," I said again and led her to the trunk of the car.

"Rabbit? What's happening?" she asked, looking around us.

I let go of her hand. "Close your eyes."

Dolly shook her head, smiling, but then did as I asked. I watched her face for a moment as she stood there with her eyes closed. Trusting me completely. My chest squeezed yet again. Forcing myself to move, I lifted the gift from the trunk. "Open your eyes."

Dolly did as she was told . . . and her blue eyes grew so huge they resembled the moon. "Rabbit," she whispered as she made to take the dress from me. Her eyes traveled up and down, drinking in its entire length. She reached out her hand, seemingly scared to touch the sparkling blue material.

"It's . . ." Tears built in her eyes. "It's . . . it's for me?"

I nodded. "For you." I nudged my head in her direction. "Put it on."

Dolly blew out a long breath, then she took the dress from my waiting hands. I reached into the trunk for the shoes. When I turned to give them to her, I paused. Dolly was silhouetted by the full moon. In the center of the field we had parked on, there was only us; she and I, and a sky full of stars.

I didn't care for them. Their beauty paled in comparison to her majesty.

Dolly had shed her clothes. The milky skin of her back looked paper-white in the moon's glow. She lifted the dress over her head and slid it effortlessly down over her body. I walked to where she stood. I knew she knew I was behind her when her shoulders tensed for a moment. Then her head tipped to the side, offering me her neck.

Unable to resist, I gently pushed her hair to the side and pressed a soft kiss on the side of her throat. She gasped, and goosebumps covered her skin.

I passed the shoes over her shoulder, and then lowered my hands to zip up her dress. I pulled the zipper up very slowly. I savored the view as I covered each inch of pale skin. I stepped back and waited for her to put on her shoes.

When they were on her feet, she turned. My eyes feasted on her as I inspected her from head to toe. The long blue dress fell to her ankles. The sparkly silver shoes sat perfectly on her little feet.

"You like?" she asked nervously, smoothing her hands over the full skirt.

I nodded and met her eyes. Moving back to the boombox, I fast-forwarded the cassette until the song I wanted came on. As the opening bars began to play, I turned and held out my hand to Dolly. Blushing, eyes lowered, she came to me.

She always came when I called.

Dolly slid her hand into mine. She waited, breath held, for what I would do next. I brought her hand to my mouth, gave it a swift soft kiss, and then bowed. Looking up from my gentlemanly position, I asked, "May I have this dance?"

Dolly's face betrayed her shock. She didn't speak. Instead she nodded her consent. Standing straight, I pulled her against my chest. I held out our hands and carefully placed the other around her waist. Dolly placed her hand on my shoulder. I looked into her eyes. They were locked on me. Her cheeks full of color.

As the song started, and a man sang about being unable to live with or without someone, I swayed us in time to the beat. Dolly never looked away as I held her close, letting the lyrics tell her how I felt. I disagreed with not being able to live with Dolly. I could definitely do that. We were never to be parted.

Not even in death, I was sure.

"Rabbit," Dolly said quietly as her blue eyes glittered against the stars. "You do not dance."

I smirked and pulled her even closer. I felt the heat coming off her skin. Smelled the roses I always smelled when she was close. "Tonight, apparently, I do."

Dolly rewarded me with a smile, then a giggle that floated up into the air. We danced as the song played out. When the next song began, one equally as slow, she looked around us and asked, "Rabbit? Is . . . is this a prom?"

Bringing our joined hands to my chest, I nodded. "Your prom, Dolly darlin'. A well-deserved prom, just for you."

"And you," she said breathlessly. She seemed overawed by it all. Dolly tipped her head back and looked up at the stars. "Rabbit . . . a blanket of stars." She looked to the right. "And the moon so full and bright."

"They came out for you," I said, and the brightness of her smile could have rivaled the midday sun.

We danced. We danced for three more songs. Dolly's face was flushed from dancing. When I stopped, I bowed low again and kissed her hand. "Thank you for the dance, little Dolly."

She giggled.

As I straightened, I saw the spark in her eyes return, the spark that had been lost destroying the Jabberwock. I saw the lightness return to her bones and saw the innocence he had temporarily stolen filter back as if delivered by moondust.

"Close your eyes again," I said.

"Rabbit!" she scolded. "No more presents. I feel utterly spoiled already!"

"One more." I waited for her to close her eyes, a stern look on my face. Dolly laughed, but then did as I asked.

I went to the trunk and took out the final present. I made my way back to Dolly and stopped before her. "Open," I said. Dolly's eyes fluttered open. She waited as I kept the present behind my back. When I decided she had waited long enough, I brought the gift from behind my back.

Dolly's eyes widened in amazement. Her hands masked an audible gasp. "Rabbit . . ." She slowly put out her hand. She ran her fingertips over the glittering stones. "A . . . a . . . a crown," she half-cried in disbelief.

I lifted it up. With Dolly's eyes regarding me with nothing but adoration, I slipped the crown on her head. "For my queen."

I fixed it in place and stood back to admire my work. I couldn't take my attention off her. My little Dolly. My little Dolly, once broken, healed by a pretty dress and a crown. Standing before her king like the royalty she was.

My queen of the dark.

"Well?" she asked nervously, placing her hands down by her sides.

I took a step toward her. Then another. I studied her crown, the bright blue of her eyes, the pink of her lips. "Perfection," I stated, my voice low and husky.

Dolly dropped her gaze, then lifted it back to whisper, "Silly Rabbit."

My lip hooked up at the corner. She was back. My little Dolly was back with me. Not lost. But by my side. Taking her rightful place as my queen.

Heeding Chapel's words, I moved my mouth toward hers. I was unhurried as I approached. Dolly held her breath as I ran my lips around hers, barely touching. I felt her shiver as I teased her mouth. Then I pressed forward, fusing our mouths. Dolly moaned lightly at my touch. Unfamiliar warmth ran down my spine as I took from her only her taste. Only her kiss, nothing more.

When I pulled away, I pressed my forehead against hers and just breathed. Dolly's hand came up and lay on my chest. The night was silent, and so were we.

Time passed; not even the ever-present tick-tock of my pocket watch could be heard. "I have something else to show you," I said and took her hand.

Dolly let me lead her deeper into the field. Farmland in the middle of nowhere. Just us, the sky and our sins. I knew Dolly had seen the blanket on the ground by the slight hitching of her breath. I didn't turn to face her at first. As I too looked at the blanket, I thought of what she had said about the movie she had watched.

I wasn't sure I could do this.

But then Dolly's hand slid onto my shoulder, and I felt her press her forehead against my back. I dropped my head forward and breathed deeply. I pushed away the dark thoughts that were threatening to spring forth. I cast out their abusive touches and sounds from my head.

And I turned, slowly, my eyes closed. Dolly's little fingers rubbed soothing strokes down my cheek. "Rabbit." At Dolly's whisper of my name, I let my eyes open. She took a deep breath.

I knew then that she was just as nervous as me.

"I don't know if I can do this . . . like you want," I admitted, my head twitching at the thought of taking her slowly. Gently. No blood. No biting or scratches down my back.

"Neither am I." She let out a pained laugh. With shining eyes, she whispered, "But we can try."

I sighed, tensing as Dolly's deft fingers began to unbutton my vest. My hands dropped to my sides as she pushed the vest off my shoulders. She untied my cravat, removing the pin that had, only few hours ago, freed her from the room of doors. The black silk fluttered to the ground as she released it from my neck. My shirt came next, and I stood before her, shirtless, and still tense.

Dolly took a deep breath, and her eyes fell to my bare chest. Her hands rested on my pecs, then they started to slowly explore. My jaw clenched as she ran her fingers over the many clocks I had tattooed on my skin. Tattoos that Chapel had painstakingly drawn with a needle and ink. Tattoos that had said goodbye to Heathan, and in his place had birthed Rabbit. She circled me, stopping at my back. I knew she was looking at her face staring back at her. Then I felt her lips kiss that spot. Her lips were like the butterflies I would catch and kill as a child. Tickling the skin.

Dolly moved around. She laid a kiss over my heart.

It beat faster in response.

I hissed as she broke away. I stared down at the black headband in her hair. That was always there—constant, familiar . . . Dolly.

This was my Dolly before me. The only person I had ever let in. The only person who had ever wanted me for me.

The killer by my side.

I could do this.

Or at least I had to try.

Dolly was a statue as I reached out and pushed her hair from her shoulder. She closed her eyes. By the time she had opened them, I was pressed against her, chest against breasts. I let my hands drop from her shoulders to her back. Dolly's breath fanned against my neck. I gritted my teeth as I pulled her zipper down. My fingertips grazed her bare skin as the zipper exposed her back. Taking a deep breath, I stepped back, and the dress that had been resting against my body fell slowly to the floor. I swallowed a lump in my throat as Dolly stood before me, naked and vulnerable.

She lifted her chin. She moved forward and placed her hand at my waist. Her fingers crept lower until they had taken possession of my button. Dolly opened it and gently pulled down my zipper. My pants slid into a heap on the ground.

I was just as exposed as her.

Dolly sighed as she glanced down. More tattoos. More clocks. No square inch left unmarked. Dolly looked at me, waiting for instruction. I took her hand in mine and led her to the blanket.

We lay opposite one another, no words being said, just air being shared. I shifted closer, my attention dropping to her lips. I moved in. I kissed her, and Dolly kissed me back. I wrapped my hand in her hair, but I did not pull. Didn't try to dominate, just let it happen; no aggression, simply feeling.

Dolly sighed against my mouth. The sound hit my chest.

She liked it like this.

I fought back my need to take her hard, and rolled her onto her back. I braced over her naked body. I stared into her eyes. She stared right back. Then I let my gaze fall. I crawled down her body, placing soft kisses on her neck, her breasts, her stomach and her thighs. Dolly slipped her hands into my hair as I moved back north. She searched my face, and then said, "Take me, Rabbit." I held back my urge to seize control. "Make love to me." A smile played on her lips. "Like they did in the movie. Under the stars. Just her and him, and their making of love."

Closing my eyes, I talked myself into doing as she asked. I felt Dolly's legs shift and open under me. I groaned when her fingers wrapped around my cock. I opened my eyes and tore them away from the vein in her neck. Instead I looked into her eyes. I kept my focus on them as she placed me at her entrance.

Dolly nodded. She was giving me permission. Dolly was giving her permission . . . to me. To us. To tonight.

I pushed forward, arms braced on either side of her head. I slowly entered her, inch by inch. Dolly's hands landed on my back. But instead of clawing, she ran her fingertips up and down, bringing bumps to my skin. Dolly moaned when I filled her. I froze above her, panting as I refrained from doing what my inner demon demanded I do.

"Rabbit," she breathed, eyes fluttering closed as I began to move. I slowly rocked into her. Gentle motions. It wasn't long before the need to take her roughly disappeared. As I studied her face, I stared at her lips parting slightly. At the flush on her cheeks and the pleasure in her eyes. I knew that I could stay here forever, just watching her pretty face lost to my touch. Feeling her hands on my back. Feeling her hands as they traveled up my side until they landed on my cheeks. "Rabbit," Dolly mouthed, no sound coming from her throat.

I had no choice but to kiss her.

So I did.

I pressed my lips over hers as my hips moved faster. But the gentleness continued. Sweat broke out on my body as I took her in the balmy night. Dolly's breathing grew labored, and I felt her pussy begin to clench. I groaned against her mouth, my tongue sliding against hers. I swallowed Dolly's moans and she swallowed mine as we built to a high. My hands hooked under her shoulders as pressure built at the base of my spine. My thighs grew tight. My chest was flush against Dolly's, my lips fused to hers.

"Rabbit," she whispered against my mouth. I felt her pussy contract, and Dolly's mouth broke from mine and her head tipped back. She cried out in pleasure, the sound and feel of being inside her carrying me with her. I groaned, eyes closed, as I came inside her. Our bodies were slick with sweat, arms wrapped around each other.

I breathed hard as I came down, my head tucked into her neck.

Dolly stroked my hair, her short, shaky breaths warming my skin.

I opened my eyes. I blinked into darkness, and then slowly lifted my head into the night. Dolly's eyes met mine. I felt a pain in my chest. The pain of knowing I could never live without her. Dolly was as much a part of me as my blood and beating heart. And I part of her.

I recalled what Chapel said to me.

My nerves returned. When I saw a smile pull on her lips, I opened my mouth and let the words spill out. "I love you."

There wasn't a part of Dolly that didn't tense. I froze, and then fucking broke apart as tears filled Dolly's eyes and fell down her cheeks. "Rabbit . . ." she said in a hushed voice. "I love you too."

My nose flared at her words. I thought of all the kills I'd

made. Of her blood that I had consumed, and all the times we had fucked . . . then the one time we had made love.

Nothing compared.

Nothing compared to my little Dolly, beneath me, telling me she loved me too. Dolly placed her hands on my cheeks and looked into my eyes. "Heathan James, you have eaten my heart and drunk my soul. I am yours. I have been consumed by you . . . happily."

I blinked, sure she hadn't noticed what she had called me. *Heathan James* . . . She had called me by my *real name*. My Dolly, my Ellis. Two very different personalities sharing the same body.

I loved them both.

Minutes passed. We kissed. Then I rolled us to the side. Dolly laid her head against my chest, staring up at the stars as her boombox continued playing all her favorite songs. Dolly's hand traced up and down my chest. I played with her long blond hair.

"We only have one more left," Dolly said, breaking the silence.

My hand stilled in her hair. "Yeah."

"The King of Hearts."

"Yeah."

Dolly didn't look up at me. "Then what, Rabbit? After we destroy the final bad man and free Ellis, what comes after?"

My eyebrows pulled down. "I don't know," I said honestly. "I never planned beyond the final kill." Not beyond our getaway, anyway.

I was lost in thought when Dolly suggested, "A tea party, I think." I smiled. "We shall celebrate with a tea party, with all the buttered crumpets one could ever eat!" She sighed happily. "Yes. A tea party we shall have. We can decide what to do after that." She giggled, and my heart stopped for a second at the sound. "A nice cup of Earl Grey. Everything is solved by sharing a pot of Earl Grey."

I smiled and ran my fingers through her hair again. I closed my eyes, inhaled her rose scent, and agreed, "Only Earl Grey will ever do."

CHAPTER 16

THE KING OF HEARTS

Rabbit

I watched from the bed as Dolly applied her makeup. Needing to feel her again, I walked over to where she sat. She smiled at me in the mirror as she applied blue shadow to her eyes. I picked her up and sat down on the stool. Dolly yelped as I placed her back down on my lap.

It was all part of her game. I'd done this every day since the night at the field. Since the night I couldn't keep my hands off her.

Dolly picked up her blusher and started to brush pink onto her cheeks. I rested my chin on her shoulder and simply watched her. Moving her hair out of the way, baring her neck, I kissed at her skin. I flicked my eyes up to her reflection. Her hand had paused midair and her eyelids had become hooded.

We were in Laredo now. The final place on my map, home to the King of Hearts—Dolly's papa. The mastermind behind the ring of rapists. The man who bet his daughter's pussy. Gave it away to whoever won a round of poker.

I closed my eyes, inhaling the rose scent from Dolly's skin. When I opened them again, she was finishing off her lipstick. She lowered the lipstick to the table and, sighing, lay back against my chest. My arms wrapped around her waist. I held her close. I ran my nose down her cheek.

"Mmm," she murmured and closed her eyes. Her hands covered mine at her waist. Her fingers ran over my skin. When I pulled back, I met her open eyes in the mirror. I played with the ribbon around her neck, the one that held the vial which read "Drink Me." It had been filled since the night at the Jabberwock's home.

My blood once again hung around her neck.

"We have to go," I said. Dolly nodded. We had been in a cabin Chapel had organized for us. It was another one of his homes. Now that the police were after us, now that our faces were splashed all over the news, we couldn't risk motels.

We couldn't risk traveling during daylight.

"The Sick Fux," the news claimed, "are highly dangerous." The Texas Rangers had declared a manhunt. A reward had been offered for our arrest.

It was never gonna happen.

I wouldn't live without Dolly.

She wouldn't survive without me.

Dolly placed all of her makeup in her bag on the vanity. "Ready," she sang. I lifted her up and placed her feet on the ground. I righted my cravat in the mirror and took my jacket from the bed. I buttoned it up and picked up my cane from where it leaned against the dresser.

When I turned around, Dolly was holding her crown. She was stroking the "jewels," as she called them. In reality, they were inexpensive colored stones.

Seeing how happy she was, just looking at that damn crown, made my black heart melt. I walked to her and stopped a few inches away. Dolly looked up and cast me a huge smile. I took the crown from her hands and placed it on her head.

Dolly stilled as I did so. She touched the crown, and her searching eyes tried to read my face. "A queen is never seen in public without her crown," I said. Tonight was the first time we had been out in the world since we defeated the Jabberwock.

"Queens are not seen without their crowns." She nodded. She turned to look at herself in the mirror. "So beautiful . . ." she murmured, never taking her attention off the sparkling crown.

I thought exactly the same thing, though I wasn't looking at the crown, only her.

Always her.

I held out my hand. "Let's go."

Dolly placed her hand in mine and I led her outside. We walked past the Mustang that had seen us through the slaughter of the "bad men." Dolly's hand came out and stroked along the door. "Bye-bye, Mustang," she sang as we left it behind.

I unlocked the garage at the end of the property. When the

wooden doors opened, Dolly gasped and stared at the large black truck that awaited us.

"It's huge!" She rushed forward to brush her hand over its hood. "And so shiny!"

I passed by her and opened the door. I bowed in her direction. "Your carriage awaits, Your Majesty."

A loud giggle burst from her throat. Slipping her hand in mine, she nodded her head regally and said, "Why thank you, kind sir."

I lifted Dolly up to the seat and shut the door. I put her makeup bag in the back of the truck with the rest of our things. I grabbed the boombox and jumped into the driver's seat; the truck was too new to have a cassette port. Dolly took the boombox from me and pressed play. She danced as I pulled out of the garage and onto the dirt road that led us out of the property.

I killed the lights, eyes focused on the dark as I led us toward our final destination. The drive was quiet but for the music. I stopped outside of the property lines, hiding the truck from sight behind an old barn.

I wasn't sure how this was going to go. But if we got out, I wanted to make sure we had the truck ready.

Out of all of the bad men, Earnshaw was the only one the PI couldn't get much on. He never left his home. Hadn't left in two years. As far as the PI knew, he had no guards. There was no sign of a housekeeper. Just an occasional delivery man. The PI didn't know what he was delivering.

I wasn't surprised. Earnshaw was always the smart one. The creator of the fucked-up life he and the uncles led. The chess player moving us all around, his fucking pawns. He had never touched me. I didn't know if he had touched Dolly. She had never mentioned him in her conversations with Ellis.

But I knew he had touched all those kids I saw being brought in at night. Delivered in trucks, for God's sake. My blood ran cold as I wondered if that was what was being delivered to his door. More kids from foster homes. Carers paid off with thousands of dollars taking kids to be raped.

"Rabbit?" Dolly's voice dragged me from my fucked-up thoughts. "Are you ready?"

I nodded, staring at her in her blue dress, striped socks and the crown on her head. Her makeup was impeccable. Then I looked at the scars on her arms. The ones she gave herself when she had begun to go insane. The ones she inflicted on herself because of what he let happen. When he had sent me to that hell, the Water Tower. Endless days in darkness, devoid of Dolly.

My blood began to boil, like a kettle bubbling with rising heat. He had been responsible for all of this. He had been the one to take me into that fucking office and ply me with whiskey. Got me so drunk, day after day, for the Cheshire Cat to fuck me. To hold me down and fuck me hard.

He had been the one to take Dolly on her tenth birthday and give her to the Jabberwock. The man responsible for so much hurt over so many years that her mind had blocked out her life, retreating into the world of a zombie. A shell of the little girl who liked to sing and dance, and hold imaginary tea parties with me.

The boy she loved . . . who was sent away for killing one of them.

That fucker had deserved to die.

"Rabbit?" Dolly asked again.

Nodding, I exited the truck. I kept my cane close. I walked to Dolly's door and lifted her out onto the long grass. The night was humid and sticky. Dolly held her doll's head in her left hand. Her knife and gun were tucked into her waist belt.

Dolly slipped her hand into mine. I stared at our intertwined fingers. We always walked this way now. Ever since the night at the field, she never let me go. I had only taken her that way once since. It wasn't in me to be . . . romantic. I needed more. Needed the blood. The fight.

Dolly needed that too. But she also needed me to be soft with her. Gentle. To keep her by my side, to have her happy after so many years of being lost, it was a sacrifice I could make.

The house had only just come into sight when I pulled us to halt. Turning to Dolly, I said, "I don't know what's waiting for us in there." I stroked her cheek over the blush she'd so expertly applied to her porcelain skin. I drank in her huge blue eyes, committing them to memory . . . just in case.

"Rabbit?" she whispered and lifted to her tiptoes to kiss my cheek. "You look sad."

I thought about it. Sadness. Shaking my head, I pushed the truth of her statement away and said, "I don't know what will happen in there, Dolly darlin'."

She blinked, long false lashes brushing the tops of her cheeks. She looked down, then back up at me. She swallowed, like she understood what I was saying. "It could be dangerous," she ventured.

I nodded, touching her face again. I ran my fingers down her cheek, her neck and down her arms. I squeezed her hand still joined in mine. "He knows we're coming," I said and saw Dolly hanging on my every word. "He will have seen us on the news. He will know that we have killed his friends." I paused when Dolly took a deep breath. "He will be expecting us."

"It will be dangerous." This time there was greater certainty in her tone. When her eyes fell and she held my hand just that little bit tighter, I knew she understood perfectly.

We might not come out of this alive.

But he had to be destroyed. It was the penance he had to pay for all the years of pain he had put us through. For all the years he had kept us apart.

"He has to die," Dolly said, as if she had heard my thoughts. I nodded and saw a sheen of tears in her eyes. She looked away, wiped her eye, then said, "Ellis must be freed . . . even if Dolly and Rabbit must die."

"Yeah," I rasped, trying and failing to imagine a world without her in it.

"Rabbit?" she asked. I lifted my chin. "Where does one go when one dies in Wonderland?"

I smirked, seeing the surge of hope in her face. "To the best part," I said. "Bright skies. Green fields . . . and lots and lots of tea parties."

Her face lit up. "With Earl Grey tea, buttered crumpets and strawberry tarts?"

"Of course," I confirmed. Leaning down, I kissed her lips, and then whispered against them, "Only Earl Grey will ever do."

I went to pull away, needing to go and face the cunt, to escape the thought of losing Dolly, but she tugged on my arm. She sniffed back a tear. "I love you, Rabbit." A smile ghosted on her lips. "Maybe even more than Earl Grey tea."

My heart fucking cracked. "I love you too." My voice was rough, resonating through my insides. Edging closer, I kissed the back of her hand. "But there is nothing to compare it to, because I have never loved anything else. It has always been you. Only ever you."

"Rabbit . . ." Dolly whispered, wrapping her arms around my waist. She held on for a few moments, and then she pulled back. Tucking her doll's head into her belt by its hair, she took her gun in hand. She held it up, slipped her other hand in mine and said, "We're going to be late."

On we walked, my cane at the ready. Dolly held her gun up as we approached the dark house. We scoured the ground, waiting for any sign of movement, of threat . . . There was none.

We reached the front door. It was unlocked. We entered the large foyer. It was as deserted as the grounds. Dolly's hand held mine tight as we searched the rooms. Each one was empty.

A lone door stood at the end of the hallway. We stood before it. Dolly looked to me and cast me a small smile.

A second later I had opened the door. I held my cane up, Dolly readied her gun . . . and sitting before us was large desk, identical to the one in the office of the Earnshaw estate.

And behind that desk was Earnshaw.

He was dressed in a suit. His hair was white where it had once been dark. He was thin where he had once been built . . . and there were two tanks next to him; clear plastic tubes led from one to his nose.

His eyes locked on us, a stand-off.

A handgun lay on his desk, nothing else. Two chairs were positioned opposite him. I darted my eyes around the room.

"Heathan James. I have been expecting you."

I felt Dolly freeze. I heard her breath stutter into short, quick pants. The King of Hearts looked at her. His face melted, a look of pure adoration gracing his sallow features. "Ellis . . ." he breathed. Tears seemed to build in his eyes. "You look beautiful." Dolly's hand began to shake in mine.

"Take a seat." He gestured with a weak hand to the empty chairs opposite him. My eyes narrowed, waiting for someone to leap out and attack. I expected him to pick up the gun and fire. But his hands lowered unsteadily to his lap, the tubes coming from them tapping on the wooden top.

I took a hesitant step into the office, then another, keeping Dolly behind me in case this was a trap. I expected nothing less. He was smart. Calculated.

I was too.

"Please," he said, his once deep, commanding voice weak and strained. I sat down. Rather than have Dolly sit on her own, to face the man who should have loved her more than life itself, I pulled her down onto my lap. I kept my cane at my side, ready to fire when the time came. I eyed Dolly's gun. She had it braced for action.

Then I studied Earnshaw. Bags of medicine hung at his side on metal poles. His skin was pale, and he wheezed when he breathed.

"Lung cancer," he informed me, clearly noting my interest.

I glared at the fucker, not giving two shits.

"Turns out all those cigars I smoked were bad for me." He chuckled, then coughed.

I sneered.

Dolly remained silent.

Still.

Earnshaw shifted in his seat, a move that made him hiss in pain. His cheeks reddened with the effort. When he reached the position he wanted, he met my eyes. "They think I only have a couple of months left."

My heart beat faster at that news. Not because I was happy, but because I wanted us—Dolly and me—to be the ones who killed him. Not cancer. Our bullets and blades. Our payment for what he had done.

"Seems your arrival here was fortuitous," he said. "Much longer and I would not have been alive." He smiled, and that was the smile I remembered. The smile that signaled he got off on the pain of children. The one he gave me as he plied me with whiskey. The one he gave me as the Cheshire Cat led me to my bedroom, changing the course of my life forever. The one he gave me when I returned and he passed me off to whichever fucker wanted my ass next.

"I wouldn't have been here to chat. To tell you why I did what I did."

Dolly remained silent. She was barely moving. My jaw clenched. "Why?" I asked, hating myself for even giving him the floor.

His stare singed mine. "Because I loved it," he gloated. I felt the temperature of my blood spike to an all-time high. "Because I really do like to fuck children. Because I like to play with people's lives. Because life is boring without plea- sure . . . and children give me so much pleasure. It's that simple."

I breathed. I breathed. I breathed as I restrained myself from fucking killing him right then.

"I have money," he went on. "I have all I could ever want. Money can buy you anything." He smiled the thinnest of smiles. "Even you, Heathan James."

"What?" I said, teeth clenched.

"Your papa," he said with a tired flick of his hand. "All it took was a few thousand to ensure that if anything happened to him, I would acquire you. I would become your legal guardian." I felt the color drain from my face. "Only took a few thousand for a desperate man to ensure Mr. James had an unfortunate accident, ending his life, right when his son was ripe for the picking. Age, you see. It counts a lot to men like me, and my colleagues." He flicked his hand again. "You hold zero appeal to me right now."

I felt sick as his words sank in. Then his gaze fell on Dolly. She was a statue on my lap. "And Ellis, my sweet, sweet girl." He beamed a smile at her. I wanted to reach across the table and rip off his predatory head. "My girl, who believed she was Alice. Who paraded around in a pretty blue dress." He nudged his head at her outfit. "Seems not much has changed."

I felt Dolly's legs twitch.

"It was a shame your mother found out about my . . . preferences." My breathing paused. Every part of Dolly tensed. "I couldn't let her know that I knew, of course. But like you, she loved her tea. Earl Grey, if I remember correctly." He looked past us. I turned and saw a picture of Dolly's mama hanging on the wall by the door. Earnshaw shook his head. "A tiny drop of arsenic in her many cups of tea ensured she would never steal my little girl away from me, like I knew she planned. *I* had plans for Ellis. I knew what my friends liked, and she was definitely it. They played good games of poker for the privilege of breaking her in."

He sighed. "The only spanner in the works was you, young Heathan. Your obsession with my daughter." He shook his head. "If only you hadn't killed one of my best friends, you would have remained by her side." He shrugged. "Perhaps she wouldn't have gone mad. Ellis, my fun little girl, became a deaf-mute." He flicked his head toward her, sitting statuesque on my lap. "Seems not much has changed there either." Dolly remained still. I panicked. Had she become repressed again?

Earnshaw took a long wheezy inhale. "I would love to hear how you escaped from the Water Tower, Heathan." He whistled low. "You and those men you escaped with have pissed off a lot of people. Important people who relied on that place to bury their indiscretions."

My lip hooked at the corner in disgust. I fucking hated this prick. He laughed when he saw my expression. "Heathan James," he murmured and laughed again. "You think we are so dissimilar?" He leaned forward, putting his hands on the table. "I like to fuck kids. You like to kill. I get hard from their screams. You get hard from your victims' spilled blood. Our tastes may differ, but we are cut from the same cloth."

"I'm nothing like you," I hissed, holding Dolly even tighter.

He smiled victoriously. "You *are*." He sat back. "You like the power killing gives you." He licked his dry lips. "You use your anger to fuel it. I guess you have me to thank for that. All those years of being fucked must have royally pissed you off."

I swung my cane up, ready to fire, but Earnshaw took hold of his gun and aimed it at me. He opened his mouth, about to say something else, something to make me lose my shit, when a bullet struck him right between the eyes.

Earnshaw's face froze in shock. His arm fell to the table, taking the gun with it. I flicked my eyes up at Dolly, arms out, her gun still in position from the kill shot.

"Time for tea," she declared coldly, then slowly lowered her gun. She shrugged. "I got very sick of him talking, Rabbit. He had such bad manners, don't you think?" She creased her brow and pouted her lips. "You know how I feel about bad manners."

Dolly jumped from my lap and dusted her hands down her skirt. I watched her, spotting Earnshaw's blood beginning to pool on the table from the corner of my eye.

I flicked the final card beside his head.

The King of Hearts was no more.

Dolly walked to the wall of pictures next to the door. Her breath hitched as the picture of her mother stared back at her, all long blond hair and blue eyes. She looked just like Dolly.

Dolly's shaking hands traced over her face. My gut twisted when I saw her swipe a tear from her eye. Then she moved to the picture of Ellis. She must have been only about eight. I remembered her like this. The little girl who sat beside me on the grass, when no one else talked to me. The girl who told me we were friends, when I never had any before.

Dolly laid her hand against Ellis's smiling face for so long that I rose from my chair. Before I got near, Dolly said, "Ellis has gone." I froze, mid-step. "Ellis is free . . ." Dolly sighed and turned to me, her hand slipping from Ellis's face. "She has gone to the part of Wonderland where the skies are bright blue. The grass is green, and there are lots and lots of tea parties."

Dolly's eyes fell. When they looked up at me through false lashes, I knew why. She was gauging my reaction. Seeing how I would react to knowing that my little Ellis, the person who lived behind a door in Dolly's mind, had gone for good.

She wanted to know if Dolly was good enough for me.

I moved toward her and cupped her face. "I'm glad she has gone. I want her to be happy. No more darkness and no more sadness." I kissed Dolly's mouth, and she sighed against my lips. "Rabbit has his Dolly; it's all that matters now."

The responding smile was blinding.

Dolly looked around the room. "What now, Rabbit?"

"The mission is complete." I reached into Dolly's pocket and pulled out her lipstick. "The last one," I prompted, and Dolly nodded.

She looked about the room. Her eyes fixed on the wall behind where Earnshaw lay dead. Dolly walked behind him and began her scrawl. "SICK FUX," for the final time, in her favorite pink lipstick . . .

Right below a picture of Ellis sitting in Earnshaw's lap.

Dolly dropped the half-used tube to the ground. She opened her mouth to say something else, but the howl of police sirens sounded outside.

"Come. We must go," I said, the pulse in my neck leaping into a sprint.

Dolly giggled in excitement and ran to me. I dragged her from the room to one of the windows. Police cars raced down the road.

"What pretty blue lights!" Dolly said in awe.

Pulling her by the hand, I raced down the stairs. I tried door after door until I found one that led down to a cellar. I knew from the PI's maps that there was an underground tunnel to the barn. No doubt the way he brought in the batches of kids he'd raped before he got sick.

We raced down to the cellar, closing the door behind us only moments before I heard the police enter the house. Muted voices came from the floors above us. I pulled Dolly through the large cellar until I found a door. I opened it to see a short tunnel. I was about to run through when I realized that it led to the storm cellar.

"Wrong one," I said and began looking for other doors. My heart pounded faster when I couldn't find one. Then I saw a large shelving unit. A cobweb clung to the top of it . . . a cobweb that was blowing like there was wind behind it.

The doorway was behind the shelves.

I pulled Dolly toward it and released her hand to start pushing the shelves out of the way. Dolly hummed behind me, dancing on the spot.

A gasp came from the bottom of the stairs.

I whipped around to see a man wearing a cowboy hat. Heart beating wildly, I pushed Dolly behind me and pulled out my cane. But the Ranger wasn't looking at me. His eyes were fixed on Dolly.

Dolly peeked around my waist and looked at him.

He stepped closer, ignoring me, until I blocked his path. Narrowed eyes glared at me . . . and that's when I saw it. Those eyes. I knew those eyes. Eyes that looked at me with hatred.

"Eddie fucking Smith," I said and watched his face tense. I looked down at his uniform and smirked. He'd got his wish after all.

Texas Ranger.

"Rabbit?" Dolly whispered from behind me. "Who is this?" She walked around me. Eddie Smith swallowed as he beheld Dolly in her full Alice in Wonderland regalia. As her blue eyes, eyes that he had once loved for many years, locked on him. By his reaction, I was sure that love had yet to fade.

Eddie didn't speak, just stared. When Dolly looked at me, waiting for me to answer her question, I said the only thing that came to mind. "The Mad Hatter," I announced, looking at the Stetson on his head. "Dolly, this is the Mad Hatter." Dolly gasped in excitement, her hands covering her mouth.

Then, meeting Smith's eyes, I asked, "Question is, what is the Mad Hatter about to do?"

CHAPTER 17

Eddie

I COULDN'T BELIEVE it was her. Ellis. In the flesh. Talking. Smiling . . . happy.

"Question is, what is the Mad Hatter about to do?"

I heard our men upstairs, searching the rooms. I knew that somewhere, Earnshaw would be lying in a pool of his own blood. He was the last target they had, the orchestrator of their abuse. The conductor of every sick and twisted movement that had occurred on the Earnshaw estate.

Only very recently had I learned about it all.

I looked at Ellis and wanted to cry for the things that I heard had been done to her. I flicked my eyes at Heathan. Even though I hated him with every ounce of my being for stealing my girl, I would never have wished on him the things that had been done to him by those evil men.

I thought back to the interview with Simon Wells. The one who made the complaint about Earnshaw and his colleagues years ago. The complaint that was ignored.

I thought back to what he told me, about the terrible things Earnshaw and his colleagues had done to him. About how he had seen Heathan, and later Ellis, being led into rooms where the same fate undoubtedly awaited them. I had run straight to the bathroom and vomited.

"You're the Mad Hatter?" Ellis's voice cut through my memory of Simon's testimony. But what he had told me remained. As I looked at her heavily made-up face, a strange clock drawn around her left eye, all I could think of was how she was taken over and over by those men . . . arranged by her own father.

The dead man upstairs, who I believed had deserved to die.

Hell, they all deserved to die.

"Yes," I replied. Ellis spoke with a regal English accent. She wore the clothes of a sexualized Alice in Wonderland and, to cap it all, she sported a crown upon her head. "I'm the Mad Hatter," I confirmed and saw Heathan breathe more easily. When I glanced at him, he was watching Ellis with the same fucked-up, possessive gaze he had when they were kids.

I realized that in his own fucked-up way . . . he loved her.

He'd come back for her.

Jesus . . . I think he'd saved her.

Wreaked revenge on those who had wronged them, no doubt . . . for *her*.

Ellis ran to me, and I lost my breath at how beautiful she was. I saw the blade in her waist belt. Saw the gun in her hand. Her old doll's head was on her waist too. "Do you hold tea parties?" she asked with excitement.

Indulging the innocence that was Ellis, I nodded. I played her game . . . one last time. "Yes." My rough voice betrayed the tightness of my throat. "I hold tea parties."

Ellis squealed and I winced, praying her voice hadn't been heard by the men upstairs. "We shall have to attend one day, shan't we, Rabbit?"

"Sure, darlin'," Heathan drawled. His eyes cut to the ceiling when the sound of footsteps came closer to the cellar stairs.

"You are very much invited," I said, and she clapped her hands. I glanced at Heathan and saw him watching me. He was trying to read what I would do.

I saw his cane. I knew from the maid that it held both a blade and a gun. And I expected that he would kill me now. Knowing he was listening, and knowing he would read the subtext, I said to Dolly, "You have to run now, for you're going to be late. You must follow the White Rabbit down a new hole. But one day . . ." I smiled, seeing her blue eyes wide and so, so beautiful, "But one day, we will have that party. And I'll bring the Earl Grey tea."

"Earl Grey!" She turned to Heathan. "Rabbit? Doesn't that sound absolutely charming?"

"Sure does, little Dolly." He nudged his head for her to come to him. Dolly did, like Ellis had always done with Heathan. Heathan pulled her to his side, then turned toward a shelving unit behind them. One that now revealed the entrance to a tunnel.

"I'll shut it behind you," I called, and Heathan's suspicious gaze narrowed on me. I removed my hat. "For her," I said. Understanding spread on his face. "For what they did . . . to both of you."

Heathan paused, eyes still narrowed, then nodded. Taking Dolly's hand, he pulled her through the gap. I rushed to the selves and watched them fade out of sight, Heathan running, Dolly skipping, holding his hand tightly. "Chapel," I heard him say into a cell. "I need that border crossing now!"

Hearing the door to the cellar open, I pushed the shelves back in place and ran to the opposite door, to what I knew to be a storm shelter. My uncle came down the steps. "Earnshaw's dead. Shot. And recently. He's still warm. They have to be close."

I pointed to the storm shelter's door. "I heard voices down here. I think it's them."

The men behind my uncle piled into the tunnel, leading them in the opposite direction from Heathan and Ellis. My uncle eyed me strangely, so I ran down the tunnel.

As I ran, I fixed my hat back on my head and thought, *The Mad Hatter. After all this time . . .*

. . . finally.

EPILOGUE

Dolly

Mexico

I WALKED over the sand to where I knew Rabbit waited for me. The large umbrella hid his face. But I spotted his tattooed forearms, shirt sleeves rolled to the elbow.

Hand on hip, I walked around the umbrella until I knew he could see me. I looked out over the sea. Rabbit and I lived in a house on a beach. We had our own private beach. We could see the public beach beside us. After all, people-watching in Wonderland was one of my favorite things in life. With every day here in this new part of Wonderland, I got curiouser and curiouser.

I heard Rabbit growl deeply in his throat.

And I smiled.

I arched my back, pretending to see something in the distance. Rabbit growled again and said, "Turn around."

Shivers broke out down my spine at his command. Fluffing my hair with my hands, I fixed my crown and spun . . . slowly . . . oh so slowly. My boombox sang a song about a fruity drink called Piña Colada. I swayed my hips to its beat.

When I looked up, Rabbit had lain back on his sun lounger. I giggled on seeing him. He dressed as he always did, only his pants were rolled up to his knees, showing off his tattooed legs. His black shirt sleeves were rolled up too. His shirt was unbuttoned to his navel, and his cravat hung loose around his neck.

And he wore a monocle on his left eye. I had bought it for him as a gift. My Rabbit couldn't be a *true* White Rabbit without a monocle.

The vial of my blood hung at his throat. My thighs clenched just looking at it . . . at thinking back to that night. And the many nights that have been just like it. I loved touching my Rabbit.

Not a night went by that we didn't touch and play.

"Here," Rabbit ordered, pointing to the small gap on his sun lounger. I kept my hand on my hip as I flounced to him. I stood beside the sun lounger and demanded, "Well?"

I waited for him to comment on my new pale-blue-and-white bikini. Rabbit's eyes flared as they tracked up and down my body. I glanced down at his crotch and smiled.

He very much liked what he saw.

Suddenly, Rabbit grabbed my wrist and pulled me down to his chest. I yelped as I fell. But I laughed when my chest hit his. When my lips hovered above his.

"Do you like it?" I asked. "The bikini?"

Rabbit's hand moved to the back of my neck, and he slammed his lips on me. He ate at my mouth, biting at my lip. Fighting back, I bit into the flesh of his lip so hard that I tasted blood. Rabbit groaned loudly as he stole more hard kisses.

When we broke away, his pupils were dilated. "Silly Rabbit," I scolded and slapped at his hard chest.

Someone cleared their throat. The server had brought our tea. "Time for tea!" I sang and pointed to the table to the side of us for the server to put it down. Rabbit's arms stayed around my waist, holding me in place. I wasn't going anywhere.

The server withdrew. I sat up and poured the Earl Grey into our cups. Milk and sugar—two lumps each. Rabbit's hand stayed on my stomach. When I turned to give him his tea, he was looking at his phone. I lay beside him and placed his tea on the table on his other side. I laid my head on his shoulder and watched him type out words I couldn't read.

"Will I ever meet them?" I asked, pouting. I wanted to be friends with Mr. Chapel, and Messrs. Henry and Hyde.

"Maybe one day," Rabbit said and pocketed his cell. "They both have their own journeys to travel first. Their own bad men to kill."

I sat back in a mood and sipped at my tea. "I'm bored," I complained, heaving out a deep sigh. I turned to Rabbit. "I miss killing, Rabbit. I miss sinking my blade into people's flesh and making them bleed." I thought about all of our lovely kills. I smiled fondly. "I rather miss hearing the loud screams our wickedness causes too."

Such sweet, heavenly sounds . . .

"I do too, darlin'," he replied, and I giggled into my cup

when his naughty part got hard in his pants. I knew he was imagining all that lovely blood on his hands.

I busied myself with drinking my tea. I had taken only four sips, Rabbit had taken only two, when a loud smack could be heard from the public beach beside us. Our heads whipped to the side. A man had a little boy—no older than eight—by his neck. His mouth was at his ear . . . then he ran his hand down the boy's back and over his bottom.

The boy cried.

My teacup shook in my hand at the sight. At the man licking along the little's boy's neck. The little boy froze, his head dropping as the man led him to a car that waited at the beach's edge.

"Dolly," Rabbit's cold voice said as we watched the car drive out of sight.

"Yes, Rabbit?"

He turned to me, his eyes just as furious as mine. "We're going on a new adventure." I felt the blood surge through my veins. I nodded in delight. He finished his tea, and then sat on the edge of his lounger.

I jumped to my feet, readying to race after the car.

Rabbit reached out and stopped me with his hand on my wrist. He messaged someone on his cell. "Chapel will have his address in ten minutes. Stupid fucker let me see his registration plate."

Smirking, he stood and yanked me to his chest. His eyes were wild, his hard cock pressing against my leg. "Go get your gun and your blade—"

"And my dress and socks and boots and lipstick," I said, interrupting him. "I can't kill without all my favorite things." My eyes widened. "Oh! And my Alice dolly too. She just *loves* to watch us kill."

Then I waited. I waited for the White Rabbit . . . *my* White Rabbit . . . to signal the start of our new adventure.

I watched him, breath held. Watched as a slow, vicious grin pulled on his lips. Watched as he reached into his waistcoat and pulled out his pocket watch.

My heart raced as he looked into my eyes. I locked my stare on him as he raised the watch to his ear.

Tapped on the metal.

And with malice in his heart and darkness in his veins, smiled and said, "Tick tock."

THE END

"SICK FUX" by Ed Williamson

PLAYLIST

Dear Jessie — Madonna

Love The Way You Lie — Eminem, Rihanna

Ballroom Blitz — The Struts

Monster — Kanye West, JAY Z, Rick Ross, Nicki Minaj

Dark Fantasy — Kanye West

The Land of Make Believe — Bucks Fizz

Poison — Alice Cooper

Living Doll — Cliff Richard & The Drifters

Savage (feat, Flux Pavilion & MAX) — Whethan (Strip club scene)

Sexxx Dreams — Lady Gaga

My Boy Lollipop — Millie Small (The Caterpillar scene)

Fragile — Kygo, Labrinth

Chitty Chitty Bang Bang: Doll on a Music Box/Truly Scrumptious — Original Cast Recording

Issues — Julia Michaels

Two Fux — Adam Lambert

Believer — Imagine Dragons
Seven Nation Army — The White Stripes
Crazy Train — Ozzy Osbourne
Two Ghosts — Harry Styles
With Or Without You — U2 (Prom Scene)
Feels — Care
One Mississippi — Zara Larsson
Many Of Horror — Biffy Clyro
If We Were Vampires — Jason Isbell & the 400 Unit
Praying — Kesha
These Four Walls — Little Mix
What About Us — P!nk
Power — Little Mix
Make Me Wanna Die — The Pretty Reckless
Monster — Lady Gaga
We Found Love — Rihanna, Calvin Harris
Escape (The Pina Colada Song) — Rupert Holmes
Dusk Till Dawn — ZAYN, Sia (The Jabberwock Scene)
Mad Hatter — Melanie Martinez
Cocaine Blues — Joaquin Phoenix

ACKNOWLEDGMENTS

Thank you to my husband, Stephen, for keeping me sane. These past few months with you, and our new little man, Roman, have been the best of my life. However, giving birth, enduring seemingly endless nights of sleep deprivation due to colic, emigrating from the US to the UK, and writing this book, has been one crazy ride! But I have loved every bit of it!

Roman, I never thought it was possible to love somebody so much. You're the best thing I have ever done in my life. Love you to bits, my little dude!

Mam and Dad, thank you for the continued support.

Samantha, Marc, Taylor, Isaac, Archie, and Elias, love you all.

Thessa, thank you for being the best assistant in the world. You make the best edits, keep me organized and are one kick ass friend to boot!

Liz, thank you for being my super-agent and friend.

To my fabulous editor, Kia. I couldn't have done it without you.

Neda and Ardent Prose, I am so happy that I jumped on board with you guys. You've made my life infinitely more organized. You kick PR ass!

Hang Le, thank you for another unbelievably perfect cover. Onto the next one!

To my Hangmen Harem, I couldn't ask for better book friends. Thank you for all for everything you do for me. Here's to another step forward in our Dark Romance Revolution! *Viva Dark Romance!*

Jenny and Gitte, you know how I feel about you two ladies. Love you to bits! I truly value everything you've done for me over the years, and continue to do!

Thank you to all the AMAZING bloggers that have supported my career from the start, and the ones who help share my work and shout about it from the rooftops—even if books like this put you through the ringer!

Thank you to all my wonderful author friends. It would be a scary world without you to lean on. And lastly, thank you to the readers. Without you none of this would be possible.

AUTHOR BIOGRAPHY

Tillie Cole hails from a small town in the North-East of England. She grew up on a farm with her English mother, Scottish father and older sister and a multitude of rescue animals. As soon as she could, Tillie left her rural roots for the bright lights of the big city.

After graduating from Newcastle University with a BA Hons in Religious Studies, Tillie followed her Professional Rugby player husband around the world for a decade, becoming a teacher in between and thoroughly enjoyed teaching High School students Social Studies before putting pen to paper, and finishing her first novel.

After several years living in Italy, Canada and the USA, Tillie has now settled back in her hometown in England, with her husband and new son.

Tillie is both an independent and traditionally published author, and writes many genres including: Contemporary Romance, Dark Romance, Young Adult and New Adult novels.

When she is not writing, Tillie enjoys nothing more than spending time with her little family, curling up on her couch watching movies, drinking far too much coffee, and convincing herself that she really doesn't need that last square of chocolate.

FOLLOW TILLIE AT:

https://www.facebook.com/tilliecoleauthor

https://www.facebook.com/groups/tilliecolestreetteam

https://twitter.com/tillie_cole

Instagram: @authortilliecole

Or drop me an email at: authortilliecole@gmail.com

Or check out my website: www.tilliecole.com

For all news on upcoming releases and exclusive giveaways join Tillie's newsletter: http://eepurl.com/bDFq5H

Subscribe to Tillie's YouTube channel: 'Tillie Cole'

Made in the USA
Middletown, DE
21 October 2023